/

THE CULT

A Novel of Two Norman Kingdoms

RICHARD DEVLIN

Published by Undercroft Books

Publisher's Note: This is a work of fiction in which actual historical persons at times figure prominently. Any other resemblance to persons living or dead is purely coincidental.

Richard Devlin. The Cult: A Novel of Two Norman Kingdoms

ISBN 10: 0990919404
ISBN 13: 978-0-9909194-0-7

Cover art by the author

Author photo on page 343 by Greg Castillo

For a list of historical and fictional characters in *The Cult* see page 340.

To Mario

who made it possible

ACKNOWLEDGEMENTS

I owe great thanks for their support to three generous and accomplished writers: Gwendolyn Womack, Jake Fuchs, and Marie Macpherson. I would also like to thank the members of my writing group whose unflagging interest in the fates of Elise, Edmond, and Martin never failed to hearten me—and finally, Mary Webb, an inspiring teacher and the author of *The God Hustlers*, a brilliant novel about a religious cult and the nature of evil.

PART ONE

The Ancient Circle

1172-1176

1

1172

The South of England

It happened so quickly—one moment she was kneeling at a shrine in Clarington Cathedral praying for her ailing aunt, the next, a pair of black-robed arms had seized her and a second pair had tied a gag around her mouth. At first, she was too stunned to struggle. By the time she did, it was too late; she was bound hand and foot in a windowless room beneath the tower of the cathedral. The only kindness they had shown her was to throw a woolen coverlet around her as they left. Crazed with fear, she lay sobbing for hours in the darkness until, at last, she fell asleep.

When she awoke, her body was numb from the cold earthen floor. Was it morning or night? There was no way to tell. If she could only untie her hands! Maybe then she could somehow unlock the door. Yet the harder she tried, the tighter the cords seemed to grow. Nor, in truth, was she anxious to move about this chamber. Just before they had slammed the door and left her in this horrid darkness, she had seen it was the charnel room, the place where they stored the old bones to make room for new burials in the cathedral yard. Inhaling a smell of damp and rot, she could feel their gruesome presence a few feet away: the skulls with their leering tooth-filled grins and gaping eyes, the filthy stacks of bones with bits of cloth still clinging to them. Yet even amid her disgust and fear, she felt the pangs of hunger. For hours, she had tasted only the salt of her tears through the cloth of her gag.

Now fully awake to the terror of her situation, she thought of Rafe, the last person she had spoken to before they took her. They had met purely by chance in the alley behind the cathedral and slipped into the churchyard. There, in a corner beyond the grave markers, he had declared himself.

"Sweet Miriam,"—she loved it when he called her that—"in a year, you'll be eighteen and I'll be twenty. Not long afterward, I'll finish my journeyman year. Once I've joined my uncle in his trade, I'll ask your father for your hand."

The words had thrilled her, but not knowing how to answer, she had merely smiled. When she spoke, it was mainly to warn him. "Dear Rafe, it's wonderful to hear you say that, but we dare not linger here. What if we're seen? My mother is nursing my poor aunt at home. Otherwise, she would never have let me come out alone. Now I have to go and light a candle at the altar of St. Catherine, my aunt's patron saint."

They parted then, but before they did, Rafe leaned over and kissed her on the lips, a thing he had never done before. Would she ever see him again? Or her aunt or her parents, or her little brother, to whom she had been unkind that very day? No, she mustn't think such things! Of course she would. She prayed now to the Virgin with all her heart, vowing never to be mean or bad again, begging her to end this terrible ordeal.

But who, she asked herself, were these men who had locked her up inside this wretched chamber? Did their black robes mean they were priests? No, that couldn't be. How could priests, God's representatives on earth, do such a thing? They must have stolen their robes and the key to the chamber. Unless it was all a mistake. Yes, perhaps that was it! They must have confused her with some wanton, a strumpet or a thief, a girl who looked like her. In the morning when they came to claim her, she would tell them who she was, and they would surely let her go.

Weary now and sick with hunger, her hands and feet still bound, she pulled the coverlet up as best she could, prayed to God for deliverance, and closed her eyes. She was nearly asleep when a hollow noise pierced the silence: footsteps outside on the stones of the cathedral floor. They came closer and stopped, she heard a key scrape as it turned, and the door swung open. A single candle, brilliant after the blackness, lit the room. It was the heavier man of the two. Without a word, he set the candle-holder on the ground, knelt beside her, and untied her gag. He must be here to undo the mistake, to free her! Yet instead of an explanation, he produced a glass vial and pulled out the stopper.

"Drink this, the whole thing. It's for your own good."

She was wrong. This was no reprieve. Instinctively, she turned away. As she did, the death's heads confronted her. Now the man took firm hold of her chin, pinching her nose with his other hand.

"Drink it all, or I'll do worse."

She struggled, resisting until her breath gave out. Once her lips opened, he forced her to swallow. The liquid was bitter with a sweet, unpleasant aftertaste. When she was done, the man gagged her again and stood with a disgruntled look, as if this task were not of his own choosing. Soon, however, his frown began to waver, his scowl melted into a grimace, and the darkness in the corners of the room expanded, sucking every-thing into itself.

*

Will set out in the cold before dawn, surprised to see a light snow on the ground. By the time he entered the woods, the morning was well advanced. Moving stealthily among the trees, he laid his traps. A few hours later, he claimed his meager yield: two hares, two squirrels, and a rabbit. He was about to start for home when he noticed something pale behind the branches of a thicket.

It was a young woman's body, naked in the space beneath a fallen tree. He had been here earlier to set a trap, but at that hour the hollow where she lay was deeply shaded. Even now, her skin was dappled by the shadows of the withered leaves above her. As he moved closer, he felt a great pity. The girl's body was marred by strange, small wounds all over, everywhere except her face. Had animals done this? No, the cuts were too clean for that. It seemed clear she had died in no natural way. What if the killer was near and watching at this moment? Will listened to the wintry silence. He heard nothing but the chirping of some birds. Scanning the forest in all directions, he saw only dark tree trunks, gray brush, and sprinklings of snow.

Still, that was not the only danger. This was the New Forest, royal land. If they caught him now with a bagful of game, things would go badly for him. In the old days they chopped off your hand or took out an eye for poaching. Now it would be a steep fine or prison. That meant prison for him; he had no money to pay a fine. It would be much worse, however, if they found him here beside the girl. They might even think he was the killer! A poor man was already halfway to guilty in this world.

Warily, he moved closer, close enough to touch her, but he didn't. It seemed irreverent somehow. Even dead, the girl was beautiful. Whoever had done this must have savored her fine features: sable eyebrows and eyelashes, smooth forehead, slender nose, dark curls still frozen to her cheeks. Last night's snow, the first of the season, had kept her body fresh.

Weary of standing, Will knelt on a bed of cold leaves and looked more closely at her wounds. Some were small and round like tiny open mouths, others larger with pieces of flesh cut away. Had she been alive for all this torture? He hoped not. Indeed, it seemed unlikely. Her eyes were closed and the look on her face was fixed, a tranquil mask revealing nothing. Seventeen at the most, he guessed, no husky farm girl but a fine town maiden. They had heaped leaves on her body to hide it, before the wind blew them away. A few still clung to her skin, bronze and gold upon pale flesh. And they were not her only ornament. As if in modesty, her hand was caught between her legs. On one finger there was a silver ring. Whoever the killer was, he had not been a thief. Finely worked, the ring widened to form the setting for a purple stone. Will stared at it, wondering how many meals it would make in his children's bellies. No, he hadn't sunk that low, not yet. He had meat enough for ten days if properly spread out. What good could come of stealing from the dead?

And now, heartless as it seemed, he would have to leave and tell no one what he had seen. There was no trusting the author·· ities. Bailiff or baron, priest or pope, they all conspired to grind you down. Christ fed the multitudes, they said, but those who governed in God's name cared little whether poor folk lived or died. King Henry's game wardens would have to find the girl and seek her family out or, failing that, give her a Christian burial themselves. But what a wicked world it was where a man couldn't do his duty by the dead!

Bowing his head, he said a prayer for the girl's eternal soul, cast a final glance in her direction, and departed.

2

1173

As she entered the gallery beside the great hall, Elise saw at once that its gray stone walls had been transformed. It was the last Sunday in May, and garlands of snowy hawthorn blossoms hung between the iron sconces; the air was thick with their heady scent. Elise's aunt, the Lady Melisande, was meticulous in all her duties as the mistress of Bourne Castle, but she was not afraid to break with custom on occasion. In honor of the feast of Pentecost, she had ignored the old wives' tale that hawthorn blossoms indoors brought bad luck.

Elise paused to inhale the sweet odor. As she did, a flood of memories overcame her. There had been a hawthorn bush beside her childhood home in Picardy. Ten years had now passed since her parents had died and her uncle, Earl Desmond de Bourne, had brought her as a child of five to England and Bourne Castle.

"Beware, my dear, the hawthorn has a lovely scent, but its thorns are sharp and, some say, deadly."

Elise looked toward the great arched doorway of the hall and saw her aunt. As Melisande approached, her gray-green eyes were bright beneath her carefully coifed auburn hair. She had not gone with her husband and his party to the parish church, instead hearing Mass in the castle chapel with a few departing guests.

"Good Sabbath, my dear. I hope you are well."

"Thank you, madam, I could not be better." In truth, Elise was feeling elated. This morning as she awoke, Margaret, her old nurse, had told her the Count de Vere was gone. The count was a widower and over twice her age. Ever since his arrival three days before, she had been afraid he had come from Normandy to ask her uncle, the Earl of Clarington, for her hand in marriage.

"Margaret and I stayed in church after my uncle left," Elise continued, "for the christenings, I mean. I love to see the village folk enjoy themselves." In fact, they could barely keep from laughing at the squalling of the infants whose long white robes gave the holy day its other name of Whitsunday.

"I'm glad you don't disdain to be among the villagers, my dear. It won't do for a lady to be partial only to her kind. When you marry, one of your tasks will be to help your husband govern."

As always, Elise searched for a proper reply. "In that regard, madam, I could not have a better model than my uncle's wife." It was flattery, of course, but also true. Her aunt played the role of helpmate to the earl superbly. Accomplished in all things, she read and wrote in both Latin and French, which, having been born in France, she spoke without the Norman accent prevalent in England. And unlike his first wife, Melisande had borne the earl a son.

"You're kind to say so, my dear, but now that we've met, I must tell you there has been a change of plans. We are to dine with the Bishop of Clarington this evening, staying over the night. They say his new residence is splendid."

"Clarington until tomorrow?" Elise queried, unhappy with the news. On Monday at the Whitsun fair in Windham, she had hoped to introduce her uncle to a fellow pupil from her lessons in the village. Edmond was the son of Baron Hugh, her uncle's vassal, but the earl had not seen him since he was a child. Now, none of that would happen. She would have liked to protest. Instead, she asked a pointless question. "Why was there so little notice?"

Her aunt was already moving toward the stairway in the gallery corner. "Well might you ask, my dear. I myself wanted to decline, pleading guests here at the castle, although in truth, they've mostly gone. Unfortunately, there was a second message, this time from the abbey. The Count de Vere is there visiting his old acquaintance, Prior Gramont. They too have been invited. His note urges us to join them."

Elise stiffened at the mention of the count, suddenly wary of this supper. Her aunt paused at the foot of the stairs. "Come with me to my chamber until it's time to dine. Margaret knows we are leaving and will pack your things."

Elise complied, as everyone did with Melisande. Beneath her aunt's careful courtesy, there lay a will of iron.

Upstairs in her solar, they sat before a leaded window in the new French style. On this sunny day, light streamed through the border of colored glass, tinting the rushes on the floor. Her aunt returned to the topic of their supper. "Your uncle also felt we should go. Ever since that business with the girl last fall, the one who disappeared from the cathedral yard, Bishop Osbert is very sensitive to slight."

"The young woman they found in the New Forest?"

"The same," Melisande replied. "The earl prefers to think the bishop had no part in it. I myself am not so sure. He has an evil reputation as regards young women. There was another girl, a servant in his kitchen some time back. She too was found dead in peculiar circumstances."

Elise felt herself shrinking from the thought. Could a priest, an ecclesiastic of high rank, be a party to such crimes? And why was her aunt speaking of these things? Was there, as usual, some lesson in it?

"In this recent case," Melisande said, "they detained a young man by the name of Rafe, the victim's sweetheart, the last person seen with her. Since there was no real evidence against him, they released him. Nonetheless, word spread that he had killed her in a fit of jealousy. From then on, he was shunned as if he were a murderer."

"Since there was no proof, that seems unjust."

"You will learn, my dear, that justice is a rare thing in this world. The boy could not bear his neighbors' scorn. One night he tried to hang himself but failed. His act was seen to confirm his guilt. He gathered his few things and stole away. Some think he went to foreign lands, others that he joined King Henry's army. Whatever the truth, let the story be a warning. A young woman must always be discreet. This Rafe and the murdered girl were seen but once alone together. In the end, only appearances mattered."

So that was the lesson. It made Elise think about Edmond. Could her aunt possibly have guessed the way she felt about him? She was glad they had done nothing indiscreet, nothing at all, in fact, except exchange loving glances. As always, Elise searched for the proper response. "A sad example, madam, but I take your point."

"Then I'm glad to have spoken. And my advice also applies to our stay tonight in Clarington. Of course, no one has linked Bishop Osbert directly to the recent disappearance. The girl's body was much decayed; they knew it from an amethyst ring. Once they had found her, two men in the bishop's employ—it's not quite clear who—left for the continent. Some say they abducted the girl at his behest, but no one has charged that openly. The bishop has too many powerful friends. Whatever the case, there's no doubt of his Excellency's weakness for young women. However charming his residence, don't walk about alone, especially at night. Once you and Margaret have gone to bed, remain there until morning."

This further warning seemed excessive. Did her aunt really think she would wander at night in a strange house? Elise almost asked, then thought better of it.

"Tomorrow, before we leave Clarington," Melisande added, "your uncle will meet with the count to conclude the discussions they began last week."

Hearing this, Elise's fears returned. "His business with the count is not yet finished?"

"Evidently not." There was no expression on Melisande's face.

Elise struggled to seem casual in her response. "Might I inquire the nature of it?"

"Of course, but I'm not at all clear about it. I believe it's something to do with a loan and some land. I really don't know the rest."

"I see." If it was only that, she was safe. "When do we leave for Clarington?"

As soon as the midday meal is over. As for our stay at the bishop's, we'll make the best of it. It's only for a night."

*

They left Bourne Castle early in the afternoon. Their party was small, comprised of her aunt and uncle, each with a servant, Elise and Margaret, and four men at arms from the castle garrison. On the way north, the fields were green, the roads pleasantly smooth and dry. Late in the day, they rode into Clarington, a busy market town. There they found the beggars in full force. After giving the alms expected of the earl's party, they made their way to the bishop's palace. Approached from a dark and narrow street, it was indeed a splendid sight. Built of smooth blocks of cream-colored stone, it was three stories high. Riding through the ornately carved portal, they entered a large central court. When they had finished dismounting, the bishop himself appeared. A plump, balding, middle-aged man, he greeted them with courteous solicitude. Looking at him, it was hard to believe the stories Melisande had told her. Still, she found it difficult to keep from flinching when he took her hand in a paternal manner and addressed her uncle.

"You've kept your niece too well hidden, my lord. I've heard tales of her youth and beauty, but they failed to do her justice. Happy the man who is able to pluck such a flower as a bride." Elise forced a smile, hoping the bishop was not referring to the count.

Unused to such florid language, the earl did not reply. Once the welcome was over, Elise and Margaret were shown to the

room they would share with two other ladies and their servants. A half hour later, the bishop led their party on a tour of his
new residence. Nearly square in plan, the palace had four wings
around an open court. On the second level, there was an arcad-
ed porch. In his Excellency's rooms, in place of rushes, richly
patterned rugs lay on the floor.

"These fine carpets are from the East, a taste I acquired from
the Sicilian Arabs. As a young priest," he explained, "I held a
position in Palermo."

The guests nodded in appreciation, and the tour went on.
Last of all, Osbert showed the earl and his wife their chambers,
separate but connecting rooms with places for their servants.
Such privacy for visitors, even noble ones, was rare. Clearly, the
bishop wanted to impress his guests.

At supper, there were eighteen people at a U-shaped table.
While musicians played, retainers wearing the bishop's livery
waited on the guests. Prior Gramont sat beside the bishop, her
aunt and the earl to his right. Elise was seated between her uncle and the Count de Vere. Tonight, the count was less oppres-
sively attentive. She listened as he talked, at times interjecting a
few words. If, during an interlude of silence, she felt his eyes on
her, she busied herself with the abundant food. The meal was
sumptuous, with oysters fresh from the coast, cooked venison,
and roasted fowl. As the night wore on, Elise drank three cups
of Gascon wine. It made her a bit dizzy but it also calmed her.

At one point, while listening to a guest at an adjacent table,
the earl and his wife leaned forward. Looking beyond them,
Elise observed the bishop and the prior trading glances. A
young serving boy seemed to be the object of their knowing
looks. She was the only one who noticed. The others were too
busy eating, drinking, or conversing. Gradually, as always happened, the company grew livelier and louder. At last, the sweets
were served, two kinds of tart along with jellied quinces and a
pudding. Finally, the first guest spoke of retiring. Seizing her
chance, Elise pleaded fatigue and begged to be excused. She held
her breath as she left the banquet, afraid she might still be

summoned back. Once out of the hall, she fairly ran up the stairs to her room. There had been no hint of a betrothal. Once again she had escaped.

As she readied herself for bed, Elise's thoughts were already back in Windham. She wondered how Edmond and Martin, her fellow pupils at the lessons taught by Canon Thomas, had spent the holy day. Once again, she found herself wishing Edmond was not the son of an impoverished baron of mixed Saxon blood. Although ruled by a king from Anjou, England was still a Norman kingdom a century after the conquest, a land where all those in power spoke Norman French. Since Edmond's mother was Norman, he of course spoke it too, just as she and Martin and all educated people did. Unfortunately, Edmond was also a second son—and worse, destined for the abbey.

Beyond that, Elise hated the fact that women, whatever their rank, were almost never allowed to choose their spouses. Queen Eleanor herself had been badly mismatched, wed too young to King Louis of France. That misalliance ended in annulment, a luxury of the great; lifelong misery was the lot of many others. Elise's parents had been an exception. Theirs had been a true love match. For her, their happiness remained a kind of beacon, a light from the past to guide her. She wanted a marriage like theirs or none at all. It was yet another reason she disliked the count. Puffed up with vanity, full of feigned affection, he could never be part of such a union. She put him out of her mind and, dreaming of a different future, fell asleep beside her faithful Margaret.

She awoke with a terrible thirst and a pain in her stomach, no doubt the result of the wine and the highly seasoned food. There was no sound but the breathing of the sleeping women and their servants. From what she could tell, it was the middle of the night. Not wishing to wake the others, Elise lay on her back and tried by force of will to make herself feel better. To no avail; the effort only made it worse. On the brink of being sick, she remembered the bishop showing off his Arab-style fountains. There was one in the wall of the porch a little distance from her chamber. She sat up carefully while Margaret snored beside her. It was a warm night, and the curtains on the bed were open. At first, Elise stared into total darkness. Then she saw a thin line of light, the edge of what must be the door. With that as her goal, she slid cautiously from the bed. Beneath the sparse rushes, the stone floor was cold on her feet. She searched for her slippers with her toes, found them, and moved slowly toward the door. Reaching it, she felt for the latch, lifted it gently, and pushed. In the next moment, she was on the porch. On the wall to her left, a lamp attached to a hook cast a feeble light. Beyond it in the darkness, she could hear the murmur of the fountain in its niche. Running to it, she bent over the basin and took a long drink from the jet of water. Only then did her stomach erupt. She was sick in the basin once, then again. Embarrassed, she wiped it clean with the help of the jet, leaned over, and took a final drink.

Better now, she bathed her face. As she stood up and breathed the cool night air, the breeze caressed her arms and legs beneath her nightdress. The feeling of sensuous freedom was strangely exhilarating. Once again, she thought of Edmond, intimate thoughts that made her blush. At the same time, she remembered her aunt's warning not to leave her room. Feeling strands of wet hair on her face, she raised her head to smooth them back. As she did, she saw a sliver of light fall on the porch across the way. What if someone saw her in this state? Alarmed, she pulled back into a recess in the wall. From there she watched the wedge of light expand and then, as if in a dream, watched her double, another female in a nightdress, step from behind a door. Who could it be at this hour?

The door opened wider and she recognized the graceful figure of the Lady Melisande. What could she be doing here? Her bedchamber was at the far end of the porch. Soon, Elise had her answer. A tall, dark-bearded man, naked to the waist, stepped from the room into the light. It was the Count de Vere. At once, Melisande put her arms around him. He held her close and kissed her on the mouth. Then, grasping her shoulders, he pushed her abruptly away. It took her aunt a moment to regain her balance. As if in defiance, she threw herself back into her lover's arms. Recoiling, he held her arm with one hand and with the other slapped her face. The sound echoed painfully through the court.

Elise was amazed to see Melisande, of all people, treated thus, but her aunt scarcely reacted. She merely turned and walked slowly toward the corner of the porch. Before she had disappeared into the darkness, the count had closed his door.

And that was all, a brief moment in the night. Yet by the time it was over, Elise understood a great deal she had not before: for one thing, her aunt's silence about the count's suit for her hand, for another, the postponement—or was it the cancellation?—of the betrothal she had dreaded. Might she owe her reprieve to Melisande's passion for the count? Harder to grasp was the count's abusive conduct. Last, worst of all, was the shame of her aunt's betrayal of the husband who adored her. Until tonight her aunt had seemed in every way the perfect wife, dutiful and faithful, devoted to the earl. And now this.

Elise stood on the porch in the darkness and tried to absorb it. All at once, the world had become a different place, one where rules observed by day were violated in the night, where nothing could be taken at face value. Her aunt's warning about late-night wandering, for instance. She saw now that her motive was not to safeguard Elise but to keep her from discovering her liaison. Thanks to the wine and the bishop's rich food, her effort had failed, leaving Elise with a number of questions. For one, how had this meeting come about? Was it long planned or an impulse of the moment? From what she knew of her aunt, the latter seemed unlikely. Did that mean her aunt had known the count before his recent introduction to their household? Elise felt she must have, but at least for the present she could only guess.

But what misery for her uncle if he knew! Still, he might never need to. Perhaps it had been a momentary lapse, a reckless act that would not be repeated. Although repellent to her, the count was undoubtedly a handsome man. He was also younger than her uncle, who seemed if anything older than his age. Elise was aware these things happened just as much among the privileged as among the poor. Except for the lovers themselves, she might be the only person who knew.

Whatever the case, Elise was sure she would never forget this night, one in which, for the first time, she had glimpsed the duplicity of the world. She also knew she could never tell the earl what she had seen. He loved his wife too much; it would break his heart. And there was another thing Elise knew for certain. After what she had witnessed tonight, she could never consent to be the bride of Gilles de Vere.

3

Martin was distracted by a rasping voice. "Tell me, where is your father, Master Martin? Too busy for the fair?"

With a leathery face framed by tin and copper wares, the tinker peered out from his stall and waited for an answer.

Martin saw no reason to conceal the truth. He had been going places by himself for years, ever since his father had become steward at Preston Manor. "He's in Winchester till Friday."

"On business during holy Whitsuntide?"

"It was a thing that couldn't wait," Martin said, annoyed at the man's prying.

"I see. Most likely some botched affair of Baron Hugh's. Without Alfred Rendon as his steward, the baron would be lost."

"I wouldn't let the baron hear you say that," Martin shouted, moving off into the crowd. His father's employer was known for a bad temper that was even worse when he was in his cups.

Next, Martin passed a dozen stalls, some newly built and painted in bright colors, others in need of repair or thrown together with discarded wood. All were full of things to tempt the people of Windhamshire: breads of all kinds, pies of beef, pork, and eels, sweetmeats made with candied fruits or honey. There were booths with cheeses, herbs and spices, stalls with many kinds of pottery, tables with leather goods and stacks of cloth in several colors. He examined them one by one, sometimes pausing to laugh at a painted mummer who kept dodging in and out among the crowd, mocking and playing tricks.

At last, Martin grew tired of being jostled by his neighbors and walked to the end of the village street. Here in the precinct of the parish church, the sounds of the crowd were muted. The old church's front tower was flat-roofed and square, its rough-

hewn stones framed by timbers in the Saxon style. Beside the
church there was a grassy yard sprouting a crop of gravestones.
Some were carved crosses, others standing slabs, most were
small stone markers overgrown with weeds. Martin's mother,
who had died when he was six, was buried here. He walked to
her grave and knelt to say a prayer beside the stone that bore
her name. Then, knowing it would please his father, he entered
the church to light a candle for his mother. Inside, the cool
darkness smelled of damp. He dug into the knapsack slung over
his shoulder and found a coin. Dropping it into the box provided, he lit a small candle and prayed once again for his mother's
soul.

When he came out into the daylight, he finally admitted he
was disappointed. Edmond had agreed to meet him at the fair at
midday. Two hours had now passed, and there was still no sign
of him. Tired of waiting, Martin decided to set out alone for the
place he had wanted to show his friend. Leaving the village, he
came to the edge of a stream and crossed the narrow wooden
bridge that spanned it. Before him, bright green in the sunlight,
lay a great open field. Inhaling the grassy smell, he plunged into
it. Gradually, the sounds of the village grew fainter. Soon the
quiet enchantment of a summer afternoon fell over him, its silence interrupted only by his muted footfalls and the distant
cawing of a crow.

As Martin moved steadily north, he thought about his absent
friend. There always seemed to be something amiss at Preston
Manor. Because of his father's position, Martin knew the situation all too well. In his role as steward, Alfred Rendon was
nearly always busy with his duties. His skills at writing and
counting were crucial to Baron Hugh, who neither read nor
wrote. This lack of learning was compounded by the baron's
love of drink. Still, whatever his faults, and they were many,
Hugh Preston was of noble birth, much higher in rank than
Martin's father.

Such distinctions meant little to Martin and his fellow pupils. On the other hand, the Lady Elise's inclusion in their les-

sons had shocked many. Martin had been told that her aunt, the earl's wife, had urged her husband to allow it. Their teacher, Canon Thomas, was a well known scholar, but because of a chronic ailment, he had retired to a cottage in the village. To those who objected to his female pupil, the old priest pointed out that both boys were destined for the Church, and that all three of his students were under his constant supervision. In fact, they all greatly loved and admired their teacher. Thanks to him, Martin's hunger for knowledge had grown immensely. He now wanted to fathom the truth of things, to know all he could of the past as well as foreign lands and distant places. As things stood, however, he would have to learn about it all from books. A year from this fall, he would enter Windham Abbey as a Benedictine novice.

Walking briskly, Martin was nearly half way through the field. Ahead of him, a sky of deep blue full of luminous clouds met the line of the woods on the horizon. Beyond them, a mile or so to the north, lay his destination, the mysterious spot he had discovered a year ago.

Less than an hour later, he had made his way through the woods and reached a clearing. Before him was an open space covered with grass, a broad circle surrounded by large standing stones. Leaving the shelter of the trees, he entered the clearing and was captured by its spell as always. Once inside the circle, he felt he could sense the presence of a past as ancient as the scarred and weathered stones themselves. Some thought the crudely carved monuments had been erected by a vanished race of giants, others that they were put here by the ancient gods, the ones men worshipped before the Christians came.

Still others believed they were dragged on sledges from afar by slaves of pagan kings. Known in the village as the clearing of the stones, the place had an evil reputation. All sorts of stories were told about it; that demons gathered here at night, that sorcerers used it for their rites, that those who touched the stones were cursed. The legends varied, but all agreed the clearing was a wicked place. For that reason, no one from the village ever came here.

His teacher had taught him to disparage all such tales, the products, he said, of ignorance and superstition. In fact, Martin was happy the clearing was shunned by all. It made him feel that it belonged to him alone. The only person he wanted to share it with was Edmond, all the more so because of a thing that had happened a month ago, something so strange Martin felt a great need to talk about it with his friend.

Standing now in the center of the circle, Martin looked at the stones in the afternoon sun. There were eighteen in all; he had counted them many times. Large and gray, with patches of moss where they met the ground, they were of three kinds. Some were over twice a grown man's height, narrow and tall. Others were shorter and wider with jagged tops, a few broad and irregular in shape. In one of these, there was a rounded hollow where he liked to sit, enthroned, as it were, in the lap of the past.

Guessing his friend might be detained at Preston Manor, Martin had brought some sheets of parchment in his satchel. Closely inscribed, they were full of Latin to be learned. One had irregular verbs, the other rhetorical figures. Climbing into his seat, he pulled them out of the knapsack and settled down to work. He stayed with it for a while until his thoughts began to wander. Laying the parchments down, he gazed out over the clearing and tried to picture it in ancient times, full of pagans in long robes worshipping the sun and moon. There was almost no wind, the sunlight was warm on his face, and gradually it made him drowsy.

He awoke with a start to the sound of his name. He waited to hear it again but it was not repeated.

Then, just as he was deciding he had dreamt it, it rang out, louder and clearer this time. "Hello, Martin! Is that you?"

Recognizing the voice, he slid from his seat, let the parchments fall, and turned to see Edmond advancing toward him.

His handsome face flushed, his brown curls askew, his friend was a welcome sight.

"Edmond! I looked for you in the village. I wanted to bring you to this very spot. How on earth did you find me?"

His friend walked up to the stone and stood beside him. At sixteen, he was a year older than Martin and taller and stronger too. "It wasn't easy. When I saw you were not at the fair, I asked one or two people if they had seen you. The miller's wife said you had gone into the field north of the village. I decided to catch you but couldn't see you as I crossed the meadow. I was about to turn back when I spotted a reddish patch, the color of a shirt I knew, and a pale dot I guessed must be your mop of yellow hair. You were at the edge of the woods. I called, but you were too far away to hear. When the reddish patch disappeared into the trees, I decided to follow. Once in the woods, I kept moving north. Now and then, a fresh footprint or a newly trodden plant revealed your path. Finally, I came to this strange place and saw two legs dangling from a rock. An odd sight, to be sure!"

Stooping to pick up the parchment, Martin grinned. "And then you shouted and woke me from a dozing sleep."

"Were you really asleep, or under a spell? I must say, it took a bit of courage coming here. They tell so many weird tales about this place."

Martin was flattered by Edmond's persistence in following him, but he found it difficult to say so. He compromised. "I'm glad you overcame your hesitation."

"And I'm delighted to have found you. Nor does there seem to be anything so frightful." Despite his words, Edmond looked doubtfully around the clearing.

"Of course not," Martin said reassuringly. "As you can see, I'm very much at home. But how do you think these great stones came to be here? Come, take a look at them all before you answer."

Together, they made a quick circuit of the clearing. As they finished, a cloud covered the sun and the place took on a more threatening aspect.

"It's growing late. We'd better go," Martin suggested, and Edmond promptly agreed. On their way back through the woods, they speculated on the stones and how they came to be there. When they reached the field leading to Windham, Martin halted. "Before we go back to the village, I want to tell you about what I saw at the clearing earlier this spring."

The two sat down on the grass, and Martin began his tale. "About a month ago, on the night of a full moon, I decided I wanted to see the clearing after dark. Worn out from a long day of visiting tenants, my father fell asleep early. It was a warm night for April. I left the house at sunset, knowing it would be night by the time I reached the clearing. Not wanting to be seen, I skirted the village, taking a path that led into the field further on. Crossing it, I reached the woods."

"Weren't you afraid?"

"Yes, I was, but I was also caught up in the adventure. I had been to the clearing by day the week before and even marked a kind of pathway through woods. The moon was full, so it wasn't difficult to find my way. Half way there, still far from the clearing, I heard a sound."

"An animal?"

"No, more like a human but indistinct. I kept going, moving cautiously. Bit by bit, the sound became clearer. It was like a low moan but with a rhythmic beat."

"You realized they were people?"

"Not quite, only that they were creatures of some kind. To be honest, my first thought was of evil spirits. I wondered if Canon Thomas might be wrong, about superstition I mean, and the people from the village right."

"I would have had the same thought! Why didn't you run?"

"I don't know why—or yes, I do. Curiosity. The more afraid I became, the more I wanted to know what was there. So I went on. Soon, I glimpsed light through the trees, a dull glow in the direction of the clearing. Step by step, I came nearer. When I reached the edge of the woods, I saw there was a bonfire in the center of the clearing. The wind was behind me or I would have smelled it earlier. At that point, I forgot about devils and spirits and thought about thieves and outlaws. Who else would be camping in such a place at night? Monsters or murderers, I couldn't decide which was worse, but I was determined to find out which it was. I crept gradually closer, hiding in the bushes as I went."

"You're driving me mad. Who or what were they?"

"I'm not sure even today, but I can tell you what I saw. Inside the stone circle, a score of figures were grouped around the fire. They were wearing long, dark robes like monks' but with over-hanging hoods that hid their faces. They had been chanting, but they had stopped."

"Were they from the abbey, then?" Edwin asked, looking re-lieved.

"I couldn't tell at that point. I still had no proof they were even human. I kept thinking they would lift their hoods and show me burning eyes and monstrous faces like the devils painted on the wall in Windham parish church. Then the chanting started again, a bit like the monks' but with a stronger rhythm, more demonic than angelic. The words were not in Latin but some tongue I didn't know. It sounded a bit like the Greek Canon Thomas has started to teach us. The louder it got, the more frightened I became."

"What happened then?"

"The worst part. In the midst of the chanting, one of the fig-ures left the fire and moved directly toward me. I felt sure he must know I was there, that these creatures had some uncanny gift that told them."

"My God, what did you do?"

"I wanted to run but I knew it would give me away. I prayed and crouched lower in my hiding place. The figure came closer and halted some six feet away at the most. Then he parted his robe—it was not like a monk's but divided in front—and took a long, leisurely piss. That's how I discovered these creatures were human."

"Did you see his face?"

"No, the hood shaded it completely. As soon as he left and returned to the group, I started back, slowly at first, then faster and faster until I was running through the woods. Finally I reached this field and crossed it. I was never so happy to see the village."

Once Martin had finished his story, Edmond grew strangely silent. He seemed intrigued but wary. As the two crossed the field, they began to speculate about the nature of the band of robed and hooded figures. Gradually, elated to have shared his secret, Martin formed a plan. Animated by it, he became more persuasive with each step. By the time they reached Windham, he had won his friend over. They would return to the clearing on the night of the next full moon. If Martin had guessed correctly, there would be another gathering then. With Edmond's help, he hoped to discover the secret of the clearing of the stones.

4

Late at night on the final day of Whitsuntide, Prior Guy de Gramont was at supper with Count Gilles de Vere. As he finished his meal, the count complimented his host. "You dine as well here as they do at the castle, my friend."

The prior was inclined to agree. Between the two, glistening in the candlelight, lay the remains of a meal of roast capon, grilled beef, and pudding. On one side lay a pile of mussel shells, on the other, barely touched, a plate of sweetmeats.

Gramont smiled faintly as he replied. "And why not? I live outside the abbey walls. I make no pretense of following their rules. I leave that and most of my duties to my sub-prior, a pious and conscientious priest. Just the sort of cleric I abhor."

The count laughed and took up the theme. "Nor from what I can see do you keep monastic hours."

"I should think not. A few hours from now, in virtually the middle of the night, the rest of the abbey will rise for Matins. You can be sure I won't be among them." In fact, the prior took little notice of the abbey's rules. As most of the monks there knew, he owed his office to an unknown patron, a man of great importance in the realm. A large gift coupled with a threat of high disfavor for refusing had been enough to conquer Abbot Philip's scruples in the matter. Indeed, not even the abbot knew the name of Gramont's patron's. Everything had been done through intermediaries.

"All the same," the count added, "you are not without your uses to the abbey."

"Certainly not. The abbot is old and unused to the world. Detesting wealth and privilege as I do, I am not awed by our benefactors. If I play on their vanity, they loosen their purses. In the course of this Whitsuntide, I've gained the abbey three substantial gifts. Tonight, with our guests finally gone, I can be myself again. I believe I've even drunk a bit too much, something much more in your line."

"A modest amount, I would say."

"For others, perhaps, but not for me. As you know, I prefer to maintain control. Speaking of wealth and privilege, you've said nothing of your negotiations with the earl."

"If I have not, it's because there's little to report. Nothing has been settled but a loan de Bourne agreed to, for the sake of his niece should we marry. And the girl is still young. Her uncle is in no haste to have her wed. I also have my own reasons for holding off."

"Does she not please you?" the prior asked. "I had the opposite impression."

"No, no, it's hardly that. You've seen her yourself. She's quite lovely, a bit too clever perhaps, but charming nonetheless."

"Too clever?"

"One might not know it from her conversation. She has little enough to say, but her aunt and uncle assure me she is quite the scholar. She reads both French and Latin and writes well in both. I could teach her more interesting things, of course, but as it happens, I have a chance for another match, a Burgundian widow with lands and a good deal of money."

"I see. Another rich widow avid for your charms. Your first wife made you wealthy, did she not?"

"Not as wealthy as I had hoped. After a year, she died in childbirth as did the child, a son. Which was probably just as well. I needed her money more than an heir."

Indeed, Gramont thought, the count and he were alike in this: their disdain for the ties of affection that governed ordinary men. This absence of feeling was hardly surprising in the prior's case. The man the world knew as Guy de Gramont was a bastard, the castoff son of a great nobleman, Geoffrey de Mandeville, the first Earl of Essex. A companion of monarchs, the earl had also been Constable of the Tower of London. As it happened, his wife was the Count de Vere's aunt, Rohese de Vere. Thus, unknown to the world, the two men were cousins, although not by blood. Oddly enough, they somewhat resembled each other. Both men were tall and lean with thick dark hair and carefully trimmed beards. In other respects, they differed. At thirty-seven, the count had the kind of dark eyes and olive skin that women seemed to favor. The prior, the taller of the two, had a long face, fair skin, and deep-set blue eyes. Aware of his imposing looks, he often used them to good effect.

Now, thinking ahead, he went over their plans for the following day. "I'll set out early for Clarington wearing the clothes you've lent me and riding your horse. Before I go, I'll dismiss my servant for the day. I've left you one of my Benedictine habits. Once the Lady Melisande is gone, you can take my mount to Clarington. We'll reconnoiter at the bishop's. Those who see the earl's wife will believe she has come to confer with the Prior of Windham Abbey, her confessor and advisor."

"Good, I shall make sure I'm not seen until I leave wearing your clothes. Caution is crucial. I don't wish to fall out of favor with the earl. He may yet be my uncle by marriage."

"I'm glad you're being careful. I, too, have a good deal to lose should my role in this be discovered." In fact, the prior had only one motive in supporting the count in his liaison; he wanted him well funded. A rich marriage alone could do that. The Lady Melisande was the key to the marriage with Elise.

Sooner or later, the prior might well have to leave Windham Abbey. When that day came, he would need his cousin's gratitude. Then and now, the more dependent Gilles was on him the better. That way, he would be able to convert his dependency into concrete support. "You know I am with you in this as in all your efforts," he added. "Luckily, your skills with women combined with your title have seldom failed you in the past."

"You flatter me cousin, although what you say is true enough." With these words, as if honoring himself, the count raised his cup and drained it.

The prior also drank, and for the first time that night the two were silent. Then one of the candles on the table sputtered out. Neither man moved to relight it. Suspecting the wine had numbed his guest, Gramont decided to revive him.

"Come cousin," he said, "you've grown dull. Let me rouse you with a ribald tale, one you may not have heard. Do you know the story of the whore of Dover?"

"A bawdy tale?

"Lascivious, in fact." Gramont saw he had piqued his cousin's interest. The count was not used to such stories from him.

"I don't think I've heard it. Go on."

For the next few minutes, Gramont recounted the lewd tale, that of a harlot of Dover who, because of a wager she had made, ended by servicing a foreign ship's entire crew, from the captain to the oarsmen in the galleys. At the end of what was, in fact, the first part of the story, the count exclaimed, "Bravo! A capital tale, and all the better if true. If so, can you tell me the name of the infamous slut?"

"It *is* true, my friend, but you're too ready with your praise. There's another part. Let me finish and then, if you like, I'll tell you the woman's name."

The second part was even more outrageous, detailing how the bawd had tricked her sister strumpets when they tried to steal her earnings. At the end, the count burst into laughter, and the prior spoke again.

"I see I've amused you. Now, if you still wish to know, I shall tell you what I've told no man before, the name of the infamous whore of Dover."

"Please do," Gilles urged. "Let's see if I recognize it."

"Very well. Her name was Jessica Redfield."

The count nodded knowingly. "Of course! Even in Normandy, I've heard the name, a byword for sluttishness."

"Indeed. And what I tell you next only one other man in England knows. That woman, Jessica Redfield, was my mother."

Gramont saw the shock on his cousin's face. Then, after a moment, Gilles grinned as if equal to the jest. "Mother, indeed, you go too far! In this case, beyond credulity."

At these words, the prior felt a rush of anger too intense to be concealed. Once again, he saw its effect on Gilles's face.

"God's blood!" the count exclaimed. Are you in earnest? If so, forgive me. How could I have known? I had no idea your mother was so lowborn. I merely assumed . . . "

"Assumptions can be dangerous, my friend, along with the desire to please. The latter, if carried too far, can have the opposite effect." Even as he spoke, Gramont's anger began to cool. Why, after all these years, had he told this story to his cousin? Perhaps it was the wine.

The count went on apologetically. "I suppose I should have realized. I knew your father did not raise you, but how is it that, left with such a creature, you were so well tutored as a boy?"

"That's another sordid tale. Once abandoned by my father, my heartless mother gave me to an aging couple in an obscure village. She sent them a pittance three times a year. They were ignorant, poor, and brutal. I was ten when she died, ending the dole. Pleading poverty, my caretakers took me to the local priest. He saw I was bright and eager to learn. He decided to take me in and teach me. His cook fed me well every day, something new for me. I made my bed in a bundle of rags near the embers of the fire and was grateful. A few weeks passed this way. Then one night, I learned the price of my education. Perhaps you can guess what it was."

"I daresay I can. The story's common enough."

"It is. But like any child, I hated his fat, smelly body invading mine week after week. At that time, my hatred of the Church began. Later, it came to include the kings and nobles whom the Church supports, men like my detested father. As I grew older, I turned into a handsome, clever boy. Endearing myself to the priest, I manipulated his desire. When that failed, I threatened to expose his sinful vice. In the end, he gave me what I wanted: first learning, then the money I needed to leave that wretched place."

"You were a resourceful boy."

"Of necessity," the prior said grimly. "As for your surprise, the fault was mine. Before tonight, I've never spoken about this. I gave no thought to your response. My mother was a whore but beautiful, they say. Years after her death, a friend of hers, a woman of her trade, told me the story. She was still young and new in her profession when she met my father. He was fifty, already past his prime. Mad for her, he decided to keep her as his mistress. For a year, she lived in luxury, adoring him, but when he learned she was with child he turned her out. When she finally understood that he would never recognize her or her bastard, her devotion turned to hatred. From then on, she reveled in her infamy, knowing each tale would remind my father that this trollop was the mother of his son. Spawned by such parents, how could I not despise the love of men and women? And what, for that matter, is this so-called love? A mere trick of nature to insure humanity's survival."

In the dim light of the two remaining candles, the prior saw his cousin had no response. "I commend your silence, Gilles. And you're right not to console me. Nor am I ungrateful for my past. It taught me early to know the vileness of humankind. Today I have something better than what men call love, which even the most wretched may possess. My father, Geoffrey de Mandeville, may he suffer eternally in hell, turned traitor to both King Stephen and that monarch's rival for the throne, the Empress Maud. He ended his life in the marshes of the Fens, surrounded by the remnants of his army. Only by dying in a skirmish did he finally escape the gallows. His legitimate children were protected by their lady mother."

"My aunt Rohese," the count interjected. "She did all she could to surmount their father's shame."

"Exactly. Today her son, William de Mandeville, is Earl of Essex, an intimate of King Henry. Prouder by far than his sire, he cannot bear to have his great name sullied by a story such as mine. He buys my silence with a yearly income, a great part of which is my stipend from the abbey."

Nodding, Gilles lifted his cup and spoke with an air of conviction. "You've done well by your misfortune, cousin. I'm proud to be the one man in England beyond your disdainful half-brother to know how well. I raise my cup to you."

Suddenly tired of the conversation, Gramont merely nodded. Sooner or later, the company of others always wearied him. As he watched the count drink, it struck him that his cousin was the only person in the world who spanned the gulf between his past and present, his public and his private selves. The thought made him slightly uneasy. The count had two salient vices: women and drink. Taken together, they made him difficult to trust completely. Nonetheless, their lives had now become too deeply intertwined to be easily separated.

5

Crouched behind a clump of bushes, he saw only a dark, looming outline with the moon behind it. The figure was holding a heavy stick or club, ready to strike. Then a voice whispered, "Martin, is that you?"

Recognizing Edmond, he stood up. "At last! Where have you been? I've been watching the meadow for over an hour."

Lowering his weapon, Edmond moved closer. "This afternoon, my brother arrived from London unexpectedly. My father and he drank even more than usual at supper, for St. James's Eve, they said. In the end, my mother became afraid and begged me not to leave. At last, my father fell into a drunken sleep. My brother soon followed, and I left. Once in Windham, I had to find a different way. Some villagers were celebrating St. James's Eve by dancing in the field. So as not to be seen, I took the path to the east of it. When I reached the woods, I followed them here to the spot where we agreed to meet. I brought the club in case we run into trouble."

"Well, you're here now," Martin whispered, "that's all that matters."

They had been unable to come in June. Tonight might be their last chance to see the gathering this summer.

Thanks to the full moon, they had little trouble finding their way. Inside the woods, Martin breathed the deep perfume of the summer night. Through the dark leaves, he could see a luminous sky full of stars. Halfway to the clearing, they smelled smoke from a fire. Before long, between the branches of the trees, the tallest stones appeared, a mottled silver in the moonlight. Approaching the circle, they saw something new in the center: a dark, dome-shaped mass like an oversized hut. Smoke rose from its roof, tinted pink by a fire inside. As they watched from the safety of the woods, Martin heard the same low, rhythmic chanting as before. Tonight, however, the gathering was inside the hut. They could see nothing. All their planning had been in vain.

Or perhaps not. Martin turned to Edmond and whispered. "Do you see the opening to the right? We might be able to look inside from there."

"Yes, possibly," Edmond whispered back. "Let's move in that direction."

Still inside the woods, they went about twenty feet on the path around the clearing. Then they heard the barking of a dog. Was it a watchdog? If it alerted the members, they were sure to be discovered.

As if reading his thoughts, Edmond came up with an idea. "The dog seems to be on the north side of the clearing. I'll stay under cover and see if I can silence it. If I'm not back soon, you might want to take a look inside the hut yourself. If something goes wrong, run to the woods and don't wait for me. I'm faster than you, I'll catch up with you at the edge of the field back to Windham." Clutching the heavy stick, Edmond was gone before Martin could object.

Impressed by his friend's decisive action, Martin felt painfully inept. As the moments passed, the stones became more menacing, grim sentinels guarding their secret. What had made him think it was his to uncover? The barking grew worse. The chanting stopped. One by one, three dark-robed figures came out of the opening. They began talking loudly.

"Go see what's making the mongrel bark!"

"Some woodland animal, surely. What else at this hour in this place? It was a mistake to bring a watchdog."

"What's done is done. Let's find the reason for the barking."

Martin's heart began to throb. If they found the dog, they would also find Edmond!

And then the barking stopped.

Martin waited, praying it was over. For once, his prayers were quickly answered. It did not begin again. The third man was speaking now, something Martin couldn't hear. A sound of murmured agreement followed. After a brief look around, the three men filed back into the hut.

Inside, the chanting resumed. Greatly relieved, Martin settled back into the safety of the woods. As time passed, more smoke appeared above the hut, redder now and laced with glowing sparks. Instinctively, he felt it was time to look inside. But where was Edmond?

Then he understood. Edmond would never have clubbed the dog to death. He must have befriended it. He was probably afraid it might start up again if he left it. Meanwhile, the chanting was growing louder, its rhythm accelerating. The time had come to look inside.

Observing the men, Martin had decided against the opening. He would try a different way. He crept out of the woods and moved stealthily across the grass. Approaching the hut, he saw its walls were composed of mud, leaves, and branches. Cut and bent saplings provided the framework. Coming closer, he surveyed the chinks of light that had first attracted him. Drawing near to one, he took a deep breath and leaned carefully forward. With one eye closed, he peered inside.

As he had before, he noted some sixteen or seventeen figures in dark robes with overhanging hoods. They were standing in a circle. On the side closer to Martin, there was a fire in a cairn made of earth and stone. Had all this been built in a night? He doubted it. Since no one from the village ever came here, it could have been done in advance. As the fire burned, the flames cast distorted shadows on the sloping walls. Viewed up close in the eerie light, the hooded figures seemed more menacing than ever. Feeling unsteady, Martin pulled back to gain a better foothold. There was a flat stone at the base of the hut. He moved it slightly and stood on it. When he looked again, he noticed a banner attached to a pole with a crosspiece on the far side of the hut. On it was a crudely painted figure in an armored breastplate. Its head was that of a beaked bird in profile. Where its legs should have been, there were two curling serpents. In its left hand, the creature held a shield, in its right, a kind of stick or whip; he couldn't tell which in the flickering light. As the chanting continued, Martin tried to catch a word or two but failed. There were no Greek words he recognized. Then a figure in front of him shifted, and he glimpsed a part of something just below his line of sight. Stretching to his full height, he braced himself against the frame, looked down, and was stunned by what he saw.

Spread out on an earthen platform some three feet above the ground, a naked youth lay on his back facing away. Martin could see only the top of his head, his chest and navel beyond, and a patch of dark pubic hair. His arms and legs hung over the side, secured with cords of twisted cloth. Despite his bonds, the young man did not seem to be struggling. As his head shifted slightly, Martin saw he was also gagged.

The whole thing was like a carving he had seen at Clarington Cathedral, an image of Abraham offering up his son Isaac as a sacrifice. Was this some strange reenactment of that story? If so, there would be a miraculous rescue. Whatever it was, the scene terrified him. Yet he couldn't bring himself to turn away.

Now a tall figure who seemed to be a leader of some kind approached the center of the fire-lit space. Standing between the banner and the platform, he bowed his head beneath his hood, leaned forward, and made some adjustment to the young man's bonds. The chanting ceased, and he recited a long incantation in a strikingly deep voice. Next, he made a sign with his hand and the chanting resumed. Then he bent forward and reached down.

Trying to see, Martin stood on his toes, lost his balance, and fell forward, making a hole half his size in the fragile crust. As he did, the leader jerked his head up—so sharply his hood fell back. Righting himself, Martin saw the man's dark, bearded face and glaring eyes. For an instant, the two were trapped in a mutually astonished gaze.

Then, summoning all his strength, Martin bolted and ran to the north, to the nearest woods. Reaching them, he took the path to the right—toward Edmond, he hoped. Behind him, he heard the shouts of his pursuers. As he ran, their voices became less distinct. Thank God, they must have taken the direction to the left! Keeping to the path, he saw a dark figure moving toward him. He darted behind a bush and hid the same way he had earlier that night. He hoped the outcome would be the same. Holding his breath, he peered between the leaves. Yes, it was Edmond, still holding the club. Jumping up, Martin grabbed him and whispered in a voice that hardly seemed his own, "The other way! They're behind us."

Turning, Edmond dropped his club and ran, and Martin followed. Soon, they came to the still-tethered dog, who wagged his tail and panted. Clearly, Edmond had beguiled him. Keeping to the path in the woods, they went on running until they came to the start of the path leading back to Windham. Fleeing the moonlight, they plunged into the trees. Barely breaking their pace, they ran through bushes, leapt over rocks, dodged overhanging branches. Just when it seemed the woods would never end, they reached the field. Winded though they were, they barely paused. Halfway across the meadow, the village appeared in the moonlight.

Badly in need of a rest, they found a large rock and sat behind it, still fearful of possible pursuers. Catching his breath, Martin told his friend how he had broken through the wall and had to flee. After resting a bit, the two crossed the remainder of the meadow. Once in the sleeping hamlet, they hid from the moonlight in the shadow of the church. There, Martin spoke to his friend in a hushed voice.

"I haven't told you yet what I saw inside the hut. If you want to know now, come back to my house where we can talk. My father is in London."

Edmond agreed, and they moved on. As they passed through the village, the whitewashed cottages were ghostly in the moonlight. Inside his father's house, a simple two-room cottage, Martin closed the shutters tight and lit the candle on the table. They sat down across from each other, and for the first time that night, Martin saw Edmond clearly. His friend's face still shone from exercise, his brown curls were dark with sweat, his blue eyes full of animation. Dipping a ladle into a bucket, Martin offered him some water. They each drank twice, taking turns. Calm at last, Martin told his friend what he had seen inside the hut.

At the end of the tale, Edmond was silent, doubtless trying to take the whole thing in. Finally, he spoke. "But who do you think these people were? And what were they doing with that boy?"

"I have no idea. Their hoods concealed their faces. At the bottom of their robes, I once or twice saw feet. One was shod in a poor man's shoes, another in fine leather. As they chanted, all the voices were male."

"Renegade monks, perhaps?"

"No, their robes were different from monks'. Besides being parted in front, they had deeply overhanging hoods concealing their identities. Only the leader revealed himself by accident. I've never seen him before, but I won't forget that face. Even worse, he saw me clearly. The fire lit both our faces. It was between us, just across from the spot where I broke the wall."

"I hope you two never meet again," Edmond said earnestly.

"We certainly won't, if I can help it! But do you think we should have roused the village, awakened the sexton and asked him to ring the church bells, if only to save the boy?"

Edmond took a long time to reply. "Perhaps, but we still don't know what they were up to, whether real harm or some strange mummery. You saw no weapon, and the young man was apparently unhurt. Shouldn't we know what was happening before we call for help?"

In his present state, Martin was easily swayed. "Perhaps you're right. They may have been miming the old pagan rites, or perhaps they were a band of outlaws dealing with an errant member."

That thought seemed to strike Edmond. "They may well have been criminals of some kind, but once you and I admit we were there, the only guilt we'll prove will be our own."

"What guilt do you mean?" Martin asked.

"That of being out late at night in a forbidden place at some strange rite. What would the people in the village think? What would our parents say?"

Martin saw his friend's point. "I'm afraid you may be right. And yet we did it out of simple curiosity. Is that so great a crime?"

"It may not be, but for me at least, the truth would be disastrous. My father is violent when drunk and adamant about that wretched vow of his. I must be a monk, like it or not. Meanwhile, I am to live a blameless life. He used to beat me, but since I've grown too big—I confess it now, this awful thing—he beats my mother for the faults he finds in me. He tolerates any failing in the future knight, my brother, in me, nothing."

"I never guessed it was that bad," Martin said regretfully. "I see now how my selfish curiosity has harmed you."

A pained look appeared on Edmond's face. "Please don't speak of selfishness. You are my best, indeed, my only true friend. I would not have done it for another, but I couldn't let you go alone tonight. Yet I took it as a given that our visit would be secret. As long as it is, you'll have done me no harm."

Chastened by Edmond's words, Martin reconsidered. "The truth is, I'm not sure of anything. If the worst is true and they intended to harm the boy, then it's already done. In that case, we may hear of it soon. If we don't, it may very well mean he was unharmed. Perhaps our interruption saved him."

Edmond's face wore a strange expression, a blend of shame and hesitation. "You don't think I've urged the coward's way?"

"I could never think that of you, Edmond. You were the one whose courage I depended on tonight."

"Then I'm glad I was there. And if we are wrong to keep silent, let the blame fall on me. Do you agree to tell no one?"

"Yes. I'll say nothing without consulting you."

"Good, but after tonight, I'm never returning to that evil place. Promise me you won't either, at least not at night."

Martin promised, then added, "We're both weary, Edmond, and the hour is late. Feel free to spend the night here if you like. You can sleep in my cot and I'll take my father's."

"Thank you, my friend," Edmond said, smiling. "It would be wonderful to pass the night here in the quiet of your house. After an evening of drinking, my brother tosses in bed and mutters fearfully. On nights like this, I sleep in my little lean-to room, but that's by the kitchen where the noise will wake me early. Still, if my mother should peer through the crack of my door and fail to see me, she would be distraught. Between my father and Geoffrey, she has enough to burden her."

"Then of course you must go," said Martin, disappointed yet oddly relieved. At the door, Edmond held him in a warm embrace and then pulled back.

"What's this? Your heart's pounding, my friend. There's no need to be frightened. Those men will never find us now, but let's both pray to the Savior to protect the young man."

"Yes, that above all," Martin said, and the two parted firmer friends than ever. Almost at once, Martin fell into bed. Although exhausted, he still could not sleep. First, he thought about Edmond's vow to take the burden of their silence on himself. That was all very well, but if they were wrong, the guilt would be equally theirs—more his, in fact, for initiating their misadventure.

Next, he thought of his friend's remark about his beating heart. It had indeed been pounding, not from fear but from another cause, a peculiar excitement he felt when close to Edmond. And that feeling was also connected to something he had failed to tell his friend, that the young man inside the hut was naked. In fact, Martin suspected the youth might have been there for a particular shameful purpose, one he could not bring himself to speak of to his friend. Indeed, he almost hoped that was the case. It might mean the young man would emerge from the ordeal alive.

*

Three days passed, and Martin was relieved that no boy had been found dead in Windhamshire. At the same time, he could think of little else but returning to the clearing of the stones. He wanted to see what remained of the hut that had so surprisingly appeared, but he would also keep the promise he had made to Edmond and not return at night. On Sunday afternoon, he set out for the clearing. The day was sunny and warm, full of the sweetness of high summer. Crossing the field, he made his way through the woods on the now familiar path. Before long, he was once again among the stones inside the clearing. There was no sign the hut had ever been there. Had it disappeared by magic? Had they imagined the whole thing? Challenged by the lack of any traces, he took the path around the clearing and looked for discarded remnants of the structure. He went completely around but found nothing. Beginning another circuit, he moved further into the woods, unhappy to have to explore in the denser undergrowth. Half way around, he found a group of boulders in his path. Ready to give up, he climbed onto the largest to gain a better prospect. On the other side, half concealed in a wide ditch, he spied the remnants of the hut: discarded saplings, broken branches, crumbling walls made of dead leaves and mud.

Having succeeded this far, he went back to the clearing. Where the members had gathered, the grass was still trampled, but in the very center it was strangely new. Then he saw the trick; pieces of grass had been cut elsewhere and replanted. Grabbing hold of a nearby stick, he dug out one piece, then another, setting each to the side. Digging deeper, he hit something hard. It turned out to be a crude knife blade, a piece of carefully chipped flint. Had it belonged to some ancient dweller? He had seen such things before. Digging deeper, he found a cache of clay shards, many darkly stained. Removing more grass, he continued to dig. There, mixed in with some shards and another flint blade, he found several pieces of hollow reed, many stained and sharpened at one end.

Puzzled, he went on digging. Then he heard the distant blaring of a horn. The sound came from the north. It might well be a party of hunters from Clarington. If they were strangers, they might not know to avoid the clearing. Alarmed, he stopped and looked at himself. His hands and arms were dark with dirt, his leggings badly stained. What if someone, seeing him, connected him to the rumors about the clearing? Or worse, to the sinister rite he had witnessed five days ago?

That would make a fine beginning, or rather ending, of his clerical career! The horn sounded again, closer now. It was time to go. Working quickly, he returned his findings to the ground. Replacing the grass, he brushed the dirt off his clothes as best he could and set out for the woods. Inside their cool shade, he looked back at the stones in the sunlight. How many secrets their silence must hold! Regretfully, he bade the clearing farewell. Somehow, he felt sure he would not return.

6

In a thin, even voice, Canon Thomas was reading aloud from the *Lives of the Caesars*. He and his pupils were seated at a round oak table with a surface smoothed by years of use. Because of his weakened eyesight, the old scholar sat nearest to the little window of his cottage, Elise next to him. At times, the priest would render a difficult Latin passage into French. At one point, the better to convey its meaning, he translated a Latin phrase into English. Amused by his use of the vulgar tongue, Elise and Martin laughed. Belatedly, Edmond joined them. In fact, he was finding it difficult to pay attention. It was a hazy September day, and in the half-light of the window, Elise's dark hair and dark eyes seemed to have a kind of glow. That glow and the enigmatic smile that sometimes lingered on her full, pink lips continually distracted him.

Interrupting his reading, Canon Thomas turned to her. "And what do you think, young lady, of these emperors portrayed by Suetonius with such disturbing candor? Are they in any way models for the monarchs of today?"

Lifting her slender chin, Elise answered at once. "Good Father, need you ask? They are the worst of examples, cruel and vicious, if not, like Caligula, altogether mad."

"Indeed. I'm not surprised you feel that way. And what is your opinion, Master Martin? Are the rulers of the present day so different from these Caesars?"

"I'd like to think so, father, but I can't say so with conviction."

"A sensible wariness, I'm sure. I wonder what Edmond thinks."

It took him a moment to realize it was a question. "I think I agree in some measure with both my fellow pupils," Edmond said, glancing at Elise, "but I find it difficult to picture any Christian king acting as badly as these tyrants."

"Spoken like a true believer, Edmond. Still, we mustn't be blind to our rulers' faults or to the virtues of some pagan emperors. Marcus Aurelius, for one, was both a philosopher and a ruler."

Edmond nodded, sensing the measured wisdom of Canon Thomas's words. He and Martin both greatly admired their teacher. A pious priest and a devoted scholar, he was as kind as he was learned. Elise felt the same, he was sure, even though they had never discussed it. As soon as their lessons were over, her nurse Margaret appeared at the door and took her home.

Now, in fact, the abbey's distant bells rang out for Sext, and Canon Thomas spoke again. "It seems midday is here, so let us conclude our lesson." Raising his hand, he blessed them as he always did in parting. "May God's grace go with you, my children."

Edmond watched as Elise bade their teacher farewell and exited the cottage. While Martin lingered inside discussing some question with Canon Thomas, Edmond moved toward the cottage window. He could smell the dust of the street in the sultry air. Trailing a little cloud of it, Margaret had just arrived. Having come from her sister's in the village, she began to lament the vices of her shiftless nephews. He had been told that the nurse's own husband and children had died of the plague many years ago. While Elise stood and patiently listened, he was able to admire her graceful figure and the charming way she stood, head tilted back, as the breeze played with her veil.

At last, the nurse ended her rant and the two started homeward. Martin and their teacher continued to talk. Unnoticed by them, he stepped outside and watched Elise walk up the street. One by one, the villagers greeted her as she passed. Edmond was jealous of them all. Feeling abandoned, he saw her come to the spot where she and Margaret turned onto the road leading to Bourne Castle. In a moment, she would be gone. This time, however, she let her nurse go ahead, looked back at him, smiled, and waved goodbye. He was so startled he forgot to return her greeting. In his euphoria, he forgave himself even that. What did it matter compared to the fact that her farewell was meant for him alone?

*

A month from the day of that tender parting, Edmond emerged from his lean-to room at Preston Manor. He and a servant had built the retreat a year ago, an attempt on his part to escape the chaos of his father's household. Before him, the manor fields extended to a row of distant trees whose yellow leaves announced the changing of the season. Beyond them, the Earl of Clarington's lands began.

"You must have sad thoughts, little brother, to be wearing such a face." Turning, Edmond saw his brother Geoffrey's head an inch or two above his own. Beneath his thick, straw-colored hair, his handsome face was flushed, from exercise perhaps, or just as likely, midday tippling, since his brother smelled of drink. Edmond said nothing, and Geoffrey went on.

"I know you don't pay much attention to horses, Edmond, but where did our father find that lout he hired as a groom? The stables are a shambles."

Tired of his brother's complaints, Edmond answered curtly. "He's from the village, the son of the widow Hawke."

"Hawk, indeed! A rare bird who knows nothing about the care of horses."

Edmond hesitated before replying. He felt strongly that his brother took his privileges too much for granted, showing little concern for the sacrifices made for him. Last spring, he had finished his service as a squire in London without distinction. At present, he was supposed to be searching for a lord to become his patron; Earl Desmond had graciously declined the offer. In reality, Geoffrey had spent the summer riding, drinking, and belittling everything at Preston Manor.

Suppressing his annoyance, Edmond attempted a bantering tone. "No doubt in London you're used to better. We country folk must make the best of what we have."

Apparently missing his irony, Geoffrey looked a bit puzzled. "Well, I envy you your tolerance. Perhaps if I had it, my time here would pass more quickly. For now, I'll make do with some wine and a nap before supper. The cook said there'll be fresh trout this evening. That has to be better than whatever wretched meat it was we ate last night."

In London, Geoffrey had acquired a taste for luxury in food and drink. "As I say, little brother, I'm having a cup of wine. Would you care to join me?"

In fact, Edmond would have liked to interrupt his studies with a cup, but his better judgment told him to avoid a longer conversation. Keeping himself in check, he responded in a cordial tone.

"Thank you for the offer, brother. I did come out for a bit of air, but I have more Latin yet to learn. I'll make do with a cup of well water and an apple from our orchard. As I say, we country folk have simple tastes."

As they parted, there was a look of pity on his brother's face. Edmond watched him go and, stooping a bit, reentered his lean-to room. Slamming the door, he sat down on his cot and bit savagely into his apple. Today, as always, everything about his brother irritated him. It was not that he begrudged him his place as firstborn. It was simply that he too wished to be a knight, to be part of some great venture, to test his courage before the world. Unfortunately, Edmond's fate had been decided long before his birth.

Two decades ago, Edmond's mother was many hours into a painful labor with his brother Geoffrey. At last, in a fit of pious panic, his father made the vow that, long before Edmond's birth, determined his fate. He swore that if both his wife and the child lived—and the infant was a boy—he would give his second son up to the Church. As a child, left with no other choice, Edmond simply accepted his fate. His mother even convinced him it made him special in his father's eyes. As he grew older, however, it became apparent his father favored Geoffrey. Gradually, Edmond became less inclined to accept the role the pious vow had forced on him, all the more so because his father, who was always drunk by evening, was as irreligious as a man could be and still pretend to be a Christian. In fact, Edmond finally learned the truth from someone who was present at the time of Geoffrey's birth. The baron had been thoroughly drunk when he made the foolish oath that now determined Edmond's path in life.

Added to that, there was Geoffrey himself. Four years older than Edmond, his brother had always been a bully. When they were younger and slept in the same bed, he would often wake Edmond by stifling him with a pillow. If, after struggling, he failed to free himself, there was only one escape. Even as he gasped for air, he had to lie still, defeated. Only then would his brother release him. And if, having regained his breath, Edmond reacted and struck back, it was always he who was blamed for the attack. Complaint was useless; his father had no interest in justice. Tall, blond, and robust, Geoffrey was now and always had been both his parents' favorite. Faced with that truth, Edmond buried his anger and went on. As they grew older, Geoffrey, busy with horses and weapons, generally ignored him. But not always.

And that was how it happened. It was a warm summer day, Edmond was a skinny boy of twelve, Geoffrey a strapping sixteen. Caught up in his thoughts, Edmond was treading the path beside his father's fields when he looked up and saw his brother coming toward him.

"Hallo there, your Reverence! How fares your Holiness today!"

These greetings seldom failed to kindle Edmond's rage. It was bad enough to be doomed to his vocation. To be taunted for it was too much! Ignoring his brother, he passed him and quickened his pace.

Changing directions, Geoffrey turned back and caught up with him. "No *good day* for your brother, your Excellency? Coming from church, I suppose? Are you feeling too sanctified to speak?"

He could not take this goading in silence. "I told you not to call me those names."

"Whoa, little brother, no orders, please. You're not a priest yet, you know."

Despite himself, the words shot out. "And if you'd never been born, I would never have to be!"

Edmond knew this reproach was forbidden; his father would certainly beat him if he heard it. Still, he was glad he had said it. It was only the simple truth.

His brother was ready with an answer. "Whining again? It's time to teach you a lesson, I think."

Before Geoffrey finished speaking, he grabbed Edmond and threw him to the ground. A moment later, he was astride him. Because of the heat, his brother had tied his cloak around his waist. Pulling it off, he folded it quickly and pressed it onto Edmond's face. It smelled foully of dust and sweat. Gasping, Edmond tried to tear it off, but his brother held it firmly with both hands.

It was happening again. Still, Edmond's hands were free. Furiously, he struck Geoffrey on the back. Reacting, his brother threw his whole weight onto Edmond and pressed him to the ground. Squirming to be free, Edmond pounded his brother's sides. Geoffrey seemed not to feel the blows. With each failed effort to throw him off, Edmond felt himself growing weaker. Specks of light had started to appear before his eyes. He would have to go limp and capitulate as always.

Then something in him rebelled. He had seen a stone on the path where he fell, oblong, smooth, and large, but not too large to grasp. He reached out and miraculously found it. With his last breath, he raised the rock and brought it down with all his might. The next moment, Geoffrey lay motionless beside him.

He had conquered his Goliath, but at what price? Suffocating, he had struck his brother's head even though he had aimed at his back. Or had he? Where the stone had come down on his skull, a red stain was spreading through Geoffrey's golden hair. His brother lay on his side, unmoving. Panicked, Edmond shook him, slapped him, pinched him, anything to revive him, all to no avail. His brother remained immobile. And he was much too large to move. Scarcely pausing to catch his breath, Edmond left him and ran to the manor. All the way there, he prayed that his brother was alive.

It turned out he was. Alive but completely unconscious. They carried him back on a litter and laid him in his parents' bed, a place of honor. The hours went by, day turned to night, and all the while his brother never moved. Edmond's crime was so great that his father did not even beat him. Once he had admitted striking his brother with a stone, a different penalty followed. From that day forward, the word *coward* would cling to him. No one saw it was Geoffrey, not he, who was the coward, a bully who always chose younger and smaller foes. While his brother lay senseless, of course, it was useless to plead his case. Instead, Edmond prayed he would be spared the fate of Cain, that Geoffrey would come back to life.

The following day, in the same hour he had fallen, his brother awoke with no evident impairment. In a few days, the scab started to dry and the lump on his head began to shrink. By summer's end, no trace of the wound was left. Nor, after that day, did his brother ever fight with him again. All the same, the harm was done—to Edmond, not to Geoffrey. It left him more desperate than ever to be something other than a cleric. How else could he erase the stain of that foul word? If God was good and there was justice in the world, he would be given a chance to vindicate himself. For that, he would need to be tested in battle, not for vainglory but in a noble cause. In the Holy Land, for instance. Men of valor were always needed there.

7

1174

Dismounting in the forecourt of the prior's residence, the Lady Melisande handed the reins to the groom who had ridden with her. Her mount was a fine gray palfrey, his an aging roan-colored mare. As he took the horses in hand, she spoke in her usual decisive manner.

"I shall be in the abbey church and afterward with my confessor. When you've secured my mount, ride back to Bourne Castle. Be here again when the abbey bell rings for Vespers.

"Just as you say, my lady." Bowing slightly, the man moved toward the side of the court where mounts were tethered.

Passing through the entry to the street, Melisande began the short walk to the abbey. It was a cold day in March, and she wore a wool cloak over a dress of fine green velvet. A soft leather purse was suspended from her belt, worn low on the hips in the fashion of the day. A gauzy veil partly hid her auburn hair, held in place by fillet of pure gold. Pierced in parts like the finest lace, the headband was the work of a master goldsmith in Rouen. As a final touch, she held a small jeweled prayer book in her hand. Aware of the effect she produced, one of pious gentility, she walked in a stately manner toward the abbey gate.

Lining the outside walls, there were the usual vendors with food, fraudulent relics, and images of the saints, particularly St. Michael, the abbey's patron. After them came the beggars. Since they were not allowed inside the gate, the mendicants crowded the entrance. Seeing her, they bowed low without daring to address her. As she approached, the reek of their unwashed bodies greeted her. Knowing she was observed, she resisted the impulse to cover her face or turn away. Eager to display their afflictions, the wretches exposed their stinking sores and withered limbs. Stifling her disgust, she loosened the strings of her purse and took out a handful of small coins. One by one, she dropped them into grimy outstretched palms. Near the end of the line, she gave the largest piece of silver to a crippled mother with a sickly child at her breast.

Inside the abbey grounds, she exhaled the odor of the beggars. Her charity, like the rest, was carefully contrived. She had her own reason for these visits. It had all begun shortly after Prior Gramont arrived at Windham Abbey. She had met him at the dedication of the newly finished choir and sensed an affinity between them. On a whim, she asked him to serve as her confessor. As they grew to know each other, they discarded the sacramental posture, becoming confidants instead. A few months later, the prior returned from one of his long sojourns with a party of acquaintances. Among the group, by a strange coincidence, she once again met Gilles de Vere. In this, although not by nature prone to superstition, she saw the hand of fate. Two decades ago at the court of France, the two had engaged in a short but passionate liaison. It ended abruptly when he left the court to marry.

She had been seventeen then. In the years since, her life had changed greatly. She was now the wife of an earl and the much admired mistress of Bourne Castle. She had also given her husband a son and heir. And yet she hated the tedious life they led. She was thirty-six, still beautiful, and there was rebellion in her heart. When her old lover renewed his attentions, she responded. They asked the prior for his help and he gave it willingly. Gilles was older but otherwise unchanged. He had the same insinuating smile, the same dark, compelling eyes. When they made love, it was as if her youth had returned, this time with even greater passion.

Now, reminding herself of her role, she entered the church through the small door in the right-hand portal. Inside, she blessed herself and moved quickly up the central aisle. She was already thinking of Gilles waiting for her at the prior's. If he became impatient, he would drink too much. In mid-thought, she was startled by a stooped black figure at her side.

"I trust I find you in good health, my lady." It was the sacristan, an old monk bent nearly in two with age. He had doubtless been informed of her arrival.

"Good day, brother. I've come to make my visits. You may accompany me if you like."

"It will be my privilege, my lady."

That said, she moved to the right-hand aisle. Starting back toward the entrance, she stopped at each shrine or altar along the way. At one, she knelt as if in prayer. At another, she remarked on a new statue of a saint. At a third, she made an offering and lit a candle. Again in the rear, she crossed to the left-hand aisle. On the way, she dropped the rest of the contents of her purse into the poor box, chained as always to a massive pillar. As soon as she left, the old monk would open it. In a day or two, all of Windhamshire would know the generous amount of her donation. In this manner, she played the role of benefactress with much greater skill than any pious milksop of a patroness would have.

Proceeding up the left-hand aisle, she came to the de Bourne family chapel. For what seemed an eternity, the sacristan fumbled with the keys, finally opening the iron grille. Inside, beneath their reclining images in stone, her husband's parents and grandparents lay. The men were carved stiffly in chainmail holding shields and swords. The women, only slightly more graceful, held prayer books beneath folded hands. They also had dogs at their feet, symbols of fidelity. One day, her effigy would lie here too. Beneath it, her heart would have turned to dust. At the moment, however, it was beating wildly and she was as alive as she would ever be. It took all her discipline to kneel for the appropriate few minutes in an attitude of prayer.

*

He stood before the fire, a cup of wine in hand. After the gloomy dampness of the church, both the scent and the warmth of the fire were welcome. When Prior Gramont had moved into the former abbot's house, he had insisted on the innovation of a fireplace despite the cost. The large room, used both for dining and receiving guests, was well but simply furnished.

So far, except for her initial greeting, neither Gilles nor she had said a word. Her lover wore only a dark red silk robe. Open nearly to the waist, it revealed his olive-tinted skin and slender body. Finally, he spoke.

"You've kept me waiting."

"I left as soon after the midday meal as I could. You knew I had to make my visit to the church."

"No matter. I'll find a way to make you pay. Did you latch the door behind you?"

"Yes." She measured her words, trying to test her lover's mood. As soon as she saw him, her connection to the world was altered. Elsewhere, she was commanding and imperious. With him she became strangely, reflexively compliant.

Before her, not far from the fire, a flagon of wine stood on a table with a cup beside it. Next to it there were two carved chairs. Gilles neither offered her wine nor invited her to sit. He spoke instead in his distant manner. "The prior has made all the usual arrangements. The servants are gone, and as far as anyone knows, he is here to receive the mistress of Bourne Castle."

"Please thank him for his caution."

"I will. Meanwhile, how are things with your niece? Is the earl reconciled to losing her if I decide to make an offer?"

This was a sensitive subject. She had long been tormented by his vacillation in the matter. "When the time comes, you may trust the earl to me."

Gilles smiled at her answer. "You don't feel a little jealous of the girl?"

"Not at all," she asserted, lying. "I assume the matter came up because you're once again in need of money. It seems you never have enough."

"Indeed? I thought it was you who never had enough—of our peculiar kind of lovemaking, I mean. I must have been wrong. Why not sit, drink a cup of wine, and return to Bourne Castle unmolested? The earl will be happy to see you home early. We know how he adores you."

"Don't be cruel, Gilles."

"Not cruel? I thought that was the way you liked me. Or am I wrong again?"

"My love, our time is precious. Let's not waste it in badinage. Come, take my cloak, give me some wine, and kiss me."

"Ah, more commands. You're too used to being obeyed. You can do all those things by yourself. Everything but the kiss. And I'm not in a kissing mood."

She took off her cloak, threw it on the chair, and poured herself a cup of wine. Her hand trembled slightly as she drank. Then she spoke again. "Go ahead. As usual, I am at your service."

"Good. Remember the whore in Beauvais whom I told you about? I'm in the mood for that sort of thing. I'll sit and drink my wine and you can imitate her."

Melisande recalled the story, one of a dozen he had told her. In public, he treated her as others did, as a woman of high position, beauty, and intelligence. When they were alone, he adopted a manner very like contempt. To her surprise, it excited her. In past meetings, he had taught her many of the tricks of his paid women. She found an odd enjoyment in them. It was all play-acting, of course, but strangely potent.

"Well, what are you waiting for, you lazy slattern?"

The game had begun, and already she felt the strange thrill that started slowly, then gradually increased until it reached a peak, but only after she had done her lover's will, performed as if she were the lowest slut whose services he paid for. Obediently, she began to remove her lovely clothing. Used to the help of a maidservant, she was awkward at it.

"You're more clumsy than usual today. Try a bit harder to be alluring." After each garment, she paused, and he commented.

"Ah, that's better," Gilles said. "I like that pose."

Sometimes the remarks were flattering, at other times insulting. Garment by garment, she unclasped, undid, or slipped off some piece of clothing, then waited. Sometimes, he said nothing, merely stared. Those were the worst times. She kept thinking he had changed his mind, that he no longer found her body tempting. She knew she was still attractive, that her figure was as fine as ever. Still, she felt humiliated. At last, he would murmur, "go on," and she would feel a great relief, remove the next article of apparel, and drop it with the others on the rush-strewn floor. She herself did not speak. That, too, was part of the game.

Halfway through, a crooked smile, almost a sneer, appeared on her lover's face. Still holding his cup, he stood and came closer. Outlined by his silky robe, she could see the result of her performance. Ignoring her smile, he said "next," and the game went on. Finally, Melisande stood naked with only her veil and the gold fillet on her head. Despite the fire, she felt a draft and shivered. Gilles seemed to like that too.

"No, not the headband," he commanded. "Keep that until last. The gauzy veil first. Yes, that's it. Now hold it tight between your hands. No, not like that. Pull it close against your breasts. They've begun to sag, the veil improves them. That's it, just so. Enough. Now you can let it drop."

Wearing only the fillet, she did as he said, impatient for the next stage of the game, the one where she claimed the reward for her obedience.

"Now take off the band and throw it down. No, not on your clothes, on the floor. There, where the rushes have thinned. Slip into your shoes and step on it. Don't look so puzzled. I want you to destroy it. Hold it down with one foot and crush it with the other. Do it thoroughly. It's pure gold. It will crumple easily."

"But my husband— "

"Your husband? It's a bit late to think of him! Or maybe you're tiring of our game. If so, you can dress and go home and keep your band intact. Which will it be, me or the fillet?"

She had a moment of terrible indecision. This was too much, it was absurd. The band was precious, exquisitely worked. A unique gift from her husband, it was worth the yearly wages of their steward. Yet it was such a long time since they had been together! What good was a piece of jewelry? It could be melted down and refashioned. Annoyed though she was, she took the dare and did as Gilles suggested, badly at first. Once again, he laughed at her efforts. Soon, however, the band lay flat among the rushes, crushed beyond recognition.

"Good girl. You can say it fell and was trampled by your horse. Now you may come and receive the reward for your obedience."

As he spoke, Gilles moved towards his bedchamber. Still smarting from the humiliation, she followed, wondering how much he had drunk. When at last their lips met, the smell of wine repelled her. Then he took her firmly in his arms and she no longer cared. Her naked body yielded, merged with his, and her surrender was complete.

Afterwards, they lay sated in each other's arms, and Gilles dozed off. After a while she pulled back the bed curtains to see him in the light. His body was still taut and slender. What flesh he had put on seemed to suit him. The years had lined his face around the eyes and mouth but not excessively. She loved his skin with its even, tawny color, so different from her husband's blotched and mottled pink. Indeed, Desmond was Gilles's opposite in every way, always so tender, so deferential. He was only the count's senior by five years, but he seemed a decade older. Gilles was like a storm at sea, a dangerous, erratic force. With his thick, dark hair, trimmed beard, and nervous body, he had almost the look of a gypsy. The earl was like a stagnant pond, with thinning blond hair and a body a bit heavier each year. For him, the act of love was a kind of homage, all the more so since she had produced a son, his only child, Roland, named after the legendary hero. The boy was now nearly ten, but his poor health and unstable disposition made it urgent to produce another heir. They had almost done so twice. The first child, a girl, had died before she reached six months. The second, a boy, was stillborn. She had not conceived since then. In truth, the act of love with her husband had lost its savor long ago.

Not that all was bliss with Gilles, far from it. Her love for him defied all reason. Most would have called it perversity. In truth, she had few illusions about her lover; she knew, for instance, that he did not make these secret visits to Gramont for her alone. There was something else he and the prior were involved in. She adored him nonetheless. She had loved him since her youth. Still, there seemed to be no remedy for their situation, only these stolen hours in which, subject to his whims, she indulged his passion and her own strange love, a craving to please him at all costs.

He was stirring now. As she leaned over to kiss him, he awoke. "Enough. Wait till I command you. You're cheating at the game."

"Am I? I thought the game was over." Once they had made love, she became less tractable.

"Very well then, fetch me another glass of wine, and we'll talk about my future aunt-in-law."

For a moment, she didn't know who he meant. Then, understanding, she pulled on his robe and went to pour the wine. When she returned, she handed him the cup and spoke to him with unaccustomed firmness. "Don't call me that again. It's absurd. I'm two years younger than you." She remained standing, challenging him.

Still half-reclining, he drank from the cup. "If you don't play that role, we may have no future. I might have to settle for a different heiress."

"The rich Burgundian, you mean? If you had been able, you would have married her already. It's she who keeps you waiting, or her family, who see through you."

"Perhaps," said Gilles, "but in fact I have another prospect, a lady from Anjou. Either way, I hope to make up my mind before year's end." Draining the cup, he handed it to her.

Rather than fill it, she set it on a nearby table. She was threatened by these other prospects but she hid her fear. After all, he might be lying. "Very well, but if you fail, know I am reconciled to your marriage to my niece. There's no other way for us, after all—"

She paused, then finished her thought by adding, "as long as my husband is alive."

A crease appeared between Gilles's dark eyes. "You're thinking of poisoning him?"

"Stop joking, Gilles. He *is* older than we are, of course. And lately his health has not been good."

"Indeed? Perhaps you've discovered a solution. As his widow and the mother of his heir, you would be in complete control. Meanwhile, I could marry Elise and gain possession of her lands. Then I could contrive to kill her. After a suitable interval, we two could marry. Together, we would be quite rich."

She looked at Gilles as he spoke. His voice was sober, his expression grave. Could he really be thinking such a thing? She was ready to ask when he broke into raucous laughter.

"You amaze me, madam. Don't deny it. You thought I meant it. My lady trollop, how can I not be charmed by you? Given the chance, I believe you'd be more depraved than me. Look, see how your wickedness excites me! Fetch me another cup, and we'll play again, this time without the game."

*

That evening before supper in the hall, Melisande put her son to bed in the chamber he shared with his tutor. Roland was calm tonight, almost lovable, with none of his usual strange behavior. She told him an invented story of the ruined fillet, for practice and to amuse him. Instead, he was terrified by the story of the rearing, trampling horse; the look on his face stayed in her mind through supper. Later that night, as Desmond snored beside her, she lay awake and thought of herself at Roland's age. She remembered her family, always in need of money, and the unhappy house she was reared in. She had hated the chaos and confusion, the way everyone deceived her hapless mother: her brutish second husband, her children, and the servants.

When she was twelve, her stepbrother Julien, fifteen at the time, had taught her a forbidden game. Later, shocked by the painful invasion of her body, she resisted. Angry, Julien threatened her and bullied her. Nor was there anyone else, it seemed, who cared if she lived or died. In the end, she always gave in. Afterward, he taunted her, called her horrid names, and punished her in nasty ways—for her wickedness, he said. Until he wanted her again. But when the two of them were discovered, it was she who was blamed. Had it not been for an uncle who saw her cleverness and took her with him to the court of France, her life might have turned out as squalid and unlovely as her mother's.

And yet with all she had gained, she had long been discontent. Now, once again, with Gilles, she felt alive. She had only two fears, losing him and losing her position in the world. She would do all she could to keep both. Whatever befell her, she would control her own destiny. She would not be like her mother, a pitiful pawn in others' games. If and when Gilles made an offer of marriage, she would see to it that both her husband and Elise consented. Her success would determine her own fate as much as it would her niece's.

8

As the months passed, Elise continued to think about the girl found in the New Forest and the young man unjustly accused of her death. Nearly a year had gone by since that fateful night at Bishop Osbert's. No killer had been caught, and whatever the truth of the prelate's involvement, there had been no inquiry into his misdeeds. Perhaps Melisande was right. Justice was, indeed, a rare thing in this world. In fact, her aunt was a good example of the maxim. Adoring his wife as he did, the earl had no notion that she had betrayed him with the count. On the other hand, that liaison might have ended. For her uncle's sake, she hoped so. By now, Elise had grown tired of wondering every time Melisande left the castle.

Then, one morning in April, she opened the shutters of her window and inhaled the intoxicating smell of spring. This year with its coming she felt a secret rapture, a quiet kinship with the season of new growth and new beginnings. Later that day, on the way back from her lessons in the village, she reined in her chestnut mare, a gift from her uncle for her sixteenth birthday. To her left, across a field thick with new grass, a small grove of alders was just beginning to turn green. Beneath their gray trunks lay a swath of purple.

"Look, Margaret, the violets are in bloom!

"Is that so, my lady?" Not without some difficulty, her nurse halted the donkey she had only lately learned to ride. "I don't see them."

Elise pointed in their direction. "Across the field beneath the trees."

"Oh, yes, I see them now. They're early this year."

"And a sure sign of spring. We must pick some!" At once, she slid out of her saddle onto the ground.

"No, my lady, please! We'll be late for the midday meal. You know how annoyed your aunt will be."

"I won't be but a moment. Just take hold of my horse!"

Clinging to her mount with one hand, Margaret frowned as she took the slack reins with the other.

Elise plunged into the field and knelt down in the grass beside the violets. Working quickly, she picked a fine velvety bunch and laid them in the woven bag she carried to her lessons. As she did, she saw something new inside, a small piece of cream-colored parchment sealed with tawny wax. She knew at once what it was: a note from Edmond.

Last January, frustrated by their inability to talk, Edmond had slipped the first message into her bag. In it, without preamble, he had declared his love and begged her not to take offense. She had not done so. By then, she knew she felt the same. Fully aware of the danger, they began to exchange secret notes. The recipient, after reading one, would take a knife and scrape the parchment clean, then use the fresh surface to reply. As a precaution, they never used the other's name or signed their own. Discovery would surely end their lessons, the only chance they had to see to each other. Still, neither could bear to stop. They compromised on one exchange per week.

Elise hid the note beneath the flowers, picked up her bag, and hurried back to where an irate Margaret waited.

"We're in a fine fix now, my lady! You'll have to lead your horse home and we're sure to be late for our meal."

"You're wrong again, my good Margaret. Watch!" She led her horse to the stump of a tree by the road. Jumping onto it, she thrust her foot into the stirrup and remounted. Margaret looked on with mouth agape, doubtless aghast at this unlady-like behavior.

Once at home, Elise finished her meal as quickly as she could and took the twisting staircase from the gallery to her chamber. Closing the door, she put the violets in a bowl and sat down to read Edmond's note. Breaking the seal, she unfolded it slowly, enjoying the anticipation. Today the message was short, four lines like a quatrain of unrhymed verse. Elise was touched by their simplicity.

From my window I see the spring
for which men wait all winter.
I pay it no heed. When you are near,
each day is another spring to me.

He had written only that, but this time for some reason he had added, "your loving Edmond." Even this once, she wished he had not. She was still holding the note when she heard a sharp knock and the door of her room flew open.

"My dear girl," Melisande exclaimed, "you can't imagine what news I bring!" She had entered the room with rare impetuosity. Now, with a single glance, she seemed to take everything in: the rapt expression on Elise's face, the note with the seal in her hand, her confusion at the interruption. Elise felt sure she understood. Who would know the effect of a note from a lover better? Prepared for the worst, Elise slipped the parchment into her bag and rose.

"Dear Elise, I know you'll forgive my interruption when you hear the news. I see I've disturbed your reading. A note from your teacher, no doubt. I'll wager he wished to commend you on your work without embarrassing your fellow pupils. Young or old, men cannot stand to be bested by a female."

Elise listened, amazed at her aunt's benign interpretation of the note. She felt sure she had guessed its nature. Why this fabrication in Elise's favor? Did she think they were partners in deceit, that Elise was as culpable as she was? Whatever the case, her aunt had not asked to see the note.

After a brief silence, she went on. "But I've not burst into your room to tell you that, my dear. Just after you left the hall, a message came from Winchester. Through your uncle's efforts, with some help from me, you've been invited to King Henry's court to serve as an attendant to the young Princess Joanna."

It took her a moment to absorb the unexpected news. Her first reaction was relief. At least it had not been an offer of marriage from the count. Still, she found the invitation quite unwelcome. Unable to think of a response, she motioned her aunt toward a chair.

"Will you not be seated, madam? With your permission, I shall do the same. Is not the princess still a child?"

"She'll be nine in the fall, nearing an age for tutoring. Your learning has recommended you."

"I see." By now, her reluctance must have been apparent.

"Surely you're pleased?" her aunt demanded. "I know it will be your first separation from your uncle, but many girls of sixteen are already wives and much further from home than Winchester from Windham."

When she failed to reply, Melisande continued, now visibly annoyed. "And think how exciting to be at court, not always so busy," she glanced pointedly at Elise's bag, "with your studies."

Elise felt herself redden. A corner of the parchment was still visible. Why had Edmond signed his name? If her aunt asked to see it, they would both be undone.

Resisting panic, Elise addressed the subject of the court. "My dear aunt, please don't think me ungrateful. It's the honor of the thing that makes me wary. The offer comes through no effort of my own. I have doubts as to whether I'll prove worthy."

Glaring now, Melisande said dismissively. "Let's not speak of worthiness, child. You're going to a court, not to a convent."

"Then it's already decided?"

"Yes, all except the formality of a reply. Don't imagine this offer came easily or, once refused, will be repeated. Your uncle and I have indulged you greatly until now. I myself have encouraged your love of learning—"

"And I am deeply grateful, madam."

"I haven't finished," Melisande said curtly. "I have encouraged your learning beyond what is necessary for a woman of your station. It's now time to acquire those refinements that, in combination with your wit, your beauty, and your lands in Picardy, will help you to make an advantageous marriage. If we've been too liberal in granting you your freedom, the blame is mine. Even so, it may not be too late to remedy our error. "

Her aunt looked again at the bag, fixed her eyes on Elise, and concluded. "May I tell your uncle, then, that you are grateful to be asked to court, that you want only a little time to grow used to the idea?"

There was no possible answer but yes. Elise said the word with as good a grace as she could muster.

When Melisande had gone, she sat for a long time without moving. Then she took Edmond's poem, memorized it, went to the box with her writing things, and scraped the parchment clean. Seated again, she thought of all she would leave behind at Windham and began to cry—but not for the loss of Edmond. She had no intention of giving him up. She wept instead for her youth, which she knew was about to end.

9

On a bright morning in September, Martin and his father set out on the road to Windham Abbey. Less than a mile to the west, the great central tower of the abbey church rose above the trees. As they walked, its majestic bells tolled, calling Martin to his future. Halfway to their destination, Alfred Rendon halted and laid a hand on his son's shoulder, a gesture rare for him.

"My son, you know I too once embarked upon the life you begin today, then later left to wed your mother. Remember that until you take your final vows, you too are free to leave. Should you wish to, let neither scrupulosity nor shame affect your choice. Be assured you will be welcomed back into our home."

Few though the words were, they were more than Martin was used to hearing from his father, and they moved him deeply.

"Thank you, Father. You could have given me no better parting gift." That said, the two began walking again and were silent the rest of the way.

That afternoon, Martin was accepted as a Benedictine novice in the abbey church. Abbot Philip, an aged Benedictine with a snow-white tonsure, officiated at the simple ceremony. When it was done, feeling strange in his long black robe, Martin paused in the aisle at the entrance to the cloister. He smiled as he nodded farewell to his father and the world. In truth, he was full of uncertainty. Life as a scholar and monk was all he had ever envisioned for himself, but in the course of the last year, he had grown much less avid for the second part of that equation. He was glad he would have a year before he made his initial vows.

It was that thought, not any pious vision of his future, which carried him through his first weeks at Windham Abbey. In fact, it was not easy for him to adjust to the novice's strict routine, a regimen of rote learning, sparse meals, and communal prayer at all hours of the day and night. He missed the freedom of his life at home, the joy of Canon Thomas's lessons, and, above all, his fellow pupils. The Lady Elise was now gone to another world, the royal court at Winchester. Edmond, although still in Windham, was in effect no closer. During Martin's year as a novice, no visitors or letters were allowed. Although Edmond's father had not relented on his vow, Edmond had fallen behind in his lessons. He would not enter the abbey until next year. As each day passed, the two things Martin longed for most were to see his friend again and to resume his studies. He hoped to do both at the end of his novitiate year.

Meanwhile, his new life was far from the one he had lived before. In fact, several weeks had gone by before he had his first reminder of the world beyond the abbey walls. One morning he was seated with the full assembly of the monks inside the chapter house, an octagon built in the new style of pointed arches and fine colored glass. Once the lector had read a chapter from the Benedictine rule, the monks all dispersed to their various tasks. Today, however, Father Gilbert, the novice master, directed the novices to keep their places. A slender middle-aged man, Gilbert had a thin-lipped mouth, a narrow face, and an irritable manner. Today he seemed even more ill at ease than usual.

"Good day, my children, in the name of our Lord and Savior. Before we begin our lesson on the Sacraments, I must address you on another topic. Although idle talk has, I trust, been scarce among you, you may still have heard certain rumors of late, tales of strange happenings connected to the abbey."

There were a few nods among the novices amid a general air of expectation.

"Regrettably, some monks at the abbey have made a false pattern of two occurrences. Both involve young clerics who left us without notice or permission. One was a young lay brother known as Wilfred. He was sixteen when he disappeared two months ago. He was a bit wild, at times unruly and lax in discipline. It is not unlike him to have run away."

A murmur of interest just short of speech rose from the novices. With a wave of his hand, the priest silenced the group. "The other fugitive was a novice like yourselves. His name was Stephen, and he disappeared a year ago last summer. He was devout and his Latin was excellent. It is more surprising that he fled. These two events occurred a year apart. The only connection, the only mystery, is that there has been no news of either."

As Father Gilbert spoke, Martin thought for some reason of the clearing of the stones, and that night a year ago when he had seen a boy of Stephen's age bound in the hut. Although there was no real connection, he found himself listening more closely.

"Such defections come from a rebellious heart, from sinful deeds nurtured in secret unconfessed. Thus we see that even here at Windham Abbey, Adam's primal sin still spreads its stain on all of humankind."

As he uttered these ominous words, Martin felt Gilbert was staring at him. He lowered his eyes, and when he looked up, was happy to see the priest's gaze directed elsewhere.

"We are all in our various ways afflicted," Gilbert's voice had a peculiar sadness now. "Be on your guard against Satan's wiles and speak no more of this. If I hear any more chatter about it, it will go hard with all of you."

Martin felt as if Gilbert had said, *we are all in our various ways afflicted* with peculiar emphasis. Did the novice master have secrets of his own, he wondered, things that made him feel unworthy of the trust he held?

That night, as he lay in bed dreading the bell for Matins, Martin wondered if he, too, might eventually want to leave the abbey. By taking Canon Thomas as his model, had he not deceived himself in his idea of monastic life?

About a month later, the novices were gathered one afternoon for their Latin lessons. Father Gilbert himself conducted them. As they were about to begin, he made an announcement that took Martin completely by surprise.

"Novice Martin, I have a message for you. This time each day, as you know, we do our Latin recitation. You have demonstrated ample evidence of skills acquired in that language. Henceforth, you will be occupied elsewhere."

Here Gilbert came to a halt, as if reluctant to continue. Then, clearing his throat, he announced, "You are hereby released to Brother Ambrose, head scribe of the abbey. The scriptorium is on the upper floor of the south wing. Your new superior awaits you there."

The scriptorium! He had prayed to be able to resume his studies. Could his prayers have been answered so quickly? For the first time since coming to the abbey, Martin felt a spark of happy anticipation. What, he wondered, had brought this thing about? Then he remembered that Ambrose, the head of the scriptorium, was an old friend of Canon Thomas from their years together at the abbey. Even after Thomas had left to become a canon of Winchester cathedral, the two had remained quite close. Indeed, it was Ambrose, with the abbot's help, who had found his old friend the cottage in the village when his health required him to leave his post at Winchester.

And now, God bless him, Canon Thomas must have recommended him to Ambrose. As Martin stepped through the door of the scriptorium, the first words he heard confirmed his supposition.

"Welcome, my boy, in the name of my old friend Thomas."

Ambrose was a plump, pink-faced monk of indeterminate age. Behind him extended a room of considerable size. In it, some nine or ten Benedictines were busy at various tasks.

"Yes, this is our scriptorium, Novice Martin, the love and labor of my life. And these are our scribes." With a broad wave of an ink-stained hand, Ambrose indicated six writing stands, three on each side of the room. Four were occupied by scribes, and all were placed by windows.

"As you see," Brother Ambrose pointed out, "our windows are covered with vellum. All year round, they admit an even light and, to a surprising degree, protect our fingers from the cold."

Ambrose went on to describe the many tasks of the scriptorium. At a front table, a monk was preparing cover boards for finished volumes. In the rear of the room, others were mixing colored pigments. Not far from them, using a knife shaped like a crescent moon, a lay brother was scraping skins stretched on a rack. At another table, a monk was applying a chalky substance to the surface of a parchment. Lining the walls of the room, there were wooden shelves. Bound codices lay on some, parchment scrolls on others. In the front of the room, a splendid book stood on a lectern open to a richly decorated page. The whole place was full of light and color, industry and craft. As he savored it, Martin felt he had come home.

As he finished looking, Ambrose turned to him. "I'm happy to see Father Gilbert has relinquished you. I can see from your face you're glad to be among us. Canon Thomas speaks very well of you, so much so that I stooped to a bit of coercion to obtain you. I asked Abbot Philip to speak to Father Gilbert. I hope your skills will justify my action." Ambrose smiled as he said it, diffusing any hint of a threat.

The monk's candor surprised him as much as his release by Father Gilbert. Until now, no one at the abbey had spoken so freely. Used to the silence imposed on the novices, Martin found himself speechless.

Ambrose seemed to understand. "I see, my boy, the rule of silence has your tongue. In truth, it's transgressed as much at Windham as elsewhere, but not in our scriptorium. So greatly does the abbot prize our work that we are permitted to speak at will. Nonetheless, you'll find that some of us, like those two scribes with brushes in their hands, say very little."

Ambrose moved toward the monks in question, introducing them by turns. The first, Brother Caedmon, was slender and seemed quite young. Brother Terence, the second, was older and more robust. They went on with their work as Ambrose talked. "These two know all the varieties of script, both majuscule and miniscule, but it is in artistry that they excel. They work with me to create our illuminated books, the ones with gold leaf, intricate initials, and wide margins full of cunning decoration."

Smiling, the artists looked up, nodded shyly, and resumed their work. Then Ambrose and Martin walked back to the front of the room. There, the monk spoke to Martin in a confidential tone. "I'm hoping you will be as expert with the texts themselves one day, their meaning and interpretation. We need someone not just to copy but to comprehend and comment, annotate and edit."

Here, as if catching himself, Ambrose paused.

"All that in good time, my boy. I'm moving too quickly. We'll begin now, but slowly."

With that, Ambrose moved to a vacant writing stand. Seated with pen in hand, he began to demonstrate some of the skills every scribe at Windham Abbey was required to master.

A few days later, Father Gilbert agreed to adhere to this arrangement until further notice. During the next few weeks, imitating Ambrose's script, Martin began to acquire some skill at copying. He also learned much else: how to measure and trim the pages, how to incise the lines to guide the letters, how to mix the ink and when to refresh it. He still spent his mornings and evenings with the other novices, but every afternoon except Sunday he was fully occupied in the scriptorium.

In this manner, autumn turned rapidly to winter at the abbey. The monastic routine was varied only by the many holy days observed. Luckily, Abbot Philip had long resisted the austere reforms begun by Bernard of the Abbey of Clairvaux that other prelates had imported from the continent. Between Christmas Eve and the Feast of the Epiphany, there was great feasting at the abbey, with fine meals served to both the Benedictines and their guests.

Then the season ended and the old routine returned, and with it the hardship of a monastic winter. In fact, there was only a single hour each day in which the monks were able to relieve the numbing cold in which they ate, slept, worked, and prayed. After Compline, the last service of the day, all those who were free gathered in the warming room around a central fire. During this hour, by permission of the abbot, the novices could talk discreetly to each other. One evening Martin was seated next to Aelred, a novice whom Father Gilbert had called out of their lessons a number of times. The young man had pale skin, dark curly hair, and full lips that made him seem always to be pouting. Aelred was talking to a novice on his other side when Martin heard him say the name of Prior Gramont, and soon afterward, the words, "Yes, that was the third time I saw him."

The keen-eared Father Gilbert must have heard him too. Coughing loudly, he cast a disapproving look at Aelred. Blushing, the novice lowered his head and spoke no more. Martin wondered what had upset the novice master. Before he had time to guess, Father Gilbert spoke again.

"Are you in the habit of listening to others' conversations, Novice Martin?"

Caught off guard, he shook his head and mumbled, "No."

The novice master seemed unhappy with that answer. "I would have preferred a word of penitence to that rude headshake. Perhaps you think yourself above such things."

Martin guessed these last words were a reference to his work in the scriptorium. He remained puzzled, however, by Gilbert's annoyance with Aelred.

As it happened, he had an explanation for it two days later. He was working at his writing stand in the scriptorium when Brother Ambrose, seated at a nearby table, asked him a question. "So how is our novice master treating you these days, my boy? Does he ever fault you for being here?"

"Indirectly, perhaps. The other day, he was annoyed with me for an odd reason." Martin described the incident, hoping Ambrose would have an explanation. Before it came, his superior had another question.

"You are sure it was Prior Gramont whom Aelred mentioned?"

"Yes, I'm certain."

"Then I think perhaps it's time I spoke to you." Raising his voice, Ambrose said, "You have not yet seen our storeroom, Novice Martin. Let me show you now."

Laying down his pen, Martin followed. The room was little more than an ample closet. It smelled of animal glue and the skins used to make parchment. There was a small shuttered window, half open for ventilation. In the dim light, he could barely make out his superior's face.

"Father Gilbert is both proud and quick to anger," Ambrose began, "but he struggles to overcome those vices. If he has a worse fault—I, with so many of my own, am compelled to name it—it is his servility to those above him. He has a strange, almost slavish devotion to Prior Gramont." Needlessly whispering, he added, "Some say that he and the prior have taken advantage of novices and young lay brothers."

Martin was silent. His mentor went on to explain. "In a carnal way, I mean. Do you understand?"

Shocked, Martin nodded.

"Others think Gilbert has only procured them for the prior. Either is bad enough, of course. It's been hushed up, I'm afraid, as such things almost always are. As is well known, the prior has a powerful protector. Had he not, his flagrant neglect of his duties would hardly be tolerated. It also seems that no one knows his patron's name except perhaps the abbot, and possibly not even him."

Despite the minimal light, Martin's face must have shown his dismay at these revelations.

"I hope you're not scandalized, my boy. I tell you this for your protection. Feel free to respond or not."

Encouraged, Martin opened his mouth to form a question but failed to. He had no idea where to begin.

His mentor seemed to understand. "You might well ask how such things could happen here at Windham Abbey. All too easily, I'm afraid. Human weakness is everywhere, my son, and great power often conceals great evil. Excepting the prior, Windham Abbey is free of most of the vices infesting the Church, greed and hypocrisy prominent among them. Outside these walls, from Rome to Canterbury, church offices are bought and sold, men made prelates because of their wealth, benefices given to nobles when others better merit them. There is also, as you know, a great trade in false relics of the saints: bones, teeth, fingernails, bits of cloth or hair, all meant to attract the donations of the faithful, often those least able to afford it. Yet despite such corruption, a great many clerics, the majority, I believe, are full of charity and goodness. There is also the wisdom of the abbeys and the schools, the universities in places like Paris and Bologna. There, scholars work to show the truth of God's creation in the light of reason."

Heartened by these last words, Martin finally spoke. "It was just such a path, that of true scholarship, that led me to the abbey."

"I've known that from the first, my boy," said Ambrose. "It's one of the reasons I've been so open with you. As for the prior, I've spoken not to scandalize you but to warn you. You are young, fair-haired and comely in appearance. Perhaps too clever to be easily subverted, but innocent nonetheless. Be wary of both Prior Gramont and Father Gilbert. If something untoward should happen, you must speak to me at once. Now I think I've said enough. A loose tongue is one of my great faults, for which I hope God in his goodness will pardon me on Judgment Day."

The rest of the afternoon, Martin thought about Brother Ambrose's words. They had opened his eyes to a new, darker, and more complicated vision of the world, religion, and the Church. They had also reminded him of other things: the disappearances Father Gilbert had described and, most troubling of all, the youth he had seen at the clearing of the stones that night and never spoken of again.

And then there was the shame of his own secret desires, surely a grievous moral failing. Despite knowing how much Elise and Edmond loved each other, he still found himself longing for Edmond to join him at the abbey. If his two friends were forbidden to unite in marriage, was it so wrong for him to want Edmond at his side? Each night in his freezing bed, what warmed him most was the vision of Edmond the way he had looked that Whitsun Monday, flushed and handsome, at the clearing of the stones.

That evening at Compline, Martin prayed for guidance and a true understanding of what his path in life should be.

*

Some two months from the day of his talk with Brother Ambrose, Martin was busy copying a manuscript when his mentor appeared, red-faced and agitated. Pausing to catch his breath, he addressed all the scribes at once.

"My dear children, I have disturbing news. Lest you hear it later in some garbled form, I shall tell you at once. They have found the lay brother, Wilfred, the one who disappeared last summer, in a fen on the outskirts of Clarington. The bog had partially tanned his flesh, helping to preserve his body. He was naked but they knew him from his tonsure and a scar he was known to have had on his arm. Not far from him was the body of a young woman. She too, I blush to say, was naked. Her body was equally intact. Once word spread, a workman from Fenbury came and claimed her as his missing daughter. She had disappeared two months before young Wilfred. In both cases, their leather-like flesh had preserved their wounds. All over the young woman's body there were small round lesions. Wilfred's corpse was similarly marked but worse. Besides the round punctures, small pieces were cut from his legs, arms, and other fleshy parts. Stranger still, they say the girl found in the New

Forest two years ago bore nearly identical wounds. It is as if the same fiend or fiends has committed these crimes, and who knows how many more?"

"Hearing the phrase *fiend or fiends*, Martin once more remembered the vision of that night inside the hut; the robed and hooded figures, the naked youth bound and gagged, the shock of his encounter with the bearded leader. On the other hand, that was a year and a half ago, a year before Wilfred's disappearance. Once again, there seemed to be no provable connection. Nonetheless, he decided to tell Brother Ambrose in private when he had finished talking. And then he remembered he could not. He and Edmond had vowed not to speak about that night to any other person. He would need his approval to do so, and letters were not allowed in the novitiate year. Perhaps if Brother Ambrose spoke to the abbot, he could gain permission for Martin to write his friend. He would think about it overnight and speak to Ambrose tomorrow.

*

Before the reading the following morning, Abbot Philip himself addressed the assembled monks. After a brief homily on the unpredictability of life and death, he requested their prayers for the soul of Geoffrey, the son of Baron Hugh of Preston Manor, recently deceased in London. At first, Martin thought the aged abbot was confused. It must surely be the baron who had died. Then he recalled that Edmond's father never traveled farther than Clarington. It must indeed be Geoffrey. At once, Martin thought of Edmond. Beyond the loss of his brother, his friend would now have to deal with his parents' grief, which was sure to be excessive, adding another burden to his life at home.

Then, feeling a sudden constriction in his chest, Martin realized something else. With Geoffrey gone, Edmond was now the baron's eldest son. His father's vow would no longer apply. He would not be coming to Windham Abbey after all. In the wake of the news, Martin felt suddenly cold, chilled by the thought of a future without his friend. Stunned by the unexpected blow, he sat without listening while the lector read a chapter of the rule. That afternoon, he took no pleasure in his work in the scriptorium. When evening fell, he merely mouthed the prayers at Vespers. At Compline, he refused even to pray for acceptance. That night as he lay in bed, it took all his strength to avoid succumbing to self-pity.

A week later, he learned the full tale of Geoffrey's death. It could hardly have been more dismal. One night in London, he had left a tavern drunk and foolishly consented to a midnight race on horseback. His mount tripped on some obstacle or other and he fell and broke his neck, dying instantly. It was this news, not the secret they shared, which led Martin to ask for permission to write his friend. He sent his condolences, then asked Edmond to visit in the fall when his novitiate year was over. They could talk then about the clearing of the stones.

10

1175

A rms held wide, Margaret stood at the foot of the stairs in the castle courtyard.

"Welcome home, my lady!"

A year had now passed since Elise had seen her nurse. Touched by the warmth of her welcome, she ran to embrace her. "Dear Margaret, how good of you to come down to greet me!" Elise saw there were tears on her nurse's cheeks.

"It's a joy to see your sweet face, my love. Your aunt and uncle would have been here, but no one knew the time of your arrival."

"Nor did I. The escorting party was delayed. They have already left in haste. Come with me now while I greet the household. Then we'll talk in our chamber as in the old days."

Once the welcomes were over, the two went at once to Elise's room. There, everything was fresh and tidy. New rushes were laid, a bowl near the bed was filled with scented water, and a manservant had carried up her bags. Soon Margaret was storing her things in a chest and chatting.

"Your aunt and uncle expected you yesterday. They have ridden out for exercise. Your uncle is in need of it. He took a bad turn just before Easter. Since then, he's been in and out of bed."

"He has been ill? Why did no one send me word?"

"He forbade it, my love, or I myself would have had someone write you, even if no one else cared to."

Her nurse was surely alluding to the Lady Melisande, whom she had never trusted. Her uncle's letters to Elise were signed by him but written by her aunt. In the end, they told her only what Melisande chose to convey.

"He was perfectly well the last I heard, quite over the winter's ague."

"I know my love, this recent bout surprised us all. He is much better now."

Elise decided to inquire no more until she saw her uncle. She listened instead to Margaret's news and, in turn, retailed the gossip of the court. She had other news herself, but unsure of her aunt and uncle's reaction, she was saving it for later. Shortly before the midday meal, Elise met them both at the entrance to the hall. She was reassured by her uncle's appearance. He was slightly thinner and his thick blond beard was longer. Otherwise, he seemed as well as when she saw him last. He took her in a great, bear-like embrace, then drew back to look at her.

"My dear girl," he exclaimed, "you've become a woman!"

It was true, Elise thought. She was seventeen now but seemed older, tall and slender as before but with a fuller figure. Her long dark hair, once gathered in loose plaits, was now stylishly arranged atop her head. In a new court dress with fashionably long sleeves, she looked fully the part of a royal attendant. She had chosen her clothes more for Melisande than for her uncle, hoping to convey her newly independent status. Thus far her aunt had been quiet. Now she reached out, kissed Elise, and spoke in her suavest manner. "Your uncle is right, my dear. Your year at court has greatly improved you. We are both delighted to have you home."

The welcoming atmosphere continued through the midday meal, as always a crowded affair. There were several guests and the usual hangers-on and all the members of the household who were not engaged in serving. Even her cousin Roland, eleven now and difficult as ever, was allowed to attend with Father Barnabas, who served as his tutor as well as the castle chaplain. In honor of her return, there was an especially fine meal. When it was over, having slept little the previous night, Elise would have loved to retire to her chamber. It was not to be. As the meal drew to a close, Melisande spoke on her husband's behalf.

"My dear, there's a matter your uncle needs to talk to you about, a thing of some importance. In fact, had your visit not been planned, we might well have asked you home because of it. Your uncle will tell you the rest."

Noting the look of concern on Elise's face, the Earl spoke up at once.

"No, no, my dear girl, don't be troubled. It's good news, not bad. Come with me now to my cabinet. We can chat there as in the old days."

Reassured but still wary, Elise followed her uncle to the far end of the gallery beside the hall. There, a wooden door led to his cabinet, one of the castle's smaller rooms. Inside, there was a table with chairs, rolled-up parchments stacked on shelves, and two great folders filled with documents. By turns, her uncle met here in private with his steward, his bailiffs, the master of the garrison, and, on occasion, the heads of local manors.

As a child, Elise had often sought out the earl in this room, a place where her aunt never came. The windowless cabinet faced north, not south like her aunt's large solar. Winter or summer, a fire burned in a brazier when the earl was present. In the past, she and her uncle had spent many happy hours here. Now her fond memories of those days were blended with a vague unease about his news. As he prepared to speak, her uncle's gentle smile broke though the heavy tangle of his beard. The earl had a way of hesitating when he talked. Today, perhaps because he held a letter in his hand, he came more quickly to the point.

"My child, the offer we all assumed was not to be has come at last. Count Gilles de Vere, using Prior Gramont as his envoy, has written to tell me the admiration which he felt for you two years ago has not diminished. Indeed, his ardor has only quickened. In short, he begs your hand in marriage."

It was the thing Elise most feared and hoped would never come. Having spoken, her uncle looked up from the parchment, doubtless anxious to note her reaction. She showed none, and he went on.

"He says he will not rest until I've given my consent to your betrothal."

By now, Elise knew her uncle was in favor of the match. It would fulfill the promise he had made her mother to secure her future and her lands in Picardy through marriage to a Frankish nobleman. With that in mind, she measured the words of her response.

"My lord uncle, you will forgive me if I express surprise at the appearance of this offer after so much time."

"Of course, my dear, of course. I myself felt as you do. Prior Gramont explains it all in the letter he enclosed." Her uncle lay the first parchment down and picked up another. "During the last two years, the Count's lands have been embroiled in a legal suit. At last, a court in Rouen has made a final judgment in his favor. He now indisputably holds assets equal to your own. Without them, he would not have made his offer."

Knowing the count's deceitfulness, Elise was suspicious of these assertions, but she could not make that point without revealing what she had long ago decided to conceal, her aunt's adulterous liaison. Instead, she tested the depth of her uncle's feelings. "Are you strongly in favor of this match, then, uncle?"

"I am, my love, for your sake and your mother's. You have lands but no title and no easy way to manage them without a Frankish husband. A match such as this was my dear sister's wish. I have now made it my own."

"I needed to know. You have never said it quite so plainly."

"Your marriage is a matter of great weight. This is a time for plain speaking. You must be candid too."

"Since you allow it, I will be, uncle. Put simply, I do not favor this marriage. I have no love for the count. Indeed, I dislike him intensely. I have my reasons but none I can disclose."

"My dear child, what reasons can there be? You saw him only twice, in company both times. He was attentive and full of flattery to you on both occasions. Did he perhaps approach you in some other way, offending you?"

"No, my uncle, it's nothing of that sort. There are other ways one learns about the character of men."

"Not from idle talk at court, I hope? One must be wary of such chatter. And even if there were some truth in it—that is, if a virile man once married and now widowed has at times been known to stray—why surely, you've learned that such things happen. They're nothing to keep him from being a good husband to a second wife. Especially one as young and lovely as yourself."

"Dearest uncle, you need not make excuses for the count. I know the ways of the world, and what I did not know before I've learned at court. That's not my reason."

A look of concern came over her uncle's face. Frowning, he offered a different thought.

"Nor must you imagine we wish to abandon you in Normandy. Your aunt has suggested we visit as often as we can, just as you and your husband will often return to Bourne Castle. For you two young people, a short sail across the channel will be no impediment."

As her uncle spoke, she saw her aunt's machinations at work. She was already arranging meetings with her lover! It made Elise more determined to resist.

"I didn't think you intended to abandon me, dear uncle. You know how much I trust your love. Indeed, because of it, I am able to say what I say now. Grateful as I am for all you've been to me these many years, I cannot consent to this betrothal, and will not unless you expressly command it. And even then, I could do so only with aversion, against my will and all the instincts of my judgment."

The earl looked at her intently, clearly surprised by the firmness of her refusal. She met his glance, knowing her resistance to be justified. In all these years, there had been no dispute between them. Now, in the midst of their first disagreement, the two were silent. Then, despite herself, tears came into Elise's eyes. Embarrassed, she lowered her head. At last, tears and all, she looked up, anxious to guess her uncle's thoughts.

"My dear Elise, your words have touched me deeply. As you raised your head just now it was your mother's face I saw. Remembering how she loved you and indulged you, I cannot resist your tearful plea."

"My dear uncle," Elise said, moved.

"Hear me out before we finish. You are still young. Many things may alter in the days to come. You will surely have other suitors, among them, one hopes, other landed Frankish lords. Whatever has turned you against this match, I shall not ignore your will and risk your happiness. I will not compel your acquiescence."

"Dear uncle, I thank you with all my heart."

"You are welcome, my child. You may consider the matter closed. I only hope you will not regret your choice. Now let's speak of it no more. This talk has tired me as it must have you, already weary from your journey. I'll ask your aunt not to trouble you this evening. You may wish to sup with Margaret in your room. If so, good rest and a good morrow."

Elise decided to do as her uncle suggested. When she found Margaret in her chamber, she threw herself into her nurse's arms, half-sobbing at what might have befallen her, half laughing at her escape.

The next morning, she learned her uncle had ridden to Clarington with his steward. Melisande was nowhere to be seen. Elise would have liked to visit Canon Thomas in the village, to see him and also to gain news of Edmond. Still, it might seem odd to ride out so soon after returning. With Canon Thomas's help, she and Edmond had been able to write several times. In her last letter, she had told him she would be home in June bearing important news. Undecided, she was on her way to her room when a maidservant, a new face to her, met her at the foot of the stairs.

"Please, my lady, you don't know me, but I am Teresa, new in service to the Lady Melisande. I am to tell you my mistress awaits your pleasure."

"I'm happy to know you, Teresa. I assume your mistress is in her quarters? Please tell her I'll attend her presently."

"Does that mean soon, my lady?"

"Yes, soon. I'll go first to my room, then come to her."

Elise wanted a moment alone to compose herself and to confer with Margaret if she could. Her nurse had been downstairs all morning. She might know something Elise did not.

Margaret was not in their chamber. Ashamed of her cowardice, Elise decided to go without her help. It was a warm summer day. Now, for the first time, she felt the heat. Washing her hands, she wet a cloth and dampened her cheeks and brow. When the water in the bowl was still, she looked at her reflection, inspecting the face she would be presenting to her aunt.

*

Melisande sat in a favorite chair beneath her fine glass window. On this gray summer day, the muted light softened her features, showing them to great advantage. Deferring to her aunt, Elise greeted her first. "Good morning, my lady, your maidservant said you wished to see me."

"Yes, my dear. I trust you're well rested. I was hoping we two might go riding on the morrow. I wanted to see if you were free."

"Yes, of course, madam." Elise wondered if that was all. Perhaps her aunt had not yet learned of her decision. Or had she learned it and, because of her love for the count, been glad? Melisande's face told her nothing. Elise spoke in her blandest manner. "Is that everything then, my lady?"

"Not quite. There is another matter, one I hoped I would not have to speak of."

So her uncle had told her after all. "Do you mean the offer of marriage from the count?"

"No, not exactly that," said Melisande, "but something else, something related to what I am told is a refusal on your part."

"I have refused, madam, but I have no idea what that something else could be."

"Since you do not, I'll explain, if you would be kind enough to close the door." Her aunt's voice had darkened. Elise did as she asked and turned to face her.

"Thank you," said Melisande. "Please be seated across from me. You'll be happy I've sent away my servant when I've spoken."

Her aunt's manner had begun to unnerve Elise. What game was she playing? Whatever it was, Elise also had other moves to make. She listened intently to Melisande.

"While you've been at court, I've learned from a trusted source that you have been secretly communicating with your former fellow pupil, Edmond Preston."

"There is no way you could know that, Madam." Elise spoke with some confidence; no one but Canon Thomas knew about their letters. He sent them care of the abbey inside his own.

"You may think so, my dear, but you are mistaken. There are ways of lifting wax seals and resealing parchments. In short, others beside Canon Thomas, your intermediary, have seen your letters."

Elise winced at the mention of her teacher.

Her aunt noted it. "You need not be concerned. No blame will devolve on him unless you make it necessary. Nor, for that matter, do I wish to expose you. If your uncle learned of this connection, he would surely feel betrayed. He might forgive you in the end, but his wrath would fall on Master Edmond and his father. The baron is, after all, your uncle's vassal. The earl has been very patient with his debts, his drinking, and his gross incompetence. Thanks to Master Rendon, his steward, things at Preston Manor have slowly begun to improve. Your uncle's displeasure could undo that, and the blame would, of course, fall on Edmond."

Aghast at these threats, Elise sat silent, too distressed to attempt an answer. Melisande continued in an even voice, betraying no emotion. "As for young Master Preston, now that he is no longer destined for the abbey, it seems he wants nothing more than to be a knight. With your uncle as his patron, he can be, once you are in Normandy and safely married. The fulfillment of Edmond's dream is in your hands. In deciding this, remember your uncle is a man of wonderful innocence. Once undeceived, his rage at your clandestine suitor would doubtless be that much greater. All this can be avoided with a single word from you."

Her aunt had bared her strategy, but Elise had her own in waiting. Nor did her aunt know Elise understood the reason for her plan, the fact that the count was her lover and wished it. Clearly, she meant to advance his suit no matter what the cost. Elise wanted no part of this travesty of a betrothal. Was it too soon to reveal what she knew? She needed a moment to think.

"And what would that word be, my lady?"

"You know very well. The time for pretense is past. You need only consent to your betrothal, one that will connect you to a noble house and bestow on you the rank of countess. It will also unite your holdings with the count's, expanding them, and lastly, restore you to the region of your birth."

Elise noticed her aunt had not spoken of the count's attractions as a man, the first thing most people mentioned to a prospective bride. Enraged at her manipulation, she retaliated. "In describing the match, my lady, you say nothing of my handsome suitor, a man I am told is desired by many women. My uncle reports that his ardor for me is great, that he has admired me from the first. Should I not welcome the love of such a man?"

Elise saw she had hit her mark. Melisande's face had finally lost its composure. Her aunt took a quick breath, then cast a glance full of hatred at Elise.

"Such things go without saying," she fairly hissed. "I'm surprised you speak of them so boldly. Have you learned to talk this way at court? If so, decorum must be sadly lacking there of late."

"Decorum is lacking of late in many places, madam," said Elise, hearing the strain in her own voice. "Perhaps it's the example of King Henry who keeps Queen Eleanor a prisoner and passes his nights with his mistress, Rosamond de Clifford. You disapprove of adultery, I presume, if only as a failure of decorum. Or am I wrong?" As soon as she had spoken, Elise wondered if she had moved too quickly.

Her aunt's face had, in fact, turned pale. She might not know how Elise had learned the truth, but she seemed to sense a threat. There was fury beneath her forced calmness. "Of course I disapprove, my dear, as does your uncle. I could never believe an accusation of his infidelity. Nor would he credit such a thing of me, no matter who accused me."

Her aunt let the words sink in. "Indeed, I feel sorry for anyone so foolish. He or she would lose all credence with the earl as well as his support and love."

Elise had made her move and lost. She saw at once that her aunt was right. The truth was on her side, but it was a truth she dared not tell her uncle. There was nothing more to say.

"You've made your point, my lady," she conceded. "Please tell me plainly what you wish."

Sensing victory, her aunt's features softened. She assumed a look of what Elise had often thought was counterfeit concern.

"I'm glad to hear you speak more sensibly, my dear. I want only what your uncle wants but is too good to insist upon, your consent to be betrothed to Gilles de Vere. Once the matter is settled, you can trust in my silence about Edmond Preston, just as I'll expect discretion in regard to me. Think of it as a pact between us."

Her aunt had made herself clear. It was time for Elise to reveal her news. She had wanted to do so just before she left for court, but she could no longer wait.

"I understand you, madam. And to avoid the consequences you mention, I might feel compelled to give my consent. Unfortunately, I am not free to do so."

"Not free? What foolishness is this?" her aunt demanded, again losing her composure. "Have you made some vow to that boy with the sanction of that interfering priest? Without your guardian's consent, it would mean nothing."

"No, madam, I have not, but something even more preventive has occurred. It seems Princess Joanna is quite fond of me. This might not in itself preclude a marriage, but in this case I fear it will. I am commanded by his Majesty King Henry to remain in the princess's service. Early next year, she and her entourage will travel to the kingdom of Sicily. There, child though she is, she will be wed to the young Norman king. I am to be part of her retinue."

"Surely, you're not in earnest?" Melisande demanded. "You've been ordered to a distant land and cannot marry for that reason?"

"Exactly, madam. The princess's attendants may not marry. If your informants were as good at court as hereabouts, you would know the truth of all I say."

"I shall certainly know it before I consent to any alteration in our plans. Meanwhile, assuming what you say is true, I see no reason why you may not be betrothed."

Elise rebelled at even this. Then she thought of Edmond and her teacher and the threats her aunt had made. For now at least, she would suppress her feelings.

"If it's what I must do to protect those I love, so be it. That said, I want to tell my uncle the news of Sicily myself. Do you agree?"

"As you wish," Melisande replied.

"Good," Elise said in a voice as devoid of expression as her aunt's. "And now, since you've succeeded in laying the groundwork for this devil's bargain, one you may live to regret, may I go?"

"Yes of course. Nor need you concern yourself with my re-grets. When you are my age, you may understand me better. I have your word that you'll agree to the betrothal?"

"Yes. That said, I must add, although it may matter little to you, that I am as innocent as the young man whose future you have so unjustly threatened. Innocent, that is, of all but the ex-change of loving words."

"I thought as much," Melisande admitted, "but as I've told you before, appearances are all that matter. The connection it-self is enough to undo you."

As her aunt spoke, there was a note of relief in her voice. Her face showed only a look of cold resolve. Whatever she felt, Elise could no longer bear to be with her. "Having been told that truth again, I'll leave you, madam."

"Yes, go. I shall not speak of Sicily until you do. One day you may see that I've done you a service." Melisande's voice had be-gun to waver, perhaps reflecting the price she had paid in win-ning. She had just given her lover to another.

"I very much doubt that, madam, but if so, it will be that I've learned from your bad example." With that, Elise turned and left the room.

11

A week from the day of her betrothal at the abbey—by proxy, with Prior Gramont officiating, Elise rode into the village with Margaret. A boy from a nearby stables took their mounts and tethered them not far from Canon Thomas's cottage. Then, as in the old days, Margaret set off for her sister's. Elise watched her nurse go, walked the short distance to her former teacher's home, and, full of expectation, rapped on the weathered door she knew so well.

At first, there was no response. Then, just as she was about to knock again, she heard the latch being raised and her teacher was there, smiling as always when he saw her.

"Welcome, my dear Elise," he said. "As you see, we're already here."

She entered and saw Edmond standing by the table. On this bright summer day, the light from the window showed his features clearly. The change from would-be monk to heir of Preston Manor had improved him. His skin was tanned, his brown curls streaked by the sun. It was as if he had grown into himself during their year apart. She felt too happy to see him to say a word.

Doubtless sensing her hesitation, he spoke first. "Welcome home, Elise! At times I thought this day might never come—our meeting again, I mean. Yet it has, with Canon Thomas's help. I can't thank him enough as I've been telling him."

"Nor can I," Elise added. "I prayed for this meeting all winter, and my prayers have now been answered by your kindness, father."

"As have mine," their teacher said, "that I might see you both again. Now I shall leave for an hour by my rear door, the same Edmond used to enter. The infirmarian at the abbey commands me to use my ailing leg lest it grow worse. I resist, but walking in the woods, limp and all, seems to help, along with a bit of quiet meditation. Meanwhile, all I know of you two makes me sure you will not betray my trust. I see this hour as an act of justice. The world has unfairly kept you two apart. Let us hope God will one day right that wrong."

Elise was silent, moved by their teacher's words. Edmond answered for them both; there was a new decisiveness in his manner. "You may trust us, Father. We will do nothing to make you regret your kindness."

When the old priest had exited clutching his staff, the two looked at each other for a moment. Then each said the same three words. "You look well!"

They both laughed at their awkwardness. Then they moved closer, close enough to embrace, but thinking of their teacher's words, Elise merely extended her hand. Edmond took it at once and covered it with kisses. His gesture spoke of a year of pent-up feeling. Touched, she held his strong brown hands in hers and pressed them to her cheek.

"Dear Edmond, how I've missed you!"

"And I you, Elise! All the more so since everything here held some memory of you. I could not leave the manor without seeing Bourne Castle in the distance reminding me you were gone."

"How cruel for you! You know from my letters how little I wanted to go and how much I missed you."

"Your letters alone gave me hope. Poor Canon Thomas! He must have grown tired of my asking if one had arrived!"

More at ease now, Elise laughed. She decided not to say anything yet about the letters. "Yes, thank God for his patience. But why are we standing? Let's take our old places at the table. No, wait. First, let me see you fully in the light."

Edmond stepped shyly back facing the window.

"How tall you've become," she said, "and sturdier too."

"It's true, I have. And you, Elise, are more beautiful than ever. I heard you'd become a courtly lady, elegant and stylish. I was afraid you might have grown too fine for me."

"Too fine!" she exclaimed as they both sat down. "What a thought. We are the same as always to each other. And today, here and now, we can at last talk freely, even look into each other's eyes. Yours are a deeper shade of blue than I recall."

"And yours a darker brown," Edmond echoed. "Soon, I hope, we'll be truly together, for good, I mean. I intend to become a knight and worthy of you."

"You're already more than worthy of me, Edmond. And I know we'll be together one day, no matter how long we have to wait." At once, she regretted the words. She had wanted to spare him until later.

Edmond's response was not surprising. "I don't understand. Why must we wait so long? In the fall, your uncle will let me begin my training as a squire at the castle. I already ride well and have begun to practice arms. After the harvest and the manor rents, I'll have enough for new armor and equipment. When a year has passed, I'll be on my way to becoming a knight. Just wait, I'll cut a proper figure!"

Elise saw she would have to admit the truth. "I know you will, darling, but I won't be here to see it, not for a while at least. And it's better for us I should not be."

"Not here?" Hasn't your year at court ended? I was hoping you were home for good."

A moment earlier, Edmond's face had displayed an exultant smile. A look of distress had replaced it. Elise knew she had to be strong. If she was not, they might sink into despair together.

"I hoped so too," she said, "but fate, the same fate which will one day unite us, has intervened. I am commanded to attend Princess Joanna on a long journey to Sicily. There she will wed the Norman King."

Looking shocked, Edmond drew a deep breath and spoke. "When will you go, and how?"

"Next spring or summer, by land and ship both. I doubt I'll be able to come home before I leave."

"Then when will I see you?" Edmond's face was flushed, his voice loud enough to be heard outside.

"I don't know when, my love, but please calm yourself. We must be careful even here. I didn't want to admit it before, but we have not even been able to write without being intercepted."

"Intercepted? What do you mean?"

"Someone at the abbey unsealed Canon Thomas's letters and discovered ours inside. I'm nearly certain it was Prior Gramont. Whatever the case, my aunt knows about us but has promised to say nothing. She has secrets of her own. We've made a kind of pact."

"A pact? And what are the terms?"

"Only what is necessary," Elise said as calmly as she could. "Yet there is one thing it breaks my heart to tell you. Before her death, my uncle promised my mother to find me a suitable husband, a Norman or Frenchman whose lands would be close to my own." Elise went on with a version of the tale she had prepared. "For this reason, before I leave for Sicily, I must seem, only *seem*, to be promised to a Frankish nobleman. While I'm away, he will oversee my lands and absorb some of the profit." It was as close to the truth as she dared to come. In fact, the count would have half her yearly income as a guarantee. She, in turn, had required that no date would be set for the wedding.

Hearing the news, Edmond turned pale beneath his summer brown. "First my father's vow and now your uncle's promise! Must we forever be cursed by these oaths from the past? Will we never be free?"

Elise heard the fury beneath his words. He had written her once of the rage that sometimes overcame him, how it took all his strength to hold it back.

"Edmond," she begged, "please don't look like that, you're frightening me." Wary of what he might say next, Elise laid a gentle finger on his lips. "You must believe me. There was no other choice. If I hadn't agreed, my aunt would have told my uncle about us. Then everything would have been spoiled, our love, your career as a knight, my uncle's trust in me."

"Who is the man?" Edmond demanded. There was a terrible tension in his voice.

"I've already said more than I intended, but I see I must go on. He is Gilles de Vere, a Norman count. Unless I agree to this seeming betrothal to a man who has no love for me, we are lost. This way, by the time I return you'll be a knight, my estates will be secure, and the count, having gained all he could from me, will surely have found another bride. This plan is our only hope. If you love me you must help me in it."

Edmond's face betrayed the battle being waged inside him. At last, he spoke in a bitter, defeated voice.

"I might have known. What made me think my fate would bring me happiness for once instead of misery and shame? Still, I didn't expect it from you, Elise. You've been the light in my life, my way out of the darkness."

Edmond seemed at a breaking point. Then, instead of collapsing, he drew back and grew expressionless and cold. Reaching out for his hand, she spoke to his silence, explaining the danger of her uncle's wrath, for him even more than for her. It took all her skill to make him see their only hope, for the present at least, lay in the course she had embarked on. At last, after much pleading and reassuring, Edmond reluctantly consented. She had regained his trust, but the price was the awful sadness in his eyes.

Having said all they could of their uncertain future, the two exchanged news of Windham and the court at Winchester. Next, they talked of how to guard their future correspondence. Finally, they spoke of Martin and the end of his novitiate year when he could write. At last, they knew their hour was drawing to a close. Simply, they vowed to love each other always and to ask for Canon Thomas's blessing. Then, no longer able to resist, they stood and reached out to each other. Feeling Edmond's strong arms, Elise threw her own around his neck. As his lips pressed against hers, she felt his warm, strong body and rebellion welled up inside her. Why could it not be like this always? Returning his kiss, she held him blissfully close, then, recalling their promise, pulled back. As she did, she felt a new force in him. His mouth was again on her lips, his hand on her breast. Feeling the quickening of her own desire, she tore herself away.

"We mustn't, Edmond. We've given our word."

He looked at her blankly as if trying to recall the pledge. When he spoke, there was desperation in his voice. "It's too much, Elise. I can't part this way, not knowing when or if we'll meet again!"

"I feel the same, my darling."

"No you don't, you can't! You couldn't go away so easily if you did."

"How can you say that? All I have done has been for you!"

"All for me, and then you leave me? No, Elise, I won't let you go like this. I'll speak to my father tonight. If he's not willing to approach your uncle, I'll have Martin's father, our steward, take a letter to the earl to ask him for your hand in marriage."

"Please, Edmond, think what you're saying! A proposal now would mean the end of all our plans. Only with time can we hope to succeed."

"No, Elise. I want no more of time, of hope, of your *seeming* betrothal to another man. It's too much to ask!"

Distressed by his manner, she tried to hold him and comfort him. Instead, as if his passion had turned to anger, he seized her and crushed her mouth against his own. Then he seemed to repent, held her gently, and spoke in a choking voice.

"If we part this way, Elise, after a single hour . . . I can't account for what I'll do."

His face was constricted. He seemed caught between pain and rage. What could she say to calm him? Canon Thomas would be returning in a moment. She had to be in Winchester within a week. They could not possibly meet again in Windham. She saw there was only one solution.

"I can't bear to leave you like this," she conceded. "I think there might be a way for us to meet. The queen's attendants may not receive male guests, but there is a place in Winchester, a private inn not far from the cathedral. A young woman I know at court has met a male friend there. I'm told the proprietor, a woman, can be trusted. It's as safe a place as we will find."

Elise did not think of the full implication of her words until she finished speaking, but when she saw the grateful look on Edmond's face, she knew she could not revoke them. He reached out to kiss her one last time and she responded, delighted to see he was himself again—up to a point. Today, in this room where they had once drunk from the springs of knowledge, they had sampled a headier brew. She had a feeling that neither of them would be satisfied until they drank of it more deeply.

12

Late on a hot afternoon in August, Martin was copying a manuscript in Greek. Mindful of his wish to be a scholar, Ambrose had found two short works in that ancient language little known in Britain. One manuscript was written in the Greek of pagan times, the other in the later Greek of the New Testament. During the final two years of his lessons, Canon Thomas had taught him the rudiments of the language. The old scholar had learned it many years ago in Cyprus, where the last holy war had taken him.

Looking up, Martin saw Brother Ambrose approaching his writing stand. "I told the others this morning," his mentor began, "but forgot to inform you earlier. We will have an important visitor tomorrow, an old pupil of Abbot Philip's, John of Oxford, Dean of Salisbury Cathedral. He is a man known for great distinction, wit, and close connection to the crown."

"Thank you for telling me, Brother. Are we to prepare for this visitor in some way?"

"Prepare? No, merely keep to your work as always. The lay brothers will tidy up tonight. I will place our newest, finest volumes in the center of the room. All else will be the same. Only be at your best and on your guard."

The next day, Martin was busy with his copying when he saw Abbot Philip at the entrance with a richly dressed, distinguished-looking prelate. The contrast between the two was striking: the abbot small, frail, and white-haired in Benedictine black, his former pupil tall, well-fleshed, and wearing scarlet robes. After a few words of introduction, the dean began to walk around the room, sometimes stooping to watch a copyist at work, at other times nodding and talking softly to the abbot. Finally, he came to rest before the gospel book on display. It was open to a richly illuminated page, an image of St. Luke the Evangelist. Brother Caedmon had painted it with special care. In it, the saint held a quill pen rendered in a myriad of colors.

Observing the striking depiction, the dean spoke aloud for the first time. "Is not this colored plume held by St. Luke a strange extravagance, along with the superfluous color in the ornamental border?"

Hearing the question, Abbot Philip looked at Ambrose, who came at once to the artist's defense. "My lord dean, might it not be that Saint Luke, who is known to have been an artist, the first, in fact, to have made an image of the Virgin, might have used his quill to test his colors?"

The dean smiled as if acknowledging the cleverness of this conceit. Then, surprisingly, he turned to Martin. "And you, young man, whose gifts, I'm told, lie elsewhere than in artistry, what is your opinion of this multicolored fancy?"

Alarmed at being singled out, Martin could think of no response. Did this great man really care about his thoughts? Or was the question a trap, a ruse to embarrass Abbot Philip? A painful silence invaded the room. He was ready to beg off replying when an idea came to him.

"My lord, I am an apprentice scribe and certainly no artist," he began, "but may I suggest that by fixing our attention on the quill, Brother Caedmon reminds us of the word of God which it conveys." Having said that much, Martin stopped, surprised at his own boldness. He glanced at Ambrose and the abbot. Both nodded their support. There was no turning back now.

"My former teacher, Canon Thomas, taught me that all beauty spoke of the Divine. So do these colors, I believe, like the many-hued rainbow in the heavens and the colored windows in our chapter house. They lead the mind first to wonder, then to contemplation, and in the end, to God."

There was a second silence now. Had he made a fool of himself? He felt his face flush as he waited for the dean's response.

At last John of Oxford responded. "Well said, young man. You lack neither fine thoughts nor the words to express them.

Pray forgive my testing you. My old teacher spoke so proudly of his scribes, I thought to humble him a bit. In fact, it is I who have been humbled. I am in debt to our young feather artist for the lesson of his colors, and to you for finding the truth in them."

Once this gracious commendation had been uttered, the rest of the visit was full of the prelate's approving remarks. When the dean and the abbot finally departed, the scriptorium erupted in a symphony of self-congratulation.

"My dear brothers," Ambrose chided, "these expressions of pride ill befit men of our calling," then quickly added, "but perhaps just this once, having shed so fair a light on our abbey, we can make an exception."

Given that leave, the scribes went on exulting in the dean's approval, at the same time expressing their admiration for the prelate. It took a great man to admit his faults so readily. Still, it was Martin, a mere novice, who was the hero of the day. Because of him, they had made the abbot proud before the Dean of Salisbury Cathedral, a man said to be a close associate of the king himself.

*

"My boy, you've moved nothing but your quill for the last two hours. Are you bewitched?"

Martin paused in his work, startled by the sound of Brother Ambrose's voice. Two weeks had passed since John of Oxford's visit. For the last few days, he had been busy with a task Prior Gramont had sent to the scriptorium, and he was finding it absorbing work.

Beside him now, Ambrose spoke in his kindly way. "I didn't mean to disturb you, Novice Martin, but as you well know, I'm wary of anything connected to our prior. I've started to wonder about these pages you're working on. When he sent them, he enjoined me to show them only to the scribe who copied them. All I know is that Basilides, the author, wrote in Egypt in the early days of Christianity—in Alexandria, in fact, where Gnostic heresy was rampant. You must tell me honestly, my boy, do these pages trouble you in any way, or perhaps tax your powers of comprehension?"

"No, brother," Martin said, "or rather, yes, they tax my brain but in a good way. In fact, I've finally begun to find some order in these rather disconnected fragments."

In truth, the sheets of yellowed parchment he was working on were unlike anything he had read before. The text was in Latin, but the number of words in Greek suggested the original was probably in that language. Having heard his superior's concerns, he tried to quell his fears.

"These are two parts, I believe, of what was once a whole. One purports to explain creation by a method rather difficult to understand. It seems to conclude that all beings proceed from one great primal source. From what I can tell, this source precedes both God and Satan, good and evil."

"Indeed! Pray don't speak of that too loudly. Perhaps these thoughts are mere metaphors, but they are surely intended for the philosophic mind, not the great mass of believers." With a slight shift of his head, Ambrose indicated the scribes behind him. Some were busy writing, others ruling lines on freshly coated parchment with their styluses.

"I'm sure you're right, brother. Even if I understood these writings better, I would hardly think of spreading them. Thoughts half comprehended can be dangerous, as Canon Thomas often said."

"He taught you well," Ambrose said, "in this and many other things," then lowered his voice. "You mentioned a second part. What does it treat of? Nothing that smacks of heresy, I hope?"

To calm his suggestible superior, Martin answered as simply as he could. "The second part consists of short verses, poems of a sort, by the same Basilides."

"That sounds a bit better, I suppose, but verses on what subject? Not the desires of the flesh, I hope? If so, you must cease at once and I'll copy them myself."

"No, nothing of that sort," Martin assured his mentor. "Besides, you have too much work already. You can be sure nothing here will tempt me or contaminate me."

Hearing this, Ambrose relented, although a look of suspicion still lingered on his face. Nodding slowly, he said, "I'm sure I can trust you, my boy. And you are correct. I have more than enough on my hands with this psalter for the earl. It must be done by the end of September."

"Yes, for Michaelmas," Martin commented. The earl was the abbey's patron here on earth, St. Michael the Archangel its heavenly patron. That fact gave his feast day great importance at the abbey.

The rest of the afternoon passed peacefully while Martin read, rearranged, and copied more pages from the fragments of Basilides. He was glad Brother Ambrose had not questioned him further on the verses. Much of what was in them did, indeed, seem to be heresy. A good deal of the rest made little sense to him. Nonetheless, he was fascinated. In one long passage, the author spoke of the *pleroma*, a kind of universal flux from which all things arose. Other parts of the writings were in disconnected pages. He felt they too might alarm his teacher.

God and Satan together give life and death, presence and absence, proliferation and degeneration, but there is also a force beyond them, one that unites creation and destruction. This great power remains obscure, concealed from humankind. We know it only by the name _____ .

Here, frustratingly, the word had been both scraped from the parchment and inked out, perhaps by someone avoiding blaspheming with the name of this strange power. Other fragments spoke of the same force.

Bow down, all you who hear that name, one greater than that of any god, a force beyond all human understanding, a power the more wonderful since mankind knows it not.

Some parts were written in verse as in a hymn or chant. In these too, the name had been obliterated.

At the beginning was_____ ,
The origin of chaos and decay,
The source of symmetry and union.

A part of a page was missing here, but the verses continued on another sheet.

It is the origin and ending.
It is the core of all being.
In life, you will fear it.
In death, you will know it.

What was this awful force, Martin wondered, and why had its name been so carefully removed? Was it too sacred to be spoken, or too evil? Whatever the case, it was no manifestation of the Christian God. Puzzled but fascinated, Martin would have liked to discuss these writings with Canon Thomas. On the other hand, Brother Ambrose would never have let him continue if he knew the truth about them. And, heretical or not, he wanted to. Nor did he wish to alarm his superior. No, he would simply go on giving what order he could to these disconnected parts, both for himself, since they intrigued him, and for their owner, Prior Gramont, of whom, in fact, Martin had not yet had a glimpse.

*

The morning of Michaelmas dawned clear and bright. Well in advance of the service, the abbey church was filled with guests and members of the faithful. This year, in a ceremony following the Mass, Abbot Philip would present the newly finished psalter to Earl Desmond and the Lady Melisande in recognition of their generosity as patrons of the abbey.

Seated with the monks and other novices behind the altar, Martin looked out toward the platform on which the important guests would sit. Just as he did, the earl and his wife appeared. Finely dressed in autumnal colors, they claimed the seats reserved for them. Across from them sat the abbot, the sub-prior, and the novice master, all three robed in splendid feast-day vestments. Then a third guest arrived, a tall, slender man in black whose trim, dark beard contrasted greatly with the earl's unruly one. The stranger sat in a chair beside the Lady Melisande. As he did, the novice next to Martin whispered in his ear, "That's Gilles de Vere, the Norman count lately betrothed to Lord Desmond's niece."

Incredulous, Martin whispered back. "To the Lady Elise? Are you sure?"

"Sure as I am that the sun rose this morning. I heard it from both the porter and the lector."

Amazed by this change in Elise's fate, Martin thought at once of Edmond, who must have been desolated by the news. Since the death of his brother Geoffrey, Martin had heard nothing of his friend. Next month, however, he would make his initial vows. After that, he would be able to write him and even see him. Once he had learned how this thing had come about, he would try to be of comfort to him.

A stirring in the congregation made Martin think of something very different, the man he would see for the first time today, Prior Guy de Gramont of Windham Abbey. During his year as a novice, the prelate had often been absent. For that matter, he seldom attended services when present. Today, however, on this most important feast day, he would be officiating at the high Mass. In anticipation of the service, the entire church had fallen silent: the monks in the choir behind the altar, the dignitaries before it, the congregation in the body of the church.

The silence continued for what seemed an endless moment. Then, all at once, a shock of thunder tore the air, filling the church with the deafening roar of the bells of the central tower. The tolling went on until it seemed it might bring the stones of the great vaulted ceiling down upon them all. At last, the sonorous din came to an end, and a very different sound replaced it: the tinkling of the silver hand bells that announced the Mass and the appearance of the prior. Now, for the first time, through a cloud of fragrant incense, Martin saw the priest preceded by two acolytes with swinging censers. Clothed in brocaded vestments like his fellows, Prior Gramont took his place before the altar as the sub-prior and the novice master rose to join him in the opening prayers.

The Mass had begun, and as it went on, Martin's glance was continually drawn to the central figure on the altar. Indeed, it would have been hard to keep from looking at him; he stood half a head above the others. He also bore an odd resemblance to the seated guest, the Count de Vere. And there was something else about the prior Martin recognized but couldn't place. Had he observed him at the abbey, not known who it was, and then forgotten? It seemed unlikely. It would be hard to forget someone so striking. Now, as he began the chanting of the Mass, the deep bass of the prior's *Oremus* reverberated down the hollow cavern of the nave. Strangely, it too seemed familiar. At last, turning toward the altar, the prior looked in the direction of the choir. For the first time, Martin saw him illuminated by the brilliance of a dozen glowing candles.

In that instant, it all came back. It was the same bearded face, the same tall frame, the same commanding voice. After two years, the scene was still branded in his mind; the firelight, the robed and hooded figures, the naked youth, the terrible moment of discovery and flight. Prior Gramont was the man who had led the gathering at the clearing of the stones.

*

Alarmed by the morning's revelation, Martin spent the rest of Michaelmas avoiding coming face to face with Prior Gramont. What would the priest's reaction be if he learned that the spy he had seen that night was now a novice here under his jurisdiction? Martin could scarcely guess, but whatever it was, he was sure it would not be pleasant. That evening he prayed for a miracle to keep the prior from recognizing him.

The result was disappointing. Two days later, pleased with his work in copying the fragments of Basilides, Prior Gramont sent word to Brother Ambrose that he wished to meet the novice Martin. On his return from a short absence, he would send for him. Martin spent the next two days dreading the encounter. On the third day, he could no longer bear the burden of his secret by himself. Surely Edmond would forgive him if he knew the circumstances. He resolved to tell Brother Ambrose that afternoon. Arriving at the scriptorium, he found the head scribe was elsewhere meeting with the abbot. An hour later, Ambrose returned with a message from the abbot requiring a good deal of thought on both their parts.

Once Ambrose had conveyed it, the two adjourned to the cloister to speak in private. At this hour, the arcade had a mellow glow; its limestone columns cast long shadows on the cloister pavement as they talked.

"Brother Ambrose," Martin began, "are you certain the abbot has not only given permission but favors this action requested of me?"

"I'm afraid so," Ambrose said, shaking his head. "It seems the impression you made on John of Oxford has returned to haunt us. As you recall, Abbot Philip and he are the best of friends. The dean is anxious to have you as a scribe. I spent an hour with the abbot making all my arguments against it, but he remained unmoved."

'But why, and why now?"

"I'm coming to that. By year's end, John will surrender his post as Dean of Salisbury to take up the vacant bishopric of Norwich. Less well known is the fact that King Henry has put him in charge of the coming marriage of Princess Joanna to the King of Sicily."

"That's all very well," Martin said, risking a disrespectful tone, "but what does it have to do with me?"

"Patience, my boy. I'm almost done. It seems the new bishop will make the trip to Sicily in person. There he will finish the negotiations for the royal marriage. It's not only your skill and your wit that recommend you but also your youth and health. John of Oxford's most trusted scribe is now too old to travel. Among the party he will take with him, he needs a clever young *amanuensis.*"

"To Sicily?"

"Yes, to Sicily, for as long as his mission lasts. That's the offer, a splendid one in many ways. He will be in London for the next three weeks. If you consent, you are to join him there."

"I see," Martin said, beginning an interior debate. He hated the thought of leaving the scriptorium. He was wary of traveling so far from everything he knew and everyone he cared for. At the same time, the idea of the journey excited him. Here, all unexpected, was his chance to see the world, something he had always dreamed of doing. Also weighing strongly for acceptance was this new and chilling threat, the danger of being recognized by Prior Gramont. Still, knowing what he did about the prior, could he in conscience simply flee? No, he would have to tell someone in authority about the gatherings. The prior would be returning soon. There was no time to hesitate.

"Brother Ambrose, I think I've decided. First, however, I must speak about something serious connected to my choice."

"Of course. Go ahead."

"I hesitate to involve you in this thing, but as a matter of conscience, I feel I must. I have good reason to believe the prior is the leader of a secret band, a cult whose rites may end in murder."

A look of horror appeared on Ambrose's face. "God spare us from evil! And how is it you know of this?"

"I know of it first hand. In fact, I believe I'm in danger because of it. I first saw the prior two years ago, late at night at the clearing of the stones. He was leading a group of robed and hooded figures in a shocking ceremony. There was a victim, a young man bound, gagged, and naked."

"Dear God! Can there be such things here in Windham so close to us at the abbey? Are you sure it was the prior?"

"As sure as I am that you stand before me. He and I met in the firelight, face to face, only a few feet apart."

"Then, despite the strangeness of your revelation, I will trust you in this. Now explain to me how you came to be in such a place and also how you came so close to him."

Martin told him the story as succinctly as he could, making no excuses for himself. "I confess I was driven by an all-consuming boyish curiosity. I was afraid of the unknown, of course, but thanks to Canon Thomas's teaching, I had little fear of malicious spirits. However shocking, the evil I found was human. Since that night, as you may well imagine, I've thought long and hard about what happened to that boy. When you spoke of the discovery of the bodies in the bog, those of Wilfred and the girl who disappeared last summer, I thought of him. And earlier too, when Father Gilbert spoke about the novice who disappeared two years ago. He has not yet been found, I believe?"

"Novice Stephen? No, nothing has been heard of him."

"He disappeared in the summer of 1173?"

"Let's see, yes. He was missing for the vigil of a saint, I can't remember which. We all assumed he was ill in the infirmary. The following morning we learned he had disappeared."

As Ambrose spoke, a new certainty came over Martin. He felt sure he knew the holy day in question but he didn't want to influence his mentor's memory. "Can you try to recall the saint's day, brother? It might be quite important."

"It's been a long while. Give me a moment. It was a notable saint, I believe, one revered abroad. An apostle, perhaps. But wait—of course! How could I forget? It was July twenty-fourth, the vigil of St. James. There were pilgrims at the abbey, ready to set out for that saint's shrine at Compostela in Galicia. *Santiago,* they call him there."

Martin had guessed correctly. He now felt certain he knew the truth. "In that case, brother, I must tell you this. It was St. James's Eve the night I encountered Prior Gramont. It seems more than likely that the boy I saw was Stephen, and that he became a victim of the evil band. Now that I'm sure of the truth, I must ask you to tell Abbot Philip about the prior's part in it, hoping he will inform the proper authorities."

"Yes of course I will, once I've had a chance to reflect on all this. Meanwhile, I'll tell you something else. You are not the first person to accuse a cleric of involvement in these disappearances and deaths. When the girl was found in the New Forest three years back, Bishop Osbert of Clarington and others attached to his office were suspected. As you may know, the bishop and Prior Gramont have long been friends."

"What you tell me, brother, confirms my worst fears."

"As your discovery does mine."

Having spoken these ominous words, the normally garrulous Ambrose fell silent. Martin waited, sorting out his own thoughts while he stood beside his mentor in the waning light. After a while, the Benedictine looked up and turned to him. "I believe what you've stumbled on, my son, may be as convoluted as the ornamental carving we see across the way." Martin followed his mentor's eyes to where the evening light had struck the capital of a column, throwing it into deep relief.

"Convoluted and difficult to follow," Ambrose said, "much like the intricate borders Brother Terence loves to paint. Now, in fact, I can say that I too have long had grave suspicions about the prior. I suppressed them as latent calumnies, foolishly, I now see. God willing, my failure of wisdom may yet be set right. Meanwhile, my boy, what of your decision?"

"Yes, of course," said Martin, still caught in a web of fearful speculation. "I'd almost forgotten. Now that I know the truth about the prior, I live in dread of discovery. It's bound to happen within a few days when he sends for me."

A look of resolve now appeared on Ambrose's face. "Then I see what you must do. You know how much I hoped to keep you here, my delight in your work, the great promise you've shown. Now, however much against my will, I agree you should go. God in his goodness has provided a path of escape. The sooner you take it, the better."

Martin nodded, moved as much by the Benedictine's good opinion of him as by his unselfish concern. "Thank you, brother. Your goodness shines through in all you say and do. In this matter, your thoughts and mine are one. I shall sorely miss my days in the scriptorium—"

"I know, my boy, I know. I will miss you even more, but we mustn't dwell on it now. Whatever Sicily brings, it seems fate has willed it. Let me hasten to the abbot to inform him of your choice. Once you're gone, I shall tell him about the prior. Next week, you would have finished your year as a novice and taken your vows. I'll tell Abbot Philip you nonetheless wish to leave at once in order to avoid a painful parting from your peers."

As he listened, Ambrose's words brought the truth home to him. He was leaving everything he knew: the abbey, the village of Windham, the land of his birth. Yet it was already too late for second thoughts. "Dearest brother," he said, his voice filled with emotion, "I shall never forget all you've done for me."

"I know you will not, my boy. As it is, you won't leave for Palermo until the spring. Let us hope things have changed for the better here by then. You will be in my prayers all my remaining days."

With those words, Ambrose went to speak to the abbot, and Martin returned to the scriptorium. First, he wrote messages to Edmond and his father, leaving a note asking Ambrose to send them. Then he made private farewells to Caedmon and Terence, leaving Ambrose to speak to the others. That evening at Vespers, he thanked God for delivering him from Prior Gramont. At the same time, he learned the prior was returning that evening. Even so, there was little chance of their meeting. Martin would leave at sunrise, long before the prior was in the habit of appearing.

The next day at dawn, showing great courtesy, both Abbot Philip and Brother Ambrose walked with Martin to the abbey gate. There they made their farewells. His mentor's words, "May God go with you," were the last Martin heard before he set off on his journey. By noon, when he sat by the roadside to eat the meal the abbey kitchen had prepared, he found himself warming to the novelty of travel. After Winchester, there would be London to meet John of Oxford, then Norwich, where his new patron would be installed as bishop, and finally Palermo, that faraway city of which he knew so little.

13

Looking up, Elise saw her friend Marianne, a bright young woman with a lively smile and reddish hair.

"My dear Elise, you've come back to a court in turmoil."

"Have I indeed?" Putting the last of her things in a wooden chest, Elise closed the lid and sat down on it with Marianne. They were alone in the chamber they shared with Joanna's other attendants.

"Well, tell me everything."

"It's the queen, or rather the king. At the end of the month, he'll be sending Eleanor to Sarum, a desolate fortress on the Salisbury plain. They say she'll be even more closely guarded."

In the wake of the recent rebellion against him, King Henry had pardoned his traitorous sons, sequestering his wife instead. Elise deplored the injustice. There was no proof that Eleanor had fostered the rebellion. "He might at least have waited until Christmastide was over."

"That's exactly the point. They say he plans to spend it here with Rosamund de Clifford. He may even bring her openly to court."

"His mistress here?" Elise thought of the queen's humiliation.

"Either here or at Westminster Palace in London."

"And Princess Joanna?"

Marianne shook her head. "She's been in tears since she found out her mother was leaving. Now that she knows she'll be going to Sicily for good, she clings to her more than ever."

Elise also felt for Joanna, who had just turned ten. "The poor child, forced to marry at her age, little more than a pawn on the chessboard of her tyrant of a father."

"Be careful, Elise, someone might hear!"

"You're right, forgive me. I'm feeling distracted and sour on the subject of marriage. In fact, I have something I need to talk to you about. Are you free at present?"

"Yes, just as you see me."

"Then put on your cloak and let's go into the garden."

The garden was small with an evergreen border, rows of herbs, and flowering plants. The queen had begun it herself. Its fate, like Eleanor's, now lay in Henry's hands. When they were seated on a wooden bench, Elise spoke in a confidential manner.

"Last spring you were kind enough to tell me about your meetings with Thomas, the friend whom you wish one day to marry. He is now in Normandy, I believe?"

"Yes," said Marianne, "but he'll be in London in a month. We're hoping that when he returns, my father will relent and allow us to be betrothed."

"I hope so too, for both your sakes. He's fortunate to have a clever girl like you."

Marianne smiled and Elise went on. "Meanwhile, I find myself in a similar situation. Could you tell me about the place you met? An inn of some sort, I believe."

"Yes," Marianne said, lowering her voice. "It's run by a widow, Dame Gertrude. She's respectable and quite discreet. She can afford to be. Her clients pay her well."

"An inn? But isn't that much too public?" Elise could barely picture it.

"I call it an inn, but it's actually the lady's home. She lets chambers on a temporary basis. There are no public rooms, and no food or drink is served except upon request."

"I see," Elise said, feeling somewhat reassured. "I would like to meet her."

"Then you shall, the first afternoon we're both free I'll take you there."

A week later, Marianne introduced her to the lady, a handsome widow in her early middle years. Having decided she could trust her, Elise laid the groundwork for a future meeting at her house with Edmond. That night, she wrote Canon Thomas care of the pastor at Windham parish, avoiding the abbey and Prior Gramont. Inside her letter, she put a note for Edmond asking him to write her through Dame Gertrude in the future. Before the end of the month, his letter came. He had done as she asked and, choosing a date from those possible for her, come up with some business in Winchester for Preston Manor. Two days after receiving his letter, she paid in advance for the room, adding extra for wine and fresh pears and apples, the fruits of the season.

Then she waited, anxious for a dozen reasons. Had she given in too easily to Edmond's wishes? If she changed her mind, what reason could she give? How great was the risk of discovery once they met? Night after night, she pondered until it was too late to change their plans. In truth, her delay was hardly accidental. She wanted the meeting as much as he did.

On a blustery late autumn day, the hour finally arrived. As she and Marianne passed through the cathedral yard, great flurries of leaves whirled around them. In the half-deserted streets, it was easy to hide beneath their hooded cloaks. Marianne had a friend in Winchester, a young woman who had married beneath her station. She would spend the afternoon with her and meet Elise for their return. The two parted at Dame Gertrude's door.

Inside the house, the widow led her upstairs to a room overlooking a narrow alley. Left alone, she waited, full of uneasy expectation. At last, when she was beginning to think Edmond might have failed her, there was a rap on the door. She said the word *yes*, heard his voice speak her name, and undid the latch. The door flew open, and they were at last in each other's arms.

*

That afternoon at Dame Gertrude's, Elise learned a great deal about Edmond and herself. Their first attempts at making love were awkward, as she supposed they must always be. Soon, however, desire overcame modesty. Touching, fondling, caressing, they yielded gratefully to each other. Despite the initial pain, she found herself thrilled by Edmond's hunger to possess her. Afterward, they lay naked in the heat of the brazier the widow had provided and she marveled at his muscled arms and thighs, so different from her own smooth limbs.

Now, for the first time, they talked without constraint, whispering all the endearments they had been forced to leave unspoken. After a while, Edmond asked her a question. "Have you been happy here at court, Elise?"

"Happy? I'm not sure I knew the meaning of that word until today. Here and now, I am happy with you, but life at court wearies me. Not Joanna, poor thing. She could hardly be better, so anxious to please, so eager for her parents' approval. It's everything else, the hunger for rank and position, the petty intrigues, the pointless rivalries. I tutor the princess, but I have few books myself and little time to read. Like Martin, I too would love to be a scholar. As a man and a cleric, he can be, but I cannot, thanks to the foolish way things are ordered in this world. After you, my love, what I miss most are our lessons with Canon Thomas."

"I miss them too. How lovely those mornings were even if you and I couldn't speak. As for our love, I know we'll find a way once I'm a knight, but I don't want to think about that now. I want only you here beside me, your eyes, your lips, your hair smelling of flowers, your loveliness like a precious gift." As he spoke, Edmond took her in his arms again. After they kissed, he pulled back.

"But how dry your lips are, Elise!" He reached for the cup beside the bed and poured some wine. "Here, drink, and I'll taste it from your lips. They're sweeter to me than any wine."

Taking the drink, Elise decided to tease her lover. "Flatterer! Did you find that phrase in some ballad?"

"No, of course not. It just came to me, truly."

Even briefly, she could not bear his wounded look. "Darling, I was only joking. Come, at least share my cup. Let's drink to the life we'll have one day."

Savoring that dream, they drank by turns. Then they kissed and made love again, this time with even more passion. The day ended with the pain of parting, relieved only by the fact that they would meet again in January.

That evening when Marianne asked her about the afternoon, Elise could barely answer. In truth, she had no desire to speak of it. The next morning, playing a word game with Joanna, she could hardly believe those precious hours had happened. That night in bed, she wanted Edmond fiercely. The following day, she was stricken with loneliness. After loneliness came doubt. Ten days passed without a word from Edmond, then another week. She knew it was difficult for him to send his letters, but she desperately needed to hear from him. Could she have been mistaken in her love? Had she been only a conquest after all, like those the young men boasted of at court? No, she could never believe that of Edmond. It was only the difficulty of their situations, hers at court, his at Preston Manor. She would trust him as she always had and wait.

Then, to her horror, her menses failed to come. They were a week late when a note came from Dame Gertrude to tell her a letter was waiting. She claimed it after going to Vespers in the cathedral with Marianne. It was from Edmond and full of loving words. He had gone to Clarington to send it to avoid discovery. All was well with him and at the manor. He even knew the date when he would come again in February. That night, Elise felt she had betrayed him. When he learned she was carrying his child, his life would be ruined along with hers. No matter what came of it, he would never conceal his fatherhood.

How foolish she had been! Marianne had said there were ways to prevent a child, but that there was no need for them the first time. Ashamed to talk of such things, she had not questioned her further. Even now, she said nothing to her friend, as if by denying it, she could keep the reality at bay. On the second night after Edmond's letter, she gave in to despair. She fell on her knees and prayed to God to intervene, to save Edmond and her both. And still she made no vow to give him up. She had been humbled, she was full of fear, but she would not repent her love.

The next day, she felt a cramping in her bowels. And then, as if on angelic wings, her menses came. She thanked God with all her heart, deciding fate had favored them this time. She was determined to avoid a repetition. She no longer trusted her friend in the matter. It was Dame Gertrude who had told Marianne how to avoid conceiving. When she saw the lady again, she would ask her how.

At court, they were already preparing for Christmas, Joanna's last in England. She would spend it with her mother. Elise was chosen to go with her to Sarum along with three other attendants and a small army of guards. As the King of Sicily's bride, Joanna's value to the realm had risen. That winter was the coldest Elise could remember, the trip to Sarum a trial. The castle was built on an arid, wind-battered hill. Yet even in these dispiriting quarters, the queen did not act like a woman in disgrace. For over three decades, she had been at the heart of European power, first queen of France, then of England. In Aquitaine, her native duchy, her life was already the subject of legend and song. Here in England, thanks to her husband, she was in eclipse. The king continued to blame her for his sons' rebellion. Yet despite her misfortune, Eleanor remained dignified, regal, and charming. Already past fifty, she was beautiful still.

She also seemed to be fond of Elise. Late one night as the wind whistled and moaned outside the great stone keep, the queen invited her to sit beside a warming fire. She offered her wine and asked Elise about herself. Then, commending her learning and skill as Joanna's tutor, she spoke about her daughter. "She is my youngest girl. After her, there is only John who is as devious as she is guileless. It breaks my heart to see her leave. She'll be a bride at eleven, what a crime! I was fifteen with Louis, that was bad enough. The king, of course, will have his way. Pliable as wax, Joanna is the seal on his alliance with a wealthy Norman kingdom. I hope Sicily won't stifle her. They are like Byzantines there, they say. The court is full of Greeks, Arabs, and eunuchs. Joanna is more docile than I ever was but not nearly as clever, I'm afraid. Men prefer that in women, of course. They think wit no virtue in our sex. I disagree, as do you, it seems, since you read and write in both French and Latin."

"I was fortunate in my teacher, a devoted scholar."

"I wish there were more like you at this barbaric court. When I think of my youth in Aquitaine—the wit and the charm, the hours of poetry and song—I remember myself as I once was. Who would think this old crone bent over a fire once dined with the emperor in Constantinople?"

"No, madam, never a crone! I'm sure you're as beautiful as ever. If I may ask, was that on the way to the Holy Land, the time you dined with the emperor?"

Yes," said the queen, "we were en route to the second holy war. Three decades ago; how quickly the years go by! I see you remember the story, unlike the others who scarcely remember last year's fashions. Yes, Louis and I were grandly entertained, but we left empty-handed. However liberal with his honeyed words, the emperor gave neither troops nor money to the Christian cause. I suppose you've heard the rest, my infamous flight from my husband to my uncle's camp?"

"The Count of Poitiers?" Elise said, wondering if she should have feigned ignorance.

"Yes, Raymond. He was handsome, virile, and courageous, just the opposite of pious, puling Louis. I took his side against my husband in the plans for war. Interfering in men's affairs, they called it. That was the start of the end of my marriage, but not for the reason people think. I loved my uncle but he was not my lover. If I had slept with every man they say, I would never have been out of bed!"

At this joke on herself, Eleanor laughed a rich, melodic laugh. One day, when the queen was alone with Joanna, Elise had heard her sing a haunting ballad in the *Langue d'Oc*, the language of the troubadours. Otherwise, in a protest against her captivity, she never sang or played an instrument. Sipping her wine, she spoke in a confidential manner.

"I am frank with you, my dear, because I trust you. I met your uncle Desmond, you know, in the holy war. An honest youth, rosy cheeked and blond, hardly more than a boy. I found him quite charming, as I recall, but he could speak of nothing but his new betrothed, the girl who became his wife. She died young, I believe."

"Yes," Elise replied. "He mourned her for a long time, but he has now married again. I remember his saying he met you once. I didn't know it was in the Holy Land."

"It was shortly after our arrival. That whole winter, Louis kept me confined in Jerusalem. It seems my husbands always end by locking me up." The queen laughed again, ruefully this time. "Men always exceed their rights, you know. I've spent my life doing womanly duty. I've borne ten children who survived. The rest of the time I've spent resisting the dictates of men."

Elise was amazed at the queen's candor. Perhaps it was the season, or the wine, or more likely loneliness. All that parenting, and she was here in this grim fortress with a single child while the king spent the festive season with his mistress. Now the queen reached for the poker and turned the log.

"Men have always believed they had the right to rule a woman's body. They're wrong, of course. They should revere us instead. It is our bodies that give them life. I'm sure you've heard of the so-called rules of courtly love that my daughter Marie now champions in Champagne. What are they but a way of reclaiming the esteem men have so long denied us?"

We could use more of such esteem in England," Elise commented.

"Indeed we could, beginning with my husband. Of course, in my youth I was fortunate. I was early made the ruler of a wealthy duchy. In one way, my riches gave me freedom. In another, it made me a target for abduction and forced marriage. As much as anything else, I married King Louis in flight from such scurrilous suitors. Rich or poor, most women are bound like chattels. When at last I claimed my freedom, I paid the price. How Bernard of Clairvaux, that hypocrite monk, railed against me! Today it makes me laugh. And he had better reason than he knew. By the time I met Henry, I was no longer shy. Why should I have been? He was young and full of life. I was a decade his senior, awaiting the annulment of my marriage to King Louis. I sent Henry a ring with the words *carpe diem* engraved in it. He was not slow to take the hint. He seized both the day and me."

Elise nodded silently, wondering what would come next. As it happened, it was advice. "Don't let them tell you your body is not your own. And if you happen to transgress their rules, don't let them know. Women survive by their strength, their beauty, and their cunning. They may do without one, but not two of these. I believe you may have all three."

"I hope I do, madam," said Elise. "It thrills me to hear you say so. I could listen to you talk all night."

"I believe you could. You have a brain in your head, unlike the others. Still, I've said enough for one evening. Finish your wine, help me to bed, and I'll wish you sweet dreams of your lover."

Elise heard the word *lover* with a shock.

"Dear child, don't be distressed. It's a way of speaking we had in Aquitaine. Nonetheless, I'll be honest. I've guessed that it's so in your case. For one, you don't trifle with the young men at court. Nor do you gossip about them with the others. Clearly, the one you love is not among them. I only hope he's worthy of you. Men so seldom are, you know."

Elise opened her mouth to reply.

"No, no, you need neither affirm nor deny the thing I've guessed. I speak of it only for your sake. I hope God will bless you in it. But never forget to be cunning."

That night Elise went to bed with the queen's words ringing in her ears. She had never said it openly, but in her heart, she hated the fetters men placed on women. That bit of flesh, for instance, named after the male god of marriage, Hymenaeus. What made men think it was theirs when it belonged to a woman's body? She thanked God Edmond was not like them. If he had thought less of her after that day at the inn, she could never have loved him as she did. As she could tell from his recent letter, his regard for her had only grown.

Elise returned from Sarum savoring the queen's advice. Full of new daring, she went alone to secure the room for Edmond's coming visit. Conquering shame, she spoke to Dame Gertrude boldly, asking her how to avoid conceiving. She learned there was one nearly certain way, but it required the cooperation of one's partner. The trick was simple, although perhaps difficult in practice. Elise felt she should have guessed, but then few ever did, it seemed.

In January, the snows mounted high in the castle yard. Word came now of people starving in the cold. Elise prayed for those suffering, then that the road from Windham would be clear for Edmond's February visit. Meanwhile, a letter arrived from Martin. He had left Windham Abbey and was serving John of Norwich, the bishop in charge of Joanna's marriage. When spring came, he would be going to Palermo with that prelate. Delighted, Elise wrote that she too would be there but later, in the fall.

*

When the day of Edmond's visit came, the roads were open. As they met, a storm of pent-up longing overwhelmed them. The weeks apart had been a trial for them both. They had three hours to make up for them. First, Elise told Edmond about her conversation with the widow. Then, pulling off their clothes, they fell into bed. Once again, Elise thrilled to Edmond's love, first gently tender, then more powerfully urgent. Caught up in the flood of his passion, she sounded the depths of her own. Closing her eyes, she felt his lips on her face, her neck, her breasts. All at once, a thrill of ecstasy filled her body. Then, quelling her rising fear, Edmond followed the widow's advice and withdrew. Shuddering, he spilled himself onto her stomach. Grateful, Elise held him even closer. Later, they laughed when they found they were stuck together by his seed. Afterward, lying with bodies entwined, they spoke of all they had felt and thought since their last meeting. They made love a second time, and then, once again, Edmond was gone.

In the weeks that followed, they planned their last meeting. It would not be until June, some weeks before Elise left for the long journey to Palermo. Meanwhile, things at court were increasingly busy. Although she was still only ten, Sicilian envoys arrived at Winchester to certify Joanna's beauty for her husband. She was her mother's child; her fair hair and fine features gained their admiration. With this final condition met, Joanna's fate was fixed, and with it, Elise's departure for Sicily.

Her final meeting with Edmond was much like the others, except that now they were separating for an unknown length of time. When Elise entered the room, Edmond was already there. The first thing he said was, "My darling Elise, please don't move. I want to keep this image in my mind—you, fresh from court with eyes shining and cheeks flushed. Sometimes at night, I wake and wonder if all this is real, that we two have met twice, that you've dared all this for me, that you love me as I love you."

Elise could think of no reply. Instead, she ran to Edmond, embraced him, and lifted her face to his. He kissed her tenderly and then pulled back. "Wait, my love, you mustn't think I've come empty-handed. Let me show you what I've brought." He dug into his satchel, took out a small parcel wrapped in cloth, and handed it to her. "I hope you like it," he said, looking anxious.

She kissed him as she took it and undid the string. Inside, she found a silver pendant with an interlaced design. "I like it very much," Elise said. "It's lovely. I can't imagine where you found it."

"In Clarington. I had it especially made. Look more closely. There are two letters concealed in the design."

As soon as he said it, she saw them, two interlocking variations of the letter E. They were apparent only if you searched for them.

"It's so clever, so finely wrought," Elise said. "I have a keepsake for you too. I hate to give it to you after this."

"Don't be foolish. I can't wait to see it."

Elise took it from beneath a pillow. It was a simple silver ring with E and E inside the band. The coincidence of the initials touched them both. She felt herself about to cry but stopped. She mustn't spoil their last meeting. Instead, she talked about her gift. "You had better not show it at Windham, of course. They would wonder where it came from. I thought you could wear it beneath your shirt. It's slender enough not to show. But first, you must try it on. I'll do it for you." She slid the ring on the middle finger of Edmond's left hand. It fit perfectly.

Edmond first kissed the ring, then Elise. Then once again, they fell into each other's arms. That day, they made love ardently but slowly, almost solemnly, as if it were their wedding night. Afterward, they talked of simple things, trying not to think about their parting. Then Elise rose and poured some wine. Before drinking it, Edmond raised his cup.

"I drink to our love, Elise. From this day forward, I consider you my wife."

"And you, too," Elise said. "From this day on, you are my true husband."

After that, heartened by their vows, they talked about the future, the day Elise would return to Windham free of Gilles de Vere. Then, lying together in silence, they held each other close for a long time. When the shadows in the room began to lengthen, Edmond rose from the bed without Elise's prompting. All too soon, he was dressed and ready. Taking her in his arms, he spoke in a rueful voice. "For the first time since Martin entered Windham Abbey, I envy him. Before long, he'll be in Sicily with you."

Elise felt her heart was about to break. She responded with all the courage she could manage. "If only we could go together, Edmond, to Sicily or some other place where we could both be free! And yet I know our time will come. Until then, having Martin there will be a comfort."

"For us both. I'll be able to write you using him as intermediary." After a pause, Edmond's expression grew suddenly dark. "For all the good it will do, as long as you're betrothed to someone else."

Elise felt herself sinking. "Darling, don't say such things. We've risked all for these precious hours. Can't we be grateful and part with hope? I know in my heart we'll be together in the future."

She watched Edmond's face as he made the great effort to alter his mood. When he spoke, she could feel the emotion compacted in his words. "Dear Elise, your courage recalls me to my own. Whatever the future brings, we belong to each other now."

After kissing her one last time, Edmond left by a door that led down the rear stairs to an alley. Once he entered the High Street, no one would know where he had been. With the widow's help, they had planned it all so well.

And now it was over.

The next moment, Elise found it difficult to breathe. It was as if Edmond had taken all the air with him. Alone in what now seemed a mean and shabby room, she forgot her brave words and gave in to her anguish. Marianne found her weeping on the bed. She tried to comfort her, but Elise would have none of it. Her friend was remaining at Winchester, her lover no farther away than London. How could she know what Elise was feeling? When she had dried her tears, the two walked back in silence through the summer evening.

PART TWO

The Shrine of Mithras

1176~1187

14

1176

Palermo, Sicily

The Feast of St. Basil
The Fourteenth of June, 1176
From Deacon Martin Rendon
To Elise de Crecy in the Party of Princess Joanna
The Port of Saint-Gilles, Toulouse

    My dearest lady, I trust this letter will greet you upon your arrival at your port of embarkation for Sicily. It will come with the royal envoys who will greet you there. Here in Palermo, we are well informed about the great size of the royal party and its progress southward through the Frankish duchies. If all goes well, we expect Princess Joanna and her entourage to reach Saint-Gilles this autumn. There, a fleet of Sicilian ships will await you.

    As for me, I am well, but before I speak of myself, I want to tell you of this strange and wondrous place called Sicily. So far my impressions are mainly of Palermo, a city with a population many times the size of London's. Set like a crown at the edge of the sea, bathed in light of a brilliance unknown in England, the city spreads out to green hills full of trees bearing oranges and lemons. The Sicilians call these slopes the conca d'oru, the golden shell. Below, at the heart of a great natural bay, the harbor is full of ships from every corner of the world. The island's other great port is Messina to the east, separated from the mainland by a narrow strait. From its harbor ships set sail for Africa, Greece, and the Holy Land. And the island of Sicily is but half of King

*William's realm. The other half is the southern part of Italy. In an-
cient times, it was a part of Greece, as was much of Sicily. Magna
Graecia, the Romans called it, a land famed for philosophers and tyrants.*

*As you know, Sicily was conquered by the Normans just as Eng-
land was over a century ago. Here, however, they won the land more
slowly, in many battles with the Arabs who had ruled here centuries
before them. Wisely, the Normans chose to incorporate the customs,
laws, and skills in agriculture practiced by their predecessors. They, in
turn, had taken this fertile land from the Byzantine Greeks. Today,
because of the many peoples who have lived here, several tongues are
spoken. As with us in England, Norman French is the language of the
court, the nobles, and the military. Latin is used both by clerics and in
official documents along with Greek and Latin. To this day, many
persons of the Muslim faith hold high positions in King William's
Court. Because of its large Arab population, Palermo has many great
places of worship called mosques. One knows them by their tall towers
called minarets. From these, five times a day, the faithful are called to
worship by a haunting chant. Imagine, in a land ruled by a Christian
king! In some parts of Palermo, however, the Hebrew language domi-
nates. Here, thanks to an enlightened policy of toleration under Norman rule, Jews do not suffer the persecution all too common in the
north.*

*As for William II, the present king, I have seen him only once and
from a distance, but his appearance will surely please the ladies of the
English court. At twenty-two, well made and fair of face, he is in the
bloom of early manhood. Unlike William I, his father, he is greatly
loved by all his people. He is, however, said to be stubborn and inclined
to self-indulgence. On the other hand, he is certainly no dullard. In
addition to French, he knows Latin, Arabic, and Greek. Like King
Roger, his illustrious grandfather, he has a taste both for luxury and
learning, along with certain oriental habits you may find surprising.*

*Sicily itself is a land of great abundance. Let us hope its smiling
face bodes well for both the princess and for you, my lady. So far, I
have been only once to the royal palace, called by the Sicilians the Palace of the Normans. It is a vast edifice shielded by tall, thick walls.*

There I saw the celebrated royal chapel, a splendid church of fine marble and wonderful mosaics. It was built by Norman, Greek, and Arab craftsmen. Their efforts are skillfully blended to surprisingly harmonious effect.

As for the royal marriage, my patron, the Bishop of Norwich, has nearly completed his negotiations, and will be returning to England soon. From the first, he has said we are free to remain if we choose. I shall stay on in the service of the Archbishop of Palermo. By the way, I am now a deacon, ordained by the Bishop before I left England. I no longer aspire to higher religious rank. I prefer the duties of a scribe— and in the future, I hope, a scholar—to those of a priest or monk.

In closing, let me call your attention to the sheet on which I write. It is neither parchment nor papyrus but an invention of the East called paper, made from the pulp of rags. My dear lady, I pray every day for your safe passage to Palermo. I hope you will receive this before the princess's party sets out for Sicily. Until we meet, I remain your devoted friend.

*

Before and after the departure of the Bishop of Norwich, Martin's host remained the same, Archbishop Walter of Palermo, a man whose power, it was said, was second only to the king's. In fact, Walter had formerly served as William's tutor. Since then, he had become a leading member of the *Familiares Regis*, the king's privy council. Imperious and gifted, the author of several books, the archbishop was said to be of English stock. True or not, it was the sort of question no one dared ask the celebrated prelate, least of all a humble scribe like Martin.

In his work for the Bishop of Norwich, Martin had attended to much of the English correspondence concerning the marriage. Once the bishop had left, he did the same for Archbishop Walter. At first, he was busy from dawn to dusk, copying documents in French and Latin, reading letters, and drafting replies. In November, they had word that the princess had arrived at Saint-Gilles and was ready to embark for Sicily. After that, there was a lull in the volume of his work. Deprived of his intensive labor, Martin began to feel terribly alone. He had long anticipated the Lady Elise's arrival, but it was Edmond, far away in England, whom he thought of every day. While at Norwich, he had written him once and had a warm reply. As yet, he had received no response to his first letter from Palermo.

One evening, just as he was about to leave the scriptorium, Brother Emeric, an aging Lombard scribe, addressed him in a friendly manner. "Have you grown familiar with Palermo, Deacon Martin? Or have you been too busy to explore the city?"

"The latter, I suppose."

"I'm not surprised. When I first came from Legnano, I seldom left the scriptorium."

"When was that, brother?" Martin inquired, as much out of courtesy as interest.

"During the reign of Roger II. Those were glorious days, although turbulent. In many respects, however, things are better now. Sicily is at peace."

Although he had never known war at first hand, Martin readily concurred. "Yes, that certainly makes a difference."

"A great one, I assure you. Now that you're less occupied, you must take advantage of your freedom. With that in mind, I advise you to do three things. First, stroll at evening by the harbor. There you can savor the great variety of people. Next, visit the churches, both Latin and Greek, for which Palermo is justly famed. Finally, go to the *souks*, the Arab markets, which are like a journey to the East."

Martin thanked the old monk, and the two parted. Hoping to alleviate his solitude, he soon took Emeric's advice. The harbor at evening was much as he had described it. Everyone seemed to be strolling there: lowly beggars and food vendors, merchants whose shops had just closed, noblemen whose retainers would part the crowd to make way for them. All had come to enjoy the fresh breeze and sea air. Still, as Martin looked out past tall masts and furled sails to the beautiful bay of Palermo, his thoughts were elsewhere; back in Windham's green fields with Edmond in the days before their dark adventure at the clearing of the stones.

One morning a few days later, Martin entered the scriptorium and found a letter from England addressed to him. His heart leapt. Surely it must be from Edmond. But it was not.

The Feast of Saint Silverius
Twentieth of June, 1176
Brother Ambrose at Windham Abbey
To Deacon Martin care of the Archdiocese of Palermo
    My dear boy, I hope you are well. I pray every day God will keep you in his care. Having said that, I will tell you the bad news at once. I am afraid our fears have been sadly realized. Aelred, whom you thought was singled out by certain suspect persons, is no more. He disappeared a month ago. Three weeks later, his body was found in a shallow grave near Fenbury. The corpse bore similar marks to those we have discussed already. If that were all, it would be horrible enough. Sadly, there is more. A few days later, just before Matins, Father Gilbert was found on the floor of the abbey church. He was dead from a stab wound to the heart. As soon as I heard the news, I recalled your warnings. Whatever knowledge or complicity the novice master had in the prior's wretched doings, it seems it has cost him his life. A chalice and some other things were taken from the sacristy, most likely to give the appearance of a theft. I'll add only this: the prior was here in Windham when it happened along with a number of guests, some of whom seemed of dubious character.
    Distressingly, although I have spoken to Abbot Philip twice about these things, my words have had little effect. He is aghast at the terrible events but cannot believe Prior Gramont is behind them. I've repeatedly told him what you witnessed at the clearing of the stones. He thinks it mere boyish imagining. And of course we have no proof. He has at least agreed to be alert to any hints of evildoing by the prior in the future. I pray every day he will do more: make the proper complaints to the Bishop of Winchester as well as the secular authorities there. Because of Bishop Osbert, Gramont's close associate, there would be no point in doing the same in Clarington. Meanwhile, left with no

other recourse, I continue my humble scribal labors for God's glory in the shadow of this evil.

Now, my dear boy, I must finish. A new psalter calls me to my work. I hope this missive finds you in good health and you are content in your situation. In the name of Our Lord and Savior, I am your faithful Brother Ambrose.

By the time Martin finished his mentor's letter, he felt as if the weight of his flight from the abbey had once again fallen on him. Had he done wrong to leave in such haste? Should he have gone to the authorities, perhaps to the earl himself? Too late, he realized he could have done so without including Edmond. At the end of a week of troubled sleep, he wrote Ambrose as discreetly as he could, afraid the letter might be opened. With nothing else to suggest, he urged persistence with the abbot and continued watchfulness with Prior Gramont. Still, the danger posed by the cult continued to trouble him. Then one morning at Mass in a small church not far from his residence, he heard an old priest give a sermon on the sin of grandiosity.

"Grandiosity," he declared, "makes the prideful soul believe itself responsible for everything, both good and evil, that falls within its province." Struck by the words, Martin listened more closely.

"The grandiose man ponders things beyond his purview, intervenes where he can do no good. And all the while he neglects his ordinary duties, failing at those endeavors proper to his sphere."

Martin thought about the sermon for the next few days. He felt it applied to him and his connection to the evil brotherhood. Little by little, the priest's words helped to lessen the guilt that had followed him from England. For the present at least, there was nothing he could do to change the situation there. What good was remorseful rumination? However it had come about, God had placed him here in Sicily. Should he not make the most of his new life?

A few days later, armed with a map sketched by Emeric, he began to visit Palermo's churches. Some were of the Latin rite, some Greek, but all were very different from the ones he knew in England. Inside, beneath their domed and vaulted ceilings, a few were nearly unadorned. Most, however, were covered with painted images and gold mosaics in the style of Constantinople. On the way, passing through busy streets and crowded squares, he heard the Babel of tongues he had written about to Elise. One by one, and sometimes overlapping, he listened to French, Greek, the Italian of the mainland, and the kindred tongue of Sicily. Yet it was Arabic with its strange vowels and aspirated consonants that struck him most.

The following week, Martin went to the *souks*. Here the language of the Arabs dominated. Beneath the shade of many-colored awnings, goods of every kind were bartered, sold, and traded in that language. There were breads in round, flat loaves and pastries made with nuts and honey, newly caught fish, meat and poultry either cooked or freshly butchered, and an abundance of vegetables and fruits, many unknown to him. Other stalls displayed herbs and spices. Cloves, cinnamon, and saffron were among the few he recognized. There were rows of richly decorated bowls in glazed and fired clay, vases and ewers made of hammered brass, stalls with colorfully patterned rugs, tables with bolts of brightly colored wool and silk along with an Egyptian fabric new to him called cotton.

The *souk's* many faces also captivated him: women with eyes lined in black above concealing veils, their fingertips oddly stained red, old people with weathered faces shrilly haggling, raucous children with great staring eyes, some playing, others hawking goods. And everywhere there were thickly bearded men in robes and turbans. As he passed, their dark eyes fixed boldly on him. He asked himself why until he understood. With his black cleric's robe, straw-colored hair, and blue-gray eyes, he was an anomalous figure here.

In this manner, between work and wandering, Martin was nearly content, or would have been but for the loneliness that seemed to lie in wait for him each night inside his residence, a dormitory for unaffiliated clerics that provided meals. Then word came that the princess's fleet had finally reached Naples, the principal city of Sicily's mainland kingdom. She and her party would spend Christmas there. The young bride had suffered all the way from seasickness. After Christmas, they would travel by land to the tip of Italy, cross the strait to Messina, and proceed to Palermo. In fact, it would be several weeks before Martin could meet with the Lady Elise. As his first Christmas in a foreign land drew near, Martin had a letter from Edmond. Breaking the seal, he read it in haste, then once again more slowly. With his usual sincerity, his friend asked him about his new life. Otherwise, his overwhelming concern was for Elise. His love for her shone through every line. As in England, he and Elise would have to keep their correspondence secret. Edmond asked Martin if he would receive and dispatch their letters inside his. In closing, he begged Martin to write him as soon as Elise arrived.

Once Christmas had passed, the scriptorium was busy again. Every few days, dispatches came tracing the princess's journey. On the last day of January, Martin learned that the royal party was nearing Palermo. Two days later, the young king met his even younger bride outside the city gate. On the thirteenth of February, William and Joanna were married in the cathedral. In the great crush of the crowd, Martin had his first glimpse of Elise. He caught her eye and she smiled, a look of relief on her face. It would not be long now before they met.

15

1177

"Were you surprised King William kept a harem?" Martin asked.

"I was indeed," Elise replied. "You didn't mention that in your letter."

Several months had now passed since Elise's arrival. The two friends were seated in the gardens of the Zisa palace, a favorite resort of the queen and her ladies. The word *zisa* in Arabic meant "splendid," and the palace, built in luxurious Arab style, was worthy of its name. Symmetrical in plan, with an elegant façade of inset arches, it sat like a chest full of jewels at the edge of a great garden.

"You're right, I didn't speak of it," Martin admitted, "but I hinted at it when I mentioned certain royal habits you might find surprising. I avoided being more specific, not wanting to prejudice you against the court. It was one of several customs of the Arab emirs the Normans chose to follow."

As they sat in the shade of a laurel tree surrounded by the bright Sicilian sun, Martin marveled again at how the last two years had changed Elise. The charming girl he had known in Windham had become a lovely woman. Her dark hair and dark eyes were complemented by her smooth, unblemished skin. Tall and slender, she had an unaffected ease in all her movements. How could Edmond not love a woman such as this?

"Still, for a Christian king," Elise continued on the subject of the harem, "and one so young . . ."

"Perhaps it's most useful when the king is young," said Martin, with a touch of the irony he and Elise often used when speaking of things Sicilian. It was a way of dealing with the strangeness of this Norman kingdom of the South. Sometimes he could hardly believe they were here. The rooms in the Zisa, for instance, were like a vision from another world. Beneath intricate carved ceilings, the walls were lined with colored marble, finely patterned tile, and gold mosaic. In the center of the paved and carpet-covered floors, jets of water bubbled into sunken pools, creating a refreshing coolness even on the hottest days.

"I wonder" Elise said, "if anyone ever asked the women what they thought of their condition? I suspect they'd prefer to have husbands of their own, or even, perhaps, none at all."

"Who can say? No doubt there's a certain prestige in being the bed partner of a king. What puzzles me most is William's vaunted piety. How can he reconcile it with keeping a seraglio?"

"Not easily, I imagine. How does one confess a sin and go on lavishly supporting its occasion?"

"I have no idea," Martin said, "but Palermo is full of such disparities. Where else can one hear the bells of Christian churches and the Muslim call to prayer in the same hour?"

"Or see Christian women line their eyes in black and veil themselves in Arab style? It's the fashion now, you know. In truth, I don't begrudge the king his pleasures. What troubles me most is the way the women are confined."

"In the harem, you mean?" Martin asked.

"Yes, of course, but now that you mention it, not only there. Are not all women, rich or poor, Christian, Muslim, or Hebrew, confined from birth to death? Joanna, still only a child, is already imprisoned in her marriage. And I am a prisoner too, a refugee from my own betrothal. Must this always be the way? Is it so wrong to wish for freedom?"

"Some may think so," Martin answered, "I do not. Freedom is what makes us human. And yet at times I think we're all imprisoned, both by the world and its constraints and by ourselves and our desires."

Elise nodded with a look of understanding. Although neither had spoken about it directly, Martin was certain she knew of his feeling for Edmond. She seemed not to be troubled by it; if anything, it had deepened their friendship. She, in turn, made no secret of her love, confiding that she had met Edmond secretly in Winchester before she left. Martin had no idea of what transpired there, nor did he wish to know. All that mattered was that his two friends loved each other and, for now at least, were forced to be apart.

Perhaps thinking of Edmond, Elise fell silent, turning toward the lush green vista of the garden. All around them there were trees and flowering plants whose perfume filled the air. Some thirty feet away, the central path ended in a pool, a great sky-colored rectangle extending far into the distance. On either side, a row of tall cypresses was mirrored in the water. In the far distance, the gardens gave way to a royal hunting park.

Martin's eye followed Elise's. "It's beautiful, is it not? An artificial paradise. I still find it hard to believe it all: you at the opulent Sicilian court, I, a scribe for the second most powerful man in the *regnum*." By now, the Latin word for kingdom came naturally to Martin. He had written *Regnum Siciliae* so often in his letters for Archbishop Walter.

As the two gazed at the pool, a sudden gust of wind disturbed its polished surface, breaking it into a thousand glistening fragments. Touched by the evanescence of the moment, they exchanged silent glances. Elise was the first to speak.

"They say the Arabs, born in desert lands, picture Paradise as a garden, an oasis of delicious fruits and fragrant flowers. But can even Paradise be happy if the one you love is absent? I miss Edmond terribly, as you know, and I also miss having a life of my own. You at least have your studies and your work."

Martin nodded sympathetically. "I pray every day you'll be able to take back your life."

"You understand me well, my friend, but I'm not only troubled for myself. I often feel I've forced this sacrifice on Edmond."

"You took the best course as you saw it, my lady."

There was a look of uncertainty on Elise's face. "Yes, sadly, I could find no other way."

As she spoke, a sound on the path signaled someone approaching, and two ladies of the court appeared. Pausing, they looked at Martin's black robe and moved on. His clerical garb was a partial safeguard against rumor. Whenever they met, Elise also carried a little prayer book. If someone's glance lingered too long, she would open it, make the sign of the cross, and pretend to be praying along with her spiritual advisor. There was no need this time, so the two went on talking of commonplace things. Then a serving maid approached.

"Good afternoon, my lady. I hope I am not disturbing your devotions."

At first, Elise seemed not to understand. Martin touched her prayer book lightly, and, half laughing, she answered, "No, Antonia, we've just finished. Have you a message?"

"The queen has awakened from her nap. She needs you to help with her lessons."

"Thank you," said Elise. "Tell her Highness I'll be there at once." As the girl ran off, Elise bid Martin a hasty farewell.

"I shall come again soon," he said, moving toward the entrance, "with a letter from Edmond, I hope. Until then, stay in Joanna's favor."

He watched as Elise strode briskly toward the palace. When she was halfway there, he spied a young face with fair hair in a window of the Zisa. Seeing her also, Elise waved gaily to the little queen upon whose childish will her fate depended.

16

1178

The sound of metal on metal rang out against Bourne Castle's thick stone walls. "Take care, my boy! You've nicked me twice already."

As Edmond knew, his zeal at arms was not yet equaled by his skill, but Dickon Breslin, the master of arms at Bourne Castle, was not in danger. He was wearing thick padding beneath his chainmail hauberk. "I'll do better this time, I'm sure," Edmond promised. Control was the object of this exercise. The aim was to fight with crossed swords, aim hard and close, and still not quite touch your opponent.

Once again, there was the jarring clash of steel on steel. The day was unusually warm for April. The two men had been at it for over an hour, but Edmond was not yet ready to give up. "I think I'm finally getting the knack of it," he said, trying to gauge Dickon's mood.

Deeply lined from years outdoors, his teacher's face wore a permanent frown. Its swarthy color stood out against his pale gray beard, itself interrupted by a scar that ran from cheek to chin. By now, the scar had turned livid, a sign of his exertion. Nodding mutely, he consented to one more round. Once again, the clash of steel sounded in the courtyard, this time with better results.

"Good work, my boy!" Dickon declared, "That's good enough for today. I'm drenched with sweat beneath this coat of mail."

"Just one more, sir. I think I've almost mastered it."

Grimacing, the old warrior relented and raised his sword. This time, in each of three successive swipes, Edmond came very close but never touched his teacher. Satisfied, he laid down his sword. Using both hands, he pulled off his massive helmet, then helped Dickon to do the same. Not bothering to call for a page, the two men helped each other with their heavy gloves and hauberks. When that was done, they took several draughts of water from a nearby pail and sat on a bench in the shade of the castle wall.

Dickon reached for a leather satchel and took out a parcel wrapped in cloth. Inside, there were several chunks of salted meat and a small loaf of bread. "Here, my boy, take half of this," he said. "It'll fortify you until supper."

Edmond accepted it gratefully. Chewing contentedly, he lifted his eyes to a porch across the yard and discovered he and his teacher were being observed. Three figures stood behind the railing in the sunlight, Roland, the earl's son and heir, Father Barnabas, his tutor, and the Lady Melisande. The earl's wife seemed to be staring directly at him. Instinctively, he looked away. His arms were bare; soaked with sweat, his shirt clung to his body and its open neck revealed his chest. While Roland, who idolized Edmond, waved wildly for his attention, the Lady Melisande stood quite still.

Observing the scene, Dickon spoke in a lowered voice. "That boy's an imp, if there ever was one. He's either ailing or in a frenzy. To look at him is to pity the earl."

To calm the boy, Edmond returned his salute, but his eyes were on the Lady Melisande. The faint smile on her face reminded him of what Elise had said before she left, that she and her aunt had a kind of pact, that the earl's wife had secrets of her own, that she would not betray them. And yet the mere fact of the power she possessed made him wary. From what he knew of her, he found it hard to believe she was really their ally. Whatever the case, he avoided her when he could. Luckily, because of his responsibilities at Preston Manor, the earl had exempted him from service as a squire at the castle. Caught in the lady's gaze, Edmond reached for his cloak. Pulling it over his shoulders, he stood and bowed respectfully. After that, he busied himself with assembling his gear. When he looked up again, he was relieved to see only Roland and the tutor.

*

That night, since the weather was warm, Edmond decided to sleep in his lean-to room. Settling into his private space, he lit a candle and set a sheet of parchment on his writing table. Once alone, as always, he thought of Elise. When he had become a knight and gained Lord Desmond's favor, he would ask for her hand in marriage. Although he had made a late start in his training, he was much better at it than his brother. He knew it, and one day the world would know it to. Nor did he want a mere token knighthood; first, he would have to be tested in combat. He had no idea when or where that opportunity would come.

The earl himself had fought bravely in the second holy war, the one led by King Louis of France. Since then, he had become the rare nobleman mainly concerned with the welfare of his vassals. His father, the former earl, was unlucky enough to have fought on the wrong side in the long, anarchic war between King Stephen and the Empress Maude. Having learned from his sire's mistake, the earl avoided all partisan alliance. Scrupulous in his fealty to King Henry, he was prompt to lend troops to the throne when his turn came. At Bourne Castle, however, the garrison was small. Most of the earl's men at arms were housed in an old fortress south of Clarington, close enough to be called should the need arise.

Turning back to his thoughts of Elise, Edmond sat down at the ink-stained table. It had been a full day of military exercises. He ached all over, his arms and legs were stiff, his rump and haunches saddle-sore. Still, his desire to write Elise was stronger than fatigue or pain. Filling the container with ink, he took up his pen.

Windham, May 27, 1178

Dearest, this will reach you as always, I hope, through our good friend Martin. I am fatigued from much exercise today, but they take a packet of letters to Winchester tomorrow, and I want this to go with them. Things continue well in my first year of training, as I hope they do with you. The manor lands and rents, too, are very slowly improving under Master Rendon's guidance and my own. My mother is difficult as ever, full of her usual fears and warnings. My father has been ailing lately. When he is sick, my mother attends to his needs, he treats her better, and the two of them are a bit more bearable.

How different our marriage will be from such misery, my love! I come to the castle now three days a week. And whatever I do, whether practicing at arms or occupied at Preston Manor, I think of you. I still miss you constantly. Tonight, I'm writing you from the little lean-to room where in the old days I composed the precious notes that you and I exchanged. Now as then, I send all my love, this time far across the sea. In my heart, there is but a single question. When will we meet and at last be man and wife? I pray for that hour every day.

For the present, Dickon Breslin is a good and patient teacher, and I make steady progress on my path. Perhaps your uncle will tell you the same when you hear from him. As for your aunt, I shall say only that I am not opposed by her in any way, in case that has concerned you.

My dear Elise, my hands are blistered from the sword and cannot hold the pen much longer. Write me of all the things you do in that strange city of Palermo. When I imagine them, it will be as if I'm there with you. Sicily is one of the principal places where ships leave for the Holy Land. One day it may well be my destination as a knight. If you are unable to leave, then I shall come to Sicily, that kingdom which holds the only treasure that I value.

By the time he had finished, he felt too drowsy to write Martin. Even so, he couldn't bear to delay his letter to Elise. Taking up his pen, he scrawled these words across a sheet of parchment.

My dear Martin, I am in haste to send you the enclosed. You will know its proper destination. My good wishes and my thanks go with it. Forgive my brevity and ask our friend to share what little news may be inside. As always, I envy you her presence in that city. To have you both with me again would be my greatest joy. With fond affection, I remain your faithful friend.

As soon as he had written the note, Edmond was overcome with sleep. He could seal and address the letter in the morning. Now he lay back on the cot, pulled the cover over him, and gratefully closed his eyes. Before long, his head was full of visions of Elise. First he imagined her in that distant land, resplendent in her fine court dress, next, lips parted and dark hair disheveled, smiling at their moment of reunion, and, finally, wrapped in his arms the way she once had been so wonderfully but briefly.

17

1180

Since his arrival in Palermo, Martin had greatly increased his skills in Greek, the third language used in the kingdom's official documents along with Arabic and Latin. At the same time, he had become familiar with archdiocesan affairs. After a while, his work gained the archbishop's approval, and Walter selected him for travel on official business. On these trips, Martin conveyed decrees and orders and met with officials and clerics throughout the kingdom. In Agrigento, which the Greeks had called *Akragas* and the Romans *Agrigentum,* he marveled at the splendid ruins of the great Greek temples with their giant fluted columns. In Taormina, high above the coast, he sat among the ruins of an outdoor theater built by the Greeks and renovated by the Romans. From that splendid site, he could see the vast slopes of Mount Etna twenty miles away. He watched as its crater poured smoke into the sky; some still believed like the ancients that it was the mouth of hell. He also went several times to Cefalu, the site of the great King Roger's cathedral, and once to Messina, whose strait, it was said, had been braved by Ulysses, the ancient seafaring hero.

Beyond his work, his travels, and his studies, Martin's friendship with Elise remained his greatest comfort. Their visits were especially rewarding when, after many months, each had a letter from Edmond, hers, as always, concealed inside his own. Still, time passed more quickly for Martin than Elise, trapped as she was in the tedious routine of the Sicilian court. Then, in the fall of the year 1180, a letter came for Martin that recalled him abruptly to the past. After his usual courteous beginning, Ambrose came to the point.

My dear boy, what we initially feared has come to pass. For a long while after the deaths of Father Gilbert and the novice Aelred, killings of the kind we knew before did not occur in our vicinity. During that time, Prior Gramont was often absent. Now, sad to say, he has returned and new crimes have been discovered, two of them, one after the other. Following the former pattern, the victims were a young man and a young woman. Their bodies were discovered in widely different places, the boy in a thicket this side of Clarington, the girl in some woods between here and Winchester. The girl was sixteen, respectable but poor, a bondservant on a farm. The young man was seventeen, an orphan and apprentice to a weaver. The state of his body suggested he was killed some time before the girl. In addition—I shudder to report it—both bodies had the same marks as before: many small, round punctures and, in other places, bits of flesh cut away. I pray God these wounds were not inflicted while the victims were alive.

Dear boy, I tremble even as I pen these words. Nonetheless, I am ready to act, whatever the cost. Before I can, I need to have your written testimony, beginning with your first observations of the cult and its meetings at the clearing. I hope to use it to make my case against Prior Gramont, first with the abbot, then, if necessary with the secular authorities. It may not be easy. We know the prior has a powerful protector, someone very close to the throne. We also know he was in league with Bishop Osbert, who has important friends in Rome and Canterbury. Still, when your letter arrives, I will do my best to convince the abbot of its truth.

Now I must finish. I send you greetings from your old teacher, Canon Thomas. I visit him twice monthly now with the permission of the abbot. He is a bit more infirm, but his faculties are undiminished. Proud of your success in the archbishop's office, he hopes you will be able to resume your studies as a scholar in the future. May Our Lord and Savior keep you in his care as I await your testimony.

Martin had been gone from England long enough to hope he had heard the last of these strange deaths. Now, however, the brotherhood had appeared again. How many members were there now? Too many, perhaps, to ever bring to justice. For the thousandth time, he asked himself the same question. Should he have raised the alarm after that night at the clearing? And later, when he had learned the truth about the prior, had he taken the coward's way by fleeing? He hated to think so, but whatever he had failed at then, his duty now was clear. He must do all he could to prevent more killing.

He spent two days writing the document, making it as thorough as possible. Then he asked the archbishop if he could include it with the official correspondence to the diocese of Winchester, insuring it would reach the abbey safely. The prelate agreed, and Martin signed and sealed the packet. Two days later, it was sent. The rest would be up to Brother Ambrose, Abbot Philip, and whatever secular authorities they turned to.

After that, weeks passed with no word from Windham, and Martin grew more anxious every day. The next time he met Elise, she discerned it in his manner.

"You seem preoccupied, my friend."

Although the weather was threatening rain, they were seated again in the gardens of the Zisa. As Martin looked up at the leaden clouds, they seemed to reflect his mood. "I am, my lady. In truth, I have a great burden on my mind. I believe it would help if I spoke about it."

"Of course," said Elise, "Go ahead, but remember our agreement. When we're together alone, please call me only by my given name, just as I call you Martin."

"As you wish, Elise." He moved a bit closer, lowering his voice as he began. "You know I left Windham Abbey with a secret. I haven't spoken of it lately, largely because of the Count de Vere to whom you are still officially betrothed. I believe he may be involved."

Martin went on with the tale of his connection to the prior and the cult, including the part of the ceremony he had witnessed at the clearing of the stones.

As he spoke, a look of concern appeared on Elise's face. "You say Edmond was with you," she inquired. "What did he make of the scene inside the hut?"

"He had no chance to decide that. He had gone to the edge of the woods to quell a barking dog and never looked inside. We met as I fled after being discovered."

Martin told the rest of his story, concluding with his flight from Windham Abbey, in effect summing up the document he had sent to Brother Ambrose. "I've heard nothing from him yet," Martin concluded, "but I feel certain this fellowship is evil. They practice vile rites which result in the murder of innocent young victims."

"Who else besides you knows about these things?"

"No one except you and Ambrose. After that night, Edmond and I never spoke about the cult again. Indeed, I deeply regretted involving him. I should not have asked him to come."

"Then what a lonely burden this has been for you. To think of all the young people who may have died! And you believe the Count de Vere is part of it?"

"I can't be sure, but his close association with the prior would make it seem so. Ambrose also wrote me about Bishop Osbert, who was implicated in the similar deaths of two young women."

"I think I can assist you there. On Whitsunday evening when I was fifteen, I had supper at the bishop's. Strangely enough, he was here in Palermo in his youth, in a clerical post he never named. And there was something else that night which now belatedly makes sense. At supper, unobserved, I saw the prior and the bishop casting knowing glances at each other and a pretty serving boy. It's well known that the bishop had a penchant for young women. The prior's inclinations were, I suspect, the opposite."

"You suspect correctly," Martin said. "I learned of it from Brother Ambrose. It seems the cult makes no distinction between male and female in their victims, requiring only innocence and youth. What you say makes me doubly glad I spoke to you. I suspect that the prior, the bishop, and the count were all involved in this vile band. Later, I learned that the boy I observed at the clearing must have been Stephen, a novice who disappeared from the abbey the day before. I have no doubt he was killed, but there's no real proof. They've never found his body."

"How terrible," Elise whispered. "And he was only one of many."

"Yes. That's why I feel compelled to try again to stop this thing."

"Of course, but since you've sent the account, you've done what you can for now. You must trust that God will do his work through Ambrose and the abbot."

"I'll try to," Martin said. "In any case, you've confirmed me in the justice of my effort."

"God willing, you'll succeed. Now I think it's also time I told you something, a secret I've kept as long as you have yours. My Aunt Melisande and the count are lovers. My uncle, thank God, knows nothing of it."

Amazed by the disclosure, Martin responded at once. "If your aunt loves the count, why would she want to see him marry you?"

"I'm sure it's his wish, not hers. Greed for my income is his only motive. It seems she defers to him in everything. I suspect they meet secretly when he visits England, but I don't believe he comes for her alone. If he's part of this evil band, that would explain his presence. You've given me one more reason to avoid the monstrous union he and Melisande have planned for me."

At that moment, the first drops of rain began to stain the garden path. Vowing to meet again soon, the two friends parted. The following week, Martin received a letter at the archbishop's palace. It was surprisingly brief and undated.

Brother Ambrose to Deacon Martin

Dear friend, a week before your letter and enclosure came, the prior resigned his position at the abbey. Three days later, he disappeared. I nonetheless gave your document to Abbot Philip. He was gravely concerned, but he delayed his response and asked me in the meantime not to speak to the authorities. For over a month, he prayed and deliberated. In the end, discretion won out over zeal. When he learns where the prior has gone, he will warn the authorities there. At present, he fears a general alarm would create a scandal, discrediting the abbey. And so, dear Martin, your document has been locked away for future use. I am as disappointed as I know you will be. For now, however, there is nothing we can do. Nor can I write more at present. We are again quite busy here. How often I wish you had not been forced to leave. At least we are finally rid of the prior. And yet who can say where he will reappear? If I learn more, you will hear from me.

In his haste, Ambrose had neglected to sign his name. The hand, however, was clearly his. Once again, Martin's desire to expose the prior and his monstrous brotherhood had been frustrated.

*

One morning, Martin was seated at work when he heard the rustle of silk behind him. Turning, he saw the archbishop himself, the celebrated Walter of Palermo. Along with the other scribes, Martin stood at once, ready to follow the custom of kneeling to kiss the episcopal ring.

"No, no," Walter shouted. "Keep your seats and go back to work! This is not an official visit. My secretary is on an errand. I've come in person to fetch Deacon Martin."

The archbishop was deeply involved in the plans for a new cathedral. Still smarting from King William's endowment of Monreale Abbey, and worse, his creation of a competing archdiocese there, Walter wanted his church to rival William's. At the same time, he wished to keep his preeminence on the royal council and the favor of his former pupil. The strain showed in the prelate's irascible manner. Walter's voice had a range from stentorian to subtle, magisterial to mellow. This time he chose the last.

"Nor is there need for those anxious looks. Your work as scribes is among the few things about which I have no complaint."

No complaint was high praise from a man as hard to please as Walter of Palermo. Clearly relieved, the scribes remained standing as their superior left the room. Martin followed, noting how splendidly Walter was dressed. It was winter, and over a red silk robe, he wore a fur-lined cloak of scarlet wool. Passing through an anteroom full of documents, they entered the archbishop's cabinet. On a shelf behind a table, there were several books, two of them written by Walter himself.

"Sit down, my good deacon," the prelate said, settling into his own capacious chair. "I have no patience with protocol today. I need your help."

Not for the first time, the archbishop's words were a surprise to Martin. What sort of help, beyond his ordinary duties, could Walter want from him? Martin listened intently.

"Notwithstanding my position on the royal council, the king and I have not been as close in recent years. For this and other reasons, I've decided to give his Majesty a sign of my regard. He is steeped in luxury, as you know, but there is something rarer I might offer him, something that depends on you."

"On me, my lord? How could that be?"

Once he had spoken, he recognized his gaffe. One never addressed the archbishop without being asked. "Forgive me, my lord. I spoke out of turn."

"Out of turn, perhaps, but to the point. Here, then, is your answer. The gift I wish to give is you."

Martin was silent. If the words meant what he hoped, it would be a splendid opportunity.

"I see from your face you may have guessed. In this past year, as you know, you've become a trusted servant. I shall miss you sorely, but I believe you have talents that will serve you well in a different capacity. I wish to offer you to William as a royal scholar. If you stay clear of intrigue and devoted to scholarship, you may have a brilliant future. And each time you compose a new work or translate a Greek volume into Latin, the king will remember my generosity. This, then, is my proposal to his Majesty and you. What do you think?"

In the effort to take it all in, Martin found himself speechless.

"You hesitate, young scholar? No fine words to confirm your rhetorical skills? If there's some impediment, tell me at once."

"Yes, my lord, I mean no, there's no impediment. It's just that I'd scarcely dreamed of such an honor at my age."

"Indeed, I believe you will be the youngest scholar there. Also the only Briton. Your merit, if earned, will stand out all the more. Do well, and you will be thrice favored—by the king, by me, and by your fellow scholars here and elsewhere."

"I'll do all I can to be worthy of your Excellency's generosity."

"I'm glad. Then I shall begin the arrangements. Nor should you be overawed or apprehensive. Like King Roger, his illustrious grandfather, William is fond of learning, but he is not nearly as exacting."

As Martin left the prelate's cabinet, Walter's voice lingered in his ears. Pausing in the antechamber, he thought about his benefactor. There was no trace of piety in the archbishop, even less of humility. Ability, yes, and skills of several kinds. Above all, he seemed to Martin a perfect example of what keen intelligence combined with great ambition could achieve, for good or ill, under the all-embracing mantle of the Church.

18

1181

Elise had acquired an admirer, Giovanni da Matera, the second son of a baron from Basilicata in mainland Sicily. One morning in October, he spoke to her outside the royal chapel.

"Madonna Elisa, how lovely you look this morning!"

Handsome, eloquent, and cultivated, Giovanni was fluent in French as well as Greek and Latin. Polyglot to a fault, he often spoke the vernacular of northern Italy. If Elise failed to understand, he translated. Out of courtesy, she sometimes replied in some phrase he had taught her in that language.

"Buon mattino, Messere da Matera."

Having obliged him to that extent, she turned to one of her companions. They were awaiting King William and Queen Joanna outside the royal chapel. "Do you know if the king and queen are on their way?"

"Yes, I believe so," a young Englishwoman answered. Along with Elise, she was one of the few who remained of the group who had come to Sicily with Joanna. "This Mass not only celebrates the queen's birthday but the holy day today, the Maternity of the Virgin. The priest will pray for an heir to the Sicilian throne."

"As will we all," interjected Giovanni, smiling suavely. With that, the king and queen appeared and preceded the courtiers into the chapel. Joanna was now a young woman, and William, about to turn thirty, had grown a beard—to look more like King Roger, his famous grandfather, they said. Inside the chapel, Elise took a seat, captivated as always by the beauty of the place.

Martin had not exaggerated in the letter he had written. In no other place had artisans skilled in manners as different as Byzantine, Arab, and Norman united their efforts so pleasingly. As the singing of the choir swelled and filled the church, Elise scanned the splendid gold mosaics of the nave depicting biblical events.

All the while, the smell of pungent incense mingled with the courtiers' rich perfumes. Between these scents, the oppressive heat of the crowd, and the innumerable burning candles, it was hard not to feel lightheaded. As she followed the ceremony, Elise found herself slipping away from the moment and drifting into the past; not just to Edmond, whom she longed for every day, but also to Canon Thomas's little cottage and her lessons. From Martin's talk, she knew fresh currents of thought were flowing everywhere. Sadly, only small eddies ever reached her, marooned as she was among the queen's attendants. As one of Joanna's tutors, Elise was able to use her position to acquire a variety of books. She read them even if her pupil never opened them. In recent months, avid for an heir despite her youth, the queen had come under the spell of an older woman, a Calabrian baroness known for her passion for relics and similar pieties. In fact, the old docile Joanna had disappeared. It was increasingly hard to predict her behavior.

To this, and to the insipid chatter of the ladies of the court, Giovanni da Matera's conversation made a welcome contrast. He was not only attractive with curly black hair and dark, sympathetic eyes but also quite learned in his own unsystematic way. More important, he lent her his books, some of them quite precious. At the same time, it took all her skill to ward off his deft advances. She made sure they spoke in public, discouraged his gallantry, and talked only of authors, ideas, and books.

Things continued this way throughout the winter. Then, one day in the spring, Elise was on her way to join the queen when she encountered Giovanni outside the king's audience hall. Detaining her in his charming way, he drew her towards the nearest window. Under his arm, he held a codex bound in reddish leather. "*Madonna Elisa*, I have a new book to lend you."

"*Messere Giovanni*, you must give it to me later. I'm on my way to attend the queen."

"Then I won't burden you, my lady, but do pause for a moment to regard the subject."

Before she could object, he opened the book to the first page. On it, in large red and gold letters, she saw the word *Ovidius* and, beneath it, *Ars Amatoria*. It was the famous book on the art of love by Ovid. She knew the Church disapproved of it, but she had long desired to read it. For some reason, however, Giovanni was holding the volume with only one hand. It seemed about to fall. Reaching up, she took the nearest edge. Then she felt her admirer's other hand around her waist. At that moment, a palace eunuch called Eusebius appeared, observed them, and passed into the hall. Furious, she slammed the book closed and handed it to Giovanni.

"Thanks to your rudeness, sir, I must decline your offer." Still angry, she entered the audience hall before he could reply.

Inside, the king sat beneath a golden mosaic of regal emblems, among them palms, leopards, and lions. Eusebius was beside him. Elise thought about the man who had observed them. She had seen him with the king more frequently in recent months. It was unclear to her how these men, castrated by barbaric custom in their youth, came to power at the Sicilian court. It seems the practice had originated in the harems, where only eunuchs were considered safe to tend the women. Tall and slender, with a beardless, sallow face, Eusebius had actually been born in Greece, but he had lived so long among the Arab eunuchs he seemed like one of them; he even dressed like them in a long full robe and turban. Known for his venomous tongue and his cunning, he had once been in charge of King William's harem. In recent years, he had advanced to a post in one the *diwans*, the Arab name for the royal offices.

As Elise stood among the queen's attendants, various visitors arrived and paid their homage to the seated monarch. All the while, Eusebius stood beside him whispering. After the last visitor was presented, Elise was distressed to see the eunuch's eyes alight on her. Bending over, he said something to the king. As he did, William looked at her and smiled insinuatingly. Then, evidently recalling his royal manners, he acknowledged her more gravely with a courteous inclination of his head. That was all, but it was the last kind of notice Elise wanted. She was thankful Joanna had missed the exchange. She had been talking to her new favorite, the Calabrian baroness.

*

A week after the incident with the book, Elise was at supper with the members of the court. The night was unseasonably hot for May. Perhaps for that reason, the King and Queen were absent. Free of royal supervision, the company became a bit too lively for Elise's taste. The banquet hall was also stifling. She left as soon as she had finished eating, returning to the chamber she shared with three other ladies of the court. She was sponging her wrists and neck when she heard a gentle rapping at the door. Crossing the room, she opened it and was surprised to see Eusebius.

"Madam, to combat the heat, " he said, speaking French with a Greek accent, "the king and queen have arranged an entertainment in a chamber of the palace with a cooling breeze. Queen Joanna has graciously invited you. There will be music, a small group of guests, and iced drinks with fruit nectars. The last of the winter snow arrived today from Etna. The queen would like your opinion of the new musicians."

There was no expression on the eunuch's face, nothing to explain the oddity of his request, let alone his humble role as a messenger. Elise *was* fond of music, however, and Joanna did defer to her in things of taste. In any event, there was no question of refusing.

"I shall be happy to come, of course. Can you tell me the place of the gathering?"

"It's in a part of the palace seldom used. I've been command-ed to escort you. If you are ready, please come with me."

After taking a moment to use a hand mirror of polished sil-ver, Elise complied, following Eusebius up and down two stairs and through a suite of rooms lit only by the lamp he carried. She would never find her way back alone. Perhaps one of the older ladies there would know the way. Finally, the eunuch opened a door and showed her into a kind of antechamber with no windows. Lit by a single candelabrum, it was sparsely but elegantly furnished.

"The queen and her guests will join you here. You will ex-cuse me. I have others to escort." Before she had time to ques-tion him, Eusebius was gone. He had closed the door behind him as he left.

Alone, Elise was struck by the oddity of the situation. Before she had time to speculate, the inner door of the room swung open and the king, richly dressed in a green silk robe, was be-fore her. Surprised, Elise bent one knee and bowed according to the custom of the court, then waited for Joanna to appear.

Instead, William spoke. "Please rise, my lady."

She did as commanded, still wondering at the circumstances, and looked at the king directly for the first time. Although heavier now than in his youth—the result, they said, of self-indulgence—William was still a handsome man. In the style of the Greeks, his mustache and beard were closely trimmed. Both were darker than his hair, no longer quite blond as it once had been. In dress and demeanor, the king seemed almost as much a Greek or Arab as a Norman.

As she waited uneasily for an explanation, Elise glanced into the room behind the monarch. Covered with small colored tiles in the Arab style, it too appeared completely empty. Only then did she understand.

"Don't be alarmed, my lady," said the monarch. "I trust you'll forgive the ruse. I've long wished for a private interview with you. Only recently did I learn you might not object."

In a moment, Elise saw the sequence: her known friendship with Giovanni, a book called *The Art of Love* and Giovanni's arm around her, a look of approving interest from the monarch. All that was needed in addition was the scheming eunuch with his whispered slurs and comments to the king. That explained why she was here, but now that she was, how was she to extricate herself?

"I am humbled by your condescension, Majesty. I look forward to seeing you soon in the company of the queen."

"As you wish my dear, but until then, will you not join me in a cup of chilled wine?"

Her heart sank as she heard the words. Was there no escape? There had to be. The king was known to be pious and a gentleman. She need only be courteous and firm. "Your Majesty, I humbly beg to be excused."

William's face grew flushed. Was it anger, embarrassment, or both? In any case, she soon learned her approach was wrong.

"I don't wish to excuse you, my lady. In fact, as sovereign of the realm, I command you to drink a cup of wine with me."

With that, the king turned and, gesturing for her to follow, walked into the inner room. The chamber had cunningly patterned tiles not only on the walls but on the floor. Inside, the king led her to a pile of cushions bordering a shallow pool. Surveying the scene, she realized she was in a private room of William's harem, a part of the palace known to very few. Reluctantly, she took the place he indicated next to him. Between them and the pool, there was a narrow table. On it stood a gold pitcher and a pair of matching cups. Pouring the fragrant, dark-red wine, William took one cup and handed her the other. In the room beyond, she could hear the sound of Arab instruments; the plaintive trilling of a flute, the sensuous bowing of the rebec, the insinuating rhythm of the tambor. The room smelled of *zagara*, a perfume distilled from lemon blossoms, a scent emblematic of Sicily.

Amid these all too obvious enticements, Elise took the cup, knowing each compliant move put her in greater danger. And yet the alternative, offending the king and being forced to leave the court, was worse. Instead, she sipped the rich, cool wine. After that, setting her cup on the table, the king leaned toward her, took her in his arms with practiced skill, and kissed her on the lips. In the next moment, he was fondling her breasts, barely protected by her silky clothing. She felt the softness of his perfumed beard, first on her cheek, then on her neck.

She pulled back just enough to dislodge his hands. She had to find a way to make him let her go. "Please, my lord, the night is very warm," was all she was able to manage.

"Of course, forgive my impetuosity. You are quite beautiful, you know."

While he spoke, Elise thought of everything she knew about the king. Deeply religious—he had spent a fortune on the abbey and great church at Monreale—he was known to be learned but also fond of pleasure. Although he had initiated foreign conquests, he had never taken part in a campaign. At the same time, he had brought peace within the realm. For that reason alone, he was loved and admired by his people.

"Come, drink your iced wine," he said in a soothing voice. "It will cool you."

As she drank, he began again, more slowly this time, coaxing her with endearments. At least it seemed unlikely he would rape her. Or was it? She must find an excuse to demur, something to put him off. His hand had moved to the cushion where she sat. Now it was slipping beneath her dress—

"Your Majesty, I beg you. If you persist, you will be my ruin. You are known as a man of faith. Do you want such a thing on your conscience?"

The reproach had its effect. Withdrawing his hand, he pulled back and looked quizzically at her. "You need not be concerned about my conscience, madam. Look, rather, to your own. I was told you were schooled in the ways of love and hated your betrothed. If Sir Giovanni has conquered you so easily, why not me?"

"My lord, the *Messere da Matera* has done nothing, only lent me books."

"You betray yourself with that *Messere,* madam. Has he taught you the language of the mainland too? The man is a known seducer. Am I to believe he is innocent?"

"I know only that he is fond of reading. That is the ground of our acquaintance."

"And I too am fond of reading. I've read the *Art of Love* in Ovid's Latin, the songs of the troubadours in French, the love poems of the East in Arabic. You will have no reason to regret an evening in my arms. Why persist in this childish resistance? I was told you were a woman of the world. More to the point, I can make sure you remain here at court, safe from the marriage you wish to avoid. I ask only a few hours of pleasure. I intend no more. Your reputation will remain intact."

I can make sure you remain here at court. The words rang in her ears like a reprieving bell. If she stayed in Sicily, Edmond could join her and be knighted here. He need never know about the king. They could marry with William's blessing. It was not as if she were a virgin. In her mind, she began to form the words. *My lord, placing my trust in your promise, I will resist no longer.* She opened her mouth to speak, then thought of the vows she and Edmond had made in the little room at Winchester. Once she had broken her pledge, made love with another as she had with him, how could she live with this thing in her heart when they were finally together? No, there had to be another way. Desperately, she tried a final ploy.

"My lord, your gentle wife has long protected me from the marriage you have mentioned. What would she think of the price you ask to keep me safe in Sicily?"

As soon as she said it, she knew she had blundered. William stood at once, spilling red wine on his gorgeous green robe. His face was flushed, his features distorted. She had never seen him so angry. As he spoke, he seemed to be making an effort to contain himself.

"You go too far, my lady! First the Church and then my consort. I see now I have made a mistake. Your cool northern beauty and the stories of your learning both intrigued me. And yes, although I am a devout believer and a loving husband, I am not a saint. It seems you, however, purport to be one. Beyond that door a dozen lovely women all await my pleasure. I chose you over them and others too, ladies of higher station than yourself."

So there were others besides the harem. Why had she not guessed? She saw now how naïve she had been. Perhaps it was not too late to remedy the situation.

"I meant no offense, your Majesty. A mistake has been made, but not by you. I was misrepresented."

"That may or may not be. Whatever the case, you are the first woman so favored to refuse. From that, you may gauge the degree of your pride. But I have never taken a woman unwillingly, and I shall not tonight."

Hearing a dismissal in these words, Elise rose from the pillows awkwardly, nearly falling without the king's assistance. Standing, she spoke in a lowered voice.

"Your Majesty, I beg your pardon for any offense I've given. Your candor has humbled me. Following your example, I too will be frank. You are a handsome man, possessed of all the allurements that great power brings. Were there not another to whom I am pledged, not the count but my true betrothed, I would never have dared resist you."

"I see. You love, and that love makes you proud. Perhaps in your learning you've read too many pagan books. Pride for a Christian is the deadliest of sins. In parting, you need have no fear of me. I will neither punish nor exile you. I myself am too proud for that. I shall leave you now and call Eusebius. He will lead you back to your maidenly bed. If, indeed, you are a maiden. If not, you have been a fool. Goodnight, my lady."

Silenced, Elise bowed as the king departed, resplendent in his wounded vanity and wine-stained robe. Safe now, she felt faintly sorry for her royal suitor, and for the first time, attracted to him. Perhaps she *had* been a fool. If so, it was now too late. Her fate and Edmond's hung on her decision.

When Eusebius came, he led her away without a word. She kept her head down as she trod the labyrinth behind him, doing her best to hide her tears. They were tears of fear and also anger. It was surely he who had arranged this vile liaison. At the door of her chamber, she lifted her eyes and saw a look of purest hatred on the eunuch's face.

19

1182

In the wake of her disastrous evening with King William, Elise grew more anxious every day. As time passed, however, he did nothing directly or indirectly to retaliate for her refusal. On the occasions when they met, he was distant but, if anything, more courteous than ever. It was not she but Eusebius who had fallen out of favor.

The king had sent for her in May. The rest of the summer, things went on as usual at court. Elise began to hope she would emerge unscathed. Unfortunately, she underestimated the eunuch's wrath. Although his position at court was weakened, he still had the power to harm her. He merely bided his time, waiting long enough so that the king would not connect him or the fatal night to what came next.

It was midwinter before he began a campaign of surreptitious slander, maligning her pagan learning and her virtue, spreading tales of her adultery with Giovanni, who, it seemed, had a wife back in Matera no one had known about. The eunuch even defamed her connection to Martin, accusing her of secret assignations with a cleric in the gardens of the Zisa. It seemed he had informants everywhere. Some of Joanna's new circle at last believed the rumors, among them the Calabrian baroness. Others did not but still felt Elise had been too lenient with Giovanni. A few thought her reading of the pagan authors might yet have a negative effect upon the queen. The rumors grew very slowly in strength and predictability. It was over a year from that fatal night before the poison had its full effect.

Late in the summer, Elise received a courteously worded letter from Joanna. She thanked her for her years of service and informed her that she need postpone her marriage to the Count de Vere no longer. The final lines seemed to preclude all possible appeal.

Since it will soon be autumn, you need not think of embarking for Normandy at present. Please take as long as you wish for the necessary preparations. You will be welcome as our guest until they are complete. You should sail by next spring but no later than July to be assured of a safe passage in the most auspicious weather. I thank you again for your faithful service. Wishing you Godspeed and happiness in your marriage, I am, as signed below—Ioanna Regina

Feeling faint, Elise sat down in a chair by the window, scarcely able to absorb the import of the note. Outside, the summer sky was blue, the air sweet with the scent of the season. Must she bid farewell to this land that had preserved her from a hated marriage and kept her safe for Edmond and their love? Somehow, after all this time in Joanna's service, she had stopped believing this day would come. Now that it had, she felt a mounting sense of panic. For the first time in years, she was unsure about her course of action. She read the letter again. Instinctively, she felt the queen had not composed it. Nonetheless, it was written in her hand and signed with her official seal. Feeling lost, Elise thought of Martin, her only real friend in Palermo. He had not yet assumed his position as a royal scholar, so she sent him a note care of the archbishop's palace.

Two days later, she was seated beside him inside the church of St. John the Hermit. It seemed the safest place to meet. From the first, she had loved this odd monastery church. From afar, its five bulbous domes made it look like a part of some Eastern fable. She had come with a servant from the palace as companion. The woman sat in the crossing while she and Martin found chairs in the rear part of the nave. Given the state of her reputation, the risks involved in such a meeting hardly mattered. Indeed, the woman seemed surprised to find Elise was here to meet a cleric, not a lover. It was a new feeling for Elise, this shame before the world. And all because she had refused a king's advances! She told the whole story of her misadventure to her friend, concluding on a rueful note.

"I had long known the world could be unjust. Now that truth has come cruelly home to me. So far, I've told only you the entire story. To speak to anyone else would, I think, be foolish."

"I'm afraid it would. Where the king's name is concerned, silence is the only prudent course. If it were known you rejected his advances, it would humiliate him, endangering you all the more."

"Of course you're right, but is there not some other answer, some way to spare me . . . Normandy?" She said *Normandy*, not *marriage to the count*, hating even to speak the words. "My mind is clouded by emotion. I find it difficult to concentrate. It's as if everything has crumbled, all the plans and hopes I've nurtured for so long."

"How could you feel otherwise? You must give yourself time to think."

"Yes, I must, but having you to talk to helps. In fact, I've been thinking a lot since receiving Joanna's letter, trying to fathom what has brought me to this pass. It all seems to begin with a memory from my childhood, one I still find oddly painful after all these years. I've never spoken of it to anyone."

"Feel free to tell me," Martin prompted, and Elise began her tale.

"As I think you know, I was a young child when my parents died. We lived at Crecy in Picardy, not far from the Norman border. My grandfather was a viscount, my father a younger son. He and my mother were deeply in love. I remember that clearly. That, and their love for me, their only child. When I was five, my father was called to Flanders as part of some military action, a payment of a debt of honor to an old friend. He was badly wounded in the combat. My mother's health was frail, one of the reasons I had no siblings. Still, she went to him at once. I was too young to understand. I only knew I had been abandoned by them both. First I cried, then raged. I would neither eat nor listen to the servants. Until my parents returned, I would do nothing I was told. At last, my nurse Iseult lost all patience. She called me a wicked, selfish girl and told me God would punish me, that if I didn't give up my willful ways, my parents would never come home."

Elise came to a halt. She had no idea how much these memories, once spoken, would affect her after all these years. She felt the old emotions welling up inside her.

Martin saw her distress. "Weep if you need to, Elise, only God and I will see you. Even your servant has fallen asleep."

"Thank you, dear friend, but I need to go on. Enraged at the nurse's threat, I continued to rebel. At last, they found someone else, a young woman who spoke soothingly and made no threats. After that, the days passed with no word of my parents. Gradually, my anger turned to fear. When the news came at last, it brought the terrible fulfillment of Iseult's threat. Not long after my mother had reached him, my father died. Grief-laden, worn out from long hours of travel, my mother too fell ill. Tended by nuns in a place called Antwerp, she lingered for a week before she died."

"How terrible that must have been for you."

"It *was* terrible, but at first I was too shocked to grieve. I did not even cry when they brought my parents back and laid them in their great stone tombs inside the local church. There were reclining figures carved on them, somber effigies with no resemblance to my parents. All I could think of was how cold and lonely they must be inside, so close and yet apart, and that my wickedness had put them there. Weeks passed at Crecy, and all the while I had this awful guilt inside me. No one mentioned it. No one spoke about my crime. Iseult was gone so perhaps they didn't know. But I did. My remorse was with me every day. Then, at last, my uncle came and claimed me. Almost at once, with a perception rare for him, he saw that I thought I had caused my parents' death. I confessed it all to him. He cursed my nurse and assured me nothing I did at Crecy could possibly have hurt my parents many miles away in Flanders. From that day forward, I loved him."

"I can see why."

"And, as you know, I've gone on loving him ever since. Yet despite his redeeming words, a fear of my own selfishness still lingered in my heart. Even as I grew older, it stayed with me. If happiness came my way, I reasoned, it must never be at the expense of others, especially those I loved. Only now do I see how that thought may have led me to this pass. First, I protected my uncle from the truth about his wife. Then, to keep Melisande from destroying Edmond's future, I consented to my betrothal, postponing the consequences of my action by coming to Sicily. Yet when the king offered to shield me from my marriage, I balked at the price, unwilling to violate my vow to Edmond. Even now, what troubles me most is the pain I will cause him when I marry. In the end, all my plans will have failed. Unless I can find another way. That's why I've come to you. I need your cooler head."

"And I want only good for you and Edmond. My mind has been racing as you talked. Let me think a little longer."

Elise nodded, and the two fell silent. Together, they watched the light stream from the narrow windows of the little dome above. Outside, Elise heard the call of a distant vendor followed by the shrill cry of a seagull. Had it strayed from the harbor, she wondered, and been unable to find its way back? She felt like the gull, lost, homeless, and adrift.

Finally Martin spoke. "I have an idea I think might work."

"Thank God. Tell me."

"It's simple enough," he said. "Before you do anything, before you tell anyone else you've been asked to leave, you must write a letter to your uncle's steward. Address it to him alone. Inside, include a note to him and a letter for your uncle. Tell the steward the letter must go only to the earl. Enclose it, sealed and labeled "For the Earl of Clarington's eyes alone." In the letter, you must say that although you cannot reveal the cause in writing, you cannot possibly marry the count. Tell your uncle you need some of the funds from your estate and his support to leave Palermo. Then implore him to say nothing of the matter to your aunt. Tell him you'll make everything clear when you two meet."

"At Bourne Castle? How can I see him with Melisande still there?"

"You can't, not yet at least. Isn't there someone else you could go to?"

"As it happens, there is." Elise had begun to feel there might be hope. "I have an aunt in Picardy, my father's sister. She has a house at Abbeville some distance from my lands. Melisande would have no knowledge of her."

"She would be a good choice, but don't mention her yet to your uncle."

"No, I won't," Elise said. "I must be firm in my letter. I have nine months before I leave. That should be time enough. I'll write to the steward exactly as you suggest."

"Addressed to him alone," Martin said, "it should elude even Melisande."

"Whatever happens," Elise concluded, "I shall at least have tried."

Having settled their plan, the two friends talked a bit more about the details of the letter. Elise was in better spirits when they parted. She wrote her uncle that night.

Then she waited.

20

1183

"You'll find books in many languages, my friend. We have works of antiquity in Greek and Latin, others in Arabic, Hebrew, and Aramaic. We have Egyptian papyri in hieroglyphic and demotic script, scrolls from the East with brush writing no one here can read."

Martin listened as Father Heraklios, the custodian of the royal library, introduced him to the collection. In the way of such things, over a year had gone by before Martin's appointment as a royal scholar had been implemented. At last, on the retirement of an aged scholar, Martin was given a place and an annual stipend, the first quarter in advance. He sat now with the custodian beside a carrel full of books. Dark-haired and dark-bearded, Heraklios was a Sicilian-born Greek in early middle age. He was said to be brilliant but without ambition, enamored only of his books. His broad face often wore a sardonic smile. Around them on shelves spread a great wealth of manuscripts. Some were *rotuli*, scrolls of parchment or papyrus, the oldest with spindles for unrolling, others thick codices with wooden covers. There were also innumerable stacks of unbound pages. The room was large, separated into sections according to the language of the books.

When Martin had finished looking, the priest led him into the adjacent scriptorium. "Our copyists labor here, duplicating the old and creating new books. Our scholars are also free to use this room."

Martin thought of his first day in the scriptorium at Windham Abbey. He felt the same excitement now. "I can hardly wait to begin."

"Naturally," Heraklios said, smiling. "I will help you in any way I can. You may take a while to discover your direction, the best path for your scholarship. Good luck." Having completed his minimal instructions, the custodian left him. Martin spent the rest of the day exploring. For the next few weeks, he felt as if he was in a scholar's paradise, free to sample the fruit of the tree of knowledge, in this case without fear of expulsion.

One morning, searching a section devoted to the early Fathers of the Church, Martin picked up a dusty volume by Clement of Alexandria, a moralist of the second century. As he did, he noticed a narrow unbound text beside it. There was no author's name, but as he scanned the pages , he spied some lines of a kind that seemed oddly familiar.

It is Demeter and Pluto,
It is Isis and Osiris,
It is Eros and Aphrodite.
It is Anu and Astarte,
It is greater than all these,
The fertile womb of creation,
A power beyond good and evil.

Who or what, he wondered, was the subject here? Laying the sheets on a nearby table, he sat down and continued to read.

It is the origin and ending.
It is the core of all being.
In life you will fear it.
In death you will know it.

To his surprise, he already knew these lines. Where had he read them? Then he remembered. It was at Windham Abbey in one of the pages Prior Gramont had sent to the scriptorium.

They were written by Basilides, the Gnostic of Alexandria. Mystified and intrigued, Martin had even copied a few of the verses. The lines that followed, however, were new to him.

Out of the infinite depths
Came dominions of darkness and light.
The devil plunged into the darkness
And God rose up into the light.
Greater than both is the force born
Of the universal seed, all-powerful Abraxas.

Abraxas. So that was the word blotted out on the pages at Windham Abbey, the name of some dark primal force or demonic god, a power greater than God or Satan. Having learned it, Martin went on reading. Once again, he found Basilides's writing both difficult and strange. Oddest of all was a long passage on numerology. Using an arcane method of assigning numbers to Greek letters, the philosopher had arrived at 365, the sum of the letters in Abraxas's name as well as the number of days in a year, the time it took for the heavenly bodies to complete a full circuit of the earth. Thus Abraxas was given another name, *Cosmokrator,* Greek for "ruler of the cosmos."

Did the prior really believe these things, Martin wondered, or was he merely exploiting Basilides's writings to deceive and entrap the members of the cult? In either case, the best person to ask about Abraxas was Heraklios. The priest's wide reading had made him the master of many subjects.

When, later that day, Martin inquired about Basilides, Heraklios was as usual a font of information.

"In the second century of the Christian era, beliefs were quite diverse, nowhere more so than in Egypt, where Gnostic heresy abounded. Basilides was one such Gnostic, but surviving works by him are rare."

Rare, thought Martin, *yet here in Palermo.* Then he remembered what Elise had said, that Bishop Osbert had lived here in his youth. Might he already have been a member of the cult? He could hardly expect Heraklios to tell him that, so he asked a more general question.

"What more can you tell me about Basilides?"

"Mainly this—that even compared to his fellow Gnostics, Basilides was considered strange. Almost from the first, he was condemned by the Fathers of the Church. It is as if in his work Greek philosophic method and the revelation of the scriptures were at first confused, then confounded with pagan superstition. Abraxas, the great power of which he speaks, may or may not be his own creation. Not surprisingly, two centuries after his death, the Church Council at Nicea declared his works heretical, banning him along with many others. Since then, his writings have been thoroughly suppressed, the reason so little remains. Indeed, we know of him mainly from the diatribes of his detractors. Having said all that," Heraklios concluded, "may I ask why you are interested in him?"

"It's difficult to explain," Martin said. "Will you forgive me if I don't answer at the moment? You have been a great help to me nonetheless."

"It is my duty as well as my pleasure, but I don't think I need to warn you. Basilides and the other Gnostics, however fascinating, will not do for your chosen area of study. Take any of the Fathers of the Church, or one of the great thinkers of the pagan past, but be wary of heresy. The court of Sicily is tolerant, but even here it's wise to steer clear of such teachings."

Martin nodded in agreement. "Your warning is already taken, father. That was never my intention. In truth, Abraxas has distracted me from my researches. Now that I've spoken to you, I'm anxious to resume them."

A few days later, however, Martin encountered another distraction. Shortly after he had come to the palace as the youngest scholar, Heraklios had asked him to perform a periodic task. From time to time, he would go to the shop of an old Jewish scholar called Isaac who dealt in fine vellum, papyrus, and rare pigments, some made from precious gemstones. Once at the shop, he would order whatever was needed in the scriptorium. The goods would be sent to the palace the following day.

Martin set out on his errand on a cloudy March afternoon. Making his way through the narrow streets, he came to Isaac's shop, disclosed only by the painted image of a scroll over a doorway in an alley. He found Isaac inside in the dim light of a hanging lamp. Framed by a silky white beard, the old scholar's fine features were subtly expressive, especially when he spoke with admiration of Maimonides, the famous Jewish philosopher from Cordoba in al-Andalus. When they had finished the order, Martin asked Isaac for the first time about his own career. His answer said a good deal about both his character and the history of his people.

"Except for the good opinion of my fellow scholars, I have never sought the world's acclaim or, for that matter, the favor of our monarch. Sicily is the most tolerant of Christian kingdoms, but as has happened elsewhere, tolerance may all too quickly turn to hatred and suspicion. In that event, my prominence would do me greater harm than good. As it is, I am content with my lot as a private scholar and a merchant of rare goods. In fact, since you've asked about my interests, let me show you two stones I have recently acquired."

His curiosity piqued, Martin followed his host to a room in the rear full of curios and books. There, lighting another lamp, Isaac opened a little compartment in a wooden chest and extracted two large cameos. The first, bluish-white on black, showed a winged female in flying drapery. It was so skillfully carved that the folds of the garment completely revealed the figure underneath.

"Exquisite, is in not?" the scholar observed. "It's made of layered onyx and dates from Roman times, not an angel but a Victory. Of course, as a student of the Hellenes, you would know that. Not quite as good but also finely worked, is this gem cut from agate, an amulet."

As he spoke, Isaac placed a large, oval-shaped stone in Martin's palm. It was a cream-colored relief on a purplish ground.

With a shock, Martin recognized the figure, the same he had seen on the banner at the clearing of the stones. The carving showed the beaked head, the torso with a whip and shield, and the strange legs composed of two snakes. In this finely carved gem, the arms were carefully carved, the breastplate was that of a Roman soldier, and the reptilian legs had tiny scales. A comb on the bird's head also made clear it was a rooster. Over the years, Martin had become more familiar with pagan symbols. The cock doubtless stood for virility, the shield and whip for power. Since the ancients believed snakes could fertilize themselves, they no doubt stood for fertility. Seven capital letters surrounded the symbol and spelled out the name *ABRAXAS*.

Evidently sensing Martin's interest, Isaac went on. "The name is usually written in Greek. It's rare to see it in Latin letters. Some inscriptions use the phrase *Lord of Hosts*, probably from the Kabbalah. Almost nothing is know of the origin of the image. Although some say it comes from ancient Egypt, that has never been proven."

"Have you seen more of these amulets?" Martin asked.

"This finely made? No, never. Other gems with this image? Yes, several. I believe they were once quite common."

"At the time of the Gnostic heretics?"

"Yes," the old scholar said softly, perhaps put off by the mention of heresy. "At that time, and since. Do you know the emblem? Many scholars do not."

"I am familiar with it," Martin said, "but not from an amulet. Would you be willing to sell it?" The moment he asked, Martin felt foolish. What would he do with such a thing?

The old man's face seemed to say as much. "To a scholar like yourself, perhaps, as a curiosity, but the price would be high. In fact, I have decided to keep it, showing it only to a trusted few. Surely you know this symbol is a part of some dark belief?"

"I thought that might be the case," Martin answered blandly, avoiding any mention of the cult.

Before taking his leave, he thanked Isaac sincerely for showing him the stones. Even so, he was strangely disturbed by the amulet. It had revived his unease about the evil brotherhood. Had the cult once been in Sicily? Might it be here again? A single stone, however suggestive, told him little. In truth, Martin was weary of thinking about the cult. Unless he banished it from his mind, he might never discover a subject for study as a scholar.

The next day, he went back to his search. By the end of the month, he had made up his mind. The focus of his study would be Aristotle, a thinker admired equally by Christians, Jews, and Muslims. The teacher of Alexander the Great, Aristotle had been the greatest thinker of his time—and many believed, of all time. Systematically, Martin began to read everything he could find by the master, whether in Greek or in Latin translation.

*

In his life as a cleric, Martin made no comparable progress. Sometimes, faced with his continuing feeling for Edmond, he was full of shame. At other times, as if in reaction, he felt only anger and defiance. Had God not made him this way? How could the Creator be wrong and the world that disdained his kind be right? Plagued by these questions, he was far from the spiritual peace he was supposed to be striving for. He hoped nonetheless that his life—simple, celibate, devoted to his work—would in time overcome these desires the Church condemned as vile abominations. Meanwhile, whenever he thought too longingly of Edmond or, as often happened, some comely youth or handsome knight rekindled his desire, Martin prayed to God to be delivered from his lust.

Then, one day in December, Elise sent a note asking him to meet her in a courtyard of the palace. After five months, a letter had come. As the two sat together in the warming sun, she handed it to Martin. The fine parchment was signed by the earl, but the letter had been penned by Melisande. From the first line, it was apparent her uncle had not read Elise's letter. Despite its clear direction to the steward, it must have either been lost or somehow intercepted.

"Could it be," Martin asked, "that the steward has conspired with your aunt?"

Elise shook her head. "He's a trustworthy man. I can't believe he would betray me or my uncle. Something else must have happened. See what you think of the rest."

With no mention of a letter from Elise, the reply spoke of how Prior Gramont had close acquaintances at the Sicilian court. Through them, her uncle had learned she was free to marry. In his capacity as intermediary, the prior had arranged an escort for Elise. Leaving Sicily by ship in June, she would make her journey with two Benedictine nuns and two Norman men at arms for their protection. In Normandy, she would meet the Count de Vere, her future husband, and the two would be married at Caen. That was all, except for her uncle's sincere regrets. His poor health would keep him and his wife from crossing the channel for the ceremony.

Dismayed, Martin looked up. "It says very little about your uncle's illness."

"Yes, it troubles me greatly, and may be what enabled Melisande to intervene again. However it happened, it's now too late. I made my devil's bargain with her long ago. With this letter, she's claimed the price."

Martin felt differently. "No, Elise, you mustn't give in so easily. In three days, a packet of letters will leave Archbishop Walter's office en route to the Bishop of Winchester. It will be easy enough to include a missive to be forwarded to Windham."

"How can I write again? I've failed once already."

"You won't have to. I'll write this time, to Edmond at Preston Manor. It's time he understood your situation. While your uncle has watched him training as a knight, he has surely grown fond of him. I believe he will listen to what Edmond says. Once he understands the situation, Edmond will speak to him. He would do anything to keep from losing you."

"But what can he tell the earl?"

"Just this: a fact he has learned from Deacon Martin, your former fellow pupil, that an important letter from his niece has failed to reach him, that you are unable to marry the count for grave reasons you must explain in person—"

"—and that, because of these circumstances," Elise continued, "I need my uncle's help."

"Exactly," Martin said, watching hope bloom again on Elise's pale face.

"Yes, we must try it," she urged. "Perhaps Edmond can do what I failed to do."

Two days later in the same courtyard, Martin read the letter to Elise. As he finished, he added a warning.

"We mustn't deceive ourselves. There is a risk. If Melisande learns of this letter or Edmond's meeting with the earl, she may renege on her bargain and denounce you both. Yet it's a risk I believe you must take. I know Edmond, for one, will not hesitate."

"I agree. This letter may be our last chance. Even God cannot help us if we fail to take it. When will you deliver the letter to the archbishop's office?"

"This afternoon. It should travel swiftly. Once your uncle understands the situation, he can put a stop to the wedding and make new arrangements for your departure from Palermo."

"Then go, my friend," Elise urged, "and God with you. Once again, I owe you a great deal. Let us pray that this time we'll succeed."

21

Sweating from the heat, the brawny sailors rowed with rhythmic grunts. As the skiff moved out of the harbor, Elise turned to the shore and lifted her hand in farewell to Martin. On the way to ship, each wave that struck the prow felt like a blow. Every stroke of the oar took her farther from Palermo, the refuge she had clung to for so long. Martin's letter had failed. There had been no word from Edmond or her uncle.

Once she had climbed the ladder and seen her baggage hauled aboard, Elise stood dazed on the deck as the ship's hands raised anchor. Before long, there was a booming sound above her and the great sail filled with wind, puffing out like the breast of a giant bird. They lurched into the waves while Elise clung to the rail and looked back toward the slowly disappearing city. When the land was no more than a line on the horizon, she turned again toward the sea and stared blankly at the merging blue of sea and sky.

After a while, she felt a gentle hand on her shoulder. It was Sister Genevieve, the younger of the two nuns who would be her companions. "I've come to tell you you'll have to unpack your things yourself, my dear, whatever you'll need for the voyage. The rest they will store below. There are no servants on the ship."

Beneath her wimple, the nun had a homely but kindly face. Her hazel eyes were intelligent and lively.

Elise thanked the nun and followed her below. How different this trip, she thought, from her journey to Sicily! She had sailed on a royal galley then, part of Princess Joanna's great entourage. This small craft was a merchant ship laden with cargo. She had seen fewer than a dozen crew members. The five persons in their party were the only passengers.

Later, she met Genevieve on the deck. The nun knew the details of their voyage.

"We will sail first to the mainland, then follow the coast to Marseilles. From there, we'll travel overland to Normandy, to Caen, where our sisters' convent is located. There are two Benedictine abbeys there. The men's abbey was founded by William, the conqueror of England. Ours was endowed by his queen. I believe you're to be married in the former."

"Yes," Elise said without comment, then changed the subject. "Have you traveled widely, sister?"

"Not until a year ago. Like the two men at arms with our party, Sister Domitilla and I are returning from the Holy Land. When she was abbess in a time of trial, she vowed to visit the holy places if God helped us. Her prayers were answered, and despite her age she was determined to keep her vow. Because of my ready wit and native vigor—I am candid about the few gifts God has given me—I was chosen to go with her. We made our journey in some haste. Many fear that the Christians of the Holy Land, divided as they are by rivalry and greed, will soon lose the holy places to their Muslim neighbors."

Surprised by the frankness with which the nun spoke of her fellow Christians' faults, Elise began to suspect she had found a sympathetic spirit. At the moment, however, she felt the need to be alone. Perhaps sensing her mood, Genevieve left her to her thoughts. In the wake of the last several weeks of sadness and regret, Elise still found it hard to understand her downfall. When, as time passed, there was no reply to Martin's letter, she had been forced to assume the worst: that Edmond had been unable to intercede on her behalf. A month before the date of her departure, Elise heard from Melisande. This time she had written in her own name. After a typically elegant preamble, she spoke without pretense about Elise's situation.

In truth, I doubt you were guilty with this Giovanni. I know how full of intrigue a court can be. Whatever the case, you are compromised. After such a dismissal by the daughter of our sovereign, you cannot return to Bourne Castle unmarried. Although he knows of your disgrace, the Count de Vere has not changed his mind about the marriage. But if for some foolish reason you try once again to evade our bargain, the results will be disastrous. As you may have guessed, I long ago intercepted your letter to your uncle, the one sent through his steward. The earl was very unwell at the time. The man had no choice but to give it to me. As it is, your uncle knows only that Joanna has released you to begin your married life. Should you balk again, he will have to learn the truth: your disgrace, the scandal with Giovanni, and worst of all, your liaison with Edmond Preston. As things stand, the latter is nearing the completion of his training because of the earl's patronage.

To make sure you understand, I am not speaking of your childish dalliance with him in Windham but of Winchester. You will recall the accommodating widow Gertrude? She and I were girls together in the Ile de France. She showed promise, as I did, but lacked my opportunities. We kept up our correspondence as time passed. When she learned you were at court, she wrote me of Marianne, her former client, then of your inquiring visit. Assured I would not interfere, that I cared only for your welfare, she told me all I wished to know. You may think me vindictive. I am not. I was happy to see you have your fling as men do, as long as you kept to the bargain we had made. And now the time has come to do so. Should you be so foolish as to try to reach your uncle secretly again—or to forward this letter as proof of my duplicity, understand you will fail. All that comes to my husband in writing I now see beforehand. I close by congratulating you on your marriage. Through it, you will reclaim your reputation, unite your lands with the count's, and gain the rank of countess, a great deal in the eyes of the world. The rest will be up to you.

Reading the letter, Elise was both astonished and, for Edmond's sake, relieved. At least he was safe. There was no mention of a failed attempt by him to intervene on her behalf. Then a slow rage began to grow inside her. At last, full of fury, she resolved to find some way to countermand her aunt. By now, however, the disdain of Elise's fellow courtiers had worn her down. Even Martin had done all he could. There was no tribunal she could turn to, no one to alter the queen's decision but the king whom Elise had mortally offended. And even he was no match for the slander that had ruined her. Thus, in the end, the unthinkable had happened. She was on her way to marry Gilles de Vere.

*

During the voyage, to her surprise, Elise began to feel a welcome sense of freedom. Once they had docked at Marseilles and commenced the long journey north to Caen, she began to enjoy the little incidents of travel, observing the variety of places they passed through. For the first time since childhood, she felt free of protocol. Sister Genevieve, a native of Anjou, proved an ideal companion. Like Elise, she was an orphan of loving parents. She too was learned beyond her peers. Unlike Elise, she lacked both a fortune and a pretty face. Against her will, her relatives had married her to the church. For her dowry, she had brought a small sum of money and a vital spirit. As the two women exchanged their stories, they found solace in each other. One night in Toulouse, in the guesthouse of a Benedictine convent, Genevieve spoke earnestly to her.

"My dear Elise, you must not despair. You know your own mind, and God knows your heart. Not the unjust God that men impose on us but the loving God who dwells within. Bide your time and when the opportunity arises, seize it. I myself have a splendid priest for my confessor, the rare man who is truly concerned with justice. When the time comes, and a bequest from my uncle allows me to live in the world, he will help me have my vows annulled. He has already prepared the petition."

"I'm so happy to hear that, Genevieve," Elise exclaimed. "You deserve the life you choose. Sadly, I see no way out for me."

"Not at present, perhaps, but you are still young. From what you say, you've already been willing to defy men's customs. When the time comes, you will know how to do so again.

Meanwhile, learn to dissemble. Avoid the rash actions men drive us to, after which they call us creatures of unruly passion. I feel sure you'll win out in the end. Meanwhile, rest assured that you'll be in my thoughts and prayers."

As she listened, Elise remembered Queen Eleanor's words that night at Sarum, oddly similar in many ways. She had spoken of beauty, strength, and cunning, at least two of which were necessary for a woman to survive. In Sicily, Elise's beauty had brought her only harm. Now, for the first time since Joanna had dismissed her, she felt her strength returning. Yet she would not depend on that alone. She would also be cunning. She would learn to dissemble and deceive as both the great queen and the wise nun had advised.

*

It was a clear early autumn day, cool and sunny with a light breeze from the channel. The great abbey church of St. Etienne was built of creamy yellow limestone. Its tall towers and high façade were simple but impressive. Their small party entered through the great front portal. As Elise looked up, it seemed as if the soaring mass of stone was tilting towards her. Had it come crashing down upon her at that moment, she would have considered it a blessing. Like so much in life, the effect was an illusion. Nothing now would intervene to save her.

Inside, the arched vaulting rose high, and light poured into the nave from the clerestory windows. A gray-bearded priest from the abbey performed the ceremony. Two monks, acquaintances of Prior Gramont, served as witnesses. The prior himself was in Brittany, they said. There was a small group of noblemen along with monks, nuns, and a few townspeople curious to see the Lord of Evremont and his new bride. The service was simple and without a Mass. Still fatigued from a journey that ended the day before, Elise felt part of a pantomime, a mummery in which her true self played no part.

All morning the count maintained a deferential manner, albeit tinged with irony at times. Afterward, the principals shared a meal in the abbey guesthouse. The setting discouraged ribaldry and there was little sense of celebration. She felt the others must know the count's pecuniary motives. The few who commented on his bride's beauty seemed surprised, as if it were an accidental bonus. Through it all, Elise remained silent except when addressed. No doubt she seemed a shy bride to those assembled.

In the evening, husband and wife went to an inn in Caen. In the morning they would leave for Evremont. That night they dined together in a private room. Their supper was more lavish than the wedding meal provided by the monks. A fawning innkeeper served them broiled fish, roast pheasant stuffed with bread and nuts and cooked in wine, desserts of honey-cake and candied fruit. If she had known how rare such a meal would soon become, Elise might have eaten better. As it was, she merely sampled each dish, fortifying herself with wine. Gilles drank a good deal and ate with appetite. He had been courteous all day, commiserating, for example, that her guardians could not be present.

Near the end of their meal, her new husband smiled insinuatingly across the table. "Is it true, my lady wife," he asked, "that you already know the art of love?"

She hadn't thought the issue would emerge so soon. She knew Melisande would have told the count about the scandal, his ironic use of the name *The Art of Love* confirmed that. Still, she sensed her aunt had continued to honor their bargain where Edmond was concerned.

"Whatever you mean by that remark," Elise said, "you are free to think it. Is it not enough to admit I am not a virgin? I suppose you know why I left the Sicilian court?"

"A scandal of some sort with a young baron from Matera, a man known for his way with women. Was it he, then, who deprived you of your virtue?"

Elise had a ready answer. "I alone am responsible for my actions. No one has seduced me or deceived me. With your permission, sir, I would prefer not to discuss the matter."

"What haughtiness, madam," said Gilles mockingly, "for a woman who admits her guilt! On the other hand, I am no moralist. I'll speak no more of your disgrace. Perhaps, in lieu of a confession, you can demonstrate the ways you've learned to please a man. With a bride schooled in such arts, I should not have to exert myself unduly."

Elise had not known what to expect tonight, but it had not included insults. "You need not exert yourself at all, my lord. In truth, I am nauseous with fatigue. As of today, you have achieved the chief objective of this union. My lands and rents are yours. With that in mind, I beg to be excused. Please finish the meal at your leisure. If you insist, we can resume this discussion tomorrow."

She had spoken in haste with no thought of the count's reaction.

"I don't need your permission to remain here, madam. Nor have I dismissed you. I am your husband, I've made a request, and I expect compliance. Not to be too exacting, I'll give you a bit of help."

With that, Gilles pulled his chair out into the center of the room. Then he walked to the door and turned the key and locked it. Wine in hand, he sat down in the chair, spread his legs wide, and looked directly at Elise.

"Come, madam, show me your skills," he urged. "There's a way to arouse a man known everywhere. And surely in Sicily, where the king keeps a harem adept in all such arts. Was it perhaps he who was your tutor? Ah, yes, I said I wouldn't ask. I won't, but since I cannot deflower you as a husband should, you will have to oblige me another way."

Elise knew what Gilles wanted, of course, but she balked at the command. He had her wealth, was that not enough? Must he also have her subjugation? Instead of refusing, she appealed to whatever was left of his courtesy. "Sir, I beg you. I am not feeling well. I've already asked to be excused."

At these words, Gilles's face darkened. He answered in an irate voice. "And I, madam, have asked a simple service of my wife. I'll not unlock that door till you've performed it to my satisfaction."

Furious, Elise answered without thinking. "If you want such service, sir, then cross the channel to my aunt. There is evidently no debasement she won't undergo for you." That said, she stood and ran to the door, intent upon escaping. The key stuck in the lock. Before she could turn it, Gilles was beside her, twisting her hand. When she let it go, he pulled it out of the lock, and, large though it was, slid it into the lining of his jacket.

"You will do as I say now, madam, or suffer the penalty. I thought to accustom you slowly to my needs, but if you fail to comply with my request, I shall take you here on this food-stained floor in your fine dress. And I'll enjoy it all the more, and you much less, if you resist. Which shall it be then?"

At first, Elise could not believe he meant it. As much as she loathed de Vere, she had pictured something different; the two of them in darkness, a prelude of some kind, and then, quickly or slowly, the culmination, not loving, of course, but at least without conflict. Perhaps if she performed this one submissive act, it would suffice. With that in mind, she watched Gilles sit down again. Hating herself almost as much as him, she knelt before him, and then, despite herself, pulled back. It was not prudery or disgust, although she certainly felt the latter with the count, it was a need to refuse this too willing capitulation. If her marriage began this way, where would it end? No, whatever the penalty, she would not give in.

At that moment, as if reading her thoughts, Gilles jumped up angrily. Moving at once to make good his promise, he grabbed her roughly and kissed her on the lips. When she failed to respond, he slapped her. Defending herself, she pushed him away with all her might. Surprised, the count lost his balance and fell against the wall. Glaring, he took hold of her and threw her to the floor. She felt a sharp pain in her arm as she tried to break her fall. She now understood the danger of resistance. She decided not to fight. Barely noticing, Gilles grabbed her dress of rose-colored Sicilian silk, her finest, and tearing the skirt, pulled it and her shift up to her thighs. Then, pushing her legs apart, he entered. The sudden agony was awful. She cried out, but he took the torn bottom of her dress and thrust the cloth into her mouth. Then consciously, it seemed, he slowed his rhythm, prolonging his pleasure and her pain. Just when she felt she could bear no more, he finished and collapsed on top of her. When it was over, her nausea returned, induced by the attack, Gilles's wine-soaked breath, and the sour smell of the rushes on the floor. She was about to be sick when he pulled himself up, stood over her, and spoke. He seemed calm now but his eyes were full of hatred.

"This will remind you to obey me in the future."

Having said that, he moved toward the door. Facing away, Elise heard the key turn, looked up, and watched him leave. After several attempts, trembling uncontrollably, she raised herself on one hand and saw the key was in the door. Crawling first on her stomach, then her knees, she reached for it and turned it until the door was locked. That done, she fell back exhausted. After a while, she rolled over on her side. Curled into a ball, she cradled the pain between her legs. As the night wore on, the candles on the table burned out one by one. At last she fell asleep. In this way, dozing fitfully and waking to the truth of her new life, Elise spent the first night of her marriage.

22

1184

Several months had now passed since Martin had waved to Elise from the dock in Palermo. No word had come from her yet, nor, for that matter, from Edmond. He was also wary of writing his friend again. What if his last letter, like Elise's, had somehow been intercepted? Until he knew, he would not send another. The situation was all the more frustrating since he had a new missive for Edmond, a farewell written by Elise before she left. Martin could scarcely imagine the anguished words it must contain. By now, of course, Edmond must have heard the news about her marriage.

Then, one day in January, a letter arrived at the scriptorium. He was about to break the wax when he saw it had been opened and resealed. It was from Elise. As he read, he soon guessed the situation. The letter, sent through the court at Rouen, was strangely reserved, as if Elise knew the count might read it. Was his chateau, then, a kind of prison? She wrote about it carefully, saying only that parts of it were very old and lay in ruins. As the *mont* in Evremont suggested, the stronghold was built on a great limestone hill. Situated by the eastern Norman border, it was not far from Elise's birthplace in Picardy. Managed well by an overseer, her lands and their income were conveniently nearby—convenient principally for her husband, Martin thought ruefully.

Taking his lead from Elise, Martin wrote back in a cautious manner. After that, months passed before a second letter came. It too bore the signs of de Vere's inspection. From this reply, however guarded, Martin gleaned what he could about her life at Evremont. Despite his new wealth, the count had made no improvements to the chateau. From the rumors at court that followed Elise's marriage, Martin had learned that de Vere was well known for his debauches and his debts. He also suspected something worse, that as a member of the Abraxas brotherhood, he was supporting its crimes with Elise's income. Martin was glad, at least, that he had warned her about the cult. Meanwhile, distressed by her plight and his powerlessness to help, he asked God to protect her in what he felt sure was a wretchedly unhappy union.

*

That year the Sicilian winter was mild and short. Once the rains had ceased, spring arrived with warm, sweet days and balmy nights. As the season changed, Martin made a new beginning, studying not just Aristotle but ancient commentators on his works. He read whenever he could in Greek, sometimes translating parts into Latin. He had his own carrel for books and a table to which he returned each day. Not far from the spot where he worked, the store of Greek volumes ended. Beyond it were shelves of works in Arabic, many of them translations of ancient Greek texts. In Sicily, Arabic was everywhere: as the third language in official documents along with Greek and Latin; carved into buildings and set in colored tiles on the walls of mosques; spoken in the voices of the Arab population. Here at the palace, some Arabic works were on scrolls, others in bound volumes. Many were written on parchment, others, mostly from Egypt, on papyrus. The newest were on paper, a recently favored surface of the East. As Martin examined them with care, he marveled at the ornamental script, amazed that something so beautiful could also carry meaning.

One afternoon as he was working at his table, he glanced toward the Arabic books and came upon a novel scene. In the light from a window set high in the wall, two well-dressed Muslims stood facing each other. The one with his back to the window had a small volume in his hand. After turning a few pages, he began to read. Now, for the first time it seemed, Martin heard the Arabic language pronounced with exquisite refinement. The distinguished appearance of the reader matched his voice. Fully bearded and dressed in a robe of blue damask, the man seemed about forty years of age.

Martin listened until the scholar had finished what he guessed must be a poem. Only then did the speaker notice him, making a courteous gesture of greeting with his hand. With that, the man's companion also turned. Dressed in a rust-colored robe, the second Saracen had a shorter, darker beard. Taller than his companion, he was also remarkably handsome. The fine features of his face stood out against a white silk turban. He too now greeted the Christian stranger with an inclination of his head. Martin nodded courteously and smiled. Then, to avoid appearing rude, he lowered his eyes and continued his work.

Later that day, Father Heraklios told Martin who had greeted him. "That was Ibn Jubair, the shorter man, I mean, the famous Muslim poet and geographer. Last year on his way to Granada in al-Andalus, the ship he was sailing on foundered near Messina."

"I remember hearing that now."

"As well you might have. The scholar had recently visited the greatest cities of the Arab world from Alexandria to Baghdad, not omitting the sacred pilgrimage to Mecca. Knowing his fame, King William's emissaries welcomed him warmly. Indeed, our ruler invited him to stay in Sicily as long as he desired."

"And the other man?" Martin inquired.

"Khalil al-Din? You don't know him? Then, of course, you would not. He is a royal scholar like yourself, but he's been away for a long time traveling with Ibn Jubair. He has now returned since the geographer will soon be leaving for al-Andalus. At first, they say the great man was delighted to find all things Muslim were still honored here after a century of Norman rule.

Lately, I've heard he's complained that, in the countryside especially, Muslims are being subordinated and oppressed, not only
by Normans but by Lombard upstarts."

"I'm sorry to hear that." Martin said. "So far, Sicily has
seemed to me a miracle of toleration. And I'm looking forward
to meeting Khalil al-Din."

In fact, Martin hoped that this newly discovered colleague
might serve as a guide to the knowledge that loomed before
him every day, all of it hidden in the undulating script Heraklios
called Kufic.

*

One morning a few weeks later, Martin spent two hours
searching for variant versions of Aristotle's *Poetics*. Almost all
were in Latin translation although there were some fragmen-
tary parts in Greek. Having found what he needed, he ate quickly at midday and returned. As he entered the room where he
worked, he was surprised to see a tall robed figure standing by
his reading table. Coming closer, he recognized Khalil al-Din.
The scholar was cradling a large Greek codex in his arms. Using
the French of the court, not the Latin he might have employed
with a Christian scholar, Martin addressed him with great courtesy, mindful that they were not yet formally acquainted.

"Good sir, please don't burden yourself with such a weight.
Pray be seated in my accustomed place. Take whatever time you
need to properly inspect your book."

Looking faintly amused, the man set the tome down, careful
not to disturb the other volumes on the table. Relieved of its
weight, he smiled and responded in faintly accented French.

"It is kind of you, young scholar, to give up your place. Nor
will I ungraciously refuse your offer. What will you do, however, while I read a few pages of Plotinus?"

"I shall do as I always do, sir," Martin answered. "Look for
works by and about my current subject, Aristotle. I wish to
learn everything I can about him."

"A commendable goal. As it happens, I too am a follower of Aristotle, although I read him mainly in Arabic translation. As you may know, we Arabs have long kept the knowledge of the Greeks alive."

"Of course. It makes me regret I do not know your tongue."

"I can sympathize. My Greek, although adequate, is sometimes weak. I had enough to do mastering Norman French, the language of the conqueror, and Latin, the tongue employed by all Christian writers."

Here, the scholar paused. "You must forgive me. I've not yet introduced myself. I am Khalil al-Din Hassan bin Ali. And you, I believe, are Deacon Martin Rendon, the young English scholar recommended to King William by Archbishop Walter."

Surprised the stranger knew so much about him, Martin was slow to answer.

"I'm flattered that you know me, sir, and pleased to meet you. We have similar interests, it seems."

"And complementary skills. Perhaps we can be of assistance to each other in the future." As he spoke, the scholar smiled again, this time baring fine white teeth.

Martin responded in kind. "I must confess I had similar thoughts, and that I also knew about you and your reputation as a scholar and a poet."

"Alas, a poet no more. My poetry began and ended with my youth."

Martin could think of no tactful response to this. For a moment, both men were silent. When the scholar spoke, there was a new note of shyness in his voice. "You have been very kind, Deacon Martin, but I think I will take this book back to my place after all."

"Of course."

Lifting the volume, the scholar bid him good day and departed. Full of vaguely promising thoughts about the future, Martin watched him go.

23

Elise sat at the little writing table in her chamber, trembling as she listened to the pounding on the door. She had barred it as she always did when Gilles was drunk. Over a year had now passed since the day of her marriage. Her life during that year had been more difficult than she could possibly have imagined.

At last the knocking ceased. For a while she had been afraid her husband would summon Mordran, his burly overseer, to break the door down. The sturdy oak it was made of and the iron rod she used to bar it were among the few things she was grateful for at Evremont. Another was Jeanne, the servant who had become her secret ally. Later, she would come to spend the night, a further discouragement to the count.

From the first, Elise's relations with her husband, marital and otherwise, had been disastrous. There had been no repetition of their wedding night at Caen, thank God, but there were other horrendous scenes, especially when the count was drunk. What she dreaded most was bearing his child. Dame Gertrude had told her what she hoped was true, the best days of the month for conceiving. At those times, Elise steadfastly resisted Gilles's advances. At last, the day after a particularly terrible night, the count approached her outside the castle hall.

"Stay your flight for an instant, madam. I am as tired of our warring as you must be. In truth, I've lost interest in bedding you. Your prudish resistance has destroyed any charm you might have held for me. Instead, I propose a truce. I will no longer insist on my marital rights or force myself on you. You, in turn, will act the dutiful wife, make no attempt to contravene my orders, and remain at Evremont as long as I desire."

Suspicious of the count's motives, Elise first thought about the offer, then replied. "I will agree on one condition, that you allow me the freedom of a monthly stipend. You can give it to Jeanne if you like."

"Too fine a lady to sully yourself with money?" Gilles queried. "Play that part if you like. I accept your terms, do you consent to mine?"

Anxious for a respite, Elise had agreed, but when, as tonight, the count drank too much, and there was no whore from Rouen or village girl at hand, he sometimes disregarded their agreement. Meanwhile, he continued to squander her income on his vices. At times, Elise felt it was only his fear of her uncle's wrath, kept dormant so far by Melisande, that protected her from greater danger.

Ready once more to begin a letter, she sat wrapped in a thick woolen cloak over a heavy dress and underdress. Although she had gained a meager income, the count's resentment had taken the form of small privations. Little wood for her chamber was one of them. Replete with hardships great and small, her life had followed the same dismal course until, a week ago, Jeanne had told her there was a way to send her letters secretly. Together, the two had worked out the details. Now all that remained was to write her letter. Chafing her hands to warm them, she took up the pen.

The Feast of St. Agnes
Evremont, January 21, 1185

My dearest Martin, this will be the first time I have been able to speak the whole truth while writing you from here. For fear of its being intercepted, I cannot say how this letter will be sent. When it arrives, examine it carefully. It should come with the seal unbroken and the outside packet written in my hand. If this is the case, please write in your next missive, "The almond trees are in blossom, surprising at this time of year." If you see evidence of tampering, write, "There have been storms along the coast near Cefalu."

That said, I must tell you at once what you may have guessed already. My life here is an unhappy one. You may wonder why I do not flee when the count is away. There are reasons. The first is the watch kept over me. Gilles's overseer, an ogre by the name of Mordran, is my principal jailer. There is also a small garrison that guards the only entrance to the castle. Like the servants, they have been told I am unstable and cannot be allowed to go out on my own. I have only a small monthly stipend from my husband, barely enough for my most pressing needs, that and a secret store I brought with me for when I sorely need it. In accordance with the unjust laws of Christendom, my husband has gained all my wealth. In this respect, as you see, Norman wives are worse off than Arab women. As I learned in Palermo, there is divorce among the Muslims. Once the contract is broken, the wife regains her property.

There is another more important reason why I stay, however. My pact with Melisande protects Edmond. If I broke it now and she retaliated, she could ruin his career and favor with my uncle. In that case, my failure would be complete. So I go on, awaiting the day when things will change. This may seem like folly. Perhaps it is, but it is all that remains of the greater folly I once committed, my attempt to control not only my fate but Edmond's and my uncle's.

Meanwhile, my husband is often away. And whether he is or not, I have the freedom of the grounds for exercise. To the degree that I'm able, I also pursue my reading and my writing. Thank God for the books I brought with me from Sicily, my own, those you gave me, and those urged on me by a repentant Giovanni. There are also a few books here, an odd leftover lot.

Elise heard Jeanne's voice behind the door and stopped. She rose and unbarred it, let the servant in, and secured the door again.

Jeanne was a woman of forty with strong arms, a careworn but kindly face, and a steady gaze. Bred in hardship in the village, she was used to the count and his unsavory guests, but she also had a grievance against him. Her dead husband had once been a servant at the castle. Toward the end of his life when he was already ailing, he had forgotten some order of his master. In a drunken rage, the count had beaten him brutally with a rod. That day Jeanne had sworn revenge. She spoke now in a lowered voice in her usual straightforward manner.

"Madam, my son is below in the kitchens. If you finish your letter soon, he will take it with him tonight."

"Thank you, Jeanne, I shall. I can hardly wait to have our plan in place."

As Jeanne left, Elise returned at once to her writing. Hurriedly, she attached a simple code for Martin to use to send news of Edmond, and went on.

Dearest Martin, how fondly I think of our talks in the gardens of the Zisa. It seems we never know how fortunate we are until our lot has worsened. In Sicily, we dreamed of the old days at Windham with our mutually beloved friend. Here at Evremont, those days in Sicily now seem idyllic. It's small comfort to know Melisande has also been sorely disappointed. Gilles sends occasional missives to Bourne Castle, lying letters to the earl that describe our happy union. He also sends separate notes to Melisande in which he promises to renew their liaison. I know all this because he tells me, mocking both me and her. He has no intention of going to England, even less of inviting my aunt and uncle here. Nonetheless, he seems sure Melisande will not reveal his treachery. No doubt he understands the abject nature of her passion. He also has her letters. Even my uncle could not deny their truth.

When I am tempted to self-pity, I think of Queen Eleanor who after all these years is still her husband's captive. She too failed by supporting those she loved, her sons in their rebellion against their tyrant of a father. Most of all, what keeps me from despairing is the thought of Edmond and the love we shared. I hope the letter I left with you has helped to heal his pain.

As you may have surmised, I can only send these candid letters, not receive them. In your reply, please use the code I've enclosed to tell me any news you may have had of Edmond. Now my friend, I must finish. Forgive me, I haven't spoken a word about you or your fine work as a scholar. When I think of how in my youth I too wished to pursue the path of knowledge, it brings home to me how far I've fallen. Still, my life is not yet over. I shall not despair. And whatever my fate, you will always have my grateful friendship.

Alerted by voices outside the door, she ended her letter there. It was Jeanne again, discussing something with another servant. When they were finished, she entered and watched in silence as Elise sealed her letter and gave her some coins from the secret cache she had brought from Palermo. Jeanne left at once to take the letter to her son. He lived in the village but often traveled to Rouen. There, he would give the money and the letter to a merchant who did business in Sicily. When there was news of the letter's arrival, Elise would again pay an equal amount. Later that night, she thanked Jeanne again as she undressed for bed. She felt greatly relieved to have written the truth to an old friend.

*

Five months after sending that first secret letter, Elise had a reply from Martin. Using the code, he explained he had finally heard from Edmond. Martin's letter to him had been lost at Winchester, misplaced for months in a corner of the bishop's palace. When at last it arrived, it was too late to act. She was already married. Elise wrote Martin at once, amplifying the code she had created. When Martin replied, he used it to tell her Edmond had received her farewell letter and now knew that she had never wavered in her love. Reassured, Elise decided not to write Edmond again. However much it pained her, she felt it was better for him to begin a new life without her. She hoped he might find contentment even if she could not. By the time this second exchange with Martin was complete, another year had passed.

24

1186

When the cold weather at Evremont was at its worst, the Count de Vere left for Rouen as well as other destinations he kept secret. Late in March, he returned with a group of guests. Soon others joined them. Elise kept to her room, happy to be excluded from their revels. One moonlit night, unable to sleep, she happened to look out the narrow window of her chamber. As she did, she spotted a tall cloaked figure walking on the castle grounds. There was something familiar about his gait. As he turned in her direction, she saw it was Prior Gramont. Here, once again, was the third author of her misery, the man who had aided the count and her aunt in all their machinations. Since her arrival at Evremont, her husband had avoided mentioning the prior. In fact, she had learned all she needed to know about them both from Martin, above all that Gramont was the leader of a vicious band, a murderous brotherhood dedicated to a power called Abraxas.

She watched him approach the castle in the ghostly light. As he came nearer, she found his long face and brooding look increasingly repugnant. Finally, he disappeared beneath the entrance porch below her window. Two days later, the count's visitors were gone. Elise hoped the prior had left with them. Most likely he had, since that afternoon the count sent her a message asking her to dine alone with him that evening. Shortly after they sat down to eat, he told her he was ready to depart again. For the rest of the meal, their desultory talk was limited to household matters. As supper drew to a close, Gilles took an almost conciliatory tone.

"As usual, I can't be sure when I'll return. Mordran has enough money for three months if necessary. Jeanne, too, has what she needs for most domestic matters. I am also leaving this purse for you to use for your expenses. The harvest was good at Crecy last year."

As always, Elise stifled her anger when her husband spoke about the proceeds from her lands, most of which he squandered on his profligate adventures. This time she merely nodded, waiting to see if this small largesse was a sign of something more. Evidently it was not, although he had been less hostile as he ate and drank tonight. When they finished the meal, she spoke her parting words. "If that's all, I'll leave now to retire. I assume you'll be departing in the morning."

"Yes, of course. There's only one thing more. I'm told you wander a good deal about the grounds. I need to warn you to avoid the exterior wall and the ramparts below. Many sections of both are in need of repair. More important, Mordran tells me a vicious breed of rats has made a home in their vicinity. They say one bite can be deadly."

"I'll be sure to be careful," Elise said, wondering at this sudden interest in her welfare. "Please thank Mordran for the warning." Her intonation was flat with a hint of sarcasm. The count knew how much the hulking overseer and she disliked each other. On the way to her chamber, Elise found herself wishing her husband and the overseer might both be gone tomorrow, a thing that almost never happened.

*

The next morning when the count had left, Elise climbed to the top of the keep to view the land around the castle. It was spring, and in the newly planted fields and woods beyond them, the first tender patches of green had appeared. Moved by the promise of the season, Elise looked out to the distant blue hills on the horizon. As she did, she envisioned her freedom, vowing one day to regain it.

The previous year, to keep her sanity and be outdoors, she had planted a small garden by the walls of the old fortress. The plot was in a distant corner of the grounds where no one ever went. Jeanne had helped her begin by gathering seeds and plants. Outside in the sun and the wind, Elise felt less like a prisoner. Still, there was no one to share her pleasure—no one but a little brown puppy Jeanne had given her, the runt of a mongrel litter from the village. Elise called him by the Latin name for wizard, *Magus*, perhaps wishing he could magically transport her from this place.

The castle itself had been built two centuries before over foundations dating back to Roman times. Beside her garden, marked by the bases of missing pillars, lay the floor of what had once been a small chapel. The only other remnant of this build-ing was a piece of wall with a niche. Inside it there was a little statue of the virgin. Jeanne had found it, scarred and battered, in the castle ruins. In front of the statue, she had set a crude lamp, a cylinder of pierced metal that held a small candle. The count permitted no pious artifacts at Evremont. As a concession to Jeanne, the only servant he trusted not to steal from him, he allowed this small shrine in a spot he never frequented. As if in exorcism of this godless place, Jeanne had the habit of lighting the lamp every morning. Before working in her garden, Elise sometimes knelt before it and prayed to be delivered from her life at Evremont.

On the afternoon of the count's departure, she began her spring renewal, planting the seeds of herbs, vegetables, and flowers. Beyond the floor of the ruined chapel, a grassy slope led to the crumbling wall. That, in turn, overlooked the ram-parts. After working a while, she turned to trim a bit of hedge and caught a sudden movement in the corner of her eye. Some small creature had darted beneath a loose stone in the wall. Could it be one of the rats Gilles had mentioned? Not waiting to speculate, Magus barked loudly and dove after it. Unable to fol-low, she listened as his bark grew fainter. When she could no longer hear him, she became concerned. There was a gap in the wall near the spot where he had disappeared. As she approached it, a sudden wind whistled around the ramparts. Once it subsided, she could hear Magus's barking somewhere far below. She called his name several times, but he did not appear. If only she could see onto the ramparts! There were firm stones in the wall on both sides of the gap. Perhaps she could hold onto them and look below. Suppressing a fear of heights, she walked to the wall and took a firm hold of both sides. Leaning forward, she called "Magus!" three more times.

Her voice echoed eerily back, but there was no answer. Disappointed, she leaned out a bit farther and looked down. Startled by the drop, at least thirty feet to the bottom, she was suddenly dizzy. Then she felt something push her from behind. Losing her balance, she fell forward until a hand caught her arm and wrenched her back. The force was so great it threw her to the ground. As she collapsed, her head hit something hard.

When she opened her eyes, Mordran was standing above her, glaring and grotesque. Then Magus was between them, yelping and snapping at the interloper's feet. Carefully aiming a kick, the overseer sent the pet flying up against the wall. Afterward, Magus lay silent on the grass. Pulling herself up, Elise ran and gathered his limp, furry body in her arms. Full of pity and rage, she wanted to murder Mordran, to make him pay for attacking this innocent creature, the last repository of her starved affection.

"Brute! There was no need for that. For that matter, why are you here?"

Mordran looked at her with disdain, making her feel it was she who was intruding. "I saw you were in danger."

"And nearly pushed me to my death!"

The man grumbled something to himself, then spoke in a harsh voice. "You're wrong," he said, and something like a smile distended his thick lips. "I saved your life."

He moved menacingly toward her and added, "You were told to keep your distance from the walls."

She had never been so near the man. For the first time, she could see the deep scars on his wide neck, his balding head and flattened nose, the black hair on his massive chest and forearms. He had evidently been working on the grounds. His clothes were heavily stained, but the smell he exuded was more than sweat. It was like the smell of rotting meat.

In her arms, she now felt the first stirrings of Magus's breath. He was alive, thank God, despite this monster. She was still angry, but she knew it would not be wise to make a greater enemy of Mordran. She said nothing, and he shrugged, picked up a spade he had laid on the grass, and walked away. When he was gone, Elise set the dog on the ground. To her relief, she saw he could walk. But where had he been while she was calling him? Wherever it was, Mordran must have heard his barking there. Or had he already been spying on her? And if so, why? There must be some other reason to keep her from the ramparts. Nor was she certain the overseer had not deliberately pushed her, then changed his mind at the last moment. What was it he and the count were hiding? She would have to be very careful if she wished to find it.

*

The next day as she watched from a window in the keep, Elise was surprised to see Mordran on horseback riding through the castle gate. A chorus of howls from the guard dogs, so different from Magus's yelps, rose up around him, reminding her of the hazards of escape. Once past the barbican, her jailor set out on the road through the fields. Before long, both the road and the rider disappeared into the woods.

An hour later, Jeanne told her the stable boy had said Mordran would be gone until tomorrow. This would be her best chance to find whatever was concealed beneath the walls. Mindful of everything Martin had told her about the cult, she decided to investigate. Nor were her motives entirely unselfish.

What she learned might not only be used to expose the cult. It could also help her gain her freedom.

That afternoon, she set out with the sack she used for gardening. She had already observed the beginning of some stairs descending from the wall onto the level of the ramparts. Now, on her way to the wall, she knelt before the little shrine and asked to be protected in her search. Next, she took the lamp, which had a handle on its side. Jeanne had already lit the candle. In her bag, in addition to her trowel, Elise had a second candle and a metal knife. She also had a small whetstone and dried moss for tinder if the lamp went out.

Anxious to begin, she took the path to the left along the wall until she reached the stairway. Looking down, she was once again shocked by the height. The stones of the staircase were full of weeds and needed mortaring in places, but it appeared that none were missing. She would not let her fear of heights deter her. With the sack slung over her shoulder and the lamp in hand, she began the descent with a good deal of trepidation. Step by step, she clung to the wall, never looking down. Exposed on three sides, she felt the wind rise up and heard the cawing of the crows above her with a rush of fear. A collision with one could send her to her death. Calming herself as best she could, she continued step by step. She was shaking when she reached the bottom. Leaning against the wall, she closed her eyes and breathed deeply, then opened them and looked out at the distant hills. She was now on the lower level. Here, a narrow, roughly paved walk led around the ramparts. She took it back to the right in the direction of her garden.

After some thirty paces, the path became overgrown with weeds and brambles. She set the lamp down, took out her knife, and, with some difficulty, cut through the worst parts of the growth. As she moved forward, she was forced to repeat the operation twice. The last time, she heard angry male voices rising from below. Were they searching for her? Her heart beat fast as she listened. No, thank God, they were merely two guards arguing about whose watch was next.

Reassured, she went on toward a small stone arch some thirty feet ahead. Nearing it, she saw it was the entrance to a vaulted tunnel. She hesitated, then spurred on by the desperation of her present life, entered the passage, using her lamp to light her way. The tunnel sloped gradually downward. As it did, it became narrower and the air inside grew thinner. She prayed only that the passage led somewhere. She was beginning to gasp when she felt a small stirring in the air. There must be a source ahead. By now, she had begun to lose all sense of time. Luckily, Jeanne had agreed to guard her chamber from the other servants, pretending her mistress was not well.

Now she came to an opening on her right, a rectangular doorway of some kind. Unlike the tunnel, it was not made of separate stones but carved from the great mass of limestone beneath Evremont. Incised over it was a crude image, a man seated cross-legged with the antlers of a stag. She knew it once as a figure of local legend, Cernunnos, a forest deity worshipped by the ancient Gauls. This must be the entrance to his grotto. Lowering her lamp, she saw there was a stairway leading downward. She was not tempted to take it. The stairs were too steep, the blackness below too forbidding. Instead, she moved ahead through the tunnel. Finally, after some two-dozen paces, she saw a barely perceptible glow ahead. Before long the passage opened up into a large, high-ceilinged room. At the top of the wall to the left, a faint light emanated from a narrow shaft. This must also be the source of the air.

The large chamber was cut out of solid limestone; four thick piers merely seemed to support the ceiling. Amid the smell of damp and mold, Elise detected another more repellant odor but could not identify it. Frightened but curious, she explored in the circle of light cast by her lamp. In the middle of the space between the piers, she discovered a marble altar on a broad stone platform. On the facing side, there was a striking figure in relief. Sculpted in the style of ancient Rome, it showed a man with a billowing cloak and a short tunic. He was wrestling a bull which he held by the horns.

The image was vaguely familiar, but Elise could not recall where she had seen it. Now, lowering her lamp to the floor, she found traces of footsteps in the dust. They seemed to be quite recent. Not long ago, she had seen the prior. Had he been here for a gathering of the brotherhood? Martin had told her about the meetings of the cult. She must look for evidence. Moving to the rear, she saw the room ended like a chapel in a rounded apse. Inside it, there was a high pedestal in the antique style. On it were marks where the feet of a statue had once stood. A crude image was painted on the wall behind it: a beak-headed figure in armor whose legs were made of snakes. He held a whip in one hand and a shield in the other. It was the symbol of Abraxas. Martin had described it to her in Palermo. Here the colors, red, black, and ochre, were clearly new. This was no antique image but a symbol painted by the cult.

Lowering her light, Elise examined the floor where it met the walls. Behind the pedestal, she found a small heap of debris. Setting the lamp down, she sorted the objects in the pile. There were clay shards from broken bowls, parts of blades made of chipped flint, and hollow reeds sharpened at one end; the same things Martin had found at the clearing of the stones. And what about the rest? Feeling a growing sense of dread, Elise went back to the altar. The marble relief had been yellowed by centuries of grime, but the slab on the altar was even darker. It was the color of porphyry, a deep purplish brown. As she approached it, she became aware of the repellant odor she had smelled before. Lowering her lamp, she saw its surface was covered with dark purple drips and stains.

And then she understood. This was the altar on which the cult sacrificed its victims. The odor was the smell of blood; both the slab and the platform were steeped in it. Recoiling, she picked up the lamp. As she did, the candle inside flickered. With a glance, she saw it was almost burnt out. Forgetting the blood, she set her lamp on the altar and reached into her bag. There she found the trowel, the knife, the whetstone, the dried moss. Everything but the thing she needed! Frantic, she emptied the sack onto the altar.

There was no candle. She followed the seam of the bag to the corner. There she found a hole. The spare candle must have fallen out. It could be anywhere between this chamber and the upper level.

At that moment, the candle sputtered out, leaving her in total darkness. Resisting panic, she recalled the faint shaft of daylight at the entrance to the chamber. She looked toward it and found it was gone. It must already be late in the day. She would have to feel her way back in the dark. Faced with the task, she felt a moment of despair. Paralyzed, she sat down on the platform, too frightened even to pray.

Then she was suddenly angry. She would not let this evil place defeat her! Standing, she gathered her things and restored them to her bag. She must leave no evidence. The lamp! She had almost forgotten it. She reached for it frantically, struck it, and sent it flying. She heard the metal slide, then stop. Searching for it with her fingers, she found it poised on the edge of the slab. Then she tied off the corner hole, put the lamp in the sack, and hung it over her shoulder. Ready to start, she took a first step in the dark, then a second—and crashed onto her hands and knees. She had forgotten she was on the platform. Still wearing her bag, she stood slowly, grateful to find she had broken no bones.

Doubly wary now, she moved gradually toward the tunnel entrance. She had to think before every move. Deprived of the ability to see, she found her other senses more acute. The smell of the blood was worse, and she heard a faint rustling on the floor. Had the count told her the truth about the rats? Groping her way toward the entrance, she finally found the beginning of the tunnel. How far was the door with the image of Cernunnos? Twenty paces? Twenty-five? She would have to be careful to avoid the stairs. Inside the tunnel, the dark seemed even blacker, the way she imagined blindness. There were cobwebs too. Had they formed so quickly, or had she taken a wrong turn? She felt something by her foot, then a nibble at her ankle. Kicking out at it, she barely suppressed a scream. If she had heard Magus's barking, she too might be heard.

A slope in the floor suggested she had reached the stairway to the grotto. It would be to her left. Avoiding it, she moved forward but somehow miscalculated. Her left foot stepped into empty space. Losing her balance, she plunged down the stone stairs. One after another, they struck her as she fell. At the bottom, she lay stunned in the blackness, afraid to move. What if she had broken a leg? She could die here in the dark, the only thing worse than being found by the count or Mordran. Slowly, she felt her arms and legs. She hurt all over, but none of her limbs seemed impaired. She murmured a grateful prayer and reached for the wall beside the stairs. It was slimy with mold, but she clung to it anyway. By now, she felt completely sightless. Holding on to the wall, she stood up. Her right hip and leg were both aching. Could she walk? She took three steps slowly, inching forward, and found she could. But she could not afford another fall.

Trapped in the airless space, she became conscious of an odor much worse than the smell of the blood. It was the same putrid scent she had noted on Mordran. Now, perhaps in delayed reaction to her fall, she felt faint. To keep from collapsing, she sat on the floor and waited for the dizziness to pass. When it did, the pain in her leg made it difficult to rise. She crawled forward in search of a support but found none. The smell had now become horrendous. Reaching out, she touched something small and cold but slightly soft. Revolted, she pulled away and tried to stand and run. Then she stopped. To flee now would be pointless cowardice. Was she not here to learn the truth? She extended her hand toward the object. Stifling disgust, she touched its separate parts, four fingers and a thumb, all stiff with death. She had found the latest victim of the cult. Mordran must have been at work disposing of the body yesterday when he heard Magus barking. This grotto was cut from solid limestone, an impossible place for a grave. He had not yet been able to bury the body elsewhere.

These thoughts flew through her head while she sat beside the corpse. Its reeking odor reminded her of her task. She must be certain this death was the work of the cult. In Palermo, in one of their conversations at the Zisa, Martin had told her about the markings on the victim's bodies. Except for this hellish blackness, she could have seen them at a glance. Now there was only one way.

Steeling herself, she found the hand, then followed the arm to the shoulder. There were no marks. She moved to the breast—it was a female—and just below felt a small, round puncture in the clammy flesh. Soon there were more on the stomach and arms. Sick from the smell, she worked quickly to be done. Moving onto the thighs, she found more punctures but also deeper cuts, wide gaps in the flesh that would never close. Then she felt something crawling. Were they insects? No, maggots, of course! Despite herself, she screamed and shook them off her hand.

Summoning all her strength, she rose without support. Staggering, she found her way to the foot of the stairs. Her bruised body hurt more with each move. Ignoring the pain, she dragged herself slowly upward. Along the way, she found the whetstone. It had fallen from her bag. She checked to make sure she had the rest of her things. She must leave no traces. She hoped they would think a member of the cult had dropped the candle. Reaching the landing, she stood again, aching but ready to make her way back through the tunnel. She was sure now of two things: the cult had a new home at Evremont and she must find a way to leave. First, however, she had to escape this wretched darkness.

Holding on to the wall to the right, she felt her way into the passage. Now it was uphill and much harder. She walked slowly at first, then more quickly. At last, ignoring her pain, she ran. Fleeing the darkness, the stench, the death, she struck the tunnel's stone walls and tore her sleeves. She no longer cared. Still, the tunnel seemed endless. Panicking, she tripped on a stone and fell again. There was a sudden sharp pain in her knee. Ignoring it, she dragged herself up and lurched forward.

At last, she burst out into the twilight. A few steps ahead, something small and pale lay on the path: the candle. In the sky above it where a turquoise glow still lingered, the evening star shone brighter than Elise had ever seen it.

25

1187

In one important way, Martin's thoughts about his Muslim colleague proved correct. Several months after their meeting, Khalil al-Din and he began a scholarly collaboration. They started by translating three sections of Aristotle's *Ethics* into Latin. For the first part, they used a Greek manuscript for a source, for the second, an Arabic translation. For the third, they found versions in both languages and used them to correct each other. Once the translation was finished, they worked together on the commentary. Alone or apart, the two rarely consulted their fellow scholars. Khalil and he loved the Hellenes for their own sake; most of their colleagues employed the ancients' philosophic methods to elucidate the doctrines of religion.

Queried on the subject, Father Heraklios was tactful. "I see the merit in both approaches. The one is approved by the Church, the other of great interest to more recent scholars. In fact, I feel sure our young king will welcome studies of the great philosophers in their own right."

In the next year and a half, proceeding on that premise, Khalil and Martin presented King William with two works, one based on the *Ethics*, the other on Aristotle's *Poetics*. Dedicated to the monarch, the books included many passages in Greek, one of the several languages William read. Some months after the second work had been accepted by the king, Father Heraklios invited Martin to his alcove. There, amid shelves filled with scrolls and unbound manuscripts, he gave Martin the good news. "It seems that, inspired by the presentation of your second book, the king has read a portion of your first and been quite pleased with it."

"The *Ethics*, you mean?"

"Yes, or at least your commentary on it. He says he hopes to read both works when time permits. That means, I suppose, when he's neither hunting nor dining nor visiting his harem." From time to time, Heraklios lifted the cloak of courtesy he considered proper to his role and bared the cynic underneath. "Or, for that matter, devising disastrous campaigns against Greece and Egypt."

Martin too was aware of the monarch's faults. One of them had brought about Elise's downfall. The two campaigns in question had yielded ignominious results. The naval attack on Egypt had ended in immediate defeat. The short-lived war on the mainland of Greece had included the infamous sack of Thessalonica, a debacle in which the Sicilian army murdered, raped, or pillaged thousands of innocent victims. As it happened, the king had not taken a personal part in either of these campaigns. That fact, however, merely reinforced the rumors of his cowardice.

On the other hand, William had his virtues. "At least our monarch reads," Martin said, "in four languages when it suits him. And he pays our stipends faithfully."

"A point well made, my good deacon. In truth, we are much better off than scholars at most courts," Heraklios conceded. "Now for my other news. I hope soon to receive a number of important volumes, copies of books from an old monastery on the Greek mainland. I have been communicating with the abbot."

"Rare texts?" Martin queried. "Are there works by Aristotle?"

"Yes, along with Herodotus and Democritus, and best of all, dialogues of Plato. You've seen the two translated from the Greek by Henry Aristippus?"

"The *Phaedo* and the *Meno*? Yes, I've read them both with great interest. In fact, Khalil al-Din and I have recently taken a much greater interest in Plato."

"I'm glad to hear it. At the time of the former King William, the man who translated those dialogues was one of our greatest scholars. Sadly, it did him little good. The victim of a vile intrigue, he died in prison blind and maimed. In that respect, too, we are more fortunate today. Here in Sicily, these years of our young king's reign have been among the happiest the realm has known."

"Let us hope they continue that way," Martin said. "As for the books, do you have any idea when they might arrive?"

"Within a few months, I believe. When they do, you and Khalil al-Din will be among the first to know. Meanwhile, I think it best not to mention the matter to Diodorus. I've begun to be suspicious of his work."

Diodorus was an older scholar who had felt the pagan Greeks were his particular domain before Khalil and Martin took them up. Although puzzled by Heraklios's remark, Martin decided to inquire no further, and the two men parted.

Meanwhile, he was anxious to tell Khalil the news about the books. Today, however, was Friday, the day on which Khalil, like most Muslim men, attended the sermon at the mosque. Martin had no idea which mosque or where. The two seldom spoke of their faiths or their lives beyond their work. Theirs was a world of thought, its locus pagan Greece, but within the confines of that world, they had now become quite close.

Courteous and kind, animated and reserved by turns, Khalil al-Din combined a poet's insight with deep philosophic understanding. Perhaps inevitably, Martin had grown quite fond of his collaborator as time passed. In truth, he had become much more than fond. In recent weeks, he had been forced to recognize the truth. At night, as he lay among his snoring fellow-clerics longing for a fresh breeze from the harbor, it was no longer Edmond but Khalil al-Din who occupied his thoughts. And therein lay the danger. This time, much more was involved than a youthful infatuation. For the two scholars, thoughts and words were all, their vocation and their passion, the path to the knowledge of the past, the key to present and future learning.

In a world dedicated to reason, there was no room for unruly desire. Or so he told himself, but even as they worked and talked, disputed and conferred, his feelings continued to undermine him.

They were still fresh in his mind when, the following day, he rose early to walk in the cool morning air. Despite the hour, many people were about: peasants with produce for the market, servants on errands for their masters, tradesmen en route to their shops. Caught up in his thoughts, he barely glanced at them. Nearing the cathedral square, he heard the cacophony of hawkers' cries in several tongues; he had entered the hubbub of a market day. Needing quiet to think, he skirted the cathedral and turned into a narrow street that led beyond it. After a while, he found himself nearing a church he knew well. As he came closer, he felt fate must have led him here. It was the parish of the priest whose sermon had helped him overcome his guilt about the cult so long ago.

The church had a single large, round-arched central portal. Martin entered through the smaller door cut into the large one. Inside, he was greeted by the reassuringly familiar smells of candlewax and incense. Knowing this was the day when the priest heard confessions, Martin waited his turn. When it came, he parted the curtain and knelt inside the darkened cubicle. At first, despite the protection of anonymity, he found it difficult to speak. He started by telling the priest he was a deacon. Then, conquering his fear, he used the words he had prepared while waiting.

"Father, I am fond of a man in a way the Church forbids."

There was a short, unnerving silence before the priest responded. His voice was low and sounded oddly weary. "Have you had carnal relations with this person?"

"No, but I have contemplated them. He is a close colleague. Our work deals with thoughts and ideas."

"And your desire troubles you, imperiling your work?"

"Yes," Martin said, gratified by the priest's understanding.

"What I say next," the confessor continued, "may surprise you. The world is both cruel and dangerous for men with feelings like your own. You have read Leviticus, perhaps, that book of the Bible which fixes the penalty for lying with another man as death. Yet elsewhere in the Old Testament, as in the tale of Jonathan and David, the love of one man for another is not condemned. Even the great Saint Augustine had such a liaison in his youth. In his *Confessions,* he called it sweeter than all the rest. In later, more benighted centuries, rulers like the Emperor Justinian and Louis, the son of Charlemagne, decreed castration, death, and even burning at the stake as punishment for what they called the sin of Sodom. Nearer to our time, Anselm, Archbishop of Canterbury, condemned the sodomy prevalent at the English court. Oddly enough, his own impassioned letters show a more than ordinary love for some of his disciples."

Here, perhaps unsure of the effect of his words, the priest paused. Then, as if in haste to be done, he concluded. "In our own day, the Church has become more lenient. Not long ago, the Lateran Council rejected new and harsher punishments for clerics guilty of this sin. Nonetheless, this tide of clemency could turn at any time and swell into a storm of persecution."

The priest's words had indeed surprised Martin. They almost seemed a kind of *apologia* for a thing the world had long considered an abomination.

"Are you saying, father, that I might pursue my feelings without guilt?"

"No, certainly not. Only that your feelings are not sinful in themselves. So far, from what you say, God's grace has prevented your straying. Wisely, you have sought spiritual aid before succumbing. Has your colleague shown any feelings like your own?"

Instinctively protective, Martin answered no.

"Then you are that much safer. Guiltless until now, you must suppress all such desires in the future. If you succumb, there may be no turning back. The torments of hell await those who surrender to this vice. If you cannot stifle your desire, you must end the relation."

"But my work is dependent on my colleague."

His confessor's voice rose for an instant, then shrank into an urgent whisper. "What good is your work if you lose your eternal soul? If you value it, surmount your lust. Think also of the shame, the disgrace to you and your colleague should you be discovered in this sin. Fasting and prayer will strengthen your resolve. The temptation can be overcome."

How easy that is to say, thought Martin. Rebelling, he forgot where he was and nearly shouted, "How can you know that, father?"

There was another pause, longer this time. When the priest spoke, his voice was full of a chilling resolve. "Because I myself have done so. I bear the same affliction. With the help of prayer and great effort, I have resisted it all these years, remaining chaste in the eyes of God and man."

His confessor's admission left Martin in confusion. Once he had heard it, the rest of the priest's words flew by, scarcely lodging in his brain; phrases like self-abnegation, chastisement of the flesh, and constant vigilance. In truth, he could hardly bear to think about the life the priest had led. When at last he heard the Latin formula of absolution, Martin stood, parted the curtain, and left. As he walked to the door, he was followed by the eyes of waiting penitents who must have heard him raise his voice. Entering the street, Martin was blinded for a moment by the sunlight. Too disturbed to return to his residence, he began walking aimlessly. As he did, several passersby stared. Was the rebellion he felt in his heart apparent in his face?

Soon, recalling his confessor's questions, he realized he had failed to admit the true nature of his feelings. His love for Khalil was already a full-blown passion, a hunger that grew inside him every day. Nor had he told his confessor the truth about his colleague. He had, in fact, come to suspect Khalil might harbor feelings like his own. A few weeks ago, they had spent two hours beside each other working at deciphering a faded Greek manuscript. At last, they were able to translate a passage that had formerly eluded them, the key to all the rest. In the midst of their scholarly joy, when the sympathy between them was the greatest, Khalil had stood without a word and left. Angry at first, then puzzled, Martin began to suspect that his colleague had fled from an excess of feeling.

The following day was Palm Sunday, the beginning of Holy Week. As he had planned, Martin attended Mass in the cathedral, a splendid ceremony with much chanting and celebratory hymns sung by a choir. All through the Mass, he prayed earnestly for guidance. By the time it was over, he had undergone another change of heart. His confessor was a kindred spirit, a fellow sufferer who understood his plight. Surely God had spoken to him through his voice.

He was already freer than most clerics, a respected royal scholar, secure in his profession and without financial need. Was not his life in Palermo rich enough without this dangerous indulgence? It would be what the Greeks called hubris to desire more. As the cathedral bells tolled, Martin heeded their call. He would do as his confessor had advised.

*

As he entered the dormitory of his residence, he was feeling a kind of moral exultation. Crossing the room, he spotted something on his bed. At the same time, a young cleric new to Palermo approached him and addressed him in a timid voice.

"A messenger brought that letter half . . . no, an hour ago, from Father Her . . . "

"Heraklios," Martin prompted, guessing the young man was intimidated by his position as a royal scholar.

"Yes, that was it," the newcomer said, losing some of his shyness. "The messenger said Father Heraklios thought it might be important."

Martin thanked him, and when he was gone, picked up the packet. As usual, Heraklios had guessed correctly. The missive was from Elise, the first in over a year. He sat down on his bed at once and read.

My dearest friend, I have discovered the place where the brother-hood meets at Evremont. Indeed, I did so many months ago. Since then, I have been afraid to write the truth. If, despite all my precautions, my husband intercepted the letter, it might be fatal for me and equally dangerous for you. Remember, Prior Gramont has no idea of how much you know about him and his vile cult. Should he find out, it would make you the object of his vengeance. As I know all too well, he has close associates in Palermo. It was they who informed him of my situation at the palace. That said, that warning given, I am writing nonetheless. I can no longer bear to think I might die a victim of my husband or the prior and leave the truth untold.

Here it is then, simply. I have found an ancient shrine at Evremont carved out of the mass of living limestone underneath the castle. The interior is a kind of pagan chapel with a bloodstained Roman altar at its center. On its front, there is a carving of a figure known as Mith-ras, a god with a cap shown strangling a bull. I know the name because I found the same image in one of the few books here at the chateau. On the rear wall of this space, there was a crude painting of the same beak-headed symbol of Abraxas you saw on the banner at the clearing of the stones. There were primitive implements, too, like those you found buried there. Last, and most terrible of all, in an even deeper rock-cut grotto, I discovered the body of a female victim of the cult.

It was all too familiar, thought Martin, all but the shrine of Mithras, the favorite god of the Roman legions, soldiers who killed a bull and drank its blood to give them courage. The prior had found another ancient site, this one conveniently owned by his cohort in crime, the Count de Vere. In place of the Church he disdained, the prior had again chosen Abraxas, the awful power that Basilides the Gnostic had proclaimed, a power greater than God or Satan.

And now Elise, with a courage that Martin had failed of as a boy, had discovered the cult's crimes. But at what price? Knowing the danger she must be in, he read the rest anxiously. At last, in tone of near-desperation, she revealed her intentions.

I pray that when I write you next I will no longer be imprisoned here. Thus far, neither Gilles nor his overseer are aware I know the truth about their gatherings. If they were, I feel certain my life would be forfeit. I have an ally, however, in Jeanne, my servant. She has her own reasons to detest the count. With her help and her son's, I hope to leave this place. When I am safely away, I will tell the authorities about the cult and all I have discovered here. Pray for me, then, and keep my welfare in your heart.

Having finished, Martin attempted to gauge the import of Elise's letter. Was her discovery the beginning of the downfall of the cult? Or would it only result in her death? If she were harmed, he would never be able to forgive himself. It was he who had told her all he knew about the cult.

That night, using the code they had developed, he wrote Elise, avoiding any hint about the cult or her discovery, both of which would be too dangerous for her. He also avoided something else, a recent letter from Brother Ambrose. Writing as usual about the abbey and the state of Canon Thomas's health, his mentor had also given him another bit of news. Edmond Preston, heir to Preston Manor, had married a young woman from Fenbury. Her name was Aeline. Like the Prestons themselves, she came from mixed Norman and Saxon blood.

Clearly, Edmond had succumbed to family pressure. Sooner or later, Elise would learn about it, but Martin would not be the one to tell her. Her life at present was difficult enough. Instead, he prayed for both his friends, but knowing the danger around her, especially Elise.

26

It was a warm summer day, and Martin and Khalil al-Din had been at work all afternoon. Three months had passed during which Martin had strictly adhered to the advice of his confessor. Difficult though it was, he had begun to feel safe inside the carapace he had constructed to contain his feelings.

Meanwhile, the rare codices promised by Heraklios had come. He and Khalil had a copy of one, a dialogue by Plato called the *Symposium.* The work narrated a discussion taking place during a banquet in ancient Athens. Since the text was in Greek, they made notes as they read it aloud to help in their eventual translation into Latin. They had just reached the part where Socrates repeats the allegory of the wise woman Diotoma. Enthralled by the tale of Love's quest for Truth through Beauty, they decided to go on reading despite the lateness of the hour. When they came to the end, there was no sound in the room. Martin sensed they were alone among the books. From where he sat, he could see even Heraklios was gone.

Abruptly deprived of Plato's words, Martin felt strangely dislocated, thrust back from ancient times into the present. As he and his colleague sat in silence, the dusty odor of the books around them blended with the scent of sandalwood, a perfume Khalil wore in the summer. For the moment, nothing seemed quite real.

At last, clearing his throat, Khalil spoke. "Are men in England familiar with the love that Phaedrus, Pausanias, and Socrates himself discuss so freely in this dialogue?"

Surprised, and wary at the import of the question, Martin was more than reluctant to answer. In all their time as collaborators, they had never spoken of this subject.

"What kind of love do you mean, exactly?"

"The love of one male for another," Khalil said. There was no expression on his face.

Martin paused, taking time to choose his words. "Men are familiar with it, certainly, as they are in every land, but as with your faith, I believe, it is forbidden."

"Is it never practiced for that reason?"

"No, like most forbidden things, it is practiced nonetheless. As many at the courts of Europe are aware, Prince Richard, the heir to the English throne, prefers men to women."

"And is he disapproved of for that reason?"

Unnerved by the interrogation, Martin tried to strike a lighter note. "My friend, are you mimicking Socrates's method with these questions?"

Khalil laughed. "Perhaps I am, all the same, will you not indulge me with an answer?"

"I will, since you insist. Yes, even with a king," Martin admitted, "men disapprove. These are different times from those of Socrates and Alcibiades."

"And you yourself, do you disapprove?"

Khalil's voice had become disturbingly intense. Martin felt endangered by the question. He knew what he thought, but it was not what his confessor had advised. Nor did he know his colleague's feelings in the matter. Nearing panic, he temporized. "I myself? I wonder why you ask. How would you reply if I asked you the same question?"

"My response would not be in words."

Unthinkingly, Martin said, "What would it be, then?" Too late, he saw the question might seem a provocation. Before he had time to retract it, the answer came. Turning to him, Khalil took Martin's face in his hands and kissed him firmly on the mouth. Then, with great dignity, he stood and left.

Once he had gone, Martin sat unmoving. Khalil's act had stunned him by its suddenness and force. Whatever it meant, it was no kiss of mere friendship. After a while, he rolled up the parchment with their notes and put it in his bag. Then he picked up the manuscript of the *Symposium* and took it to his carrel. He felt sure a few days would pass before Khalil returned, and he was glad. In a moment, the resolve Martin had clung to for three months had been undone. He too needed time to think.

*

As he had expected, Khalil was absent for the next three days. On the third morning, Father Heraklios asked Martin to go again to Isaac's shop. Grateful for a diversion, he arrived there late in the afternoon. After greeting the scholar, he picked out the papers and pigments. Today, there was no mention of cameos or Abraxas.

Perceptive as always, Isaac appeared to sense his mood. "You seem preoccupied today, young scholar."

"I am, my learned friend. You must excuse my taciturnity."

"Of course," Isaac said, and the two parted cordially.

Afterward, free to wander, Martin took the direction toward the harbor through the Muslim quarter. Once called by the Arabs al-Halisa, the place of the elect, it was now simply known as the Kalsa. Martin had not been there for several months. As he entered the district, he was as always fascinated. He passed first through a bustling market with its shouted cries and haggling, then entered a labyrinth of narrow streets and whitewashed walls where silence gradually replaced the noise. After a while, the silence was only occasionally interrupted by the closing of a gate or distant crying of an infant.

As Martin walked, his thoughts kept returning to Khalil al-Din. His colleague's kiss had awakened his deepest yearnings. Had it been a mere impulse, a rare lapse into reckless indulgence? Although he had come to love him, Martin knew very little about his fellow scholar's life beyond their work. At first, he had assumed that like all Muslim men of a certain age, Khalil was married, but as time passed, the scholar never mentioned a wife or children. Nor did Martin ask, preferring to keep the world they shared apart. Was he now ready to enter his colleague's world? Was the scholar ready to admit him?

At forty-one, Khalil al-Din was both his mentor and his senior by twelve years, a man of fastidious habits, full of probity and honor. Would he be willing to betray the trust entailed by their connection? From what Martin knew of him, it seemed unlikely. When Khalil returned, they would simply ignore the incident or perhaps make some scholarly joke about the influence of the Greeks. They had the joy of their work, their success as collaborators, the amazing good fortune of being royal scholars. It would be madness to upset that balance.

Martin was so full of these thoughts that he failed to take note of his direction. He saw now he was lost. Unsure where to turn, he continued down a narrow street that ended in a tiny square. There was a fountain attached to one wall, a wooden bench against another. Tired of walking, he sat down on the bench. As he did, a gray-bearded man in a turban appeared, dipped a cup in the water, and took a drink. Martin could read perhaps two hundred words of Arabic, but he knew few phrases of the spoken tongue. Addressing the man, he used them to little effect. Resorting to pantomime, he tried to explain he was lost. Seeming to understand, the man indicated the proper direction. Bowing in thanks, Martin set out again. This time, he tried to take note of his way.

Soon he came to an alley he thought he recognized. He took it to the next street, turned right, and ended in an impasse. Here, half-concealed in the dark opening of a door, two bearded men glared angrily at him. Startled, he drew back and fled. As he rounded the corner, he remembered how odd his black cleric's robe and blond hair and beard must look inside this quarter. After a few more turns down narrow streets, he found himself back in the little square. The old man was now seated on the bench. Meanwhile, the light was growing dimmer. Most of the houses were at least two stories high; the day would soon turn to evening in these shadowed streets. Belatedly, he realized he was hungry. Twice, drifting from ovens in inner courtyards, he had smelled the enticing aromas of cooking food. The sounds he heard now were mysterious and muted, faint women's voices deep inside their dwellings.

Seeing the stranger again, the old man shrugged his shoulders and approached the fountain. Facing away, he washed himself methodically. Just as he finished, Martin heard a voice cry out. The cry turned into a wail, the wail into a song. It was the muezzin calling all Muslims to evening prayer. Hearing the sound, the old man took a folded cloth out of his bag. Kneeling on it, he began his prostrations. Knowing he must be facing east, Martin took note of the direction south, his way home. At the same time, he knew how difficult it was to keep a straight course in these winding streets. Once it grew darker, it would be even more hopeless.

As the old man prayed, Martin wondered why he was here and not inside a mosque. Whatever the reason, he felt painfully like an intruder. Then an idea came to him. It was the merest chance, but it seemed a possibility. He had been told that Khalil al-Din had a house in the Kalsa. If he could find it, his colleague could show him the way back. When the man finished, Martin approached him again. In his best Arabic accent, he said "Khalil al-Din."

Looking attentive, the man spoke a few words and shrugged again. He had heard part of a name, it seemed, but not enough to be of help. Frantically, Martin struggled to recall the rest. Khalil seldom spoke his full name, nor did he use it in their writings. Still, Martin had heard it and seen it written more than once. Why could he not recall it? The old man had folded his cloth and was ready to leave.

Desperate, Martin spoke again. "Khalil al-Din—" The man shook his head. Martin struggled for the rest. Then, all at once, it came. "Khalil al-Din Hassan bin Ali!"

Even in the gloom of the darkening square, he could see the recognition in the old man's eyes. Nodding, he murmured something and gestured for Martin to follow. After that, they moved silently through the streets. Gradually, the salt-smell of the air informed him they were closer to the harbor. At last, they stood before a portal in a whitewashed wall. Smiling, the old man turned toward him and knocked on the darkly painted wooden door. As he did, Martin's heart began to beat faster. After what seemed an endless wait, the door creaked open. A bearded man, broad-shouldered and of average height, stood in the entrance. The old man murmured something to him and motioned Martin forward.

The man who had opened the door, evidently a servant of some kind, looked inquiringly at Martin, waiting for him to speak. For some reason he could not. Just as the man was about to close the door, he said the name. "Khalil al-Din Hassan bin Ali." Once he had, the servant nodded, thanked the old man, and watched him disappear into the street. Opening the door, he led Martin into a little forecourt. In heavily accented French, the man asked him to wait. The next few moments were the worst. Then the inner door swung open and Khalil al-Din was there.

At first, the scholar merely stared. Next, as if to make sure they were quite alone, he strode to the outer door, barred it, and turned to Martin. Only then did he speak. "So you have found me. I prayed to be shown the way and you have come. I shall resist no longer."

As he spoke, there were tears in his colleague's eyes. Taking Martin by the shoulders, he kissed him in the Arab manner on both cheeks. A third kiss on the forehead was like a benediction. Without another word, he led Martin into the house. As the door closed behind them, Martin sensed that his life was about to change forever. He felt a curious blend of fear, excitement, and relief. In the next moment, he realized he had failed to pray for help while lost. Now at last he prayed, but only to thank God for having let him lose his way.

PART THREE

The Fallen City

1189~1192

27

1189

Windham, England

"You've the look of a knight who's ready to embark, my boy."

Seated fully armed on a fine new horse, Edmond smiled at Dickon Breslin's words. The two men had met in the courtyard of Bourne Castle on a warm September day. It was now a year and a half since the Pope had issued his call to holy war. The previous spring, King Henry and Philip of France had suspended their quarrels and begun to prepare for war along with other Christian rulers who had been inspired to take the cross.

"Not yet a knight, Master Breslin, but I hope to be before too long." In fact, he knew it would be spring before things at the manor were settled, and he would be free to cross the channel and join the Christian army. Thanks to Earl Desmond's generous support, he and his gear were ready in advance. "First, however, I need you to approve my equipment."

"Well, better dismount then, sir."

Edmond did as asked, stepping onto the mounting block a servant had provided. Armored and weapon-laden as he was, he could hardly have done so otherwise. Next, moving to a corner of the busy castle yard, he unfastened the parts of his equipment one by one, handing each to Dickon for inspection: first helmet, shield, long sword, and lance, then gauntlets, chainmail hauberk, axe, and mace. As each was proven worthy, Dickon passed it to a serving man for temporary storage in the castle armory. Next, he moved on to the gear on Edmond's horse, then to the mule behind, slowly examining its burden of supplies. Finally, he turned to Edmond. "I find no fault with any part of your equipment, sir."

"I'm glad to hear it," Edmond said, grateful for Dickon's expert approval.

"As well you might be. The Earl's armorers have done their best by you. God speed you, my boy. My heart will go with you to the Holy Land."

"I thank you for that sir, and for your patience in the past. I came late to you as a pupil, but you made up for the default."

"Not I, but you yourself, my lad, with hard work and persistence. I know very well the years have kept you here against your will. Your time has come at last, and well deserved, I say."

Standing by Dickon in the sunlight, Edmond reddened at his instructor's words. He was past thirty now, but he still blushed when complimented. There had been so little praise in his childhood and youth.

"It has been long in coming, well deserved or not. In truth, I have you and the earl to thank for everything."

"And you shall make us proud, I know. Now, before an old soldier lets his feelings run away with him, let's part. It has made me young again to know you all these years."

Equally stirred by emotion, Edmond reached out to embrace his teacher. Dickon would be leaving on the morrow on a mission for the earl that might well last until the summer. Who knew if or when the two would meet again? Despite his apparent robustness, Dickon was well past sixty, afflicted by injuries suffered four decades ago in the second holy war, the campaign during which he had first met the earl.

When they had parted, Edmond rode back to the manor through fields full of the scent of freshly gathered hay. Looking up at the cloudless sky, he thought of all the events, great and small, that had finally led him to this moment. It might never have come about had not the Muslim general Saladin conquered Jerusalem two years before, conquered it almost at once when, unable to defend the holy city, the Christians who held it had exchanged it for their lives. Outraged, Pope Gregory had called upon the kings and knights of Christendom to wage another holy war, the third in a century.

Few in Christendom were ready at that point, least of all Henry of England despite his announced intentions. Now things had changed. Traveling overland, Frederick Barbarossa, the famed German emperor, had already departed for the East with his great army. King Henry was dead, and King Richard, his son and successor, was brimming with valor and bristling for combat. That too seemed a sign to Edmond. The new king and he were birthmates, born the same day and year, the eighth of September, 1157.

The armies commanded by Richard and Philip of France now hoped to sail for Palestine by summer's end. And although Edmond would be among them, his path had not been easy. Ever since he had finished his training with Dickon, there had always been something, some obstacle or pressing difficulty at the manor, to keep him from the path of knighthood. During those long, trying years, he had learned the news that altered everything. One morning in the castle courtyard, the Lady Melisande had told him. Dressed in the velvet she often wore, she had just mounted her horse. "Master Edmond," she said, "allow me to detain you for a moment. I've had news that may be of interest to you."

"Of course, my lady, I am at your service." He always used a tone of careful courtesy when speaking to Lord Desmond's wife.

"My dear niece, your former fellow pupil, has left the Sicilian court. She has been married at Caen to her betrothed, the Count de Vere. Sadly, my husband and I were unable to attend."

Hearing her words, Edmond was dumbstruck. First, he stood staring, unable to speak. Then his shock turned to disbelief. How could it be, after the vows they had sworn, after all her loving letters from Palermo? Had Elise not repeatedly assured him she was safe in Queen Joanna's service?

On the other hand, it was nearly a year since he had received a letter from her. Recalling himself from his stupor, he glanced up at the earl's wife. For a moment, her face seemed to be softened by a look of pity. Then she was her distant self again. "You seem surprised, Master Preston. Indeed, after all this time you might well be. The wedding was long overdue."

Even now, he could not bring himself to speak.

His tormentor seemed to understand. "I'll take leave of you, then, my young squire," she concluded. "You seem a bit preoccupied today." With that, spurring her horse, she rode off toward the castle gate, as usual followed by a groom on horseback.

Once she was gone, Edmond came slowly to his senses. Desperate to be alone, he pushed through a flock of retainers at the entrance to the keep and took the stone stairs to the lowest level. There, alone on a bench damp with mold, he sat and wept like a child as his world collapsed around him. He stayed a long while in the silence. Gradually his tears dried up, and a terrible new rage replaced them. How could Elise have betrayed him so completely, without a word, without a cry for help? Had she finally forgotten him? No, it was impossible to believe that. Still, there it was. She had chosen the count with his wealth and position over him. And yet he could not bring himself to hate her. The next day, he awoke to a sense of desolation. For weeks after that, it was the same every day. Gradually, his misery closed around him like a vise and left him with an endless, sullen ache inside.

Then Martin's letter came. By some wretched mischance, it had been misplaced at Winchester for months. As he read it, he learned the truth, but by the time it arrived, Elise was already married to the count. The earl was also ailing at the time. There would have been no way to see him without the Lady Melisande's consent. And if Edmond had seen him, what would have been the point? If he had spoken in belated protest, it might only have made Elise's situation as the count's wife worse. Instead, he wrote Martin to explain that his letter had been delayed. Martin wrote back at once, enclosing the letter Elise had given him before she left. In the years since, Edmond had memorized it.

My dearest Edmond, by now you will know that the thing I believed would never come has taken place. I leave Sicily soon to be married to the Count de Vere. Believe me when I say I did all I could to keep this dreadful thing from happening. Because of the machinations of my aunt, a letter I sent to his steward was never given to my uncle. Then Martin came to my aid and wrote you for your help. We can only assume that you never received his letter. This may also be a long time reaching you. When it does, I hope you will find it in your heart to pity me, and one day, perhaps, to forgive me. In my heart I shall always be yours.

Reading the words, Edmond felt Elise's anguish had been added to his own. As time passed, the injustice of the thing weighed heavily on him, made worse by the fact that there was no one he could speak to of his loss. Meanwhile, life in Windham went on as ever. At Preston Manor, things had gradually improved under the stewardship of Alfred Rendon, but not nearly as much as they might have without the baron's interference. In the years after Geoffrey's death, his father's drinking had grown even worse. He had also conceived a great fear of being left without a future heir.

With his dream of love defeated, Edmond no longer had the strength to defy his parents' demands that he marry. The chosen bride was a young woman he had known since childhood. Her father, a merchant, had later moved to Fenbury. Modest and well bred, Aeline idolized him. Soon after their betrothal, she confessed she had fallen in love with him as a girl on the day she had seen him, as she said, "curly-haired and handsome," fighting bravely against an older boy who, as she later learned, was his brother Geoffrey.

And so they were married. In less than a year, a child came, a daughter, Rosalind. They cherished her all the more because her birth had disappointed both their parents, already anxious for an heir. Two years later, a boy was born. Demeaning as ever, the baron wanted to call him Geoffrey after the son he had adored. Compliant until now, Aeline would have none of it.

"My darling Edmond," she said after the boy was born, "your brother was a drunk, a braggart, and a spendthrift. You are a better man in every way. Someday even your ignorant parents must see that. It's bad enough we have to live with them. I will not let their foolishness contaminate my children."

Edmond agreed, happy to see Aeline coming into her own. They called the child Godfrey after Godfrey of Bouillon, the first Christian conqueror of Jerusalem. Having produced an heir, Edmond gradually took the baron's place in all but name. Slowly, with Alfred Rendon's help, the manor began to prosper.

Then—it already seemed long ago—the Pope had issued the call to holy war in Palestine. First, there was family resistance. Both his parents and Aeline's were united in their opposition to his going. His father, of course, was beside himself. The mere mention of his son's departure sent him off into new bouts of drinking. More sanely, Aeline's parents said Edmond was needed to stand against his father's interference in the running of the manor. He weighed their words carefully, but he was not persuaded. This was not only his chance for knighthood, it was also a mission with a noble goal, the reclaiming of the holy places. As for his duty to his children, in the years ahead, what would young Godfrey think if he learned that his father had stayed at home while others, full of courage, had fearlessly fought the holy war?

No, for once he would do what he thought right.

That left only Aeline. Sweet Aeline, the only one who would miss him entirely for himself. She alone had not said a word in opposition. She knew he was unhappy with his present life, knew he might end as a bitter old man without a chance to gain honor and see the world. And yet it broke his heart to watch her helping him prepare, knowing she would spend every day of his absence worrying about him, dreading his being killed or maimed. Before he put out the lamp at night, he would look into her eyes and see the pain of her impending loss.

"What is it, darling?" she would ask. "You mustn't think I'm fretting. Once I'm beside you, all my worries fly away."

Hearing her lie for his sake, he would lean over and kiss her tawny, freckled cheeks and smooth the reddish tangle of her hair. And then she would smile in a way that nearly broke his heart. God forgive him, he had never lain beside her without wishing it was someone else, a woman whose dark hair and lovely face concealed a mind and a will any man or woman would admire. That wish, his secret, was a constant source of shame. He tried to make up for it by being faithful to Aeline in every other way. He had never looked at another woman even though many had done more than look at him. And over time, he had come to love Aeline in his own way. When he held her now, he could feel their years together in the flesh around her hips. She had carried four children, too many for her tiny frame. The third had miscarried, the last had issued dead from the womb. After that, the local midwife and a physician from Clarington agreed it would be dangerous for her to have another child.

And still she clung to him in the night and, despite himself, he responded. Afraid for her life, he would try to pull away before he finished as he once had with Elise. Aeline would have none of it. It was as if she knew, as if she believed he was only hers completely in that moment. Afterward, he felt guilty for having lain with her at all. Or rather, freshly guilty. Since the day of their marriage, he had lived with a double infidelity: to Aeline for loving another woman, to Elise for betraying her with his wife. Sometimes he felt it was this as much as the desire to prove himself in a great cause that had decided him to take the cross.

28

"Could you ask Zia Pina to make something special for supper tonight, Hamid? Deacon Martin will be here." Pina was the name of Khalil's cook, *zia,* aunt in the Sicilian tongue. As he spoke, the scholar sat cross-legged on a cushion in his study. Before him lay a writing stand with ink and pen, sheets of paper and parchment, and a large bound book in Arabic.

"Pina must have guessed," Hamid answered. Some eight years younger than Khalil, he had a dark, curly beard, broad shoulders, and a wide, ingratiating smile. "She is making the lamb with her special sauce."

"That will be perfect. Could you ask her to prepare her eggplant too, and if possible, the almond pudding?"

"Once again, she's anticipated you. She has already made the pudding."

"Amazing. Sometimes I think you two are wizards, or in Pina's case, what is the Sicilian word?"

"*Maga,* a sorceress. But don't say it in front of her. You know how superstitious Christians are. An old woman like her who lives alone and disappears into the Arab quarter every day has to be careful of her neighbors' gossip. Some fool might use her skill with herbs and remedies to spread the rumor she's a witch."

"Our good Pina, what a thought!" Khalil said, smiling. "And as for what you say about the Christians, they think it's we Arabs who are superstitious."

"That seems strange, when they pray to idols and believe dead people's bones work miracles. One man's belief is another man's folly, I suppose."

"Very true, Hamid. You're quite the philosopher today."

"After all these years, I hope I've learned a bit from you."

"You flatter me. Since I laid down my poet's pen, I am but a humble scholar, a student of the great philosophers. I learn more from them every day."

"Still, Deacon Martin has told me how much he depends on your wisdom as a collaborator."

"As I do his," Khalil said, "and I'm vain enough to take the compliment. Now, my good sage, please let Pina know he's coming."

"Of course, but first, may I say you look a bit worn out? An afternoon nap might do you good."

"Enough solicitude, my friend. I have work to do before our guest arrives."

Hamid lifted both hands as if to say, "It's up to you," bowed his head slightly, and quit the room.

He was right, of course. Khalil had slept very little the previous night. That was the maddening thing about Hamid. He was almost always right. He had been a boy of fourteen when Khalil saw him being beaten by his master in the market in Palermo. Then and there, he had paid the full cost of his freedom. It was an extravagance, but in those years he was enjoying his first great success as a poet and budding scholar. He had never had cause to regret the gesture. From that day until this, Hamid had never failed in his devotion. Even now when, having married and fathered three children, he worked in his wife's family's business, he came to Khalil in the afternoon three times a week.

As a boy, Khalil himself had benefited from an intervention not unlike his with Hamid. In the early days of their marriage, Khalil's parents had been servants to a wealthy childless merchant. Years later, they went to tell him of their son, a student at the Madrasah skilled in reading, writing, and recitation. The man asked to see Khalil, was pleased with him, and soon became his patron. With an eye to a wider future under Norman rule, he found him a teacher who knew not only Arabic and French but also Latin. From that beginning, Khalil made steady progress except for a single crucial interruption.

At the age of sixteen, he had been seduced by a guest of his patron, the eldest son of a merchant from Marrakesh across the sea. Because of his friendship with Rashid's wealthy father, Khalil's patron overlooked his guest's advances. Older than Khalil by a decade, Rashid beguiled him with gifts and stolen kisses. Flattered and infatuated, Khalil offered little resistance. When his patron was absent, they made love in secret. For Khalil, it was like a marvelous adventure. Then one day, the two were seated in his patron's garden when a letter came from Marrakesh. He watched Rashid read it, and as he did, a shadow came over his lover's face. When he spoke, it was with a different voice, not that of a seductive playmate but a sober man.

"My father is ill. It is not the first time he's been stricken, but this is evidently worse. I must return at once."

Khalil had never thought about the possibility of Rashid's leaving. Shocked, he forgot to commiserate, quizzing his lover instead. "How long will you be gone? Will you come back to the business here again? If not, how and when will I see you?"

Rashid looked at him with his soft, dark eyes and smiled. "Whatever happens to my father, I am the eldest son. If he recovers, I shall return. If he dies, the business will be mine, and I will do as I wish. I will come for you then and take you back with me."

Khalil had never doubted his lover's word, but once he was gone, a terrible loneliness assailed him. He returned to his studies in earnest but also began to read the poets, first in Arabic, and then in French and Latin. From them he learned that the anguish he felt was the pain of love, a sickness the beloved alone could cure. Unable to write to Rashid, he began to compose love poems of his own. Those who read them years later assumed they were written to a beautiful young woman across the sea.

In this manner, two years passed. Then, one spring afternoon while he was in the garden where Rashid had courted him, his patron interrupted his studies. "Rashid's father is dead," he announced. "Rashid will now be in charge of the business. Perhaps we will see him before too long."

That was all his benefactor said. He had never admitted the love that Rashid and Khalil had shared. Khalil had been too elated to reply. From that day forward, he waited, full of hope. Six months later, his patron showed him a letter announcing Rashid's marriage to the daughter of another wealthy merchant. Crushed, Khalil gave up waiting. The poems he wrote now were about lost love.

When he was twenty-two, his work attracted the attention of a Muslim scholar at the Norman court. By that time, Khalil had already begun to read philosophy in Arabic and Latin. When, after several years, the old scholar retired, he recommended Khalil to fill his post. Thus, at the age of twenty-eight, Khalil al-Din, the son of servants who could neither read nor write, became a scholar at the palace of William II, Sicily's young king. Then, as if fortune had not already smiled on him enough, his patron died and bequeathed him a substantial inheritance. Not long afterward, Khalil had bought this house. A year later, he married. The marriage had been arranged by his patron before his death. The young woman's name was Abira. She was shy, intelligent, and charming, slender as a boy and graceful as a cat. Khalil admired her, was fond of her, but did not love her in the way she came to love him. Still, with children to bind them, they might have been happy.

But it was not to be. Abira gave birth with difficulty to a stillborn son and never quite recovered. She died of a fever at nineteen. Afterward, they said her narrow hips had not been meant to carry children. Chagrined at her death, Khalil felt strangely at fault. Might she have lived if he had loved her better? Unfounded though it was, the idea tortured him. The truth, which he had known all along, was that he would never really love a woman.

Nor, since Rashid, had he loved another man. Alone again, he sometimes assuaged his lust with one of the young men who prowled the harbor by night near the houses where women were sold for pleasure. For the rest, he had his work, his only love and greatest solace. Nor had he ever stopped hoping fate would one day bring him someone he could truly love. Now, after all these years, he had found him, a lover as unlike Rashid as possible, a fair-haired Christian from the North, a cleric and scholar, a man serious and earnest in all things. And despite the obstacles surrounding them, they had been lovers for over two years. In fact, it often seemed to Khalil that they were living in a kind of dream, a fantasy from which, sooner or later, they must surely be cruelly awakened. Yet they had taken every precaution to avoid discovery; no one at the palace knew of Martin's visits or the love they shared. Nor did anyone else, only Hamid and Pina, whose discretion he trusted completely. And even they only knew Martin as a Christian friend and colleague.

Fortified by that fact, Khalil took up his pen and went back to work. He was composing a commentary on a book by Ibn Sina, the great Arab thinker and interpreter of Aristotle. Known as Avicenna in the West, he was greatly admired by both Christian and Muslim scholars. Seized by a thought, Khalil penned several lines with rapid strokes. Pleased, he finished that idea and began another. After a while, searching for the proper phrase, he looked out the window of his study. From where he sat on the upper floor, he could see the topmost branches of his lemon tree. Another gift of the Arabs to Sicily. Were the Normans aware, he wondered, of how much the abundance of this land was owed to Muslims? On this fine autumn day, the dark green leaves and yellow lemons hung in bold relief against the blue Sicilian sky. A breeze from the harbor gently stirred the branches . . .

*

Khalil felt the touch of a gentle hand. He had fallen asleep after all. He looked up from the cushions where he lay and saw his lover's smile. A year ago, Martin had shaved his fair beard to attract less attention beneath the hooded burnoose he wore into the Kalsa. He had already shed that garment and his cleric's habit and donned a blue silk robe Khalil had given him. Now he was kneeling beside Khalil, kissing him on his brow, his cheek, his chin. Over time, the innocent deacon had become an ardent lover. Khalil reached out to return the embrace, then stopped, alarmed.

Martin grinned in response. "Don't be anxious. Both Pina and Hamid are gone. As always, Pina left our meal under a cover. And so for a night, the world is ours again."

"A night only?" Khalil asked, already disappointed.

"I'm afraid so. I hope to manage two next time." Frowning slightly, he added, "You look a bit fatigued, my love. Have you been working too hard again?"

"I worked today but in the end got very little done. I slept poorly last night."

"What kept you awake?"

"Your coming, I suppose. I couldn't stop thinking of you, of me, of us. When I finally fell asleep, I dreamt you were on your way here in the midday sun."

"But I never come until evening."

"I know, but this was a dream with its own logic. I seemed to be near you and watching, but I was unable to touch you or tell you someone or something was behind you. Every time you looked back, there was no one, but when you turned and continued to walk, a sinister figure in black appeared. Soon other dark figures joined him. In the end, they were like a flock of wingless ravens, a vengeful band of priests and nuns. Then, just as I touched you and opened my mouth to speak, you looked around and saw them all."

"And then?"

"Nothing. I awoke in a sweat and could not go back to sleep."

"My love, why dream such things? None of our colleagues know anything about our meetings. The clerics at my lodging think I'm visiting an aged monk, an expert on Aristotle. I told them I couldn't reveal his name because his abbot frowns upon the study of the pagan authors."

"So I've become an aged monk. That's good to hear!"

Martin laughed. "I don't consider it a lie but an expedient. I could never go back to the way it was before that night I found my way here."

"Nor could I," Khalil admitted. "Our days of study at the palace are a joy, our rare nights together sweet beyond description, but when I am here alone too long, my fears return. I must learn to exist in the present, to conquer my constant unease about the future."

Martin nodded in agreement. "The philosophers say there is only the present. The poets advise us to seize the day and live it to its fullest. We must listen to both, we two above all since our time together is so precious."

"Shall we have Zia Pina's supper, then?"

"Yes, certainly," Martin said, smiling, "but I'm not hungry for food quite yet."

Khalil needed no further hint. While he slept, Martin had lit a nearby lamp. Now, with the help of its light, Khalil looked into his lover's eyes. They were blue-gray, the color of a rainy sea, of fog clouding an azure sky. He closed them each with a kiss and let his mouth slip to the spot where Martin's fine blond hair trailed off into the smooth pink column of his neck. It was always like this when they had been apart; the greedy urgency of desire, the need to make up for lost time, the risk of squandering all their passion with the first embrace.

He kept them from it now, lifting Martin from the cushions where they sat. Their lips met, their bodies pressed against each other. They pulled apart just long enough to walk together into Khalil's sleeping chamber.

29

1190

Edmond rode through the manor fields at a meditative pace. The previous night, a heavy rain had awakened the fallow soil. Drenched and darkened, the earth now exuded the rich, loamy smell he loved. Unlike his dead brother, who had liked nothing better than to kill, wound, or maim the wild creatures he seemed to think were created solely for his pleasure, Edmond was by instinct a farmer. This year, however, he would not see the manor crops turn green. For the first time in his life, he would be gone, part of King Richard's army on the continent en route to holy war. Feeling a twinge of regret, he stopped and gazed at the fields in a kind of farewell, then continued on the path to Preston Manor.

It remained an unimpressive place, wood in parts, brick in others, cut stone only in the front. Even so, recent changes had improved it. The stonework, roof shingles, and a deep porch sheltering the entrance all were new. In the shade of the latter, Edmond now noticed Alfred Rendon's close-cropped hair and ruddy cheeks. As Edmond came closer, the steward raised his hand. Reining in his horse, Edmond stopped to greet him.

"Good day to you, Master Rendon. I hope you are well. Is there something you wish to tell me?"

"Yes, as a matter of fact. I have had a packet from Palermo. It was sent by Martin to the abbey where I claimed it. There was a letter from Martin for me and also one for you. He writes that yours is quite important. He begged me to speak of it only to you and to deliver it myself."

With that, Martin's father produced a folded parchment from inside his cloak. Edmond reached down from his horse and took it.

"Thank you, Master Rendon, for your care in this as in all things. I trust Martin is well?"

Nodding, the steward said, "Yes, quite well, thanks be to God." Then, doubtless intent on his next task, he moved off towards the manor outbuildings.

After stabling his horse, Edmond walked quickly to his lean-to room. It had been enlarged and rebuilt, but as even Rosalind and baby Godfrey knew, it was the place he went to be alone. Somehow, he suspected the letter might concern Elise. Inside, he sat down at his old writing table and opened it.

Palermo, Sicily
November 20, 1189

My dear Edmond, I pray this reaches you in Windham. I am distracted as I write since the two Sicilies have suffered a great blow. At the age of thirty-six, King William has died without an heir, leaving the succession to the throne uncertain. Dark days may lie ahead for everyone from Queen Joanna, his young widow, to the humblest peasant. Please keep our kingdom in your prayers.

Yet I am writing about a very different matter. I have just had a letter from the Lady Elise. She has left the Count de Vere because of his mistreatment and her grave suspicion of abhorrent crimes at Evremont. You can reach her by letter at Abbeville in Picardy, at the home of her aunt, Madam Elisabeth Dufresne. Having told you that, I must make it clear Elise has no knowledge of my writing you. I have learned from my father that you will soon leave for the holy war in Outremer. Before you join Richard's army, you may wish to see Elise. Since the earl and his wife know nothing of her flight, I must also caution you to keep her situation confidential.

For the rest, I send you my fond regards. As one who has lived in peace among Sicilian Muslims, I must say this also. I disapprove of this third holy war fomented by the Pope. That does not keep me from wishing you well in it or praying for your safe return. You have your

*path in life as I have mine. The Lady Elise's wellbeing concerns us
both. Now, as ever, I remain your loyal friend.*

Above Edmond's writing table, a small window faced
Bourne Castle in the distance. All through his youth, he had
looked that way and thought about Elise, so close yet unavaila-
ble to him. For years, she had been entirely beyond his reach.
He was stunned at the thought of seeing her again. Could it really be so simple as a ship across the channel and a few day's ride
to Picardy? If he arrived there unannounced, what would her
reaction be? Whatever the outcome, he knew he had to go. She
had been through terrible trials, taken flight, and was alone
now except for her aunt. He found a piece of parchment, took
up his pen, and wrote.

March, 1190

*My dearest Elise, Martin has written me of your situation. In three
weeks I shall be in Normandy on my way to join King Richard's army on its journey to the Holy Land. Write me in Dieppe care of the
harbormaster. I shall inquire of him, whoever he may be, as soon as I
arrive. I wish to do whatever I can to help you. In any event, I am resolved that we should meet. As always, I am your devoted Edmond.*

He rode to Windham Abbey the day he wrote it. Brother Ambrose agreed to send the letter with the abbey's continental correspondence. The next few weeks were so busy with
arrangements and farewells Edmond scarcely had time to wonder if Elise had received it. Then, as the day of his departure
grew near, he could think of nothing else. If there was no letter
from her at the harbor, he would still go on to Abbeville. One
way or another, he had to see her. Once he had, there would be
time to think about the import of their meeting.

*

On a fine April morning a month from the day he had written Elise, Edmond landed at Dieppe. As a child, he had crossed to Calais from Dover with an uncle. He remembered the confusion then and it was little different now. It took him a while to claim his horse and mule and find an inn. It was mid-afternoon when he returned to the docks and inquired about the harbormaster. After two false leads, he found the proper place, a low wooden building near the entrance to the wharf. The harbormaster was gone, but a surly assistant remained in place. When he learned Edmond was bound for Outremer, he became a bit more cordial. Edmond waited tensely as the man searched among the shelves to no avail. Edmond asked him to look again. The man pretended to, then shrugged and looked him in the eye. Finally, Edmond understood. He had been in Windham so long he had forgotten the customs of the world. He offered a coin, the man took it, and after a show of searching further, produced a small sealed parchment addressed to Edmond. Elise had written.

Outside the harbormaster's door, Edmond could wait no longer. He broke open the seal and saw the long familiar hand. There was neither signature nor salutation, and less than a half page of writing.

Your words touched me like a fragrant balm, like manna in the desert. I too feel I must see you, but it is not possible here at Abbeville. I have contrived to leave at the end of March with Jeanne, my former maidservant, ostensibly for Evremont. Instead, I will make my way to an inn on the coast east of Dieppe. The name of the inn is the Golden Gull. I shall look for you on the fourth of April or soon after. The proprietor is Jeanne's friend and can be trusted. When you arrive, ask for Jeanne Michot. All else I'll explain when we meet.

As he finished the note, Edmond tried to remember what day it was. If it was the fourth, he was already late! Even when he learned it was the third, he wanted to set out at once, assuming Elise would have arrived the night before. Still, he was tired from the journey, dirty, and unkempt. Tomorrow, he would wash and dress, ask for directions to the Golden Gull, and set out along the coast. Tonight he would eat a good meal and sleep in a decent bed. At least he hoped he would sleep. His heart began to beat faster every time he thought about Elise.

The next morning everything went more smoothly than he had expected. First he rounded the deep harbor, then proceeded up the coast on horseback. The trip took less than two hours, and when he arrived at the inn, he gave the stable boy a coin to take his mount and feed it. Inside, he asked for Jeanne Michot. The innkeeper, a balding man in his late fifties, was expecting him. He sent a serving girl upstairs. Shortly afterward, Jeanne appeared. She was a kindly looking woman perhaps five years younger than the man. She greeted Edmond cordially and asked him to follow her upstairs. Opening the door at the end of a passageway, she spoke his name. As he stepped inside, Jeanne closed the door behind him.

The first thing Edmond saw was a window with shutters half open to the hazy afternoon. Then he saw Elise. In that moment, he recalled a kindred vision from their youth: Elise in the light of the window of Canon Thomas's cottage. Seated then, she stood now to one side of the light. Taller and slimmer, with her dark hair gathered in a long, loose braid, she was wearing a coral-colored dress whose hem just touched her slippers. She was older, of course, a year younger than he was, which made her thirty-two, but he could see in the glow from the window she was as lovely as ever.

She spoke first as he had hoped she would. "Is it really you, Edmond?" She started forward—then, as if uncertain, stopped.

Noting her diffidence, he also hesitated. "Yes it's me. When I learned what you had gone through, I knew I had to come." He moved forward until he was close enough to see her eyes, as darkly radiant as ever.

Perhaps embarrassed by his searching gaze, Elise smiled ruefully and spoke again. "Yes, since we last met, life has taken its toll on me. Each day now, however, I improve. I see you are even stronger, Edmond, taller and more handsome in your prime."

He said what he had thought. "And you are as beautiful as ever. Time has merely refined your features. Still, Martin writes that your marriage has been terrible for you."

"It has, but I have endured it and am well. It's been a long time since I fled Evremont. Since then, the Count de Vere has left Normandy, supposedly for Outremer, so you need not be concerned about my safety. For now, your being here is all that matters. I can hardly bear the joy of it."

"Elise, my sweet Elise!" Edmond said in response.

She said his name, and as she did, her voice seemed to hold all the frustrated passion of their separation. In that instant, he too felt the pain of the intervening years: his undimmed love, his fury at fate's cruel blows, his frustration, year after year, at not knowing what Elise had felt or thought. But Edmond was also feeling something else—desire, insistent and unyielding. He looked at Elise and saw she understood.

In the next moment, they were in each other's arms, kissing, embracing, reclaiming each other's bodies. They moved from the window to the bed, quickly undressed, and pulled the bed-curtains shut. The drapery was made of some thin green stuff; it bathed them in a kind of underwater light. Borne on wave after wave of passion, they swam with abandon in their little sea, do-ing their best to make up for all their years apart.

When they awoke, evening had fallen. While they slept, Jeanne had brought a meal beneath a cloth and laid it on a table near the window. Aware of Elise's every movement, Edmond watched as she dressed, lifted the cloth, laid out the food, and poured the wine. Here before him was the woman he had loved for nearly half his life. Once they parted, he wanted to remem-ber everything about her. They sat down and ate with appetite. When they were done, Edmond smiled and spoke. "Now you must tell me about your life, Elise, both good and bad."

"I will if you like, but first, have you become a knight as you so wished to?"

From anyone else, the question would have irked him, but he knew how little Elise cared for rank or honor. She had asked him only for his sake.

"No, Elise, not yet. My time will come in the Holy Land. I shall take the cross before I leave with Richard's army. It's my chance to excel after all these years, to test myself in combat."

"Then you must go, no matter how I feel about this venture."

He had guessed Elise might disapprove of this third holy war, but as long as she understood his need, there was no dispute between them.

"I have the earl to thank for my equipage. I'll wear a badge with his coat of arms. It's yours as well on your mother's side."

"Badge or no badge, you've always been my champion, Edmond, but your talk of the earl leads me to my second question. How is my uncle's health?"

"He is better again of late, but he depends a great deal on your aunt."

"As he has for too long. I'm still unable to write him without her intervention. Because of her, I can't yet think of going back to Windham. I fled Evremont with Jeanne's help. She left the chateau before I did. She hated the count for the way he had treated her husband. After I left, we met and went together to my Aunt Elizabeth's in Picardy. Then Jeanne returned to this inn. The man who owns it is a widower, a sweetheart of her youth. They will be married in the summer. As for the count, as far as I know, he has no idea where I am."

"How can that be?"

"I never spoke of my aunt in Abbeville. Nor did I write the earl and Melisande that I had fled from Evremont. Afterward, I learned there had long been rumors of strange gatherings there. I'll tell you more about them later. There was also another scandal, this time with a young woman of good family. Departing from his pattern of paid women, Gilles had seduced her and left her with child. When I fled Evremont, she had just given birth to a still-born child. The family has sworn to avenge her.

Beyond that, the count had many debtors, all pressing him for payment."

As he listened, Edmond began to see the ugly fabric of Elise's marriage. Still, it was hard to believe a man could live with a woman like her and not care for her in some way. "Was he so easily reconciled to your leaving?"

"Except for his anger at my flight, I doubt he needed much reconciling. From the first, what he cared for were my lands, their value and the revenues. When I went to my aunt's, I was not only ill but desperately short of money. Although I knew nothing of Gilles's plans, I made up a similar story, that he had gone to Outremer and left me with some debts."

Edmond could hardly bear to think of what Elise had gone through. All he felt was hatred for the Count de Vere. "If we meet in the Holy Land, I shall kill him."

"My love, don't think of such a thing!" Elise exclaimed. "Nor do I believe you'll find him there. It's only another of his lies, a ploy to divert his pursuers. He cares only for his vices and his pleasures, and hates anything that smacks of piety. He won't be part of any holy war if he can help it."

"Were you unhappy the entire time?"

"From the first. At Windham, I already loathed him, but I had no idea then how truly vile he was. It took the long night-mare of my marriage to find that out."

He saw the tears in Elise's eyes, reached out, and took her in his arms. "My love, how terrible for you! And all the while I was only a few days away, knowing nothing, unable to aid you, yet loving and dreaming of you."

"It was the same with me, darling, and worse because of my marriage. Now I need to speak to you about Melisande. Despite the grave harm she did us, she seems to have kept her word and not revealed the truth about our love. I've kept a secret of hers in return, one I dared not tell you while you were in training at the castle. She and Gilles de Vere were paramours before my marriage. Although he's neglected her now for years, she's still crazed with love for him.

"How can that be, when he's treated her so badly?" Edmond asked.

"It's a kind of abject madness. Nor could she betray him to the earl without revealing her own guilt."

"Will you ever tell your uncle?" Edmond asked.

"The truth about the count and Melisande? No. I made up my mind about that long ago. If and when I see him alone and apart from Melisande, I'll reveal the truth of my unhappy marriage, not the rest. Now I should tell you about the awful thing I found at Evremont. The same evil you and Martin spied on long ago."

"At the clearing of the stones?"

"Yes. He has long known the rites there ended in the death of innocent young victims. I will omit the details of what I found at Evremont, but there was clear evidence of murder. Some time ago, I wrote to a cousin of my aunt's, a lawyer at Rouen, about these crimes. If murder only were involved, the secular authorities might be in charge, but the members of the band are heretics, devotees of a dark power called Abraxas, so the archbishop's office in Rouen will take the lead. All this I've learned from Master Severin, my lawyer."

"My God! Your life at Evremont was even worse than I imagined. But why did Martin never tell me the truth about these men? He could have written me from Palermo."

"He has always regretted involving you. For that matter, the cult left England long ago. Now, in fact, since the count has disappeared, Master Severin says I can reclaim the income from my lands, the ones at Crecy that belonged to my parents. I've been dependent on my aunt, a condition that pains me greatly."

"How difficult your life has been!" Overwhelmed by compassion, Edmond rose, knelt by Elise's chair, and took her in his arms. He soon felt her tears against his cheek.

"It *has* been terrible," she whispered. "I won't deny it, but with you here beside me, I once again feel there is sanity and goodness in the world."

"What will you do next?" Edmond asked.

"For now, I'll continue to stay with my Aunt Elizabeth. Later, I'll go back to England, eventually to Windham. I can't think of that yet, however."

As if clearing her mind, Elise paused for a moment. "Now, no more of me. You've still said nothing about yourself."

There was a sweetness in Elise's voice that made him want to tell her everything about his life: the children he already missed, the parents time had not improved, the adoring wife whom he could never love as she loved him. And yet something held him back. This could well be the last time they met; he already had a feeling the war would claim his life. To his surprise, it seemed Elise knew nothing of his marriage. What was the point in speaking of it now? These two days were for them alone, a time apart from the world that had so cruelly, blindly kept them from each other all these years.

He answered her question as simply as he could. "My parents survive. With my help and the slow, steady work of Alfred Rendon, things at the manor have gradually improved. Except for my longing for you, I have been neither happy nor unhappy, but when the call to the holy war came, I did not hesitate to answer." Edmond stopped here. Elise seemed to be waiting for more so he went on. As he did, his own words surprised him.

"That was my life until yesterday. Now everything has changed, and I can think of nothing but our love. To be worthy of it, I must pursue my fate, following in the footsteps of my birthmate. Did you know King Richard and I were born the same day of the same year? The eighth of September, 1157. It's become a kind of good omen for me."

"And why not?' Elise said, "As long as you don't give it too much weight."

"No, of course, I try not to. As Canon Thomas would say, such things are mere superstition. In fact, the moment I saw you today, I forgot the war. This afternoon, for the first time in years, I was completely happy."

Edmond saw his words had touched Elise. He heard a tremor of emotion in her voice. "I too, am happy, Edmond. Here in this moment we have each other, and for the future, the fact of our unchanging love."

They embraced again, as gentle now as they were passionate before. Soon, unable to resist, they found themselves making love again. Afterward, they fell asleep in each other's arms. Much later, they woke and began to talk. They went on dozing and talking all night until, slightly parting the bed-curtains, they spied the first faint glow of daylight through the shuttered windows. Only then did they sleep. When they awoke it was late, and Jeanne was at the door with a belated breakfast. They ate heartily and, laughing at their greediness, made love a final time.

That afternoon as he prepared to leave, Edmond saw the tears beginning in Elise's eyes. He reached out to her and kissed her on both cheeks. Then he begged her not to be afraid. "I don't think I truly cared about my life until today. Now all that has changed. I shall do all I can to survive the war."

Elise smiled, clearly happy with his promise. When she spoke, her voice had a prophetic sound. "I shall pray for you every day. Still, in my heart I feel sure you will survive. The great torrent of our love, dammed up so long, could not be cut off again so quickly. A loving God, the only God I believe in, could never be that cruel."

Persuaded by Elise's words, Edmond felt a surge of hope. With all his heart, he did now want to live. Then, nearly as quickly, the old belief returned, the dread conviction that the thing he longed for, the proof of his worth in combat, would come at the price of his life. With that in mind, he dug into the pouch he wore and found the ring Elise had given him at Winchester.

"I've kept it all these years, my love. Let me return it to you now for your safekeeping."

"No, darling. I don't want it. I still have the pendant you gave me. Keep the ring and wear it as a pledge of your return. Now we must say farewell until we meet again."

"Farewell, Elise. I shall love you always."

"As will I, my love."

They kissed tenderly one last time.

"Now, no more words," Elise whispered, "or my courage will fail me."

He did as she asked. Feeling his heart about to break, he gathered up his things in silence. At the door, he paused for a moment to savor Elise's beauty. Her image must last a long time, forever if she was wrong and he was right. Yet whatever the future held, they had stolen a day and night of happiness from fate. Not even death could take that from them.

30

As Martin trod the familiar route to Khalil's house, a warm April wind was blowing from the harbor. Despite the heat, he wore the usual burnoose to blend into the Kalsa. Lowering his head, he thought of the recent unrest in Palermo and moved more swiftly through the streets. Since King William's death, there had been conflict between Christians and Muslims throughout the kingdom. The last time Khalil and he had been together, they had discussed its repercussions at the palace. Unlike his predecessor, Tancred, the new king, had little interest in learning. He had fought hard to win the throne, and would need to go on fighting to retain it. Resourceful as ever, Heraklios had done what he could to protect his domain, courting favor with the more enlightened nobles and the wealthy clerics. Thanks to him, there was no danger yet of their losing their livelihood as royal scholars.

Martin arrived at the house just as Zia Pina was leaving. Khalil and he sat down to eat while the meal was still warm. In his honor, Pina had outdone herself. First, a delicious seafood soup, then *cuscusu* seasoned with saffron, and finally lamb with fennel in a tasty sauce. They had just finished their meal when Khalil addressed him in a somber voice.

"My dear friend, I have something to say which I can postpone no longer. I wanted us to enjoy our meal first."

Disturbed by his lover's manner, Martin tried to ward off bad news by anticipating it. "Don't tell me. Let me guess. You're weary of Plato's *Lysis,* or rather our collaboration on it. Now that the translation of the dialogue is done, you'd rather write the commentary by yourself. I understand completely."

"No, no, it's nothing like that," Khalil said, a note of impatience in his voice. "Please hear me out before you speak. I'll begin at the beginning. Do you remember the day we first saw each other at the royal library? I was with the great scholar Ibn Jubair."

"How could I forget? I thought you the handsomest man I had ever seen."

He had caught Khalil off guard. He too began to reminisce. "And I was charmed by you. Your hair was pale from the summer sun, your beard like golden wheat. You seemed to me half man, half angel, like a picture in one of your Christian books."

Martin was about to reply when Khalil held up his hand to stop him. Clearing his throat, he began again.

"Please, no more memories. I mentioned that day for a different reason. It was that very evening that Ibn Jubair first told me I should leave Palermo."

"Leave Palermo? For where?"

"For al-Andalus,"

"Al-Andalus, of course," Martin said, stung by jealousy. "To join him there. I always thought he fancied you."

"Don't be foolish. Of course there are others like us among Muslims as well as Christians, but Ibn Jubair is not one of them. He lives in Valencia and suggested Cordoba to me."

"Still, you ignored his advice. You stayed in Palermo and made a great success. Why speak of it now after all these years?"

"I have been fortunate, I know, more so than most of my fellow Muslims, but I didn't stay for that reason."

"Why did you, then?" Martin asked. Although he was afraid he knew the answer, he needed to hear it from Khalil.

His lover's eyes were on him now, and they were full of sadness. "I stayed because of you."

At another time, Martin might have felt flattered. Tonight he merely felt accused. He was still hoping to avoid the blow he feared was coming. "Why did you never tell me?"

"Because I loved you. Our situation was difficult enough. I couldn't bear for you to think you held me back. Nor was it only for your sake. The truth is, I didn't want to leave you."

"And now you do," Martin said, putting his fear into words.

"How can you say that?" Khalil demanded, raising his voice for the first time. "It's not I that have changed but Sicily. You know how things have been since William died, the new distrust of Muslims, the strife between the greedy barons and the Arabs, the slurs against Muslim officials and the palace eunuchs, all exacerbated by the so-called holy war in Palestine. Ibn Jubair saw it coming."

"Saw what, exactly?" He was still hoping he was wrong about Khalil's intentions.

"That the days of the Arabs in Sicily were numbered. It may take a decade, it may take a hundred years, but each month more Normans and Lombards and other Christians—you, for instance—come from northern lands. They seize our farms and turn their owners into tenants. The Abbey of Monreale, King William's great pious gift, gains its income from countless fertile properties once owned by Muslims. Many of those who cultivate the soil, the Arabs who made Sicily a rich and fertile land, are now little more than serfs. Each year, the portion of the harvest left to them declines."

"But you are no serf, no bond-slave," Martin protested. "King William himself admired your poetry and read our books."

"He did, and I was flattered just as you were, but William is dead and the Sicily I knew is dying too. Ibn Jubair put it well. Those Muslims who remain at court, a few officials and the royal bodyguard, will turn into a kind of decoration, souvenirs of a once-proud Arab kingdom."

"But Sicily is not alone in such a mixture," Martin parried, groping for reinforcement to his argument. "The kingdom of Jerusalem is Christian and is full of Arabs."

"Was Christian, you should say. Now that the Franks have broken the long-held truce, another war has begun. You seem to forget Salah al-Din has reconquered the Holy City in retaliation. In fact, you've made my point for me."

"Then forget Jerusalem," Martin pleaded, "and think of us. Do we not still have each other?"

"We do, but how often and how truly? You come here in disguise, hiding your habit in a burnoose. In all these years, we have never walked together in the sunlight. And it's not only because of our love. Christians in general no longer fraternize with Arabs. Now, indeed, I can hardly walk alone. A week ago, on my way home from the palace, I was jeered at by the Christian rabble. It seems they objected to the richness of my garments. They blame Muslims, not the rapacious Norman barons, for their poverty."

"You need only dress more plainly to avoid such things."

"And I need only collaborate with you, a Christian, to have my work accepted. Don't you see the wrong in that? I, who was your mentor, must now depend upon your sanction."

"Is it vanity, then," Martin demanded, "that calls you to al-Andalus? If so, I've misjudged you. You have always seemed to me the wisest, kindest, least self-seeking of all men—"

Martin stopped, hating the sound of his own reproaches.

"You know it's not vanity," Khalil protested, "I'd be content to work with you forever. It's much more than that. Sooner or later, each Arab in Sicily must make a choice for either Norman rule or insurrection. The rich merchants, officials, and those who still own lands will swear allegiance to the king and either convert to Christianity or feign conversion. Yet in their hearts, they will wish for revolt and watch in anguish as the most courageous or foolhardy of their fellow Muslims die. I cannot live with such duplicity. I would have to choose, and I cannot. I believe in neither cause, and least of all in warfare in God's name."

"Then you've decided?"

"I have no choice. Nor have I told you the worst. You know how resentful our rival Diodorus has become since our success. It now seems he has unearthed a secret dangerous to me. Years ago, long before I met you, I sometimes assuaged my loneliness with young men I met near the harbor, often for a price. He has spoken to one of them, older now, of course, but still in need of funds. Diodorus would like us to give up our work on Plato. If we don't, he has threatened to expose me to our peers—or worse, denounce me as a sodomite to the authorities. Luckily, he seems not to have guessed the truth about us."

"My God, has it come to this?"

"I'm afraid it has. Of course it's well known he envies us. His accusations would in themselves be suspect. He is vulnerable too. He has presented an essay at court they say is not his but the work of a scholar in Bologna. Still, that might not help us. Threatened, he could try to divert his detractors by exposing me. Now, don't you see, he won't be able to."

"Because you'll be gone."

"Yes," Khalil admitted, "but I was ready long before the threat from Diodorus came. Ibn Jubair has been kind enough to write to Cordoba for me, to Abu Yusuf Yaqub, the Caliph, a celebrated patron of the arts and learning. The great Ibn Rushd, now advanced in years, is also there. I've written him and had a letter back. He welcomes me."

"Ibn Rushd—Averroes?" Martin asked, astounded. "The famed interpreter of Aristotle?"

"Yes, Averroes, as the Christians call him."

"Then I'm truly lost. I can't compete with such renown."

"You've already competed and won. I chose you until I lost the power to choose. And there is also another way, another choice. You too could come to Cordoba."

"To a Saracen kingdom?"

"Yes, just as I'm here in a Christian one. Except that in al-Andalus there is no such strife as here. Cordoba is a tolerant place, just as Sicily once was. Maimonides, the great Jewish thinker, also lives and works there. Although few in number, Christians and Jews are welcome, especially scholars like yourself. We could live there in peace and go on with our work."

"You want me to go with you? And you've not said a word until now?"

Khalil looked directly at him. "Yes. Until tonight, I couldn't bring myself to tell you. Our days together were too few, too precious. And I knew I would have to go first, then send for you."

"And when do you plan to leave?" Martin said, hearing defeat in his own words.

"My ship sails in ten days for Cartagena on the border of al-Andalus."

This was the cruelest blow of all, thought Martin, that there should be so little time. Indeed, this might be the last night they would spend together.

"So soon?"

"It's the best time of year to sail." Khalil's face betrayed no emotion. When Martin said nothing, his lover reached for his hand across the table. "Dearest friend, can't we be grateful for what we've had? Don't you see how fortunate we've been? We have had both our love and our wonderful collaboration."

Martin could hear Khalil's voice collapsing into weariness and sorrow. How difficult it must have been for him to keep this to himself. And even harder to reveal it. He looked at his lover across the table. At the age of forty-four, he still seemed younger than his years. His olive skin, more used to shade than sun, was smooth except for a few lines in his forehead. His dark hair and beard were scarcely touched by gray. Even so, the effort tonight had altered him. He seemed to have aged a decade in an hour. Forgetting the shock of what had struck him as a terrible betrayal, Martin found himself moved by pity. He spoke now with a different voice.

"You are right, my love. Few have dared what we have, and even fewer have succeeded. It's just that I never thought about it ending."

Khalil seemed heartened by this glimmer of agreement. "Nor did I at first," he said. "When I realized I had to leave, I hoped you too would understand. It's not as if everything has ended. Whatever fate decrees, we will always have our love.

And once I'm settled, I will send for you from Cordoba. By then I hope you'll be ready to join me."

Having concluded his speech, Khalil lowered his eyes and was silent.

Martin, too, had run out of words. As for al-Andalus, it was too new, too far away, too much like a dream. He couldn't think about it now. Outside in the night, he heard a distant shout, then two men on the street talking loudly in Arabic, then nothing. After a while, he spoke his lover's name. Khalil looked up, revealing the tears he had tried to hide. Martin had not seen him cry since that first night three years ago.

It ends as it began, he thought, *with tears.* Whatever had made him think it would be otherwise? But it was already too late for regret. His time with Khalil was now vastly more precious. Martin rose and joined him where he sat cross-legged at the table. There he laid his head on his lover's breast, and as he had so many times before, Khalil began to stroke his hair. Lulled into silence by each other's touch, they stayed that way for a long time. All the while, Martin listened to the beating of his lover's heart, memorizing it against the day he would no longer hear it.

31

The first weeks following Khalil's departure were the worst. For a while, Martin could hardly bear to be in the rooms where they had worked together. And there was still Diodorus, who seemed to be gloating at his carrel with its great stacks of Greek manuscripts. Although Khalil was gone, their rival might still spread his stories, tainting their scholarly achievement.

One morning as Martin entered the scriptorium he passed Heraklios's alcove. The custodian seemed to be helping a scribe with some pages spread before them. Looking up, he raised a finger as if signaling *we need to speak.* When he had finished, he came to Martin at his table. Together, they walked to a quiet corner of the room. There, the priest spoke in a lowered voice. "I wanted to tell you Diodorus is gone. I thought you might welcome the news."

"You knew about his threats?"

"There's little here I don't know one way or another. It was a scurrilous thing, but the would-be accuser has now been exposed. His best work, it seems, was stolen from a scholar in Bologna nearly word for word. A week ago, a messenger brought a copy of it. Diodorus has left us in disgrace."

"Thank you for telling me, father. I should be pleased, but I find I am not. If only he had gone three months ago ."

"Then Khalil al-Din would have stayed?" Heraklios asked. "Was it only Diodorus's threats that made him leave?"

"No," Martin admitted, "there were other reasons too. These have not been good times for Muslims in Palermo."

"It had become difficult for him, I know," Heraklios said sympathetically. "You've lost a fine collaborator."

And much more, Martin thought, wondering if the custodian had guessed the truth. He knew everything else, why not that too? In any case, Martin felt sure he could trust him. Still, the unspoken truth of his love for Khalil was no help. It left him no one to confide in.

Martin spent the rest of the day at work, then left the palace to walk through the city. There now seemed to be fewer Arabs in the streets. They said many had gone to the mountains outside the city. It was a sad turn of events. Because of Khalil, Martin felt it all the more keenly.

Coming to the cathedral, Martin crossed the square full of vendors and idlers and entered. Inside the dim, cavernous space he found a small side altar lit by candles. Above it hung a large, flat wooden cross. On it, Christ's body was painted in simple but powerful lines. With remarkable skill, the artist had expressed two contradictory things: Christ's great pain and the triumph of his sacrifice. He had also conveyed something rarer, a note of tender compassion. A teardrop suspended from the corner of the Savior's eye said more about the suffering of humanity than the crimson gashes painted on his hands and feet. Touched by the moving depiction, Martin once again felt that the God preached from the pulpits was a vengeful fiction, a wrathful figure intended to make men submit to authority. It was to a different God, benign and loving, that he now turned for solace. From now on, he would pray to that God alone, begging him to keep his lover safe.

Still, it continued to be difficult to work. Day after day, Martin read and tried to write, but he always ended by wanting to share his ideas with Khalil. Finally, he understood. It was too soon to begin a new work alone. Instead, he undertook a plan of reading on a wide variety of subjects. In this way, the weeks slowly turned to months, and still no letter from Khalil arrived. Each day Martin left his residence early and hurried to the palace hoping he would find one. Each time he was disappointed. And there was another frustrating complication. Because of the strife between Normans and Muslims, the gates of the palace were often closed. The same pattern continued into the fall.

Finally, one day in July, Martin set out for the Abbey of Monreale in the hills above the city. It was a walk of several miles, most of it uphill. Along the way, from time to time, a novel vista opened up between the trees. When it did, he would stop and admire the great bay of Palermo and the sea beyond. For some reason, the distant view brought back thoughts of those far from him: Elise, Edmond, and now, above all, Khalil. When the memories became too painful, he moved on.

At the new abbey, already famed for the beauty of its cloister, he asked to see the monk in charge of the scriptorium. He was disappointed to find that the latter was absent on a journey. The porter said he would speak to his assistant and asked Martin to wait in a small anteroom. Here books produced by the abbey were displayed on a stand nearly the length of the chamber. He was studying one when he heard a voice behind him. "Welcome to Monreale, Deacon Martin."

Turning, he saw a man of roughly his own age in a black Benedictine robe. He was slightly plump with a smooth, balding forehead and, Martin noted, a clean-shaven face. Since he had stopped visiting the Kalsa, Martin had let his own beard grow again. He thanked the monk, who introduced himself.

"I am Brother Paulinus, the assistant head of the scriptorium. I've read and admired your writing on Aristotle." The monk's French was correct but accented. Martin guessed he was Sicilian, a native of either the island or the mainland kingdom.

"Thank you for your kind words and your welcome, brother. Since you know my work, I will confess that I'm here to request your help."

As they seated themselves, the Benedictine inquired, speaking Latin now, "Help of what kind, may I ask?"

"Because of the recent unrest in Palermo," Martin said in Latin, "I am often kept from the royal scriptorium and library. I need an alternative place to work."

"I see," the scribe said, directing a searching look at Martin. "It would be an honor to have you among us, but I myself am not able to grant permission. I shall convey your request to the head of the scriptorium when he returns. If you tell me where you reside, I will send you word of his decision."

Two weeks later, Martin received the good news of his acceptance. On his first day in the scriptorium, Paulinus assigned him a place and introduced him to the other scribes, most of whom were engaged in copying. Soon Martin was making the trek to Monreale once or twice a week. Thanks to the walk of several miles uphill and back, his physical vigor and mental energy improved. Later, when the daily trip became too time-consuming, Brother Paulinus arranged for him to stay a night or two as needed in the abbey guesthouse. Martin was grateful to have the Benedictine as a guide and ally in the same way he had Heraklios at the palace.

Meanwhile, the royal library was available again, so he also worked there frequently. And however indifferent King Tancred to learning, Martin intended to dedicate his future works to him. This was no time to fall afoul of royal vanity.

Not yet ready to write, Martin went back to his reading, moving on to works describing the religions of ancient times. From these he learned the roles of the Egyptian gods, the beliefs of the Assyrians and Persians, the rites of the mystery cults of Greece and Rome. The more he read, the more fascinated he became. Soon he found himself envisioning an ambitious work, a treatise on belief. Not just the beliefs of Jews, Christians, and Muslims, but also those of ancient pagan faiths. Inflamed by this idea, Martin read with new fervor. And all the while, he went on waiting for a letter from Khalil.

When at last several months had passed without a word, Martin's feelings began to change. Gradually, worry and concern gave way to anger and frustration. Then one morning a letter for him arrived at the royal scriptorium. He took it, retreated to his reading table, and tore the packet open. It was not from Khalil but from Edmond in Messina. He was in Sicily on his way to the holy war.

*

Martin stood overlooking the luminous blue of the Strait of Messina. Before him, a few miles away across the water, lay the mainland of Italy, its low hills tinted purple by a morning mist. Behind him, King Richard's army spread out as far as the eye could see, a confusion of smoking fires, moving wagons, horses, mules, and men—ten thousand of them were in temporary shelters, tents, and great pavilions.

Beside him stood his oldest friend. "My dear Martin, I can hardly believe I'm here, on my way to Outremer at last, and that I've now met both you and Elise. How often I feared I would never see either of you again."

Moved by Edmond's words, Martin thought how much, despite the years, his friend remained the same, as affable, open, and honest as ever. At the same time, there was a look of sadness about his mouth and eyes, hardly surprising after all the disappointment he had suffered. In all other ways, Edmond made a striking figure, as robust and handsome as any man in the camp. Indeed, when Martin had first seen him that day, he had felt a twinge of his old desire. Then he remembered Khalil and was grateful their love had now replaced the futile passion of his youth.

Edmond had also been appraising Martin. "You look quite distinguished, my friend, in your cleric's robe. Even so, I can still see the face of the boy I knew behind your scholar's beard. How well I remember those days. How full of curiosity you were! You seemed to question everything."

"In that regard, I hope I haven't changed. But what of our fellow pupil? How is she? How glad I am my letter reached you!"

"And I too, my friend, more than I can say. As for Elise, you are aware of a good deal already. The rest I can tell you in a word. She has left that monster for good. He himself has fled both Evremont and Normandy. She is out of harm's way with an aunt in Abbeville. Sooner or later, she plans to go back to England."

"I thank God she's safe," Martin said. "I've prayed for her since she left Palermo. I still do every day. As I will for you in this terrible venture on which you've embarked."

"Terrible?" Edmond seemed surprised and a bit indignant. "How so, my friend? Rather, glorious! You should have been here when the king arrived. As Richard's great fleet of galleys rowed his army toward Messina, I stood in the harbor along with countless others. Flags emblazoned with noble crests hung from the masts; each ship gleamed with a hundred lances sporting brightly colored pennants. And there in the prow of the finest ship stood Richard in his shining armor with his red-gold beard and hair. How heroic he was, how much taller and nobler than all the rest! None but the Savior himself could have commanded so much admiration!"

This hyperbole, so unlike his friend, made it clear the king had cast a kind of spell on Edmond. Martin could not resist objecting.

"You believe, then, that Richard will be the savior of the Holy Land? Why should he succeed where past kings failed? It was not they but the men who stayed, the Knights Templar and Christian inhabitants, who secured the holy places. Thanks to them and the great Sultan, Salah al-Din, Christians were formerly able to make the journey to the holy city unmolested. It was the infamous Frankish adventurer, Reynald de Chatillon, who broke the peace. His crime led directly to this so-called holy war."

"Great Sultan? Salah al-Din?" Edmond said, mimicking Martin's pronunciation of the name. "You sound like one of the infidels!"

"This is Sicily, Edmond, where Christians and Muslims have long lived beside each other. Here I've discovered the learning of the Saracens in history, philosophy, and science, and also learned many words of their language."

"And King Richard will learn them too, no doubt, when, in the name of Christ, he has defeated and captured the enemy."

"In the name of Christ, or the Pope?" Martin demanded. Despite his affection for his friend, this boasting irritated him. "What makes you think Christ would have wanted this war waged in his name?"

"What's this? Are you now a heretic too? Is the Pope not the representative of Christ on earth?"

"Not in every case. As history proves, popes are often wrong, especially in worldly matters. Seldom do they speak with that unerring voice which claims the inspiration of the Deity."

Raising an eyebrow, Edmond smiled at his friend. "I see you've become a theologian too. No need to dispute with me. I surrender to your expertise. You may have your high thoughts and your toleration of the infidel."

However disarming his friend's capitulation, Martin was not quite ready to give up. "You find me a bit ridiculous, no doubt. Surrounded by thousands of men who disagree with me, how could I seem otherwise? Yet all I have learned has taught me there are better ways to seek the triumph of the good than war. Still, I have no wish to weaken your resolve. In truth, your safety alone concerns me, as it surely must Elise."

Edmond colored at this second mention of their fellow pupil. "You're right," he conceded. "She *is* greatly concerned. On the other hand, she told me she felt strangely sure I would return. I myself have no such conviction. Your prayers and hers will serve me better than your arguments."

"And you shall have them, Edmond."

"I'll depend on it."

Having ended their talk, the two started back. On the way, Martin noted the high wooden palisade around the camp. Arriving in Messina, he had heard nothing but grumbling about Richard's army. At first wary, then angry with the foreigners' ill-treatment, the Messinese had finally rebelled, provoking the king to attack the Christian city. Although part of the Sicilian kingdom, Messina was dominantly Greek.

"Just one thing more," Martin said as casually as he could, "why did Richard assault Messina? Was it merely a kind of practice for the Holy Land?"

"You're too distrustful of our ruler and your countrymen, my friend. Our king could not allow these foreigners to treat him and his army with contempt. Can you imagine, these ignorant Greeks believe we Englishmen have tails?"

Martin laughed. "That's merely the local humor, Edmond. They were simply suggesting you act like devils."

"Well, the joke was on them. They ran with *their* tails between their legs. Nor do they any longer bar their gates to us. As for Richard, he seeks nothing for himself. He has wagered the wealth of England on this holy war."

"How gallant of him!" Martin said. "Does he ever think about his English subjects, those poor wretches he visited only to be crowned? Are they not hungry, ill-clothed, and without decent shelter after all the taxes levied on them?"

"You've been too long in this cynical land, my friend. All England is united in its love of Richard and support for his campaign. Or almost all."

Martin sensed something more beneath that *almost*. He attempted a guess. "But not your family?"

Once again, a faint flush tinted Edmond's face. "My wife Aeline has never said a word against my going, but my parents and her parents have."

"And your children?"

"Of course they cried to see me go, but I've provided for everyone. I've spent a decade doing little else. My whole life has been passed in duty, duty extorted from me by my wretched parents, duty given freely to my wife and children."

Martin was touched by the truth of his friend's avowal. "Forgive me, Edmond. It's not you but the war I mean to question. I have no right to preach to you."

"If not you, who then? You are my best friend, my one true brother. To you alone I can confide the truth. I have long been discontented with my life and full of guilt because of it. It was hard to leave my children and their mother, a faithful wife who loves me, and even harder . . . "

To leave Elise, Martin thought, finishing Edmond's sentence. His friend came up with a different thought. "Even harder to find a proper place in Richard's army. Although trained in the art of war, I am not yet a knight. Nor do I wish to become one until I've earned that rank in battle. As you know, I feel fated to follow the path of my birthmate."

"Ah yes, King Richard and you."

"No doubt you find it foolish. Elise did too, I believe, although she was too kind to say it. And yet it reassures me, like a talisman. Our king is a knight without peer, wholly dedicated to the cause. Whatever the motives of the other Christian leaders, I feel certain his are pure."

His motives perhaps, but little else, Martin thought, recalling the king's reputation. Yet who was he, after all, to question a man for proclivities he shared? He had to smile at his own hypocrisy.

Edmond noted the look on his face. "I see you're suppressing a grin. Are you concealing some trenchant remark you're afraid might wound me?"

"No, quite the opposite. My smile is turned inward on myself. I'm afraid I'd rather look at other's people's faults than take the measure of my own."

"In that regard, you differ little from your fellow men," Edmond said, laughing.

Glad to be in good spirits again, Martin also laughed, so loudly two passing soldiers stopped and stared, perhaps surprised at the raucous behavior of the cleric in their midst.

*

That evening at supper, Martin had a taste of military life. They ate seated outdoors at a long plank table made from freshly felled Sicilian trees. Somewhat removed from the camp, they dined on a berm where they could see the firelights of Italy across the strait. Here Martin was surrounded by a score of Englishmen of varied ranks. For the first time in years, he heard the several accents of his native tongue. After speaking only French and Latin for so long, the words seemed both foreign and strangely familiar. As he ate, he did his best to join in the banter, drinking the strong wine the English had commandeered from their Sicilian hosts. When, much later, they rose to go, he became aware he was drunk, so much so that Edmond had to help him to their tent. Inside, on a cot vacated by Edmond's page, he fell asleep at once.

He awoke in the dead of night. The camp was silent, but his head felt like a hammer on an anvil. He rose and, staggering, left to find the ditch that ran beneath the palisade. Like the thorough commander he was, Richard had placed it as far from the tents as possible in order to prevent disease. There was no moon that night. In the feeble light of a distant lamp, Martin nearly fell into the ditch. He emptied his overfull bladder, then found his way back with some difficulty. Inside the tent, he lay gratefully in the dark. After a while, he heard Edmond's voice. "Are you feeling better?"

Martin answered softly, trying not to make his head ache more. "I think so, but this drumbeat in my skull says otherwise. You know I've never been drunk before? Did I make a great fool of myself before your comrades?"

"Nothing compared to what they do as often as they can."

"I'm not used to such strong wine," Martin said, stating the obvious.

"I'd keep it that way if I were you."

Martin laughed at his friend's wry advice. He could sense Edmond smiling in the darkness. Awake now, the two dipped into the well of reminiscence, recalling their youthful years. Yet when Martin spoke of Elise, Edmond said little. Only later did he mention her again. "I've put off telling you this till now, my friend. It's a thing that concerns us both, something I learned from the Lady Elise."

Martin's interest was piqued. "Go on."

"She told me about the secret brotherhood that met at Evremont. Both the count and Prior Gramont were part of it. It was the same strange gathering that you and I discovered at the clearing of the stones. You know all about it, I suppose."

"I do," said Martin. He saw no reason to disclose the rest, not on the eve of his friend's departure for the Holy Land.

"She said you regretted involving me. Is that why you never spoke of it again?"

"Yes. I used all my skill at argument to make you go that night. You went as a friend, against your better judgment. Afterward, I vowed to leave you out of it."

"You went back to the clearing, then?'

"Only once, and by day. As you may recall, I promised you I wouldn't go at night. In truth, there was little enough to tell you at the time. It was two years later when I discovered the man who led the rites was Prior Gramont. Then I learned that the boy I saw was a novice who had disappeared from Windham Abbey. He was almost certainly murdered."

"You tell me this now, after all these years!"

"Yes," Martin said, wounded by his friend's accusing tone. "In fact, during my year as a novice, I was ready to ask for permission to write you about it. Then your brother died, and I wrote a different letter. Soon, advised to avoid a confrontation with the prior, I left the abbey for Norwich and journeyed to Palermo with its bishop. There was no point in involving you."

"I don't mean to blame you," Edmond said. His voice was full of emotion in the darkness. "Still, you must allow me my regrets. It was I who convinced you to keep that night a secret. It was an unworthy choice. I was afraid of a scandal that might damage me in Elise's eyes. Had I done otherwise, we two might have spoken out together. Instead, this wretched brotherhood went on with its foul crimes, and Elise, for whose sake I wished to guard my reputation, might very well have perished from the wickedness I chose to hide."

Martin saw the ironic truth in Edmond's words, but also felt compelled to disagree. "That may well be, but you are wrong to accuse yourself so broadly. What makes you think they would have credited the story of two boys? Abbot Philip distrusted my youthful memory even when I wrote the truth from Sicily. As for Elise, she's safe now as you yourself have seen. In her last letter, the one after which I wrote you, she told me she had decided to reveal the presence of the cult at Evremont to the authorities."

"In fact, she already has."

"I'm glad to hear it. She is now a countess, and may bring about what we could not as youths, the end of this pernicious evil. In any case, it's time to stop blaming yourself."

"Since you urge it, my friend, I'll try. Nonetheless, I still regret my cowardice."

"Not cowardice, Edmond, rather, caution."

"By whatever name, I shall carry it with me to the Holy Land, one more thing to redeem by my actions there."

Foolish as this seemed, Martin said nothing. He was glad, at least, that the secret of the cult no longer stood between him and his friend. Soon, he heard Edmond's steady breathing, then the sound of the waves in the strait as they broke softly in the distance. After a while, Martin succumbed to the lateness of the hour and fell asleep.

He awoke to an amber glow, the morning light through the fabric of the tent. A little later, Norbert, Edmond's page appeared with a breakfast of oranges, bread, and sardines, Sicilian staples. Later that day, the two friends made their farewells near the entrance to the city. As they embraced, Martin felt the melancholy burden of another parting, one which had a new and darker aspect. Despite his bravery and his years of training, Edmond was new to warfare. This, his first campaign, might very well be his last.

32

1191

After Khalil's departure, Martin had continued to bury himself in his scholarly work. Sometimes, as he searched
among the authors of the early church, he would wander into
Gnostic territory. Twice, he discovered drawings of the emblem of Abraxas, the same strange creature depicted at the
clearing of the stones, at Evremont, and on the ring Isaac had
shown him. Martin had also found another refutation of Basilides, this one by Tertullian, the influential Early Christian
writer. According to him, Basilides falsely believed that Abraxas, not God the Father, had sent Christ into the world, a Christ
who was neither god nor man but a kind of phantom or illusion. This was heresy indeed, but such arcane discoveries did
little to better Martin's knowledge of the cult.

Both the count and the prior had disappeared, but did that
mean the wretched gatherings had ended? He had no way of
knowing. He could only hope the inquiry initiated by Elise
would bring an end to the cult's vicious crimes. Still, over time
he had learned to be wary of the Church's methods in such matters. Charged with rooting out evil, the ecclesiastical authorities
were not always particular about the guilt or innocence of those
accused. And if, as sometimes happened, the facts of the case
proved inconvenient, their goal often became the suppression
of scandal instead of the discovery of the truth. Abbot Philip
had provided an unhappy example of that policy at Windham
Abbey.

Late in the summer following Khalil's departure, Martin had
given a name to his treatise on religion, *Concilium Fideorum*, "A

Meeting of Beliefs." He had worked on it through the autumn and winter, mainly reading but also writing a bit more each month. Too often, however, just as he was most involved in forming his ideas, Khalil's face would appear and fresh tides of sadness and recrimination would sweep over him. At last, ten months after his lover's departure, Martin decided to finish the commentary Khalil had insisted he take as his own. It was on a dialogue of Plato called the *Lysis*. At Heraklios's request, they had not written on the *Symposium*. The custodian thought it might offend some Christian sensibilities. The *Lysis* dealt not with love and beauty but fidelity and friendship. Perhaps if Martin kept his commitment to their work, Khalil would also keep his promise, and a letter would arrive from Cordoba explaining everything.

Having made up his mind, Martin began work on the *Lysis* at the end of February. Writing mainly at Monreale, he threw himself back into the commentary. To his surprise, he found the translation incomplete, the notes they had made unclear. After so long a time, he needed to study the text and review the related commentaries. In the end, it took him much longer than he had expected. At last, in the middle of April, he finished it. The next day he set out for Palermo to take it to the palace scribes to copy. The last thing he did was to write Khalil's name beside his on the opening page.

As he entered the library, manuscript in hand, Heraklios looked preoccupied. "I was wondering when you would come," he said, "I've had something for you for several days. Here, take it now. It will be one less thing for me to think about."

Without a word, Martin followed Heraklios to his alcove. There the priest pointed to a battered parcel bound in linen. On its scarred surface there was writing in Arabic, Latin, and French. As soon as he saw it, Martin knew. Heraklios too must have guessed, whence his impatience. He alone understood how long Martin had waited for this missive. Thanking him, Martin took the packet to an isolated table. Seated some distance from a window, he opened it carefully. Despite the dim light, he recognized Khalil's hand at once. He had left the previous April. Now, a year later, the letter had come at last.

It was long, written on paper in a small, precise script. Nearly faint with anticipation, Martin read the first few lines. They told him that Khalil was safe and well in Cordoba. Having learned that much, he decided to read no further. He could not trust his reaction among his fellow scholars. Folding the pages, he slipped them into his satchel beside the commentary. He would see about the copying tomorrow.

He arrived at his residence by midday and waited until the others were at their meal. Seated in a chair beside his bed, he took out the letter and began where he had left off. First, Khalil asked Martin to forgive him for leaving Palermo, then he begged his pardon for the long delay in writing. It had been caused initially, he said, by a dozen misadventures, all of them too tedious to detail. There were also two other reasons he would speak of later.

It was a disappointing beginning, but Martin deferred judgment until he had read the rest. Khalil went on to describe the charms of Cordoba, the richness of the city, the lushness of its gardens, the quality and beauty of its buildings, especially the monumental mosque, one of the wonders of the world. The royal palace, too, was splendid. Most wonderful of all, in Khalil's opinion, was the library.

Here, as in the east, many books are on paper, much less expensive and more plentiful than parchment. Perhaps for that reason, this collection of books is the largest on the continent of Europe. Its volumes number in the thousands, among them rare Hellenic works unknown in Christian lands.

After that, Khalil spoke of his position as a palace scholar, the largesse of Caliph Abu Yusuf, and the atmosphere of culture and refinement at the court. With these and other allurements, he gradually made the case for Martin's joining him.

Having a Christian scholar here would add to the court's distinc-
tion. In Cordoba, both Christians and Jews are welcome. There is even
a thriving Christian church. As a deacon, you could assist at the ser-
vices there. And as for your work, you would have the unparalleled
pleasure of meeting Ibn Rushd, the greatest living expert on Aristotle.

As Martin read, a flood of painful emotions swept over him.
Khalil had let a year go by without a word, and now, with barely a mention of his neglect, he was issuing a glowing invitation
to al-Andalus! He had spoken of it before he left, of course, but
Martin had not allowed himself to think about it since. Now,
after all that had happened, he was still not prepared to do so.
The second part of the letter had a different tone.

Having I hope tempted you to join me, I come to the difficult part
of this long-postponed communication. I will begin by admitting my
fear. I now dread that you, having failed to hear from me, have made
your peace with our separation. Whether or not that is so, I shall con-
fess the truth about my dereliction. I have not written until now for
two reasons, both unworthy. The first is that after my departure, I
could not bring myself to think about our separation. If, on any day of
the voyage to Cartagena, the tiring journey overland to Cordoba, or
the difficult weeks that followed my arrival, I had considered the love
I left behind, I would not have been able to go on. And so it was that
from week to week I put off writing, always unable to come to terms
with my remorse. It is still with me every day, along with hatred of
myself for having sacrificed our love to circumstance.

My second reason is an offense I have committed, the breaking of
a pledge I made. Before I left, I convinced myself that my reasons for
going were unselfish, that I had no other choice. Only after my arrival
did I realize how great a part ambition played in my decision. Once
here, I was graciously welcomed. I learned that Cordoba was indeed a
scholar's paradise. Still, even in paradise, envy and rivalry hide like
snakes beneath the fruits of erudition. From the first, I was caught up
in the politics at court. It took a while merely to gain the attention of

the Caliph and his advisors. I soon understood it was up to me to make my place among my fellow scholars.

I decided I had to show my worth at once. I had given the Lysis to you, urging you to begin your new career with it. Instead, I took it back. I convinced myself that you would understand. I had the text and a nearly complete translation, more complete, I believe, than the version you kept. I also had my copy of the notes we made, along with the unfinished commentary. Thanks to the library here and my memory of our discussions, I finished it all in a matter of weeks. As I had hoped, it made a great success, at once establishing me at court.

Now, however, I fear there are two versions of our work, the one you will have completed and the one I presented here. I've written more since, but my reputation is fixed to this particular dialogue of Plato, formerly unknown in Cordoba. Thus, having admitted my crime, I must further humble myself. If by some chance you have not completed your version or made it public, could you not do so for my sake? Should your commentary come to light, my situation here would be imperiled, much like that of Diodorus, our plagiarizing rival in Palermo.

Dear friend, that is the sum of my confession, the kind you Christians make in the dark corners of your churches. Now I, who have always been so proud, must beg you to pardon the pain I've caused you. You deserved better of me. You are the person in the world I wanted least to hurt, yet I have done so. I can only humbly ask you to forgive me.

And despite it all, I believe that you and I could still be happy here together. In Cordoba, I am known as a childless widower, a scholar wholly dedicated to his work. If you came as a fellow scholar you would be my guest. That you should reside with me would be expected. Yet even in al-Andalus, where poets praise the beauty of young boys, it would not do for us to let our love be known. As in Palermo, it would be our secret. This time, however, we would truly be together, free to love and work. Is that not a dream worth your consideration? For the present, that is all I ask, that you consider it. That, and your pardon for the faults I have at last disclosed. I end by affirming my unchanging love.

When he had finished reading, Martin put the letter away and, midday though it was, lay down on his bed to think. Gradually, tears filled his eyes. He had read his lover's letter patiently, giving due weight to his excuses, but none of them could calm the hurt and anger he now felt. He could forgive Khalil's taking back the *Lysis* but not the delay in writing it had caused. How many nights had he lain awake imagining his lover drowned at sea or killed by bandits on the road? And all the while, Khalil was not thinking of him but of his reputation at the Caliph's court. What was it he had said? That he dared not consider the love he had left behind? He had succeeded very well! Was this, then, the man he had come to love so deeply? Until today, his lover had seemed a superior being, a man devoid of faults. This new Khalil was vain and selfish, weak and fearful. He as much as admitted it. Even so, how could he have, month after month, so cravenly, cruelly delayed his letter, knowing how Martin must have hoped for word of him?

That night, lying sleepless among his fellow clerics, Martin felt a frustrated rage growing inside him. Was he alone to sacrifice, to smother his pride while Khalil, having failed in both his vows—to write and to give him the commentary—enjoyed the acclaim his duplicity had won? Did Khalil really expect that after such neglect, he could so easily leave his life here in Palermo? Martin would write him at once and tell him he could not.

Nonetheless, he would begin his reply in an elevated manner, explaining how he had finished the dialogue in both their names, in fact taken it to be copied that very day, but would now, complying with Khalil's wishes, suppress it. That would demonstrate that he at least valued loyalty above the world's opinion. Content with that beginning, Martin lay awake forming the rest of his answer, inventing one stinging reply after another to the explanations Khalil had made. At last, worn out by the whirlwind of the bitter phrases forming in his head, he fell into a troubled sleep.

33

It was mid-morning as Edmond crossed the city. The air was fresh in the English camp outside the walls, but here the stench of death still lingered. Now and then it grew worse and he peered into a vacant house and saw a body left unclaimed. Clinging to the shade to avoid the searing heat, he passed windows agape with broken shutters, doors flung open to the street, thresholds littered with debris. It had taken two years and thousands of lives, but the great port of Acre had finally fallen. A month and a half after Richard's forces joined the siege, the Muslim defenders had surrendered.

It was only a few days since the enemy had yielded, but over two thousand prisoners had already been sequestered in a separate quarter of the city. There, they would be held as hostages and used in bargaining with Saladin. The rest of the population had been forced to leave, taking only what they could carry. The soldiers in the Christian camp had lined the road to watch the procession of defeated unbelievers. For most, Edmond included, it was their first look at a large number of those whom the Pope had called the scourge of Christ.

They had expected a mob of exhausted victims, men, women, and children worn out by the siege and weighed down by their bundled possessions, wailing, perhaps, in the oriental manner to bemoan their fates. What they saw was quite different. All who passed with their burdens, including the old who had survived the siege, were surprisingly calm in the face of their misfortune. It seemed these Muslims were not demons after all, only humans accepting their lot with as much dignity as they could muster.

Ready to leave the city, Edmond drew near the wall where the fighting had been fiercest. As he did, a breeze from the sea stirred the sultry air, reviving the stench of death. Here and there, a rotting horse or cow still lay embedded in the rubble. When they had run out of stones, the Christians had catapulted dead animals' carcasses over the walls. It seemed a cruel thing, but less cruel than the deaths of the men who had fought on both sides, not to mention the innocent women and children who had died inside the city. Had the victory been worth it all, he wondered, the two years of agonizing siege, the horrendous toll of death, the exhaustion of the forces of the Christian Kingdom of Jerusalem?

After posing the question, Edmond realized he had no answer. Instead, he thought about the magnitude of this campaign and felt a strange exhilaration. How long he had waited to be part of such a great endeavor, to fight bravely, to give his all, to risk his life beside his fellows, and to triumph! And at Acre, he had proved his worth. When the mangonels hurled their rocks and crushed the walls, he had been among the first to storm the stronghold. When the enemy rose to fill the breach, he had driven them back in a kind of frenzy, plunging with shield and sword into the turbaned host. And as his reputation grew, Edmond was ever more grateful to his teacher Dickon Breslin, a hero of the previous holy war. It was his tireless training that had, in the end, gained Edmond the praise of many, among them the Earl of Leicester, a young nobleman who had taken particular notice of his skill and courage.

Now, grateful for a moment of shade beneath the gate, Edmond stepped over a patch of earth still black with blood. As he did, he looked up and saw a fellow soldier on his way into the city. Shielding his eyes from the glare, he recognized Harold, an Englishman he had known since Messina. Well-spoken and skilled as an archer, he came from York.

"Good morning, Harold, or is it afternoon?"

"Still morning, I think, my lord." Out of courtesy, the man used a title that Edmond still lacked. "Pardon me, sir, but may I ask if you've heard Duke Leopold has threatened to withdraw his troops?"

"No, for what reason?"

"He wants his Austrian flag put back beside our own."

"I heard it had been removed," Edmond said without commenting.

"By order of the king, sir, as was only just. From the first, it's been Richard's army, Normans and Angevins, English and Welsh, who took the lead and bore the brunt. Philip of France barely showed his face. The Germans and Austrians did even less."

"Still," Edmond suggested, "it might have been more politic to let the banner stand."

"Surely, sir, you don't disagree with the king's decision?"

"It's not my place to agree or disagree. Nor would it matter if I did. Our king keeps his own counsel and does as he wishes. And so far, he has done quite well. It took him only six weeks to conquer Acre, a thing the Knights Templar and King of Jerusalem had been trying to do for years."

"And about time it was, sir! We Christians held Jerusalem for eighty years before that devil Saladin decided it was his to take. We showed him, sir, did we not?"

"Yes, we did," Edmond conceded, omitting the fact that Saladin still held Jerusalem and most of Palestine. "Let's hope the rest of our campaign succeeds as well."

"With God on our side, it's bound to, sir," said Harold, crossing himself in farewell.

Moving toward the camp, Edmond once more reminded himself of the greatness of the cause he was enlisted in. He found it helped him to ignore the greed of men like Guy of Lusignan, the unprincipled King of Jerusalem, to overlook the rivalries that threatened to devour the Christian forces, to forgive King Richard his own egregious faults. Peerless in battle and the ways of war, his hero was also afflicted with arrogance and pride. Had he only shared the glory of this first great victory, he might have created a crucial solidarity among the Christian forces. Sadly, he had not. Lacking both humility and wisdom, he also was cursed with a temper like his father's.

Hadn't one of King Henry's infamous outbursts caused the murder of Archbishop Becket?

Entering the camp, Edmond made his way past men celebrating the victory for Christ with wine and wenches. Halfway to his tent, he encountered Norbert, his page. "Good morning, sir. I came out to meet you."

"So I see," Edmond said, smiling. "And to what do I owe this courtesy?"

"An official matter, sir. I have a message for you from the Earl of Leicester."

"In writing?"

"No, sir, it was given me by his page. The earl asks that you attend him in his tent an hour after noon."

"Indeed? Then I'll eat my meal now. Meanwhile, please go and tell the page I shall come as asked."

Norbert went at once, returning in time to join Edmond at the midday meal. They took it at a table filled with men Edmond had fought with. To shield them from the burning sun, the soldiers had made a canopy from an old tent. Tomorrow, they would move into the city. Afterward, Norbert helped Edmond dress. Then Edmond proceeded to the portion of the camp assigned to noblemen. Arriving at the earl's pavilion, he spoke to the page at the entrance. "Please tell the earl Edmond Preston is here in response to his request."

The page opened his mouth to reply, then faltered. "Is it Master Edmond Preston, then?"

Edmond responded sharply. "Yes, Master Preston of Preston Manor in Windham, son and heir of Baron Hugh. I am here, as I say, at your lord's invitation."

Chastened, the boy spoke more civilly. "Just as you say, sir. I shall tell the earl at once."

Annoyed with himself for explaining, Edmond waited to be called. Still, the boy's slight had given him a clue as to the company inside.

The page came back quickly. "My lord earl awaits you. He also begs of you the same indulgence he has asked of all the others. Please neither speak your name nor ask those of the gentlemen assembled. He himself will explain the reason."

Puzzled but intrigued, Edmond followed the boy inside. There, in the light of twin lamps suspended from the tent pole, he found the young earl seated at a table. No one was speaking, so Edmond quickly surveyed the scene. Two older men sat to the earl's left and right. Six younger men facing him occupied folding stools. Their faces wore expectant looks. The silence had an air of conspiracy. The page led Edmond to the last empty seat. Before taking his place, he remembered the earl's injunction. He bowed and greeted his host as simply as he could.

"My lord, I am at your service."

Lord Robert's reply was equally plain. "You are welcome, sir. Please be seated."

The earl, a distant cousin of King Richard, was a stocky young man with a ruddy face and chestnut-colored beard and hair. Despite his youth, his voice resounded deeply, the voice of one born to command. When Edmond was seated, the page reappeared and handed him a cup of wine whose fragrance filled his nostrils. Then the earl spoke again.

"Thank you, gentlemen, for keeping your names and ranks a secret. You'll understand why presently. First, since our group is complete, let us drink to our country, our noble sovereign, and our holy cause. When you have heard my proposal, you may want a cup more of this heady wine of Hebron."

They all did as asked, drinking to England, King Richard, and the holy war by turns.

The wine was delicious. Besides quenching Edmond's thirst, it seemed to put him at ease at once. After the toasts, the earl paused, heightening expectation. More curious than ever, Edmond set his cup on a little hexagonal table and waited.

At last Lord Robert spoke. "You all know that our king has no equal in combat, whether on horseback or on foot. Each of you in his own way has also excelled in battle. I have either observed you or otherwise learned of your prowess. You are all young and strong and skilled as horsemen. Here, then, is my proposal. I have been asked by King Richard to form a scouting party. If you choose to join, you will trail Saladin and his army on the path the enemy has taken south of Acre. This will be no ordinary expedition. To assure each man's freedom to react to danger, you will all be as equals save one, the leader you your-selves choose. For that reason, all names and ranks will be con-cealed. At first, those of high estate may well object. If so, I beg you to recall that we are in the Holy Land to do God's will. In his eyes we are all as one. With that in mind, I hope you will be persuaded to relent. I myself would have wished to be among you, but since you know me too well, I have been disqualified."

With this, a groan of disappointment issued from the group. The earl was admired for both his courage and his spirit of fel-lowship. He had become the Earl of Leicester in an unfortunate manner. The father with whom he had left for the war had died along the way. At Acre, his son had fought as if for two. Hear-ing the protest, he laughed, displaying the good nature that en-deared him to his men. "You gentlemen are too kind, either that or gross flatterers! My work will be done if I persuade you to undertake this expedition. Completed successfully, it will surely bring you fame and honor."

At this point, the man on the earl's left cleared his throat. The old warrior's head was bald, his face scarred from battle. At once, the earl turned to address him. "Forgive my bad manners sir. I invited you two veterans to gain your good advice. In-stead, I've rattled on without consulting you."

The man replied in a courteous voice. "You've rattled on quite well, my lord, and made a good case without our help. You've omitted one thing only, but it's something that will make a difference. These men should know that to complete the mission, they will have to go in disguise, outfitted like Saracens and riding Arab steeds."

Once more, there was a general murmur, this time less ap-proving. Wearing the garb of the infidels might seem a sacrifice to some. Edmond's own reaction was more practical. He saw at once that Arab clothes might be their best safeguard. Would it be easy, however, for men used to the protection of armor to fight with only padded clothes and curving swords requiring new skills?

The gray-bearded man to the earl's right was now speaking. "My comrade and I are here because we've lived and fought for many years inside the Kingdom of Jerusalem. A party like this can best survive by mimicking the Arabs. Their horses race across the desert sands, their layers of clothing shield them from the burning sun, their light armor allows them flexibility of movement, unlike ours which protects us but also imprisons and impedes us. Before these men depart, my lord, they must look, think, and act like Saracens."

Turning toward the assembly, Lord Robert spoke to them directly. "You must take care, in particular, of the fine new horses you shall mount, all captured from the enemy. Treat them well and I'm told they will fly beneath you—and also quite possibly save your life. I pray to God you will all return in triumph, bearing the information that King Richard needs before we move south toward our great goal, Jerusalem."

The men greeted this speech with a burst of applause. By now, the page had replenished their wine. Seizing the moment, the earl lifted his cup and stood, bringing them all to their feet. "To Jerusalem!"

In a single voice, they all repeated, "To Jerusalem!" and drained their cups. It was hardly surprising that when the earl asked for a count of those agreeing to the mission, not one of the seven declined.

34

There was a path in the hills above Monreale where Martin often walked. Sometimes he would sit on a rough stone bench beneath a fragrant pine and contemplate the splendid vista. To his left, beyond Palermo's broad plain of limestone buildings, Monte Pellegrino's rocky mass rose like a fortress from the shore. To his right, purple and green in the distance, Monte Grifone sloped more gradually toward the sea. Between the two promontories lay a vast expanse of blue, its color shading from emerald to ultramarine on the horizon. Sometimes, enchanted by the play of sunlight on the water, Martin half expected Aphrodite to appear, born from the sea and carried on the waves as in the ancient fable. Sicily induced such visions. Here, among Roman, Greek, and Phoenician ruins, one breathed the air of antiquity.

Today as he gazed, Martin remembered another view, the one at Messina the year before. That day they had thought Richard's army was ready to depart. In fact, five more months would go by before the English fleet set sail to the immense relief of their Sicilian hosts. Would Edmond return by way of Sicily, he wondered? More pointedly, would he return at all? Nothing was certain in this world. By now Martin had learned that lesson well. A year ago he would never have guessed he would be living here at Monreale, but after the death of his powerful patron, Archbishop Walter, he had been forced to give up his former lodgings. Bartholomew, Walter's brother and successor, had found other uses for the building.

After learning the news, Martin had spoken to Brother Paulinus at the abbey. The Benedictine applied on his behalf to Abbot Carus. The abbot was a Cistercian, a member of a new and stricter branch of Benedictines. Admired by his brethren, he was the first abbot of Monreale elected by the monks themselves. Fortunately, the new leader was learned as well as pious. He believed Martin's scholarly gifts would be an asset to the abbey. Treating him as an honored guest, Carus gave him a room of his own, a great luxury in any monastery.

Now, fifteen years after its founding, Monreale's great cloister was finally complete, as were the large nave and chancel of the abbey church. The magnificent mosaics covering the church's walls were also on their way to being finished. All the same, the abbey was not without its difficulties. Its founder, King William, had given to it lavishly. Tancred, his successor, wanted money more than prayers in order to defend himself against his rival for the crown of Sicily, the German emperor, Henry VI. It was not long before the new king had relieved the royal monastery of a good deal of its treasure. Fortunately, as the seat of an abbot-archbishop, Monreale was protected by the Pope. Thanks to him and the devotion of the faithful, the life of ministry and study, work and prayer went on.

For Martin, the move to Monreale was a new beginning. Indeed, his work seemed to thrive amid the calm and beautiful surroundings. There were also changes, of course. In Palermo, as an unaffiliated cleric, he had been unusually free. Here he took his meals with the Benedictines, went daily to Mass, and attended morning prayers at Prime and evening services at Compline. And yet in the midst of it all, he felt oddly alone. He had come to the abbey some months after writing his angry letter to Khalil. Almost at once, he regretted sending it. He also fervently wished he had made a copy. That way, instead of wondering what his words' effect had been, he could have read them with a cooler head and tried to estimate the damage he had done. Sooner or later, of course, he would have a reply. If none came, that too would be a kind of answer.

Meanwhile, Martin went on with his work on the *Concilium Fideorum*. Yet even when he was deep into the writing, he would sometimes recall some caustic phrase or scalding epithet used in his letter to Khalil and wince with new regret.

In this way, the months passed until on a warm day early in September, a reply from Khalil appeared at the library. As he broke the seal, Martin was equally grateful the letter had come and afraid to read its contents. Perhaps his lover had rejected both him and his letter, putting an end to everything. In fact, Khalil had done neither. Instead of resenting the attack, he blamed himself for inciting it. And once again, he asked Martin's forgiveness.

My dear friend, dare I hope that by now your just anger has run its course? You alone can tell me what I long to hear, that you forgive me and will come to Cordoba. Remember the joy of our work, the precious hours we shared, our long nights of tenderness and passion. We can reclaim it all and more in a new life together.

As Martin read the last words, he felt his heart beating faster, the start of a struggle that lasted several days. At the end of a feverish week of indecision, he sat down at the table in his room and wrote. This time he made a copy of the letter. The final pages summed up his complicated feelings.

As you see, my love, I had begun to forgive you long before your second letter reached me. As with most of us, your faults are linked closely to your virtues, in your case, pride in your scholarly work. It was your desire to shine among your Muslim peers that led you to appropriate the Lysis. Now that the terrible year inflicted on me by that pride is over, I know again what I did before, that I love you as I will never love another.

That said, I must speak now of my own weakness. Believe me when I say I long to be beside you. I can barely imagine the joy of the life you describe. However, I too have my ambition. During the long year of our separation, I found myself unable to pursue the kind of work we shared. As a result, I began to study new realms of learning, among them the beliefs of humankind. The result, put simply, will be a three-volume work I shall call the Concilium Fideorum, a meeting of beliefs. In it, I hope to use reason to demonstrate the principles that all religions share. If I succeed, I shall have struck a blow against the conflict that pervades the world of Christians, Jews, and Muslims, the conflict that spawned the hate that separated us. That, my love, is the ambitious task I've set myself. For now, I am unable to think beyond it. Nonetheless, I beg you to go on writing. I will respond in turn. Meanwhile, please believe me when I say my love for you remains unchanged.

Afraid to say more, Martin ended his letter there. Blotting the ink, he folded the pages and sealed them. The moment he did, he felt a new regret. With this letter, he had assumed the burden of their separation. A few days later, ambivalent about the decision, he prayed for a sign he had done the right thing. When none came, he went back to his scholarly work, the only remedy for all that troubled him. Once caught up in it, he seemed never to tire of his labor. There was so much to be learned, so much truth to be culled from the past, so much ignorance on which to shed the light of reason.

The next day Martin rose at Prime, joined the monks at morning Mass. During the service, he prayed earnestly for guidance. After Mass, he wrote all day, pausing only for the midday meal. The following day, he made the long trek to Palermo and read and made notes until late in the afternoon. All the while, he continued to feel an aching loneliness. On the third day, missing Khalil acutely, he reminded himself of all he needed to be grateful for. How many thousands were suffering this very day, crushed by the yokes of oppressive masters? How many others had seen their livelihood and property destroyed in warfare, their families maimed or killed by men who never ceased to lust for land and power? The *Concilium* would be his way to pay his debt to both his fellow creatures and the Creator who had given him his privileged life.

Nonetheless, he continue to ask himself if he had made the right decision. Perhaps he had, perhaps not. In his heart, he suspected the wounds from his lover's long silence had not yet completely healed.

Then, another letter came, this time to Monreale.

Winchester, June 23, 1191
Elise de Crecy to Deacon Martin Rendon
    Dearest friend, you have not heard from me for a long time, and with good reason. For one thing, I have returned to England. For another, I have a child, a boy, already half a year old. I learned of your new residence from Canon Thomas. He, in turn, knew of it from Brother Ambrose at the abbey. Our dear old teacher is full of wisdom still despite his age. He is the only person at Windham with whom I have so far communicated. You may wonder how I came to be at Winchester. The reason is simple enough but also sad. My aunt Elizabeth, with whom I was staying in Picardy, fell ill and died, and I was left without a home. Although the count was gone, I never thought of a return to Evremont. After all that had happened there, the place was odious to me. By a fortunate chance, I learned that Queen Eleanor was in Rouen, having just returned from Sicily. There, as you know, she came with Berengaria, Richard's bride and met her daughter, the widowed Queen Joanna, and King Richard.
    Desperate, I wrote her at once about my plight. She remembered me from the days at Winchester and Sarum, the painful time before King Henry died and she was liberated. She responded graciously, inviting me to join her in Normandy. I did, and found her at the age of sixty-nine remarkably unaltered. What a woman she is! There is scarcely her equal in Christendom. Quite rightly, King Richard has placed her in charge of his realm along with his justiciar. She told me that Joanna, older and worldlier now, has long regretted my dismissal. To make sure I was safe from my husband, she suggested I return to Winchester with her protection. As you see, I gratefully accepted.
    Now I must tell you what has happened in connection to the cult at Evremont. Shortly after Edmond left for Sicily and Outremer, they found the bodies of three young people, all in shallow graves beside the ramparts of the fortress. By then, my husband had fled. Perhaps he and the prior had been warned in advance. That left only Mordran, the overseer, one of the members of the cult, at the chateau. Rather than reveal the truth to the interrogators, he killed himself in a horrid

manner, slicing his throat with the kind of flint blade the cult used in their rites.

As you know, I had escaped Evremont much earlier. Through the good offices of an advocate, Jacques Severin, a cousin of my aunt Elizabeth, I have now regained the income from my holdings at Crecy. This has given me much greater freedom. My aunt trusted Severin completely. With his help, I have now made a complete account of what I saw at Evremont and what I know about the cult from you. Severin has presented it to the authorities in Rouen. Through this effort, I hope to bring some justice to the victims of the cult. I also enlisted Queen Eleanor's assistance. Her influence should assure that the evil brotherhood is properly pursued.

So as you see, my dear friend, I am past the worst of my trials and miseries. My happiness now is in my child. I must confess that I have named him Martin after one whom he will love as I do when he knows him. And I have another confession, a thing I shall admit to you alone. Tell it to no one, not even to those whom it concerns. Little Martin is not Gilles's son but Edmond's. My aunt at Crecy never knew. She believed the child was born at Evremont, conceived at a time when the count had not yet left and could have fathered him. He was, in fact, born in the same inn at Dieppe where Edmond and I met.

All I pray now is that Edmond will survive the war. Somehow, whether from wanting it badly or some finer intuition, I believe he will. As for myself, I've already grown tired of court life at Winchester. Were Queen Eleanor here, I might stay, but she is almost always abroad in one of Richard's Frankish duchies. I know my uncle will welcome both me and my child. Since I must, I will find a way to deal with Melisande.

Now, my friend, I must finish. The other Martin is calling me, and what a loud cry he has! Please write me here and not yet at Bourne Castle. When I depart, I shall make sure my letters are sent to Windham. I am now a countess and command some deference. How foolish people are! If only they knew the price that title cost me and how gladly I would have foregone it. This letter will travel by royal courier with several others for the court of Sicily. It should reach you more quickly for that reason.

Please write with your news from that other great island. Above all, tell me how things are with you.

Martin found himself deeply moved by Elise's letter. She had confided the truth about her son to him, even given the child his name! He would of course respect her confidence completely. What troubled him was something else. Years ago, knowing the hardship of her life at Evremont, he had decided not to tell Elise the news of Edmond's marriage. Now, on the eve of her return to Windham, she still made no mention of his wife and children. Was it mere tact, or might Edmond have kept it from her? Martin could only guess. Time alone would reveal what the lovers knew or did not know. Meanwhile, Martin dared to hope that what Elise had done might mean the end of the Abraxas cult.

35

"Your chamber is the same, my lady. We kept it this way all these years for when you came to visit, but you never did. I pray the Lord you're home for good now."

It was the same old Margaret Elise remembered, equally full of admonition and affection. As she entered the room, the memories overwhelmed her. Here was the curtained bed where she had hidden Edmond's notes, the window where she watched the Count de Vere's arrival, the chest which had once held the clothes she took to court at Winchester. The room was full of the ghosts of her youth, melancholy visions of past hopes and dreams.

In the midst of her sadness, Elise reminded herself that she had not returned alone. In her arms, she held her sleeping son, Now seven months old, he was a constant joy, the one great gift that fate had given her in compensation for the rest.

Drawing her near to the light, Margaret made a closer inspection. "My darling girl, any fool could see how worn out you are. They shouldn't have let the servants tire you with their greetings. Here, let me take the child."

Despite her age, perhaps sixty-five, Margaret took little Martin with practiced ease. Time had altered her, of course. Her face was lined, her limbs were heavier, she stooped now when she walked, but she did not falter as she lowered her new charge into his roomy crib.

"Come see your little bird's nest, my love. I've put it here in the corner away from drafts. A pretty thing, ain't it? As soon as the earl knew you were coming, he had the castle joiner make it. It's big enough to last him till he's three."

The crib was, indeed, a fine one. The sides were strong, the linen soft and spotless. On both head and foot boards, birds and flowers were carved into the wood and brightly painted. As Elise watched Margaret lay a little cover on her son, the tender pairing of her dear old nurse and sleeping child touched her deeply, and her eyes began to fill with tears. Seeing them, Margaret took her old charge in her arms. She spoke in the same crooning voice she had used when Elise was a little girl. "No, no, my sweet, no need to cry. You're home safe now with Margaret watching over you."

*

Elise had returned in October. On the day of her arrival, she had seen Melisande briefly. In the midst of her uncle's heartfelt greetings, exclamations over little Martin, and the rest, she was able to conceal her animosity towards her aunt. Melisande was much older, of course, perhaps fifty, although she had never revealed her true age, but her beauty was still apparent. From that day forward, the two avoided each other, meeting only in company. It helped that Elise was often in her chamber with her child. Melisande, in turn, kept to her solar in the winter months. Thus, for the present, she was spared close contact with the woman who had worked for so long to destroy her happiness and Edmond's.

Over the years, beneath the lies and half-truths of the letters penned by Melisande, one thing had clearly emerged, the fact that the earl was often ill. Elise had been distressed and puzzled by it. The uncle she left was a typical ruddy-cheeked Norman, large-boned and sturdy with a thick blond beard. Now nearly sixty, he was thinner, gray-haired, and balding, all of which might be the effects of aging. Yet he seemed also to have shrunk, not just in breadth but in height, to be a somehow diminished version of himself. This, she felt sure, was the effect of repeated illness.

That was all that she knew until, late one evening, she was seated alone in her room with her sleeping child. Brigida, the serving girl who helped to care for Martin, had just left. Elise was reading a book of selections from the philosophers, a parting gift from Queen Eleanor. In her youth, as was the custom, she and Margaret had shared a bed. Now, because of her age and irregular hours, the old servant slept in a nearby room. Elise was deep in her reading when she heard a sound that stirred her memory, three knocks in succession followed by a single tap. It was the signal Elise had invented for herself and Margaret as a child. Surprised to hear it at this hour, she walked to the door and admitted her nurse. Stepping inside, Margaret closed the door firmly and began to talk at once.

"Forgive me for disturbing you so late, my lady. It's long past my bedtime, but I couldn't sleep. There's something I've wanted to say ever since you returned. I believe it's time I did."

Concerned, Elise had Margaret sit in the chair beside her, and her nurse went on.

"The long and short of it, my love, is this: during the years you were gone, I watched as a terrible crime was nearly done, not just once, but three times to the best of my knowledge."

"What crime, Margaret? And by whom?"

"I quake as I say the words. Even here in the dark of night, I must whisper them. Murder, against the earl by his wife, the Lady Melisande."

Elise was shocked, of course, but knowing her aunt as she did, not as much as her nurse might have expected. "Go on."

"During the years you were gone, they sometimes put me in the kitchen. I worked beside the cooks and made the dishes I was good at. It was there I first noticed the Lady Melisande would sometimes come and make a fuss over some special dish, some treat to be served to the earl. So awed were they all that no one saw what I did, that after a few of these visits, the earl often fell ill. When he did, his wife would feed him in his chamber. From then on, things would grow worse and worse. Three times this happened by my count. The last time, it was so bad he nearly died. The strange part is that just when the earl was most ill, the Lady Melisande would stop making her dishes. After that, he would gradually improve, but each time it took longer. In the end, it left him the way you see him today."

"Let me understand you, Margaret. You believe that my aunt tried to kill my uncle using poison, and each time, just when she nearly succeeded, changed her mind?"

"I do, my lady. Once, the time before last, I caught her in the act. My eyes are not so good up close, but I can see very well from a distance. Your aunt had no notion I was watching. As she leaned over a dish meant for the earl, she unstopped a tiny vial, poured in the contents, and mixed them in. After that, she left. Luckily, I had time to make the same dish before they served it. From that time on, I often did the same, making a similar dish in my own little corner and substituting it when no one else was looking."

"How brilliant you were, my dear Margaret. Thank God you were there if what you say is true."

"It is true, my love, I'd stake my life on it. What I can't understand is why she always changed her mind. As for myself, each time your uncle worsened, I decided to speak to his steward, an honest man. Then I realized it would do little good. Who would believe an old nurse who had lost her charge, a creature already out of favor with her mistress? I knew I was here by the earl's grace alone. All it would mean is my banishment from the kitchen. And I needed to be there to change her dishes when I could. I went on doing so. In truth, I believe I helped to keep the earl alive."

Elise was extremely distressed by Margaret's revelation, but she also wanted to understand her aunt's behavior. "When was the last time my uncle was ill?"

"Four years ago, my sweet, about a year before Roland died. The boy was always a sickly and nasty thing. He only got worse as he grew older—mean and rebellious, fond of every vice. By the time he came of age, not even the Lady Melisande could deal with him. They found him dead in the lowest kind of inn, a bawdy house in Clarington. Dead at the age of twenty-two. They say he drank himself to death."

As she listened to the wretched tale, Elise began to make some sense of it. If the earl had died after Roland came of age, the boy would have been earl, leaving his mother at his mercy. Or if Roland had died, the title would have fallen to the next male de Bourne in line, a cousin of some kind. She spoke that last thought to her nurse. "Melisande knew that Roland might not live. With him dead, she would have lost her husband's income. Perhaps that's why she changed her mind."

"True enough, my love, but what drove her to this madness in the first place?"

Margaret had clearly thought about the puzzle for a long time, but Elise knew something she did not, the troubled connection between the Count de Vere and Melisande. Its fraught nature had surely caused both her crimes and her vacillation.

"Dear Margaret, I think I know the reason, but I'd rather not speak of it for now." Elise did not want to further prejudice her nurse against the count, the man she thought was little Martin's father. Not yet, at least.

"That's up to you, my lady. I'm sure you have your reasons. I've told you all I know, and now it's off my conscience. If you've no more questions, I'll leave you to your thoughts."

"After what you've told me, my dear Margaret, I have a good deal to think about. First, I must thank you for your wisdom and your courage. I am immensely in your debt. I believe you saved my uncle's life. Rest easy now, and leave this thing to me. The nightmare you were forced to live is over."

Despite her reassurances to Margaret, Elise gave in to distraction once she was gone. Pacing the room, she knocked her book from the table beside her chair, waking little Martin. She took him in her arms and rocked him gently as she walked and thought. Although she had guessed the cause, she was still bewildered by Melisande's actions. Had she hoped in her madness that Gilles would kill Elise, leaving them free to marry? Had the count let her believe that? If so, he had nearly cost the earl his life. Thank God her uncle had kept Margaret on despite the fact that Melisande disliked her. As was the case with so many prideful people, her aunt had underestimated those beneath her.

The next day, having absorbed the first shock, Elise began to feel complicit in all the earl had suffered. If, years ago, she had told him the truth about the count and Melisande, she might have averted so much suffering! And not only her uncle's but hers and Edmond's. On the other hand, as Melisande had warned at the time, he might not have believed her. Why torment herself with thoughts of what could no longer be undone? The earl had survived, little Martin and she were safe, and Edmond had found his great cause in the Holy Land. Still, when she looked at her uncle in his present state, it was hard to say what she felt most, loathing for Melisande or remorse at her own silence.

It took another unexpected revelation to divert her from these morbid thoughts. A few days after her talk with Margaret, Elise was seated with her uncle in his cabinet, the room where she had always gone to be alone with him. Since her return, there had been little time to talk in private. She asked him about his affairs. He responded by speaking about his tenants.

"Despite disappointing harvests, Alfred Rendon has kept Preston Manor intact and even made improvements. Baron Hugh is no use, of course, because of drink, but now at least he seldom interferes. His fretful wife is no better, but Mistress Aeline, slight in stature though she is, remains a bulwark. She is determined to protect her family's interests."

Happy to hear some good news from the manor, Elise was puzzled only by the unfamiliar name, *Mistress Aeline*. Who was it, she wondered, some cousin come to Preston Manor to attend to Edmond's hapless mother? She turned to her uncle. "Mistress Aeline? I don't believe I know her."

"Indeed? Hasn't Margaret mentioned her? After all, Edmond Preston was your fellow pupil. She might have thought you would want to know about his marriage."

"Marriage?" Elise's first reaction was disbelief. "Who is it you say is married?"

"Edmond Preston, of course. Married and father of two children. The boy was named after Godfrey of Bouillon, the first great conqueror of Jerusalem."

When at last she understood, Elise was overcome by shock, then shame. Why had Edmond not told her? Why had no one else? Martin, for instance, who must have known for years.

Her uncle saw her puzzled look. "Melisande did not write the count and you about it? I myself was not well at the time."

She made an effort to calm herself. "No, no one ever wrote or told me." Even as she spoke, she began to understand. Melisande had a reason for not writing the count about Edmond. She had kept their pact, just as Elise had; neither had revealed the other's lover. Martin, aware of her unhappiness at Evremont, had also spared her. Margaret, recalling her youthful love for Edmond, had also put off telling her the news. However well meant, their silence had only postponed the truth. Having learned it at last, Elise needed time to think.

"Dear uncle, I find I am a bit fatigued. You will forgive me if I go?" She could think of no better excuse.

"Of course. I myself have to meet with my steward. Take care you don't become ill. This wasting fever in Windhamshire has claimed more victims. Your child needs you, just as I do. You can't imagine how happy I am to have you here."

Elise forced a smile in response and left. She felt an overwhelming need to be alone. Brigida and Margaret were tending little Martin in her chamber. She could not go there and act as if nothing had changed. Instead, she walked toward the stairway to the court below. Reaching it, she saw there were too many people; servants, petitioners, guards from the garrison. Where could she go? Was there no quiet place in Bourne Castle?

The chapel, of course! Since the death of Father Barnabas, a priest from the abbey had come to say Mass on holy days and Sundays. Otherwise, it was little used. Reversing her steps, she took the stairs leading there.

Inside, she sat in one of the chairs the household members used at services. The dark interior smelled of damp. The chapel was old with narrow windows. They had only recently been filled with leaded glass. Through the colorless panes, she could see a bit of sullen sky. All the while, she kept thinking of Edmond's marriage. Why had he not told her? Bewildered, she tried to pray, begging to be reconciled to the truth. But it was no good. There was no comfort in her ungrateful prayers. Feeling the cold, she decided to go. Then, just as she stood, a new thought came to her. Edmond might have thought she knew already, that she had preferred not to speak about his marriage. Their perfect day and night had happened in a kind of dream, a time and place apart, a world no larger than a little chamber on the Norman coast. That dream had now ended. Her child, the fruit of their love, was but one of the three children Edmond had sired.

But who was the woman he had married? Slight in stature, her uncle had said, but also a bulwark at Preston Manor. All at once, Elise was seized by a desire to see her, to meet her without delay. Not today, of course. It was already too late, and she was still too agitated. She would ask to visit on the morrow, sending a message to that effect. In fact, nothing could be more fitting. Elise was a young mother too, the earl was her uncle's liege lord. It was only right that she visit the wife of the man who wore her uncle's colors in the holy war. She would do her duty and, at the same time, satisfy her curiosity.

*

The next afternoon, Elise did as planned—and returned in the evening defeated. As soon as she saw Aeline, a small, freckled woman with reddish hair, she was disarmed. The late autumn day was strangely warm, an early St. Martin's summer. Devoid of pretense, with a ready smile, Aeline suggested they sit in the manor garden she had planted. She was five years younger than Elise, but childbirth and family cares seemed to have aged her beyond her years. Still, when she spoke of her husband in Outremer, her face lit up like a girl's. Her oldest child, Rosalind, was six, sweet, shy, and strangely grave. She had Edmond's deep-blue eyes. Her mother said that she missed her father greatly. Young Godfrey, at four and a half, had his father's brown curls and smile. At first, he hid behind his mother. Later, warming to Elise, he gradually grew bolder. A loose silver band around her wrist intrigued him.

"I wear little jewelry," Aeline said, "he is fascinated by your bracelet." There was neither flattery nor envy in her voice, merely a statement of fact.

"Then allow me to give it to you as a present." At once, Elise was afraid this might seem condescending. "For Godfrey's sake, I mean. I have four, all bought in the market in Palermo. I never wear more than one."

"Thank you, my lady. I'm afraid I might never wear it. As for Godfrey, his tastes change every day. He likes shiny things at the moment."

Elise smiled but did not insist. Inside the neck of her gown, she had another silver thing. She was about to take it out for Godfrey when she stopped. What if Aeline asked her how she came by it, or worse, had a similar pendant with *E* and *A*, Edmond's initial entwined with hers? Elise's fear made her see the falsity of her position.

Yet she was already fond of this young woman. Aeline, in turn, wanted to know all about her, especially her life at court in Winchester and Sicily. By now, Maddie, the serving girl, had taken the children to the bottom of the garden. Elise talked for a while, then asked Aeline about her life at Preston Manor. Aeline answered sincerely, not complaining but frankly admitting the difficulties posed by Edmond's parents. Then she spoke about her loneliness without her husband. Towards the end, with great intensity of feeling, she talked of the things she admired about him. Her love for her husband seemed close to adoration. Elise felt both sympathy and envy. How could it be otherwise, with the woman who was married to the man she loved?

Aeline must have seen a look of sadness on Elise's face. She leaned forward, as if to grasp Elise's hand, and then pulled back, perhaps feeling their difference in rank. She spoke instead. "Has my talk made you think of your own husband, my lady?"

There was a cruel irony in the question. "No, it's not that," said Elise, feeling strangely humiliated. "Perhaps it's just that I envy the life you have had with your husband and children. In truth, I dislike speaking about my marriage. It was not a happy one. I was alone much of the time, friendless and isolated."

"And the count?"

"He was often away, and I preferred it when he was. It's too long and too sordid a story to tell. He's gone now, it's uncertain where. I intend never to see him again or to let him see my child. It is one of the reasons I've come back to Windham."

"I'm sorry to hear that, my lady. You deserve better. Still, even the happiest marriages have their sorrows."

Elise wondered what sorrows Aeline might mean. After a moment's thought, she guessed them. However deceived Elise had been about his marriage, she felt sure it was she, not Aeline, whom Edmond truly loved. That thought should have made her happy. Instead, she felt guilty and also wary. What was her purpose here, after all? She stood up and embraced Aeline.

"I must leave you now. You've been very kind. I hope you feel you've found a friend in me. The next time, I'll bring little Martin. When he's older, Rosalind and Godfrey must come to Bourne Castle to play. Martin has known so few other children. For now, I would like to send some things for you and them."

"There's no need for that, my lady. We're well provided for."

"I'm sure you are, but the earl himself wishes it. Your husband is his champion in Outremer. The war has deprived you of him. These are gifts of gratitude."

"In that case, I'll accept them in my husband's name. Please thank the earl for me."

*

Before going back to Bourne Castle, Elise decided to stop at the church in the village. Once again, she felt the need to be alone, this time to calm the feelings her visit had provoked. As she rode, she nodded to the villagers who were abroad. Despite the years, they all seemed to remember her. As she passed her old teacher's cottage, she thought briefly of visiting, but she was in no proper state. Her thoughts were too unsettled and confused. She used the stone block by the church to dismount, tying her horse to a nearby post. Entering, she was grateful to find it was empty. She knelt and prayed earnestly this time, not for herself but for her son, that he might one day know his father. Then she thought for a long time and prayed again. When at last she emerged into the amber light of evening, the shadows of the houses nearly spanned the street.

Inside the church, Elise had made up her mind about her future. She and Edmond had pledged their love three times, at Canon Thomas's cottage, in Winchester, and at the inn before he left for Outremer. The last time, she had been strangely sure that God would bring her lover back, but that was before she had learned about his marriage. Now, for some reason, her certainty had disappeared. For the first time, Elise feared he might die in battle, and she was unable to bear the thought. Kneeling on the floor of the church, she had made a solemn vow. If God would let Edmond return alive and well, she would give up her own selfish desires and surrender him to his wife and children.

*

The following morning, Elise made sure that the gifts she had promised were sent to the manor. She remained firm in the vow she had made, however unhappy the thought of giving up Edmond made her. The next day was All Hallows' Eve, bringing October to a close. With it, the first breath of winter arrived, spreading a chill through the walls of Bourne Castle. The following day was the Feast of All Saints, the next day, All Souls, the day for remembrance of the dead. After Mass in the chapel, Elise joined the earl at the midday meal. Amid the din of the assembled household, she spoke of her visit to Preston Manor, telling her uncle about her fondness for Aeline.

Afterward, a serving girl stopped her in the gallery. "I have a message for you, please, madam, from Preston Manor."

Very likely a note to thank me for the gifts, Elise thought as she took the small parchment, moved toward the light of a window, and broke the seal. The message was written in a crimped, unsteady hand.

My dear Lady Elise, presuming upon our short acquaintance, I must ask a sad favor. I beg you to inform the earl, my husband's patron, that Edmond was killed on a sortie south of Acre in the Holy Land. The news came today from a returning soldier who arrived last night. Alfred Rendon, the steward of Preston Manor, will attend the earl tomorrow morning to inform him of the circumstances of the death. I myself will be leaving on the morrow with my children for my parents' home near Fenbury. I will begin my mourning there. I thank you for your kindness in this and all other matters.

As she finished reading, Elise felt her head growing light. She reached out to the window ledge but somehow missed it. When she opened her eyes, she lay on her back on the cold slate floor. The serving girl was beside her, telling her Margaret was on the way. Above her, the stone vaulting of the gallery seemed suspended in the air. Staring up at it, she had a single thought: she had made her vow too late.

36

The stairs creaked loudly as, candle in hand, Gilles climbed to the attic room where he would sleep that night. Inside, he smelled rosemary mixed with the rushes and saw at once the room was clean. There was a chair, a low bed, and a pitcher and bowl on a table. He set the candle beside them. After months spent hiding in shabby inns, damp undercrofts, and stinking barns, it was a relief to have decent shelter. Weary, he sat on the bed. It smelled of lavender, a welcome contrast to the soiled straw and dingy bedding he had lain on for so long.

Anticipating a restful night, he dug into his bag and took out a leather flask. It held a new drink he had come to favor, a rich liquor distilled from wine. The taste was sweet and strong. He swallowed a mouthful, letting the flavor roll over his tongue. He took a second drink, delighted that this hiding would soon be over. After the cult at Evremont had been discovered, he and Gramont had fled first briefly to England, then to Brittany. When the latter, too, became unsafe, they had departed for Flanders. Now, finally, they had returned to Rouen for a single night. As he lifted the flask to his lips, Gilles heard a noise on the stairs. Instinctively, his hand gripped the knife at his waist. He let it go as Gramont appeared. Stepping into the room, the prior stood at the center, the only spot where his head failed to graze the rafters.

"Tomorrow night, using darkness for cover, we'll leave Normandy and ride south. I didn't want to speak before our host at supper, but I have had news about our members. More have been arrested."

"In Normandy?" Gilles asked.

"Yes, and in Brittany also. I have no idea who betrayed them."

Not Mordran, Gilles thought. After being arrested, he had slit his own throat rather than yield to torture. "It may have been one of my servants. They were a surly lot, always complaining I paid them too little."

"Which you probably did," Gramont noted dismissively, "not that it matters now."

"Speaking of betrayal," Gilles countered, "are you certain our host can be trusted?"

"Although no longer among us," the prior said, "he has never flagged in his support. He is much esteemed in Rouen as a wealthy merchant. It would mean his ruin if someone exposed his past."

Reassured, Gilles motioned toward the chair. The prior sat and went on. "Two members with horses will meet us outside the city gate. We'll skirt the city of Paris on the way."

"And our destination?"

"Burgundy, outside Norman jurisdiction. Then, very likely, in stages, Marseilles."

"And after that?"

"I can't be sure. There'll be time enough to discuss that later."

Gilles had not expected an answer. The prior always kept something to himself. Nor, at the moment, did he care. With the help of the liquor and the wine at supper, he was suffused with a pleasant glow. Now that he knew they were leaving, he was in a reminiscent mood.

"Do you recall when we first met each other, cousin? Having heard of your humble beginnings, I was greatly surprised at the man you'd become."

"I had worked hard to erase the misery of my youth. However I loathed it, the Church was the easiest path to the power and influence I craved."

The prior seemed more talkative than usual tonight. Gilles asked another question. "Had you already encountered the cult before you chose the Church?"

"Yes, as a young man in Outremer, in Syria. I've never told you before, but it was Reynald de Chatillon who introduced me to the brotherhood."

"The famous knight of the Kingdom of Jerusalem?"

"Famous or infamous according to your taste. Without noble rank, he had caused a great scandal by marrying the widow of the King of Antioch. He was the secret leader of the cult in Outremer, but the rites of Abraxas are much older and obscure. Many believe they go back to pagan Egypt."

Gilles hazarded one more question. "What was it that first drew you to the brotherhood?"

Gramont replied without hesitation. "Besides the influence of Chatillon, three things: the allure of forbidden pleasure, a love of the pagan past, and perhaps most of all, a deep-seated hatred of the Church."

"And it was you who began the meetings in the west?"

"Myself and a few men of influence. Gradually, others joined us. We met first in Brittany before you were a member, then in Windham, and later, of course, at Evremont."

Gilles had more questions, but Gramont seemed to sense them coming. "That's enough of the past for tonight. We have an eventful day tomorrow."

With that, careful to avoid the sloped ceiling, the prior stood and withdrew, leaving Gilles with his unanswered questions and his flask. Fatigued but still alert, he lay down on the bed. Reminded of Evremont, he thought about Elise, his errant wife. Full of pride though she was, he had done his best to humble her. He had been furious when he found her gone. Still, her income was all that mattered. Luckily, Mordran had sent him a full year's revenue before he was arrested. It was hard to say when he would see so much again. Now his thoughts drifted from Elise to Melisande. Faithful despite his neglect, she would have written him if her niece had returned to Bourne Castle. To no avail; only Mordran had known how to reach him. Now no one did, or so he hoped.

A year and a half had now passed since he had enjoyed the dark pleasures of the cult. Closing his eyes, he summoned a vision of those he had savored on the altar of Abraxas: blue-eyed maidens with golden hair, farm girls with ripe breasts and ruddy cheeks, pale beauties with dark hair, full lips, and captivating eyes. He had always both loved and hated women, ever since his childhood when the mother he adored had run off with a cleric, a young priest called to attend to the spiritual needs of her dying husband. Years later, Gilles heard she had died in a village where the priest, long since defrocked, had learned some trade, a degradation for a woman of her birth. When his father died, Gilles's kinfolk took him in begrudgingly. They made him suffer for his mother's shame. Even after his fortune had altered and he had become the Count of Evremont, he had never forgiven his mother for leaving. Nor had he ever stopped hating both her and the hypocrites of the Church.

Whatever the cause, he had grown up consumed by a desire for women, and never more keenly than during the rites of Abraxas. When, in his early years, he was first chosen to deflower the victim, he had taken the prior's advice; to seduce, not rape, to caress, not crush, to give his victim pleasure even in her terror. He often wondered if he had succeeded. There was no way of knowing. Bound, gagged, and drugged, the victims were mute until the end. All he knew was that his own desire had been immense, enough to carry him through to the gruesome conclusion. At first, of course, it shocked him, a blasphemous mockery of the Mass in which the members, many themselves deranged by drugs, had sampled portions of the now dead victim's flesh and blood. After that night, he knew there was no turning back.

That was the great gift of the cult. It had freed him from the prison of good and evil. And as the years passed, his need for its rite, like his need for strong drink, only seemed to grow. Tonight, in this proper burgher's house, it was hard to imagine such things. However, once they were safe in the South, the gatherings would resume. Then he would once again know the unspeakable joy of the total possession of another lovely victim.

*

In the morning, waking long after sunrise, Gilles felt the familiar aching in his head. Once again, he had drunk too much. He would be better after he ate. Rising, he used the pitcher and basin to wash, then dressed and prepared to go down to break his fast. Stepping out of the room, he paused to adjust to the darkness of the stairs. Halfway to the bottom, he heard a loud shout, then voices raised in confusion. Head throbbing, he entered the room below and saw Gramont restrained by two armed men. Two more were binding his hands, another was giving directions. There was no sign of their host. They had been lured into a trap.

Now two men seized Gilles's arms and took his knife. Without a weapon, it was useless to resist. Soon he too was restrained. Panicked, he looked pleadingly at Gramont. The prior moved his head slowly from left to right, compressing his lips as if to say *tell them nothing*. Still, it was hard to see how even the wily Gramont could save them now.

*

Huddled in the corner of his cell, Gilles lay in the filth of the stinking straw and listened to the screams. He was in total darkness, shackled and chained to the wall in the spot where they had thrown him the night before. Even his feet were confined, separated by an iron bar that made it difficult to stand, impossible to walk. So this was the end of their journey, not safe in the South but here in Caen, locked in the stronghold of the castle. Two days hence, from what he surmised, the prior and he would both be dead. Meanwhile, the screams went on. Once or twice, he thought he recognized a member's voice, but when their agony grew too great, they all sounded horribly the same. As they were put on the rack and flogged, their shrieks grew more piercing until they peaked, then subsided into moans and sobs. How slight the suffering of the victims of the cult had been compared to this! At least the pain of their repeated violation and slow death was soothed by drugs.

Here at Caen, for whatever reason, he and Gramont had so far been spared. The day they were taken at Rouen, they were locked in a room, fed decent food, and questioned separately. Gramont had been clear on the tack they must take, denying everything. He told him they had powerful friends, that before long they would be released. As always, Gilles did as his cousin commanded, denying all knowledge of the cult.

The next day, the pretense of civility was over. Gramont and he were bound and gagged, thrown into a covered cart, and jostled about in the darkness for days until they reached Caen on the Norman coast. Here in the stronghold of the castle, they were separated. When he had last seen Gramont, there was a strangely serene expression on his face. It was then that he understood. There would be no rescue. The prior had decided to die a martyr to Abraxas and expected him to do the same. Gilles wanted none of it. Since that moment, he had thought of one thing only. If he confessed fully, betraying the prior and the cult, would it make a difference in his fate? He had already denied everything. If he told the truth now, would they believe him?

From what he had learned, these Christian tormenters gave no respite to their victims. At Rouen, they had already executed seven of the cult. The shrieks he heard now were from four Breton members who had recently been taken. He had learned about their capture from his jailer, a pockmarked brute with a thick, top-heavy body. He had also told him that the men in charge, both the clerics who interrogated and the torturers appointed by the secular authorities, took great pleasure in their work, displaying a zeal that went far beyond the discovery of the truth.

At last, the distant screams came to a halt. Grateful for a respite, Gilles lay his head on the straw and fell quickly asleep. Later, how much later, he had no way of knowing, he awoke as the door to his cell creaked open and a light appeared. It was a lamp held by his jailer, blinding after hours of darkness. As Gilles slowly grew used to the light, the man spoke in a hoarse, gloating voice.

"You and the priest are known to be leaders of the cult. Tomorrow, you'll both be tortured—flogged or put on the rack or both. They'll question you in between. You'll be separated from your friend, of course. If your answers don't match, they'll begin again. They'll tell you that if you repent, the priest will absolve you of your sins but don't believe them. Your crimes are too grave for that."

Why, Gilles wondered, was this man telling him this? Was it sheer cruelty, or some kind of trick? Now he came nearer. Bending over, he lowered the lamp, examining Gilles close at hand. Lit from below, the man's pitted face was grotesque. Gilles watched as he opened his thick lips and roared. "Heretic! Blasphemer! Ravisher, murderer, spawn of the devil!"

He tried to avoid the man's spittle but failed. A thick spray landed on his face. A moment later, he felt a sickening pain in his groin. The jailer had kicked him there. Screaming, Gilles joined the others who had now begun again. Writhing, he tried to curl up into a ball, but his pinioned legs stopped him. Then came another searing blow, the full force of a chain mail glove across his face. He tasted blood on his lips as his tormenter left, slamming the door behind him.

When he was gone, Gilles lay in the darkness, wondering at the man's venom. And still the real horror had not yet begun. There was only one thing that gave him pleasure, a bit of revenge on his cousin for deceiving him. Earlier that day, the jailor had told him. He and Gramont would not be executed publicly. The prior would be no martyr to Abraxas. Neither he nor the cult would gain fame by his death. Tortured and murdered in secret, he would soon be forgotten, his body discarded like offal, his name and the name of Abraxas obliterated. *Small comfort,* Gilles, thought, since he would meet the same fate. Where pain was concerned, he was a coward and willing to admit it.

But what he wouldn't give for a flask of wine! He was over the worst horrors of the craving, beyond that first night of hell-borne visions in the wagon on the way to Caen. Now his thirst had returned, worse since he knew it might never again be quenched. Cursing Gramont, he vowed to expose him as the single author of Abraxas's crimes. Then he would tell all he knew and abjectly repent. He would swear that he too was a victim, a slave to the opiates used in the cult rites.

Once more, the screaming! He could bear it no longer. He gnawed at the edge of his shirt till it frayed, tore off small strips and stuffed them in his ears. He wadded two more for his nostrils, hoping to stifle the odor of excrement. The stench improved, but the screams did not. They seemed to bore deeper and deeper into his head until his brain seemed a mere function of their penetration. Somehow, in the midst of it all, he fell back to sleep.

The loud crash of his cell door awoke him. In the glare of a torch, he slowly made out two figures. One carried a sword, the other something that sounded like keys. In the next moment, Gilles found himself calling on God, on Abraxas, on any power in the universe that might still listen, praying that once he successfully betrayed the prior, he would be spared the worst horrors of the torture and go swiftly to his death.

37

From the first, Elise had been forced to conceal the crushing sorrow she felt at the news of Edmond's death. The day she heard, embarrassed to have fainted, she insisted on taking the note to the earl herself. She watched him read it and asked to be present the following morning when Alfred Rendon related the circumstances of the death.

For once, the earl refused her. "As a young man in the second holy war, I saw things I could never speak of to a woman. It would not be fair to Master Rendon to ask him to repeat the stories of a battle-hardened soldier with a lady present."

Elise was not so easily put off. "Mistress Aeline is much younger than I and has seen much less of life, and yet she has been told the truth."

"My dear Elise, she was his wife. You were merely a fellow pupil."

She winced at the words, unable to deny their seeming truth. Reluctantly, she deferred to her uncle's wishes. He, in turn, promised to give her the information afterward. The next day, when Alfred Rendon had gone, she went to his cabinet, warmed as always by a welcome brazier. A bitter cold had struck Windham overnight. The change seemed to echo the chill in her heart.

Her uncle began in his usual hesitant way. Then, as if resolved to have the thing over with, he plunged into the tale. "It seems that after the great victory at Acre, Edmond was chosen as one of seven for a sortie to the south. To deceive the enemy, the scouting party dressed as Muslims and rode Arab steeds. Their band went as far down the coast as Caesaria, making constant forays inland. On the last of these, a large contingent of the enemy attacked. During the engagement, four men were killed. Afterward, two men were missing and one made his way back to Acre. It was he who told news of their defeat. Edmond was one of the missing two. Ten days later, his body was found several miles from the place of the engagement. Because of the heat, it was already much decayed. They recognized him from his bloodstained clothing. With heroic strength, he had torn it to bind his own wounds, which were severe. On one piece there was a badge."

Her uncle paused, clearly moved. Then, bracing himself, he went on. "It was my arms, the colors of Bourne Castle, that identified him. They say he always wore a badge with my escutcheon. It was almost as if he knew he might be found in such a manner in a place where no one knew him."

He had always believed he would die, Elise thought. She had felt it that day when they parted but denied it. She had tried to imbue him with her certainty, her conviction that he would live, but he had known better.

"He died a hero's death," her uncle concluded. "Those on the mission were chosen for their valor. They went courageously despite the danger. The one man who returned conveyed the information they had gathered, greatly assisting the Christian forces."

As Elise sat by the brazier and listened, words like *valor, courageous*, and *hero* worked on her like burning coals, each adding to the growing fire inside her. She wanted to scream in protest, to upend the brazier and burn down the room, to destroy men's belief in the nobility of war. Foolishly, she had asked to learn the truth. Now she wished she could eradicate her uncle's words, forget the way her lover died, and wash away the image of his rotting body with her tears. Thanking her uncle for the information, she said nothing more and left.

That night, alone with her sleeping child, Elise remembered the vow she had made in Windham parish church. Despite all Canon Thomas had taught them, she had tried to bargain with

God out of superstitious fear. What had made her think the promise of her sacrifice could save her lover's life?

The next few days were a living horror, harder for her because, unlike Aeline, she was forced to conceal her grief. Her life had been irrevocably altered, but she had to act as if a mere acquaintance of her youth had passed away. Had Aeline been at Preston Manor, Elise could have at least joined in her mourning. As it was, she felt suffocated by her hidden sorrow. Were it not for her child, she was sure she would have sunk into despair, but when she held him close and looked into his smiling face, she saw Edmond and their love, a love that would live on in him.

Then, little more than a week after learning of Edmond's death, she had a visitor from abroad. When the servant spoke the name, Jacques Severin, she was surprised and puzzled. Since Gilles's disappearance, the lawyer had cared for her interests at Crecy and Evremont, but she had only met him once. Now, with no warning, he was here in Windham.

"Take Master Severin to the small room off the gallery," she told the servant. "And tell him I shall join him there."

The room was poorly lit and sparsely furnished with a table and three chairs. When she entered, she saw a small, bearded man in somber clothing standing by the only window. She asked him to be seated and took the chair across from him.

"You've come a long way, sir. Let me welcome you to Bourne Castle. You will stay the night, of course."

"Thank you, my lady. I've come from Winchester, stopping one night along the way. I'm afraid I must set out again this afternoon."

"I am sorry to hear that. Should you change your mind, please feel free to tell me so."

"You are very gracious, madam. Let me say first that I've come for your sake but also because of the memory of your Aunt Elizabeth, who was greatly concerned for your welfare. She was very dear to me as you know."

"She always spoke of you with great fondness."

"It gladdens my heart to hear it. May I tell you my business at once, since my time is short?"

"Yes, certainly."

Extracting two documents from a leather bag, the lawyer handed them to Elise. "These pages contain an account of the questioning, judgment, and execution of the cult members who were apprehended from the brotherhood that met at Evremont. You may not know that a few years back, his Holiness the Pope became distressed by fresh outbreaks of heresy, notably those of the Cathars and Waldensians. At that time, he issued a decree that enjoined all the bishops of Christendom to take the necessary measures to combat these heretics. Besides the usual spiritual tools, deprivation of the sacraments, excommunication, and the like, the decree allowed the dioceses to call upon the secular authorities for help in their interrogations. The result, described here in connection to the cult, may well offend you. You must use your own judgment in reading these pages. They were written by the chief interrogator at Rouen. This copy was given to me by the dean of the cathedral there. It is intended for you as the Countess de Vere and the mistress of Evremont. There is also a copy for you to send to Deacon Martin Rendon. As you have told me, and the authorities are now aware, he has long had an interest in the apprehension of this vicious band. His copy, like yours, has a short preamble written by the dean himself. Neither of you may repeat or otherwise disseminate the information here. The penalties for doing so could be severe. Is that clear to you, madam?"

"Yes, certainly, but before you go on, I have a question. What news has there been of my husband and the prior?"

"I was coming to that, my lady. The count and the prior were among those taken. As of November eleventh, the feast of St. Andrew, they were executed for their crimes in Caen. As heretics, they should have been burned in public, but in order to keep their arrest and execution secret, they were hanged inside the stronghold. That also is in the account."

Elise was astounded at the lawyer's words. She had hoped to see the monstrous cult suppressed. She had not thought it would happen so soon and in so violent a manner. For the moment, however, the fact of her husband's death eclipsed all else.

Still amazed, she asked, "Why in secret?"

"The Archbishop of Rouen is Walter de Coutances. He is also, as you may know, Justiciar of the Realm during King Richard's absence. The Dean of Rouen, John de Coutances, is his nephew. Although not a participant, he was in charge of the interrogations. It was he who gave me these documents. The Archbishop wished to avoid all scandal in this matter. Things are bad enough with King Richard in the Holy Land and his brother John doing all he can to undermine the kingdom here at home. The death of two men of the rank of your husband and the prior would bring too much attention to this evil brotherhood. As you know, they are a heretical sect of Gnostics dedicated to a godless power called Abraxas. Sometime during the months to come, news will appear from the east by way of a returning traveler, tidings of the deaths of your husband and the prior killed by bandits on their way to Outremer. In addition to quelling rumors of the cult, this fabrication will relieve you and your son from the stain of your husband's crimes. To make sure you are spared, I gave a generous donation in your name to the cathedral chapter at Rouen. Neither the world nor your infant child need ever know the truth about the Count de Vere."

Amazed at this windfall in little Martin's favor, Elise thanked the advocate profusely, assuring him that her funds had been well spent. Beyond that, she was too stunned to comment on his news. When he was gone, Elise remained in the dimly lit chamber for a long time pondering it all. The husband she loathed was dead, but so was the man she loved. The news of both deaths in such swift succession had left her depleted of all emotion. Nor could she bring herself to read the documents at present. She was still full of the images of Edmond's death. She wanted no more scenes of horror, even horror committed in the name of justice. She would read them later, before she sent Martin his copy. He would be happy to know of the cult's defeat. All he had told her in Palermo had at last come to fruition. The Abraxas cult as they had known it was no more.

Now she thought about little Martin, her dear friend's namesake. If the count had lived and learned she had a child, he would surely have denounced her and declared her son a bastard. She thanked God there was no danger of that now. Her son was safe, as was his inheritance, her lands at Crecy and what would be left of the count's estate when all his debts were paid. For little Martin's sake, if for nothing else, she must begin to live again.

*

A few days after Elise's meeting with the lawyer, Melisande for some reason began to take all her meals in her solar. She said she felt only fatigue, but the earl was afraid it might be the wasting fever that had broken out in Windhamshire earlier that fall. He called in a physician who assured him she did not. After that, a week passed during which her aunt never left her room. Then she grew suddenly worse.

"There's no question now that she is ill," her uncle said as he sat down to a hurried supper in the hall. The next day, he summoned Elise to his cabinet. As she took her accustomed seat, the earl addressed her in a somber voice.

"I need to speak to you about the Lady Melisande. Once again, the physician is sure it is not the fever, but he is at a loss to explain it otherwise. He wanted to bleed her to relieve the ill humors, but she refused, and yielding to her, I did not insist. I tell you all this because I need to ask a favor. As time has passed, a great distance has risen between you and your aunt. No doubt it's because she supported your unhappy marriage. She might not admit it, but I'm sure she has long regretted it."

"I thought perhaps she might have." It was all she could say without hinting at the truth.

"At any rate, she now wishes to see you." Her uncle hesitated. "She is weak and in pain and should not tire herself, but as always, I have acceded to her wishes. Would you be willing to go to her?"

"Of course, whenever you wish, my dear uncle." In truth, Elise wanted only to hear her aunt out and be done with it.

*

Over the years, taking refuge from her husband's ailments, the illnesses she herself had caused, Melisande had begun to use her solar as a sleeping chamber. This, too, Elise had learned from Margaret. Now Melisande herself was sick, and she was using the solar again. Teresa, her faithful maidservant, admitted Elise that afternoon. The beautiful chamber was dark, the window in the French style veiled in black. Her aunt could no longer bear the light. Growing used to the gloom, Elise saw the bed-curtains were open. Between them, so changed she scarcely recognized her, lay Melisande. Her eyes were closed. There was a chair beside the bed. Teresa motioned her toward it.

"She falls into short sleeps. She's begun to awaken from one now. She will be able to speak to you soon." With a final quick glance at her mistress, Teresa departed.

Seated, Elise felt strangely anxious. To calm herself, she studied her aunt. Melisande's skin, always pale, was now ghostly white. Her cheeks, once smooth and pink, were sunken. The sockets of her eyes seemed hollow. Her hair, which Teresa had tried to arrange, was the greatest surprise. It was almost completely gray, matted in parts and sparse in others. The last time Elise had seen her aunt, it had been its usual rich auburn.

With her eyes still closed, Melisande parted her lips. Her voice was thin but clear. "Does my hair surprise you? Until recently, Teresa kept it the color it has always been. She's quite skillful at these things."

Wincing with pain, Melisande opened her eyes. Their color was startling in the pallor of her face, like green stones set in white marble. They were all that was left of her beauty.

Staring, she examined Elise and spoke again. "I suppose I should thank you for coming although I'm sure you've done it for my husband's sake. I know death is growing inside me. That's why I've called you here."

Any pity Elise might have felt at this news was dispelled by what she had learned from Margaret. "Did you feel death growing in your husband also as you slowly poisoned him?"

She had surprised her aunt; she could tell from the altered expression on her face. Not for long, however. "No one can prove that. Was it that meddling old nurse who said so?"

"That hardly matters. As usual, I've kept the truth from my uncle. For his sake, not yours."

"In any case," Melisande gasped again, "he would not believe it."

"That may or may not be so. There's no point in discussing it." Angry now, Elise raised her voice. "Why have you asked me here?"

"To learn the truth," her aunt said in a weakening voice. "Or perhaps I should say, to affirm a truth that I've surmised. I've seen your child now several times, a handsome little boy. He is Edmond Preston's, is he not?"

Elise caught her breath. How had she guessed? Then she saw the way. She alone knew of Elise's past with Edmond. Aware of the date when Edmond left for Outremer, she had put the two things together. Still, she had no proof. Elise decided to deny it. "What an odd thought! And untrue, of course."

"Strange, then, that even here in this half-light, I saw your panic as I said it. You needn't be alarmed. Have you forgotten our agreement? We've each kept the other's love a secret all these years. Yours never stopped loving you despite his marriage. Now he has died a hero's death. Mine abandoned me for every slut who struck his fancy, then sank into the madness of a bestial cult." Once again, Melisande was forced to stop. She grimaced, then took a number of short breaths. "Now he too is dead, hanged as a murderer and heretic. I'll leave it to you to decide who has had the better of our bargain."

The last words were uttered in a kind of hiss, but they startled Elise for a different reason.

"How do you know the count is dead?"

"It was simple. I was still well when your lawyer came. I entered your room when I knew it was empty and found the document. It's what I feared might happen. Gramont was a brilliant man but also, I believe, quite mad. Gilles was in thrall to him to the end."

Elise recalled that her aunt had withdrawn from the world a few days after the lawyer's visit. "Since you know all," she demanded, incensed at this endless interference, "why have you asked me here?"

"I believe your child is Edmond's, but I cannot be sure. I am proposing another exchange. Two secrets of mine to your one." Gasping, Melisande clenched her teeth and her entire body shook. When she had recovered, she went on in a rasping voice. "Roland was not the earl's child but Gilles's. The earl never suspected. It's what first puzzled me about your son. I could see nothing of the count in him. Roland was doomed from the day I conceived him on a visit with your uncle to Rouen. During two decades apart, Gilles and I met on that one day only. It was my fate, as was our meeting again in Windham. Some loves bear only evil fruit. Our love . . . "

Her aunt started to choke. She took a deep breath and calmed herself, then closed her eyes for a long time. When she opened them, she spoke in a whisper.

"Whatever the nature of my love, Gilles's love was neither true nor lasting. So good at deceiving others, I deceived myself in this alone. You and I are alike in one thing. For us, there can be only one great love. I had mine twice, first in my youth, again in my prime. From the look of your child, you've done the same. To me, a day with the man you hated was worth years with any other. Disdain from him was sweeter than another's adoration. There was no right or wrong about it. I was simply made that way. Now he is dead, and I too am about to die. That is my second secret. I've taken a fatal poison little known in England, one that mimics natural death. I got it from Gertrude, my oldest friend. She still keeps that private inn at Winchester where you and Edmond met so long ago. In the usual dose, the poison acts slowly. It's quicker when administered in three re-peated doses. I took the third dose today. I should be dead by tomorrow. The pain is terrible but intermittent, alternating with bouts of sleep. Until the last sleep, from which I will not awake."

Elise listened, at first horrified, then angry. Her aunt had won again. She knew Elise would never tell her uncle either of her secrets. He had lived happily in ignorance so long, why de-stroy his illusions now?

Melisande was clearly in pain again. "As you see . . . I've told you everything." She reached for a pillow and clutched it to her stomach. As if calling on all her strength, she spoke in a harsh, emphatic voice. "I want only the truth, a truth I shall carry to the grave. All I have left is my vanity. Assure me that I, and I alone, ever bore the Count de Vere a son, that Gilles was not the father of your child."

Repelled by the selfish request, Elise responded with a ques-tion. "And if I refuse?"

"Before I die, I shall tell the earl what I believe, that your child is Edmond Preston's, that you two have deceived him all these years."

"You would violate our agreement?"

"Our old pact was not concerned with offspring. This new one will be. I shall keep it as I did the other, but first you must admit the truth."

The treacherous words filled Elise with rage. How dare this woman groping at death's door continue bargaining? She was like some monstrous polyp reaching out to poison everything she touched. And even if Elise complied, her aunt could still be-tray her. In her last moments with her husband, she could speak the fatal words, words that would follow little Martin all his life, turn him into a bastard, and negate his title and inheritance. Her uncle had trusted his wife all these years. Why would he doubt her now?

There had to be a way to stop her, to countermand her threats. Then Elise saw it, the only certain way. Until a moment ago, Melisande had been staring at her, waiting for her answer. Now she had closed her eyes. Had she lapsed into one of her periodic sleeps? In any event, she had let the pillow go. It lay beside her now. She would be dead soon anyway. It would take only a moment's work. A single act and the thing would be done. Her son would be safe, and she would be free of her persecutor. She thought of Edmond, dead in the Holy Land, of the happiness her aunt had taken from them both. A new flush of anger gave her strength, but her hands shook as she rose and grasped the pillow. Clutching it firmly, she pressed it onto her victim's face, bracing herself for a struggle. There was none. Her aunt's body lay inert beneath the covers. Trembling, Elise lifted the pillow. Melisande looked the same. Only her hair had been ruffled. She shuddered as she smoothed it, already concealing her crime. There was still no reaction. Her aunt was dead. How could she have killed her so easily?

At once, Elise was stricken by a terrible remorse. Would her uncle think she had murdered his wife? No, he would not believe her capable of it. Teresa, who would know the situation better, might. And what of her son, for whose sake she had done it? What would he think if, some day in the future, he learned his mother was a murderer?

But perhaps she was wrong. It might be that her aunt was still alive. Stifling revulsion, she laid her head on the shrunken breast. There was no sound beneath the finely woven fabric. But wait—there *was* a rhythmic beating. No, that was her own pounding heart! Holding her breath, Elise pressed her ear closer. Nothing. Then, barely perceptible, she heard it, the faint throbbing that meant Melisande was alive.

Alive but unconscious. She must already have been so when Elise picked up the pillow. That was the reason she had not reacted. Still trembling, Elise ran to the door and called Teresa. As the servant arrived, she left the room. In this state, at least, her aunt could not harm her.

*

Two days later, Melisande was dead. She had succumbed to the poison at dawn with the earl and Teresa at her side. The night before, the priest had come and anointed her for death. She had no choice in the matter. She had never reawakened. November, the month that began with the day of the dead, had become a month of death. With the fever still abroad, the funeral rites at the abbey were swift and simple. The earl did not know it, but he and Elise were united in mourning for the ones they loved.

Ten days passed while he kept to his quarters, seeing no one but a single servant and, infrequently, Elise. Then one morning he sent for her. As she entered his sleeping chamber, he was seated at a table holding a small book. He appeared more rested than he had since Melisande fell ill.

"Sit beside me, my dear. I've been reading this little prayer book to assuage my grief. Father Barnabas, our old chaplain, used to read it to me when I was ill. I still haven't filled his position, one of many things to be done. Now that your aunt is gone, they hardly seem to matter."

Elise kept her expressions of sympathy separate from her loathing for her aunt. She assumed a consoling tone. "My dear uncle, you must mourn without despairing. Take comfort in all you were to her, a loving companion, an exemplary spouse, a husband attentive to her every wish. My aunt said so many times." And it was true. Melisande had often said it. When she was old enough, Elise understood the irony behind her words.

"Thank you, my child. You are a great comfort as always. I've called you here on a different matter, something that might or might not be of importance. Although I know this little book nearly by heart, I still read Latin poorly. This letter has come from a learned monk in Palestine. I'm not yet ready to see my steward or his clerk. Would you read it to me? It may have something to do with Edmond Preston's burial."

The words *Edmond* and *burial,* thus linked, were like a sudden blow, but there was no way to avoid the reading. To disguise her emotion, Elise turned her chair toward the window, pretending to need more light. Facing away from her uncle, she read aloud, translating as she went.

To the Lord Earl of Clarington, from Matteus, Scribe and Brother of the Monastery of Elias, Mount Carmel, the Kingdom of Jerusalem.

"Mt. Carmel?" The earl interjected. "I was there in the last holy war. Go on, my dear, go on."

She did so, trying to conceal her emotion.

My lord, I have news that I hope will please you. It concerns your vassal and champion, Edmond Preston.

What pleasing news could there be, she asked herself, with Edmond dead? Irate at the thought, she went on reading.

It was believed that he perished in a battle south of Acre.

It was believed. Could that mean . . . no, she dared not hope!

That report, however, was mistaken. In short, he is alive.

Incredulous, she read the words again in silence, then fairly shouted, "He's alive, uncle, Edmond is alive!"

In her joy, she had forgotten to use his surname.

The earl's response was more subdued. "Yes, my dear, I heard you. It's truly a wonder. We must thank God for this great mercy. Please go on."

Calming herself, she read to the end.

He is here with us now at the foot of Mount Carmel in our tempo-
rary quarters. Soon we hope to return to our monastery on the mount
from which the infidel expelled us. As I write, Master Edmond is by
my side. Because of his injuries, he is not yet able to take up a pen.
Upon receipt of this missive at Bourne Castle, he begs you to share the
news with his wife, Mistress Aeline of Preston Manor.

Now I shall briefly explain the unfortunate confusion. After the
attack of the infidels on his party, Edmond, although injured himself,
came to the aid of a badly wounded comrade. In an effort to treat his
wounds, he removed the young man's blood-soaked tunic. Tearing
apart his own, he bound up his fellow's wounds. Sadly, the man died
less than an hour later. Half-delirious, Master Edmond heard the en-
emy approaching. Despite his injuries, he mounted and rode toward
the sea and Acre. It was nightfall when he collapsed on the banks of
the River Kishon. We found him there the next day, having ourselves
only recently left the reclaimed Acre.

By communicating with the Earl of Leicester, we discovered the er-
ror made by those who found the body. You will easily see how it hap-
pened. After ten days in the heat and burning sun, the man killed, a
baron from Kent, could no longer be recognized. The corpse was
known by your badge, my lord, sewn into the tunic that Edmond had
torn apart.

Under our care, your champion has steadily improved. Thanks to
the grace of the Almighty, he will soon return to Acre to rejoin the
Christian forces. He sends his regards to his wife, to you, his liege, and
in the event of her having returned to Bourne Castle, the Lady Elise.

That was all, the entire letter. But it had brought the news
Elise most needed to hear, that Edmond lived. Those words
were enough to bring her back to life.

38

As autumn turned to winter in the *regnum*, the two Sicilies rejoiced. The kingdom had been spared a dreadful fate. The Emperor Henry had failed in his campaign against the mainland kingdom. The German monarch claimed the Sicilian throne through his wife Constance, the last posthumous child of the great King Roger. The previous summer he had launched a campaign in Apulia with Naples, the principal Sicilian harbor on the mainland, as its object. As fate would have it, his troops had been mortally weakened by the unaccustomed heat, malaria, and dysentery. In August, Henry's fleet departed, unblocking the port of Naples. At least for the present, the Norman kingdom of Sicily had been preserved.

That winter in Palermo the rains fell steadily and gently, refreshing the slopes of the *conca d'oru*, preparing the way for the lush Sicilian spring. When Christmas came, interrupting his work as a scholar, Martin thought of those he loved, all absent. He had not seen his father since entering Windham Abbey; Edmond was in Palestine and Elise in England, most likely back at Bourne Castle by now. Most of all, he thought of Khalil whom he still longed for every day. Reminding himself of his work on the *Concilium*, he tried not to torture himself with dreams of a new life in al-Andalus.

February arrived, and the rains grew more infrequent. As Martin trod the long road to Palermo, there were puffs of white among the green, almond blossoms, the first in bloom each year. Early in the month a large packet addressed to him came to the abbey. That evening, he opened it in his room at Monreale. Inside, there was a letter from Elise and, beneath it, a document sealed with an official stamp. Noting the date on the letter, he saw it had traveled more quickly than usual.

Bourne Castle, Windham,
November 16, 1191

My dearest Martin, I hope this letter will reach you quickly. Since her husband's death, Queen Eleanor's power is again at its zenith. Although she is abroad, I've made use of her influence to have this included with the royal mail from Winchester. I am back at Bourne Castle, having returned here early in the fall. Since then, so much has happened I scarcely know where to begin. The worst was a false report of Edmond's death in combat in the Holy Land. A month later, a letter came and reversed the news. You can imagine my feelings during that month. They were complicated by the fact of Edmond's wife and children, of whom I knew nothing until I returned to Windham. I guessed at once you had chosen to spare me the pain of the news of his marriage while I was still at Evremont. Nor did Edmond speak about it when we met. Quite possibly, he thought I knew already. In retrospect, I am glad. Had I known, I might never have borne his child, my greatest joy.

Next, as you will learn from the documents enclosed, my husband has been executed for his crimes along with Prior Gramont through whom he all too willingly became a member of the vile Abraxas brotherhood. The document enclosed will tell you all the rest. It was written by the chief interrogator at Rouen and sent to Jean de Coutances, the dean of the cathedral there. His office made copies for you and me, the two most interested parties. Jacques Severin, my advocate at Rouen, brought the packet to me at Bourne Castle. There is also a preface by the dean that enjoins us both to silence on the subject of the count, the prior, and other details of the document. That silence also ensures that my son, the new Count de Vere, will not bear the stigma of Gilles's crimes. For that reason alone I beg you to observe it. It will be no hardship, I hope, since, as the account makes plain, you too are now free of the evil you discovered long ago.

In the first part of the document, I learned with sadness the name of the young woman whose body I discovered in the darkness of that ancient grotto at Evremont. She was poor, like so many victims of the cult. By chance, her parish priest had heard about the bodies found at *the chateau. It was he who connected them to her disappearance. As for the rest, I read some of it and stopped. The tortures employed by the Church disgusted me. They use the secular arm, of course, but it is their work. Where is Christ's love for the sinner in all this? I shall say no more on that subject lest I too be accused of heresy.*

Now for the news of Bourne Castle. Melisande is dead. Scheming as ever, she went to my room and read the document in question. Learning of her lover's execution, she took her own life by a poison that mimicked illness, a fact she confessed to me during our final bitter meeting. Her love for the count was a madness that finally came to nothing. Clever to the end, she guessed the truth about my son before she died. For reasons of her own, she threatened to reveal it. Death took her first. I confess I was happy when it did.

My dear friend, that's the sum of my revelations—more than enough, as you see. For the moment, my life with my child is tranquil. I console my uncle for his loss, and dear old Margaret cares for me and little Martin both. When I recall the misery of my life at Evremont, I am glad that one good thing at least has come of it, the defeat of the Abraxas brotherhood. Without the knowledge of the cult you shared with me, that might never have come about.

Lastly, despite the strangeness of our situation, I have befriended Aeline, Edmond's wife. She is a fine young woman and suspects nothing of me in connection to her husband. Like her, I pray only for Edmond's safe return as I am sure you do. From the first, we three friends have been bound by the deepest affection. Whatever the future brings, I feel certain those bonds will not be broken.

When he had finished, Martin sat for a while in the gloaming, once again thinking of his friends. Elise's final words had touched him deeply. He had also been astounded by her revelations. What an autumn she had spent! Anxious to see the document, he lit a candle and unsealed it. The Dean of Rouen's warning was on a single sheet. The rest of the pages contained the account of the chief interrogator at Rouen. In the first part, he spoke of the evidence found at Evremont. Then he went on to the capture and interrogation of the members of the cult.

Seven miscreants were taken in the region bounded by the cities of Amiens and Rouen. Of these, three were beaten and flogged and confessed to their crimes at once. All three pleaded an addiction to the drugs used at their hellish rites. These were employed both by the members and to sedate their victims. When told to name the drugs, they answered mandragore, henbane, and a third, the most addictive, but said they were never told its name. The foul ritual was held in a grotto carved into the stone beneath the old chateau, a shrine long ago polluted by the pagan rites of Mithras. At these gatherings, the three agreed, a young innocent, indifferently male or female, was first drugged, then violated by the members of the cult, then killed. Despite being beaten a second time, none of the three gave the names of other members of the cult. They said they knew only the count and the prior, the leaders of the cult, since at their meetings names were never used. In addition, all members were garbed in robes with overhanging hoods. Important members wore masks to conceal their identity.

At these despicable gatherings, all present recited blasphemous prayers to Abraxas, the heretical power they served. Some, learned by rote, were chanted in the language of old Egypt known as Coptic, a form of Greek. The words, they believed, were those of Basilides of Alexandria, a Gnostic of the early days of Christianity. It was he who proclaimed the heretical rule of Abraxas, a power greater than God and the Devil.

All three members, having admitted their crimes, were allowed the sacrament of Penance. They confessed to a priest and were absolved. After that, they were mercifully hanged, not burned as heretics, by the secular arm in the public market at Rouen.

Two of the remaining four prisoners were more resistant, admitting to neither wrongdoing nor knowledge of the cult. They were first beaten, then put on the rack, then flogged. They ended by hurling curses at their interrogators, reciting their pernicious prayers aloud, proclaiming the end of Christ's reign and the birth of the reign of Abraxas. After that, their tongues were torn out, which silenced them. The other two, having witnessed the fate of their fellows, confessed profusely. Both said that at the conclusion of their rites, those present drank their victims' blood. For that purpose, small punctures were *made in their flesh with hollow reeds sharpened like pens. From these, the members either imbibed the blood directly or siphoned it into little bowls. Then, once the victims were dead, they used flint blades to cut off small pieces of their still-warm flesh and ate them. Thus body and blood were consumed in a sacrilegious mockery of the Mass, another sign of the cult's diabolic hatred of the Church.*

At first, the interrogators suspected the latter details were perversely created for their benefit. Flogged and put on the rack, the two retracted them. Falsely, it seems. They were later confirmed by Breton members of the cult. At Rouen, all four malefactors were justly condemned, led to the stake, and burned alive in public. The last thing they breathed was the stifling smoke, the last thing they felt was the heat of the flames as it seared their skin and gradually devoured their flesh, a fitting prelude to the fire they will endure for all eternity in hell.

Here Martin stopped. Nearly nauseous, he felt profoundly repelled by the apparent enthusiasm of the writer for these tortures. In fact, they seemed to him crueler than the cult's. If this was the Church's justice, he was glad to have had no part in it. On the other hand, the account had finally revealed the horrid function of the fragments he had long ago found buried at the clearing of the stones: the flint blades, the hollow reeds, the darkly stained shards of small terra cotta bowls. He also understood now why the novice he had seen that night had not been struggling. Like the other victims of the cult, he had been drugged.

Anxious to be done, Martin skimmed the last part of the document. It was concerned with four Breton members of the cult, all of whom had been taken to Caen and subjected to similar ordeals. Two were hanged as murderers, two condemned as heretics and burned to death. After that, there was an addendum. It spoke briefly of the torture, interrogation, and execution of the two leaders of the cult, Prior Guy de Gramont and Count Gilles de Vere. The two had been taken to Caen from

Rouen and hanged in secret, avoiding the scandal their prominence might bring.

As he finished the document, Martin was not only disturbed
but strangely unsatisfied. For one thing, he was troubled by the
news about the secret execution of the prior and the count.
Could he really be sure they were dead? Gramont had evaded
punishment many times before. Might he have done so one
more time?

Then he checked himself. He had spent so many years in expectation of the prior's downfall it had become a part of him,
like an unpleasant companion one is nonetheless reluctant to
give up. It was he, not the authorities, who found it difficult to
kill the prior. More to the point, although the two leaders were
dead, how many others members were there still at large? And
what about the countless unnamed victims? Would there ever
be retribution for their awful deaths? The answer seemed clearly to be no. Indeed, if he had once had a vision of the world in
which all crimes were punished and all wrongs redressed, he
had abandoned it long ago. What mattered most, he supposed,
was that the brotherhood's meetings had ended. Lacking a leader, aware of the terrible fate of those arrested, the remaining
members would surely disperse.

That night, with the document fresh in his mind, Martin
was plagued by lurid dreams in which Abraxas's rites were mingled with the Church's brutal tortures. A few days later, however, he began to feel strangely liberated. With the cult
vanquished, he was finally free of the shadow that had followed
him to Sicily and never left him: the shame of his youthful failure to expose the prior and his evil brotherhood. Still, rid of the
cult though he was, he was not yet free of the need to understand it. Perhaps Brother Paulinus could help him. So far, the
Benedictine had proved a good friend and wise advisor.

That afternoon he asked him to step into the anteroom of
the scriptorium. "With your permission, brother, I would like
to speak to you in private."

"Of course," Paulinus said, and the two sat down together. Briefly, Martin described his long involvement with the cult, avoiding whatever the Dean of Rouen had forbidden. He finished with a description of a gathering of the brotherhood.

"They meet at ancient sites where pagan rituals were celebrated long ago. In their foul rites they use crude implements: reed tubes, crude clay bowls, flint blades like the ancient artifacts plowmen sometimes find beneath the soil."

Taking time to absorb it all, Paulinus responded carefully. "It seems these heretics look back with longing to the pagan past. From what you've said, they are also driven by a burning hatred of the Church. Their primitive tools rebuke the treasuries of our cathedrals, storerooms laden with precious artifacts of gold and silver while starving beggars linger on the steps outside."

"I see the sad truth in what you say," Martin commented, "but I have a second question. The philosophers often maintain that all creatures pursue the good. Do you agree, or do you believe there are those who deliberately seek evil?"

"I believe that most men seek the good, or at least what they perceive as good, and that very few love evil for its own sake. Yet there have always been those with no concern for good or evil, men devoid of morality. They wish only to gratify themselves, despising everything that keeps their appetites in check."

"Are such people inherently evil?" Martin queried, aware of a certain illogic in his question.

"No," Paulinus answered, "not evil but amoral, completely indifferent to right or wrong."

Martin thought of the cult's Gnostic writings. The power known as Abraxas was certainly amoral. Basilides had called it *a power beyond good and evil.* "And for those who are truly amoral, is nothing forbidden?"

"Nothing. Their own lusts and desires, whether for power or for pleasure, are all that matter."

"And if the power they desire is monstrous, the pleasure perverse and vicious?"

"It makes no difference," the monk declared with finality.

Paulinus had made his point succinctly. Martin saw it was up to him to think about its implications. He thanked Brother Paulinus and they parted, but for the rest of the day, he continued to think about the monk's conclusion. The cult had succeeded by promising liberation, freedom from morality. Yet the rites of Abraxas, full of blasphemy, lust, and blood, had ended in slavery to drug-sated horror. Was this only amorality, or something worse, a monstrous love of evil buried deep inside men's souls, a savage proclivity only waiting for some pretext to appear and satisfy itself?

If so, the Church had long provided such a pretext. For a millennium, it had inflicted a burden of guilt, teaching the faithful to live in perpetual fear of damnation and the fires of hell. And all the while, the Church had nurtured its own evils. In thrall to wealth and power, mired in the buying and selling of offices and relics, it had increasingly ignored the message of the Gospels. The cult's crimes were abysmal, its pleasures horrific, but unlike the Church, it was without hypocrisy.

Despite these new insights—or perhaps because of them—Martin's thoughts about the cult continued to disturb him. Then one day toward the end of the month, he awoke with a redemptive thought. If he was able to convey the truth in his *Concilium*, might it not help to correct the evils in the Church that helped to breed the cult? And other evils too, including what seemed to him the worst: the madness of war between religions? He knew, of course, it would not be easy. He was well aware of the gulf between truth and the comforting lies men clung to with such passion. That did not make his goal less worthy. Inspired by it, he returned to his work with new resolve.

*

A week later, needing to consult a volume in the royal library, he went to services at Prime and set out early for Palermo. Belying the coming of spring, the weather had again turned cold. Beneath a sky full of threatening clouds, the harbor was cloaked in a heavy gray mist. Then, just as he rounded a corner of the road, the sun broke through, piercing the clouds with its brilliant rays. Both the light and the sudden warmth felt like harbingers of something good.

At the royal library, he found the volume he wanted, a book by Origen, an unorthodox father of the early church. Later that day, he sat reading it in the Greek section of the library. Resting his eyes for a moment, he looked up and saw another stream of sunlight, a more modest one this time. Falling from a window set high in the wall, it was gilding the myriad motes of dust suspended in the air.

Struck by the effect, Martin stared, unthinking. And then he had a strange sensation, one he had not experienced in years, the feeling he had lived this moment once before. As quickly as it came, it disappeared. Only then did he remember how the light had fallen the same way in the same place on the day he first glimpsed Khalil, splendid in white turban and rust-colored robe, listening to the reading of the famed Ibn Jubair. Swayed by the force of his recollection, Martin experienced a total change of mood.

During the year he had waited to hear from Khalil, he had learned to suppress the full power of his desire for his lover. It had returned to him now with redoubled force. Confounded, he sat without seeing the pages of his book. In his mind's eye, the treasured days and nights came flooding back. Before long, the memory of their love had totally possessed him. Overwhelmed, he made a great effort to break the spell, forcing himself to return to his reading.

The harder he tried, the more useless it seemed. Origen's words had been drained of all meaning. After a while, in a kind of trance, he left the scriptorium, descended to the palace gate, and moved into the city. At midday, the streets were full of people; among all their faces, he saw only one face, and it was a thousand miles away. At last, he came to the spot where he sometimes met a wagon on its way to Monreale. Until it arrived, he stood unmoving, stunned by the force of his recovered need.

That night in his room at the abbey, Martin once again questioned his choice of remaining in Palermo. Did he really need to be here to complete his work? Why could he not abandon all restraint and leave for Cordoba as Khalil had so often urged? His lover had assured him he would be welcomed as a Christian scholar. From what he had learned, the great library there had everything he needed: works on the myths and beliefs of the Greeks and the Ancient East, the learned books of Judaism, Christianity, and Islam. It would not be the end but a new beginning. The more he thought about it, the more alluring the prospect became. Nor could he bring himself to pray for guidance. In truth, he felt only rebellion in his heart, a desire to break the bonds that had constrained him all his life. A single daring act and then the prize, a lifetime with the man he loved. Consumed by the thought, Martin tossed in his bed most of the night.

When he awoke at dawn, his desire was as strong but his mind was clearer. He saw now why he had so far resisted Khalil's invitation. He had been afraid, frightened to leap from everything he knew into an unknown world. And yet he had made such a leap before. At the age of eighteen, he had come to Sicily and changed his life. At that time, his flight had been compelled by fear. This time he vowed it would not be. He would go to Cordoba impelled by love.

All the same, he knew he could not suddenly forsake the Sicily that made him, the library that formed his thought, the abbey that had given him a home. Not until he had left behind something of value: the first volume of his *Concilium*. But when that book was complete, he would leave to join Khalil. He would write today and tell him so.

39

1192

To the distress of all, Windhamshire had suffered poor harvests for the last two years. The county had also been burdened by heavy taxes to support King Richard's holy war. Perhaps worst of all, the wasting fever that came in the fall had continued unabated through the winter. One day in February, the earl told Elise that he and his steward were called to Winchester on a matter of importance. It would be the first time he had left Bourne Castle since Melisande's death.

"The master of arms will take charge of the castle. The steward's clerk will attend to business matters. If something untoward should arise, both men will defer to you. I leave the day after tomorrow. Have you plans of your own that might interfere with your being in charge?"

During the long weeks of her uncle's mourning, Elise had grown used to his increasing dependence on her. "No, nothing, uncle, or perhaps one thing. I have been planning a visit to Mistress Aeline. I shall do that tomorrow before you leave. I haven't seen her since the dreadful fright that I—that she, I mean—had over the false news of her husband's death."

She had slipped again, but she saw it scarcely mattered. Her uncle had never suspected her and Edmond. He could never have imagined that his champion in Outremer was little Martin's father.

"Ah yes, the false report of Master Preston's death. What a dreadful shock that must have been for her," the earl said with the voice of shared grief, no doubt thinking of Melisande.

For her. not for me, thought Elise, wanting again to assert her right to Edmond's love. Yet she knew she could never do that, not without endangering her son's inheritance and title, and also losing her uncle's regard for her and Edmond. She spoke instead about Aeline.

"When we last met, I promised to bring little Martin to meet her children."

Her uncle nodded approvingly, and they parted. After leaving him, Elise sent a messenger to Aeline to ask if she could visit on the morrow. The man returned with an affirmative reply.

The following day, a servant drove her, little Martin, and Brigida to Preston manor in a covered cart. Margaret seldom left the castle now. Both the ride in the cart and the visit would have tired her. Fortunately, the day was warm for February. As they drove through the Preston Manor gate, Aeline was waiting in the courtyard, her two children beside her. Elise stepped down from the wagon with the driver's help.

Aeline greeted her warmly. "My dear lady, welcome again to Preston Manor!"

"Thank you, Mistress Aeline. It's been too long since we last met." With that, she turned to take little Martin from Brigida in the cart. When she had set him down, their hostess bent over to welcome him.

"So this is your son. What a fine boy he is!"

Aeline knelt to kiss the child and, rising, spoke the words Elise had hoped never to hear. "It may seem a bit vain to say it, my lady, but your son very much resembles Godfrey at his age. How old is little Martin now?"

Elise hesitated, trying to fashion a reply. She decided to concur. "Just over a year. Godfrey is five now, is he not? Even at that age, I too see a resemblance. We are fortunate to have such handsome boys!"

There was, indeed, a likeness. Luckily, Martin had her coloring, not Edmond's: pale skin, dark hair, and dark eyes. Her great fear was that he would resemble his father more as he grew. "Of course, little Rosalind outshines them both," Elise added, hoping to end the subject.

"She'll be delighted to hear that from you, my lady. Oh dear, I'm afraid she's blushing." The girl had, indeed, turned a deep pink. She retreated now behind her mother's skirts. Once the topic was changed, curiosity brought her out again. Now, feeling the cold, the group, including Aeline's maidservant, Maddie, moved into the manor house.

As the great wooden door closed behind them, Aeline spoke again. "I've never thanked you for sending the letter to Fenbury so promptly, the one the monk wrote from the Holy Land. And for translating it from the Latin."

Elise remembered her own misery in that moment. "I could scarcely do less."

Aeline smiled, and they moved into a large, low-ceilinged room. At one end, a fire was blazing. The Baron and his wife were nowhere to be seen. The two serving girls took the children to a spot a little distance from the fire. There, Godfrey, less shy than his sister, began to show Martin his toys. The two women sat by the fire, and Elise returned to the subject of the letter.

"By rights, it should have come to you. I'm sure your husband believed, in this case correctly, that it would travel more swiftly addressed to the earl."

"Yes of course, I understood that. Even now, I can hardly bear to think of that month when I lived with the thought of him dying in desert . . . " She broke off, clearly unable to go on.

"Don't think of it now," Elise prompted, knowing her feelings all too well. "Your husband is alive and safe. Soon the war will be over and he'll be home." She said it also for herself, needing to believe it.

Aeline thanked her for her words, then redirected the subject. "Forgive me, I haven't yet given you my condolences, first for the Lady Melisande, then for your husband. I only recently heard the count was killed on his way to Outremer."

As on her first visit, the mention of the count annoyed Elise. At the same time, the news also meant that the Dean of Rouen had successfully spread the false rumor about his death.

"As I said when we met, my husband and I are estranged. I believe what you say is true, but I know little more than that. The subject remains a painful one for me."

It was Aeline who blushed now, a slightly fainter shade than Rosalind. "Forgive me, my lady, I forgot."

At once, Elise regretted her remark. "No, no—you did nothing wrong. I merely gave in to unhappy memories of my marriage."

"Still, I *was* at fault. You told me about your marriage in October, that you hoped never to hear from your husband again. Two days after our meeting, word came of Edmond's death. After that, I'm afraid I forgot everything."

"Of course. I understand completely," Elise said reassuringly, conscious of the irony in what she said. As she was speaking, Rosalind left the boys and came to stand beside her. Aeline smiled at them both. "I think you've made a conquest."

"I believe it's Rosalind who's conquered me," Elise said, disarmed to see Edmond's blue eyes in the tender young face. Soon, both the boys came too. Touchingly, Godfrey took his little brother's hand to guide his footsteps. They came and were kissed by their mothers, then toddled off again.

"It's at times like these," Aeline began, "that I sorely miss Edmond, these moments with the children he will never know. Godfrey was three when he left. He speaks his father's name, but I'm not sure he would know him if he saw him. Rosalind is like me. She still thinks of her father every day. Why do men have this terrible need to go to war? My heart nearly broke when my husband left, but he never knew."

Elise listened with painful emotion, mutely complicit in Aeline's feelings. For the present, at least, they were united in loneliness, longing, and hope, but how would it be when the man they both loved returned? Picturing it, Elise was aware of the truth. Fond as she was of this fine young woman, it was dangerous to become too close.

*

The earl seemed improved by his trip to Winchester. Elise was happy to see him active again. Then, three weeks from the day of the visit to Preston Manor, word came that Mistress Aeline had fallen victim to the wasting fever. Elise wanted to go at once, but her uncle forbade it. The illness was most contagious in its early stages. Every day Elise sent a servant to the manor gate. There, he was able to inquire about Aeline's condition. From him she learned that, fearing contagion, Aeline had sent her two children to stay with her parents in Fenbury. On the sixth day, the servant returned with a small sealed parchment. Inside, ten words were painfully scrawled.

Come if you can. I need to speak to you.

Elise knew at once she had to go. Despite years spent deceiving her uncle about Melisande, she still hated lying directly to him. She did so now, however. Since her return, she had twice written Canon Thomas but had not yet seen him. She told her uncle she planned to visit her old teacher on the morrow.

The next day, she set out with Brigida on foot. When they arrived, Brigida, avoiding possible contagion, visited with Maddie in an outbuilding of the manor. With the children gone, the latter had less to do. Inside the house, she met the woman they had found to nurse Aeline. She was one of the few who had survived the fever, making her proof to its advances. Elise found Aeline in a dimly lit bedchamber, weak but lucid. She thanked Elise for coming and dismissed the nurse.

The chamber smelled of illness. As she settled into it, she felt a thrill of distaste at the memory of Melisande's sickroom. For her son's sake, she hoped Aeline was no longer contagious. She took her friend's hand. It was dry from the fever and rough, as if from recent work.

Aeline spoke in a voice that was hoarse but calm, at least at first. "You're very kind to have come, my lady. They say I am beyond contagion at this point, that the fever is most catching at the beginning. I wouldn't have asked you except for the urgency of what I have to say. First, let me tell you what happened just after our last meeting. I had news of Edmond's return from a friend in Winchester. When the word came, it made me overwrought. For a day or two, I barely slept. Then I set about making frantic preparations, but always without saying why. I knew the news might be false. I did not want to unduly excite either the children or Edmond's parents. The latter of course interfered with my campaign of cleaning and improving, seeing no need for it. I ignored them both, commanding the servants to listen to me. I even hinted at the news to one, then swore him to secrecy. I worked alone when there was no one else to help."

"If I had known, I would have sent someone to help you."

"Thank you, but your being here now is enough. At any rate, my exertions were unwise. As I may have said, I have never been robust. I was unable to stop myself. The thought of my husband's return to the chaos his parents had wreaked on this house was too much to bear. Finally, the manor and the grounds surrounding it were almost ready. Then I learned that a knight whose first name was Edmond had arrived in Winchester. He was on his way to Salisbury, his home. All along, it had been a different man! That night I felt a sudden weakness. It was followed by nausea and stomach pain. The aches and the fever soon followed."

As she was telling her story, Aeline's speech gradually slowed. Now she came near to halting. "My body . . . had rebelled . . . or perhaps it was the disappointment. Whatever the cause, I was ill of the fever I had refused to think about."

Elise had stifled her tears as she listened. In fact, she was once again angry at the toll, indirect in this case, that this pointless holy war had taken. Having heard Aeline's story, she sat in mournful silence. At last, she roused herself. She was no good to her friend in this state.

"You will recover, Aeline. You are still young, you have your life and your children and Edmond to live for. Don't tire yourself now with talking. I'm happy to sit here silently beside you."

Aeline rested for a while, then spoke in a near whisper. "Does your uncle know you're here?"

"To be honest, he does not. He thinks I am visiting Canon Thomas. I felt I had to come. However short our acquaintance, you have become a good friend, the only friend of my age and sex in England. So you see, you must get well! I can't afford to lose you."

Aeline managed a feeble laugh, then spoke in a slightly stronger voice. "I shall be calm now, I promise, but I need to talk. Let me begin with Canon Thomas. I knew he was Edmond's teacher once and also that of Alfred Rendon's son."

"Deacon Martin, whom I knew in Sicily," Elise volunteered.

Aeline nodded. "Exactly, but I only recently learned that you too were Canon Thomas's pupil. Edmond never spoke of it."

Feeling caught, Elise struggled for an explanation. "Nor have I, as you know. It was so long ago. So much has happened since."

"And yet you knew him?" Aeline asked.

They were entering dangerous territory. Could she lie on what might be Aeline's deathbed?

She settled for a half-truth. "It would have been difficult for us to know each other well. It was a rare thing, my being allowed to take lessons at all. The Lady Melisande had urged it, one of the few things she did in my favor. Outside of our lessons, the two boys and I were forbidden to speak. We were there to learn and that was all."

"Of course," Aeline said. "Since I saw you last, however, I have had time to think. From the beginning, I had an uncommon feeling about you. When we first met, if you recall, I spoke of the sorrows in every marriage. The last time we talked, I already knew about the lessons."

Elise said nothing, afraid of what might be coming next. Then Aeline's face grew flush and she began to cough. Reaching for a cup, she almost knocked it over. Elise filled it with water from a nearby pitcher and held it to her lips. When Aeline finished drinking, Elise took her hand again. Formerly hot and dry, it was clammy now.

Her invalid's voice was even weaker. "I begged you to come. Now I must ask another favor. Will you oblige me by not interrupting what I have to say?"

Puzzled and more than a little afraid, Elise agreed.

"Good, I will try to keep you to your word. When we first met, as I say, I had no idea Edmond knew you. Yet even then I felt you were the kind of woman he had always dreamed of . . . "

Forgetting her promise, Elise protested. "How foolish, Aeline! It was you whom he married, you who bore his children. Has he not been a good husband and father?"

Aeline seemed to rally in response. "Yes, of course he has. No woman could ask for better. My love for him, however, has been all-consuming. A love of that kind is not content until it fully knows its object. For a long time, I've suspected there was someone, perhaps only a distant ideal, a woman unlike me in every way, someone tall, beautiful, and gifted. I myself, as you see, am quite ordinary, from my simple skills in writing to my freckled cheeks and frizzy hair."

Again, Elise objected. "My dear friend, you are not at all ordinary. You are a remarkable young woman."

"Do you really think so? In any case, it's kind of you to say so. In one respect, perhaps, I am unusual, my love for Edmond. I have loved him since I was a child and saw him fighting bravely with a boy much bigger than himself. Later, I learned it was his wretched brother Geoffrey. Ever since, my love for him has been everything to me. Were that not so, I might not be able to say what I say now. If I succumb to this fever, I have only one wish for my husband. I know he will be a fine father to our children, a good master to his tenants, a hero in peace as he has been in war. For his sake, however, I want something more, something that may seem unusual to you. So far, you've broken your word twice and interrupted me. Now I must beg you to keep your promise. My strength is waning. Don't let it be drained by your protests. From this moment on, you must agree not to speak, neither confirming nor denying what I say. Do you promise?"

Elise saw the matter was out of her hands. "I do."

"Good. Then I will say it freely. What I would like, if I die, is that Edmond should marry the woman he has always dreamed of. And I believe that woman to be you."

Stunned, Elise finally kept silent.

"Good," Aeline said, then spoke in a voice that seemed torn from inside her. "Thank you for making no reply. A denial would not have convinced me, a confirmation would have crushed me. I am content in my ignorance. I've told you what I needed to. Now I can rest happily."

Elise seized on one word. "Yes, rest, my dear friend. I've indulged you in your whim because you're ill. Say and do what you like, as long as you defeat this malady."

"Thank you, my lady. Perhaps with my mind at ease, I will. Yet whether I live or die, I must ask one more thing—that you never repeat what I've said here today, especially to Edmond. I would hate him to think he had failed me. He alone has made my life happy."

Once again, Elise was too moved to speak. At last, she forced a reply. "I give you my word."

Then, overwhelmed by pity, she could not resist dissembling one last time. "And you and I, dear Aeline, will look back on this day in the years ahead and laugh, recalling only the bond of friendship sealed here."

These words, which neither she nor her listener probably believed, were the last Elise spoke before saying farewell that afternoon. But she left Preston Manor humbled, aware that his wife's love for Edmond was in one respect—its selflessness—superior to her own.

*

A few days later, Maddie returned with the sad news. After a fretful night, Mistress Aeline had died as morning dawned. Elise and the earl both attended the services in Windham parish church. Edmond's wife was buried in the graveyard there beside the other Prestons. The baron and his wife had acceded to her final wish, that until their father returned, the children would remain with her parents in Fenbury. Elise wrote Martin the following day to inform him of the events. She ended her letter with these words:

> *My dearest friend, I have tears in my eyes as I think of this fine young woman whom I knew so briefly. Who could have guessed that when the final barrier to Edmond's and my marriage was removed, it would leave me in such desolation? When, at the funeral, I kissed Aeline's children goodbye for the present, I desperately wanted to claim them for their father, but of course I could not. All I can do is continue to wait for Edmond's safe return. And for the day—dare I say it so soon after Aeline's death?—when he and I will be free to be one at last.*

That night, Elise decided it was time to visit Canon Thomas, the one man in England to whom she could fully unburden her heart.

CHARACTERS OF THE CULT

PRINCIPAL FICTIONAL CHARACTERS

ALFRED RENDON (b. 1137, England) steward of Preston Manor, father of Martin

BROTHER AMBROSE (b. 1138, England) Benedictine monk, head of the scriptorium at Windham Abbey

BROTHER PAULINUS (b. 1152, Sicily) Benedictine monk, assistant head of the scriptorium at Monreale Abbey

CANON THOMAS (b. 1118, England) priest, scholar, and teacher, former Benedictine monk at Windham Abbey, former canon at Winchester Cathedral

DESMOND DE BOURNE (b. 1127, Windham, England) Earl of Clarington, uncle of Elise

EDMOND PRESTON (b. 1157, Windham, England) son of Baron Hugh Preston

ELISE DE CRECY (b. 1158, Picardy) niece and ward of the Earl of Clarington

FATHER HERAKLIOS (b. 1145, Sicily) custodian of the royal library, Palermo

GILLES DE VERE (b. 1136, Normandy) Count of Evremont in Normandy, secret cousin of Prior Gramont

GUY DE GRAMONT (b. 1132, England) Prior of Windham Abbey, bastard son of Geoffrey de Mandeville

HAMID (b. 1152, Sicily) faithful servant to Khalil al-Din

HUGH PRESTON (b. 1133, Windham, England) Baron of Preston Manor, father of Edmond

KHALIL AL-DIN (b. 1145, Palermo, Sicily) Arab poet and scholar at the court of William II of Sicily

MARTIN RENDON (b. 1158, Windham, England) son of Alfred Rendon

MELISANDE DE BOURNE (b. 1138, France) wife of the Earl of Clarington

MARGARET (b. 1122, Windham, England) Elise's childhood nurse and adult companion

PRINCIPAL HISTORICAL PERSONS IN THE NARRATIVE

ABU YUSUF YAQUB AL-MANSUR (c. 1160–1199), Caliph of Cordoba, 1184–1199

BASILIDES (active 117–138) Gnostic teacher and writer from Alexandria in Egypt

CARUS (c. 1159–1233) Abbot of Monreale Abbey, 1189–1233

CONSTANCE (1154-1198) daughter of Roger II of Sicily, consort of the Emperor Henry IV, 1191–97

ELEANOR OF AQUITAINE (1122-1204) Queen of France, 1137–1152, Queen of England, 1154–1189

GEOFFREY DE MANDEVILLE (c. 1082–1144) First Earl of Essex, Constable of the Tower of London

GUY DE LUSIGNAN (c. 1142–1194) King of Jerusalem, 1186–92, Ruler of Cyprus, 1192–94

HENRY II (1133–1189) King of England, 1154–1189

HENRY IV (1165–1197) King of Germany, 1190–1197, Holy Roman Emperor, 1191–1197

HENRY ARISTIPPUS (c. 1100–1162) noted scholar at the court of William I of Sicily

IBN JUBAIR (1145–1217) Arab poet and geographer from al-Andalus

JOANNA OF ENGLAND (1165–1199) daughter of Henry II, Queen of Sicily, 1177–1189

JOHN OF OXFORD (c. 1135–1200) Dean of Salisbury Cathedral, 1166–1175, Bishop of Norwich, 1175–1200

RICHARD I (1157–1199) King of England, 1189–1199

REYNALD DE CHATILLON (c. 1130–1187) crusader and adventurer in the Holy Land

ROBERT DE BEAUMONT (c. 1165–1204) Fourth Earl of Leicester

ROHESE DE VERE (1110–c. 1170) wife of Geoffrey de Mandeville

ROGER II (1095–1154) first Norman King of Sicily, 1130–1154

SALAH AL-DIN (1137/1138–1193) leader of the Muslim forces in the Third Crusade

TANCRED OF LECCE (c. 1134–1194) King of Sicily 1190-1194

WALTER OF PALERMO (c. 1120–1191) Archbishop of Palermo 1168-1191

WILLIAM II (1153–1189) Norman King of Sicily, 1166–1189

WILLIAM DE MANDEVILLE (c. 1126-1189) Third Earl of Essex, second son of Geoffrey de Mandeville

ABOUT THE AUTHOR

Richard Devlin is a writer and artist who lives in the San Francisco Bay Area. He has had fifteen solo exhibitions of his paintings in California and Pennsylvania, where for many years he was chair of the Art Department at Carlow University. A published art critic, he has been a lover of medieval art and architecture since boyhood, making secular pilgrimages over the years to Romanesque and Gothic churches and monasteries in France, England, Italy, Spain, and Germany. But it was a journey to Sicily that inspired *The Cult*, the first novel of *The Abraxas Chronicles*. There, along with a rich and varied past, he found a unique medieval style of art and architecture, a blend of Arab, Norman, and Byzantine Greek influences. Later, he continued his on-site research in Normandy and the South of England, the two other locales featured prominently in *The Cult*.